Fire

Honeybridge
Book 1

Lucy Lennox

May Archer

Ali – Happy reading! Lucy Lennox ♡

Ali – enjoy your time in Honeybridge! Love, may archer ♡

Copyright © 2022 by Lucy Lennox and May Archer

All rights reserved.

No part of this book may be reproduced in any form or by any electronic or mechanical means, including information storage and retrieval systems, without written permission from the author, except for the use of brief quotations in a book review.

Cover design: Natasha Snow

Cover Photo: Michelle Lancaster @lanefotograf

Editing: One Love Editing

Proofreading: Lori Parks and Victoria Rothenberg

Beta Reading: Leslie Copeland, Chad Williams, Shay Haude

Chapter One

JT

"I feel like you left here in a *mood*." Alice's voice through the Porsche speakers sounded way calmer than I felt at the moment.

My assistant wasn't wrong. She rarely was.

"Mood. *Mood*," I said through my teeth. "Yes, I think you could call it that. After three fucking years of working my ass off for Conrad Schaeffer with his promise of a promotion to vice president, I actually believed it was finally going to happen."

"No shit, JT. The man's an..." She lowered her voice. "An insufferable ass. But rumor has it he said you'd get promoted to VP as soon as you close the Honeybridge Mead account up in Maine. Which, let's be honest, is practically a done deal considering you grew up in Honeybridge. Surely you have connections that can help..."

Her voice faded away while my head took me to a million places, none of which were compatible with my sanity.

Green eyes bright with arousal.
Bare, freckled shoulders.
A smile rarer than a sun-shower in June.

Anger so hot it burned, even in my memories.

Connections? I definitely had connections. But they were the opposite of helpful.

"Conrad made it sound like you know the guy who owns it, right? You two went to school together or something?" Alice continued, breaking me out of my memories.

Or something.

I swallowed around my nerves. Flynn Honeycutt was six feet of walking temptation wrapped in a barbed-wire coating of *stay-the-fuck-away-from-me*.

My boss couldn't have given me a more difficult challenge if he'd tried. Not that Conrad Schaeffer knew anything about Honeybridge Mead or Flynn Honeycutt. No, he'd most likely found out about the brand the same way the rest of the world had—through some viral social media posts.

Frankie Hilo had made several posts from the Honeybridge Tavern and Meadery. One duck-faced mirror shot of the singer being her ridiculous self in the men's room. One orgasmic selfie of her holding a half-empty glass with the simple caption "bussin." And one reel she'd shot in front of the Tavern, in which she panned the entire length of sleepy, old-fashioned Fraser Street, declared that she was "absolutely sliving the savage vibe" of Honeybridge, Maine, and instructed her Hilo-lovers to come see for themselves.

And apparently, they had. According to my mother, who served on every town development committee (because god forbid that anything should happen in Honeybridge without her input), tourism in the quaint lakeside town was up eighteen percent over the town's best summer previously, and new artisans and chefs were moving in, bringing their talent and entrepreneurial spirit. "The club has even had to hire an extra gate attendant," she'd sniffed, which was Patricia Wellbridge's genteel way of saying the town had been overrun with riffraff.

If this was true, that was great. Flynn Honeycutt deserved the boon to his business, and Honeybridge itself could use the additional tourist traffic.

Personally, though, I had my doubts. Honeybridge was a tiny town that was a little too proud of its quaint traditions and local legends. Nothing ever changed there, including the people. The life you were born into was the life you were expected to lead, forever and ever amen.

That was the reason I'd deliberately escaped the place years ago in search of bigger and better things—a life on my own terms. It was a large part of the reason I hadn't even been back for a visit in three years, too.

Now here I was, tasked with spending time in Honeybridge—"A few weeks at least, Jonathan. Heck, maybe the whole summer!" Conrad had suggested, to my utter horror—to court a new client into signing a distribution deal with me at Fortress Holdings.

A client I'd known my whole life and who'd hated me nearly as long.

A client whose naked body felt like it had been crafted to fit against mine.

A client whose prickly exterior hid a vulnerable underbelly of need.

A client whose soft cries in bed still haunted me most nights as I took myself in hand and searched for relief.

I had strong suspicions about why I, of all the people Conrad Schaeffer could have chosen to represent Fortress, had been chosen for this mission, and I was extremely displeased.

"Alice," I said, clearing my throat and trying to put the past where it belonged—deep, deep down in a lead-lined vault. In the ocean. On another planet. "I need you to get me everything you can on Honeybridge Mead's competitors. If we take them national, I want to know who they'd be up against besides Lotus and Fairchild."

This was *business*, I reminded myself, no matter how personal it felt. A deal like any other I'd done for Fortress over the years. Sure, it was way more important since Conrad was so fixated on this particular deal that he'd placed it squarely between me and a VP title, but a deal nonetheless. And I was really, *really* good at closing deals.

Alice's keyboard clacked in the background. "Will do. I've already put together a dossier on Flynn Honeycutt. He's—"

"Don't need it," I said sharply. "I know Flynn. I've got that part handled."

This was, of course, a giant lie. I might *know* Flynn, but I'd never understood the man. Still, no dossier was going to give me any additional insight.

What I knew for sure was that my usual methods with clients—building a relationship, figuring out what they truly wanted, and making sure they got a fair deal—were not going to work here. Not when we had a lifetime's worth of misunderstandings and antagonism between us...

And one incredible night of the opposite.

Instead, I was planning to go for shock and awe. Throwing out my most generous, most unrefusable offer first so there'd be no need for any back-and-forth.

"Okayyy," she said hesitantly. "So I'll pull together comps and keep an eye on everything else in progress. I'm assuming you'll be working from there for the time being? Mr. Schaeffer implied you'd be out of the office for a long while."

I clamped my teeth together to keep from shouting an expletive into my poor assistant's ears. "Conrad's wrong. I plan on being back in New York with a signed contract in a week at most."

The smile was obvious in her voice. "Ah, there's the Rainmaker talking. Go get 'em, JT!"

After ending the call, I added the stupid office nickname—*Rainmaker*, gah—to the vat of shit I was irrationally angry about.

That anger was the reason I'd chosen to drive to Maine instead of flying to Portland and taking a helicopter to Honeybridge, like my father often did. I needed to take out all that negativity on the winding two-lane roads and let the sun and wind wash it away before I gave in to my desire to tell my boss where to shove it.

As much as I disliked certain things about Honeybridge, I couldn't fault the natural beauty of the place. Skirting the edge of an enormous lake in the middle of the Maine woods, where the moose outnumbered the people three to one, it was half a day's drive—or a billion light-years, depending on your point of view—from the city I called home. And as I cruised down the sun-dappled road, inhaling the deep, heady pine scent that was like no other fragrance in the world, I couldn't help but leave a tiny portion of my New York stress behind.

Before I had a chance to put the top down on the Porsche and really enjoy it, however, my phone rang again.

"Jonathan, darling, how are you?" My mother's voice was loud enough to make me jump and nearly knock my iced coffee over. "Things here are *wonderful*. Rarely have I had a better day."

I contemplated ending the call. Dealing with Patricia Wellbridge's socialite melodrama was a frustrating experience at the best of times. Since I'd had to cancel my trip to an all-inclusive Mexican resort (and deal with the theatrical rantings of my friend with benefits, Massimo, who'd now be enjoying the trip without me) before banishing myself to this place, it was safe to say this was not remotely the best of times.

And given the mounting evidence that my mother had been involved in that banishment—the sharp uptick in her hounding to "come home for a nice visit, darling," added to my parents' brief visit to the city recently and multiplied by Patricia's need to control things she had no business controlling—my anger ratcheted high enough to make the steering wheel leather squeak in my tight grip.

We're getting rid of anger, I reminded myself. *Anger is not productive here.*

"Mother," I said carefully. "I've got to be honest. I've had better days. In fact, I need to get on a very important business call right now."

I wasn't proud of the lie, but if I stayed on the phone with her for long, it wasn't going to end well.

"Nonsense." Her laughter sounded breathless, and she punctuated each word with a loud puff of air. "Nothing's... more important... than family." She panted heavily. "In fact... most of *your* family... is coming home... for the summer kickoff this weekend. Redmond. And Thomas. Your brother, Reagan. You know your *brother* always makes an effort to get back home."

Easy enough for Reagan since I wasn't sure he'd ever officially moved out. My brother was a sweet guy but way too caught up in my parents' social sphere.

"Good for them," I grumbled. "But I really do have to go."

"I understand! I understand! You're focused on your career. You're a Wellbridge." She heaved another breath. "Success. Is in. Your blood. But *family* is our strength, sweetheart. Why, your father, the Senator, often says —*ooofumowowow!*"

She let out a bellow like the warbling wail of a loon, and I sat up straighter in my seat, my temper yielding to concern.

"Mother? Are you alright?" I demanded. "Are you having chest pains? Should I call—"

"No, darling, I'm fine! Just doing my yogaerobics. It's a newer, more *refined* form of yoga. I'm simultaneously meditating to lower my heart rate *and* doing cardio, all while talking to you," she said proudly.

Yogaerobics? Had she made that up herself?

"But if you're doing cardio, doesn't that defeat the whole..." Belatedly, I remembered why it never paid to engage with my mother. You couldn't have a productive conversation with a person who refused to hear you and could never admit they were wrong. It was as useful as... well, as screaming your frustration at the inside of your car.

Which I badly wanted to do just then.

"Never mind," I sighed.

"Where are you, sweetheart? You sound perturbed. Are you perturbed? You're not still driving, are you? Driving while perturbed can be *so* dangerous. And I do believe it's illegal in Maine."

Aaaaand there was my suspicion confirmed.

I narrowed my eyes at the pastoral country road ahead of me. Cows dotted the field past the tree break to my right, and bright green leaves shivered in a gentle breeze to my left, but I was only peripherally aware of any of that. "I live in New York, Mother. Why would you assume I was anywhere near Maine?"

"Well, I... Er. Didn't you say so?" Mercifully, the huffing and puffing cut off.

"No. In fact, why would you assume that I'm driving at all?"

"The, ah..." She cleared her throat noisily. "Mothers

just have a sense about these things. We love our children so deeply and want their happiness—"

"Mother," I interrupted with saccharine sweetness. "What have you done?"

As if I didn't already know.

"There's no need to take a *tone*, Jonathan," she tsked. "I didn't *do* anything." After a brief hesitation, she admitted, "It's possible that when your father and brother and I were in New York last week—at one of your father's political fundraisers, you remember? The fundraiser you were too busy to attend?" She gave a sad little pause. "The governor's race won't be for another year, of course, but everyone in Augusta thinks the Senator will be a shoo-in for lieutenant—"

"*State* senator," I corrected automatically, rolling my eyes. "Dad is a *state* senator."

"My goodness. There's no need to be uncharitable, Jonathan," she chided. "After all, it's only a matter of time until—"

"Still waiting for the explanation," I gritted out.

"*Hmph.* Well... as it happens, we ran into your boss while we were there, and would you believe, Conrad and the Senator knew each other back in college! He wouldn't have made the connection to you, of course, since your father hadn't taken my last name yet back then. But he said you never even mentioned you were related to the Senator."

I ran a hand over my face. Conrad had said something during our conversation earlier today that had tipped me off to this, but I'd hoped to god he'd been joking.

He hadn't.

"Why on earth would I?" I gritted out.

"Darling, why *wouldn't* you? You're proud to be a Wellbridge, aren't you? To have a father who's a senator?"

I gave up correcting her dubious use of the word "senator." She was never going to change. "Of course I am. I just..."

Having a family with wealth and connections was a privilege, but I'd wanted a life where it didn't matter that I'd been born Jonathan Turner Wellbridge III, the firstborn son of Patricia and Trent. The only way I'd managed to get away from their hopes and expectations for me was by moving to New York after college and staying there.

Though apparently, that hadn't worked either, damn it.

"So, of course, Conrad and your father got to talking," she continued, undeterred as ever. "Conrad mentioned how very well you're doing, bringing so many vineyards and craft breweries under the Fortress Holdings umbrella for distribution deals. How you've made them the fastest-growing consumer products group in the country. How they call you the *Rainmaker*, the man who can close any deal with ease—"

"Not any deal," I said grimly, thinking about my most challenging prospect yet, the one waiting for me at the end of this drive.

"—and I may have mentioned how very difficult it's been for us, having you so far away and too busy to visit the way you once did. Reagan would do so much better with your influence. I told Conrad how very grateful we'd be if there was any way he could manage to get you home."

I thumped my head back against the leather seat. Sometimes I worried that my mother was delusional. But then I remembered that, no, she was just Patricia Wellbridge.

"The truth is..." Mother hesitated for a long moment, then admitted, "We miss you, Jonathan. We love you."

I sighed, my anger easing a fraction.

I knew she genuinely missed me. And I missed my family, too.

Sort of. Sometimes.

But there were very good reasons why I'd avoided Honeybridge for as long as I had... including one incredibly hot, unforgettably passionate, very poorly timed night that my mother didn't—and absolutely *wouldn't*—ever know about.

"I love you, too, but—"

"Which is why," she cut in, innocent as a lamb, "it was absolutely *providential* that your brother happened to mention to Conrad that some *upstart brewery* here in town has gotten a small following on the social medias. That piqued Conrad's curiosity enough to agree to send you home for the *entire summer* to sign a deal or whatnot. Isn't it delightful, darling? I have *so* many events and entertainments planned."

Reagan had put this idea in Conrad's head? I changed my mind—he was not a sweet, decent guy deep down; he was a mischief-trolling curse of a sibling, from his five-hundred-dollar haircut to his pedicured toes.

My mother wasn't any better. She knew exactly which "upstart" brewery Reagan had mentioned to Conrad Schaeffer—and exactly who owned it.

"I wouldn't call Honeybridge Mead an upstart," I said, mostly to provoke her. "Not when Flynn's Grandpa Horace started it forever ago. And according to everything I've read, it's doing a booming business under Flynn's leadership."

"Yes, well," she scoffed. "Perhaps amongst the *tourists*."

"After ordering samples, Conrad said this could be the most important contract I get all year."

"Oh, surely not."

"Mmhmm. I'd think a loyal Honeybridger like yourself would be proud that a homegrown business is so successful—"

"Proud? Of a Honeycutt-owned business?" My mother

sniffed. "Not hardly. Though I'm sure those Honeycutts are thrilled to have gotten one over on us yet again."

I rolled my eyes. There it was. My mother's *raison d'être*. The Wellbridge-Honeycutt feud.

The rivalry between the two largest families in Honeybridge was hardly new. It had been raging since seventeen-hundred-and-who-the-heck-knew, when a pair of best friends had traveled north from Boston to settle the fertile land near a lake and make their fortunes. Sounded wholesome and idyllic, and it had been... until Peregrine Wellbridge had decided to dam up the town river to irrigate his crops, cutting off his best friend's water supply, and January Honeycutt had lost his ever-loving mind and chopped down Peregrine's favorite oak tree in retaliation to make a mantle for his fireplace.

Since then, the Wellbridges and the Honeycutts were required, by birthright, to disagree on absolutely everything, from the color of the sky to the name of the lake near the town, which was known as either "Kiss Me Quick Lake" or "Lake Wellbridge," depending on who you were and which camp you found yourself in.

As a result, competition in the town was fierce. I'd like to have said that the people my age weren't as obsessed with the feud as the generations before us had been—and they were definitely less mean-spirited about it—but the competition between the clans raged on intensely, and the other folks in town knew enough to stay out of the way.

I'd never bought into it and had always had plenty of Honeycutts in my Contacts list. But the most important two had always been Pop Honeycutt, who ran the General Store, and... one other number I should have deleted three years ago.

A number that belonged to a man with green eyes,

freckled skin, and the prickliest disposition I'd ever encountered.

"Ah, well. I'm confident the *Rainmaker* will carry the day at the negotiation table," Mother assured me proudly. "Even if it means getting in bed with Flynn Honeycutt."

It was a good thing no one else was on the road around me, otherwise I might have run head-on into oncoming traffic. The images those words conjured—lean muscles and sloppy kisses, the scent of mead and sex thick in the air, Flynn's low voice urging me to *"Use your mouth. Just like... fuck."*—were ones I'd thought I'd purged from my memory years ago.

"The important part," my mother said, "is that you'll be home for weeks and weeks. You can see your friends. Revisit all the places you remember best—"

"God, no," I squeaked out.

"Pardon?"

"I won't be staying that long," I said more firmly. Calmly. *Controlledly.* "There's no reason. I'm going to make Flynn a very fair offer, so this should all be settled very quickly, and I'll be back in the city again before I know it."

I willed myself to believe it, no matter how much I might enjoy the summer sunshine on my arm and the clean air blowing in through the windows.

"Nonsense. Once you get here, you won't want to leave. The softball tournament is starting Saturday, and you'll be here to lead us to victory. Redmond's girlfriend is coming for a few days, and Aunt Louise is in raptures. Oh, and I've invited the Penningtons to visit through Regatta Day, so they'll be here for the Fourth of July, too," she went on merrily, as if perhaps all the yogaerobics had destroyed her powers of comprehension. "You remember the Penningtons, Jonathan. Brantleigh is such a lovely, lively young man and the heir to his father's real estate investment portfolio. And then, of course, this weekend..." She paused dramatically. "...is the third weekend in June."

"The... oh, *fuck*." I squeezed my eyes shut.

Box Day.

"Jonathan! *Language*."

I came around the final curve into town and saw a long row of taillights backed up in front of me. Dozens and dozens of cars were stopped on the country highway, trying to take the main Honeybridge turnoff.

"The Box Day Parade is today, isn't it?" I sighed, banging my forehead on the steering wheel.

"Why, yes. Obviously." Mother sounded almost offended that I might not have remembered the festival during which the good citizens of Honeybridge went to great lengths to create lavish floral arrangements for their window boxes, which were then judged by a mostly impartial (which was to say completely partial) panel of other Honeybridgers, all for the glory of earning a small rocker on the bottom of the Welcome to Honeybridge sign. "Your cousin Henrietta and I have been working on our theme for ages."

Right. Good old Cousin Henrietta.

Box Day was my mother's personal Valhalla, during which she tried in vain to best Willow Honeycutt at something, *anything*, generally by bringing in a rotating cast of professional floral designers from the city, pretending they were long-lost Wellbridge cousins, and getting them to put together her boxes.

It still never worked.

Remembering the town welcome sign reminded me of the hidden road behind it. I had just enough time to veer off quickly on the small side road as I passed the Welcome to Honeybridge sign. Dangling from twin chains below it were smaller signs that read "Honeycutts: Ice Festival Heroes" and "Honeycutts: Blueberry Day Winners" and "Honeycutts: Softball Tournament Champions," which really was laying it on a bit thick when I thought about it.

The lone "Wellbridges: Best Leaf Peepers" rocker seemed extra pathetic in comparison. Since when was Leaf Peeping a competitive thing? Was that really the best we could do? Surely there had to be some sort of—

Whoa. No. I brought that train of thought to a screeching halt as the tourist traffic disappeared behind me. I was not here in Honeybridge to get sucked back into the competitive fray. No way.

I was here to sign a distribution deal with Flynn—with *Honeybridge Mead*, which was not the same thing—and get the hell back to my real life. The life where eventually Massimo would get over being angry, and Alice would help me remain at the top of the Fortress sales ladder.

The life where Patricia Wellbridge didn't get to boss me around.

I took a deep breath and slowed the car to put the top down so I could truly enjoy the drive through town despite my mother's continued babbling about the Outdoor Lantern Supper, the Intimate Cocktail Fete, and the Joyous Summers-End Regalia she was planning. It was a gorgeous day, and the sight of all the familiar landmarks gave my heart a tiny, nostalgic squeeze.

Okay, maybe there were *some* things I'd forgotten I'd missed about this town.

As I drove behind the redbrick town hall and caught glimpses of children and parents laughing and eating ice cream cones from the General Store along Fraser Street, I gave myself a firm talking-to.

I would not fall back into old habits of letting my parents control where I went and who I spent time with. I would not let the old family feud lull me into an *us* versus *them* mentality. And I would not, under any circumstances, allow myself to look at Flynn Honeycutt as anything but a former classmate and current potential client.

Apple Street was closed to traffic, and Pinehurst was blocked with delivery vans. I finally had to acknowledge to myself there was only one reasonable way remaining to get to Wellbridge House.

I turned onto Fraser Street and took a deep breath.

I almost didn't recognize Honeybridge Tavern when I came upon it—a gleaming white clapboard building with a jaunty sign where a dilapidated pile of brown shingles had once stood. And I sure as hell didn't immediately recognize the man unloading a box truck on the sidewalk outside, even though he had shoulders that looked extremely familiar.

Suddenly, one of the children outside Ollie's Fudge Shoppe—a boy with curly, Wellbridge-blond hair—began screaming in panic as the puppy he'd been holding jumped out of his arms and darted into the street, trailing its leash like a comet's tail... directly in front of my car.

I hit the horn and slammed on the brakes. At the last second, I yanked the car to the right, away from the pair, plowing through a gigantic pothole right outside the Tavern, and rocked to a stop inches away from the sidewalk.

Muddy water sprayed up like a mushroom cloud, blanketing the hood of my Porsche, the windshield, the sidewalk... and the man standing there with a wooden crate in his hands.

Horrifying.

More horrifying still was the way my stomach clenched and the whole world faded to white noise as my brain thought, *Yes. Fucking finally. There you are.*

It had been three years since I'd laid eyes on that face. On that dark hair and defined jaw, those broad shoulders and tree-trunk legs. On the man who'd forever be at the heart of my personal I-knew-I-was-gay-when story.

Flynn Honeycutt looked good. Better, even, than he had three years before. The kind of good that even a dousing of filthy water couldn't wash away. And for the faintest nanosecond, as he shifted the crate to one huge arm and lifted his hand to wipe the mud from his eyes, his biceps bunched, and his lips twisted up in a half-smile, like he was ready to laugh at the ridiculousness of it all.

In short, he was devastating... and doing business with the man was the furthest thought from my mind.

But then the moment passed, and time sped up again. Flynn's eyes—leaf green, emerald green, *Honeycutt* green—flared in recognition and then flashed with rage.

"*Frog!*" He growled my silly childhood nickname like it was the dirtiest curse he knew.

He took a single threatening step toward my car before one of his coworkers rushed up to pat him with a towel and blocked my view.

"Jonathan? Jonathan, are you alright? What's happening?" my mother demanded.

Part of me wanted to get out of the car and run to him. To apologize and explain, preferably while toweling Flynn off. But I was pretty sure that would only make things more tense and awkward, which was pretty on-brand for me and Flynn Honeycutt, and would absolutely, positively ensure that I would never get him to sign the contract I needed.

So, instead, I did what I always did. I sighed and drove away.

"Nothing, Mother. I, ah... I just reached Honeybridge."

"Wonderful! So you'll be here shortly. The place never changes, does it?" she sighed fondly.

"No," I said, casting a glance in my rearview mirror. "Some things don't change at all."

Achilles had his one weak heel.

Samson had his hair.

And in an entire career built around closing deals and understanding what other people wanted, I had Flynn Honeycutt... the one person I'd never been able to charm.

At least not yet.

Chapter Two

Flynn

Frog.

AKA Jonathan Turd-face Wellbridge the millionth.

AKA the man who'd gotten my hopes up way more times than I should have allowed and then crushed them every time.

AKA *asshole*.

It figured the jerk who splashed me with muddy street water would turn out to be some rich tourist in a convertible sports car, swanning into town for the weekend. But seeing who was driving it? That put the cherry on the shit sundae.

The man didn't stop or even call out an apology, which was exactly what I'd expect from him.

"Fucking *Wellbridge*," I muttered under my breath like the vilest of curse words.

Some of the Wellbridge clan lived in town year-round, but "the Senator" liked to fly in on his private helicopter every Friday to golf a round of eighteen at the club and take a sail on his vintage wooden catboat. JT hadn't visited in years—according to his mother's incessant gossiping, which was impossible to ignore no matter how much I'd tried, JT had been far too busy excelling at his extremely prestigious *dream job* to take time off—but apparently, he was old enough to play Man of Leisure with his father and his cronies now.

Lucky him.

"Flynn?" Dan, one of my bartenders, rushed over in concern and began ineffectually swiping at me with a bar rag that smelled like stale beer. "Man, who was that guy?"

"That..." My gaze followed the little red car down the street. "...was an entitled dick in a douchemobile."

"Seriously," Dan agreed, his eyes still fixed on the rear end of the Porsche. "But, like... sweet ride, eh?"

"No." I rolled my eyes, grabbed the cloth from Dan's hand, and mopped at my shirt. "Nothing about that man is sweet."

I was not impressed by JT and his fancy car. I never had been. I also was not moved by the fact that he'd looked just as good, if not better, than ever.

Mpfh. Definitely not.

In fact, the whole thing was just... excessive.

No one needed to drive a car like that. And for sure no one needed to look that good in a boring white Oxford shirt, even if the sleeves were rolled up to show his fancy watch and his stupid crown tattoo.

Which they might have been.

Though I absolutely had not noticed.

At all.

"Flynn?" Dan said, blinking at me like he'd been saying my name for a while. "You okay?"

"Perfectly fine." I scowled. "Why wouldn't I be? Help me finish unloading these cases."

If JT had swanned into town for a family visit—*finally*—then he needed to stay the hell away from me and my business.

But it only took me a minute while hauling now dripping-wet cases of beer to realize that if JT had driven into town in his own car, he was most likely here for longer than a weekend.

Fuck.

When I got the last of the cases inside and around the back of the bar, my brother Castor noticed me and stopped in his tracks. "What happened to you? Is it raining?"

I grabbed a fresh towel from behind the bar and finished wiping the mud off. "JT Wellbridge happened. What else is new?" I muttered before washing my hands quickly in the bar sink and reaching for Castor's order to fill it.

Castor set down his tray and leaned across it with a dreamy grin on his face. "Aww, JT's back? That's amazing. That's—"

I glared at him as I poured a Sprite for a customer. "No. It's not. And don't give me those eyes. Keep your heart-eyes to yourself. No eyeballs."

Our brother Alden came racing in from the street the way he always did when he'd picked up good dirt at the beauty salon where he worked. "You will never guess who's back!"

I gestured to my dirty shirt. "Pretty sure I'm wearing the evidence. And no," I added before he got any ideas, "I don't want to talk about it."

Castor continued with the dreamboat eyes. "I always thought JT had a thing for you. Like Romeo and... Other-Romeo. Two star-crossed lovers from feuding families. So romantic." His eyes widened. "Oh! What if he's here to finally sweep you off your feet and carry you away to your very own deserted island to... to..." His voice trailed off.

I snorted. Castor was the youngest twenty-three-year-old I'd ever met. The carrying-off was probably the extent of his fantasy library.

Alden was the opposite. At thirty, his eyes sparked with

knowledge and judgment. "To *fuck*, Cas. To fuck. But Flynn needs to stay away from JT because that way lies madness, as we've already learned. Right, Flynn?"

"Mmm." My brother had no idea the kind of madness JT and I had engaged in.

"In fact, any sane person would avoid all things Wellbridge," Alden went on. "They'll try to give you their magic peen and then take it away when they leave."

Castor's eyebrows furrowed in confusion. "Why do you sound like you speak from personal experience?"

Alden shut down that line of questions with a dismissive wave. "You don't need to experience it to know it's true. Just stay away, Flynn. Nobody needs to be thinking about dick right now anyway when we've got the Brew Fest to prepare for."

I felt a surge of fond affection for my brother at his use of the word "we." And he was right—who the fuck needed magic peen when you had your family and a common goal?

The Brew Fest was an expo of independent Northeastern meaderies, cideries, and breweries that took place over in Portland every August— a kind of All-Star Game for local brewers, where we served samples of our very best varietals in hopes of being named Best of the Fest. More importantly, it was also the place where the largest local Renaissance Faire organizer came to make their annual featured mead selection.

Landing the Ren Faire had been my dream for a while now, not just for the bragging rights but because it meant a steady income that would allow me to expand my operation and get a distribution deal. And if I wanted a shot at being chosen, I needed to take as much inventory as possible to the expo, which meant brewing more to replace the lost inventory, as well as ramping up production in anticipation of winning the contract.

All of this while continuing to run the Tavern during peak season and help my parents with their business.

Alden was right. I couldn't let JT's sudden appearance distract us from our goals.

"*Pfft.* Don't be insane. No force on Earth could make me wanna fuck JT Wellbridge. He's not even that good-looking," I lied, reaching for a glass to fill with vodka rocks to add to Castor's order. Someone at table twelve was celebrating early. It wasn't remotely five o'clock yet.

Castor shot me the eyeballs again like he wanted to argue or maybe call me on my lie, but Alden cut him off with a head shake. "Drop it. Flynn said no eyes, bro."

Castor sighed and rolled his eyes instead, but Alden's gaze met mine. He reached across the bar to grab a soda off Castor's tray.

"So... Why do you think he's here?" Alden asked, not dropping the subject of JT despite telling Castor to.

I shot him a look and reached for a fresh glass to replace the soda in Castor's order. "Well, gosh, Alden, let me think. His last pen pal letter didn't say a darn thing."

Alden snorted.

"Seriously, how would I know?" I demanded. "I haven't heard a word from the man since..."

Since Thanksgiving weekend three years ago. Right after my grandfather's funeral. When the world had seemed incredibly large and scary, and I'd let myself believe that JT was someone I could anchor myself to.

A special moment in my personal history I liked to refer to as the Night of Regrets.

Except you don't really regret his hands on you, do you?

"...shit, who can even remember?" I lied again.

Castor shrugged. "Probably just having a cozy visit with family. I'm sure Patricia and the Senator are thrilled to have him home."

I wanted to scoff at the idea of the Wellbridges being a tight-knit sort of family like ours—Patricia Wellbridge, in particular, was the opposite of warm and fuzzy, and their mansion on a hill was more like a museum than a place you could kick back and relax—but I supposed that might be what Wellbridges considered "cozy."

And it was for damn sure none of my business.

"Patricia most likely issued a command," I muttered, finishing the last of Castor's order and handing it to him.

He nodded a thanks and headed back to his customers.

Dan handed a check folder to a woman finishing her lunch at the bar and then turned to us. "Okay, I'm completely lost. Who is this guy? Why don't I know him?"

"Because he hasn't dragged his ass back to town in all the years you've lived here?" I shrugged.

"No, I mean..." Dan hesitated. "What's his story? What's he like?"

Castor returned in time to hear the question, and all three of us Honeycutt brothers answered at the same time. "He's a Wellbridge."

Dan wrinkled his nose in confusion but nodded along anyway.

"Dan hasn't lived here long enough to know what we mean, and he's not a Honeycutt, so Patricia Wellbridge is probably nice to *him*." Alden tapped his chin. "Let's see. Imagine... Attila the Hun plus Dracula plus the Grindr guy who leaves before the..." He realized how close he was standing to one of my customers. "*Shower water*... has dried. That's JT Wellbridge."

Dan glanced at me, eyes wide. "That's... wow. What did he do? To Flynn, I mean."

"Nothing," I began, but Alden interrupted.

"JT's jerked Flynn around for years. Cheated, lied, gotten him in trouble with teachers. One time in high school, he actually pretended to ask Flynn out. As if a Wellbridge would lower himself to *date a Honeycutt*," he said in an imitation of Patricia Wellbridge's upper-crust accent. "*Pfft.*"

I couldn't help but remember a Wellbridge lowering himself to do something else to me. The warm, yellow light from the old pendant lamp in the storage loft had shone on JT's dark blond hair, turning it gold as he'd dropped to his knees at my feet. His face had turned up to me then, skin flushed with heat and blue eyes glazed over with need.

I swallowed and nodded. "*Pfft*," I agreed feebly. I could still taste the memory of warm whiskey on his lips as he'd begged me to give myself to him.

Just once, Firecracker.

And fucking Christ, now I was hard.

I cleared my throat. "Anyway, it doesn't matter. Weren't you the one who just said we weren't gonna let him steal our focus?" I lightly cuffed the side of Alden's head. "We need to spin up the new fermenters without disturbing the aging barrels. I have a design sketched out for the brew room expansion, but—"

Dan held up a hand. "No, wait. What do you mean this guy 'pretended' to ask Flynn out?"

I cast my eyes to the recently redone ceiling and the new seating area that ringed the second floor. "Jesus. It's old fucking news, Dan. Not worth rehashing—"

But my brother Alden was an asshole, and rehashing was his favorite pastime. "I mean that JT was an entitled prick who thought he could toy with Flynn's emotions, even back when they were teenagers, before JT had attained his final, evil form. All Wellbridges are the same," he said bitterly. "They want what they want when they want it, and they fuck right off when they don't get it."

Dan frowned. "I get why the guy'd be interested in

Flynn. Obviously. But... shit. Why not actually take you out instead of pretending?"

I narrowed my eyes at Dan. What did he mean by *"obviously"*?

Castor shot Dan the dreamy eyeballs this time. "Personally, I think JT was too intimidated by Flynn's rugged masculinity."

I stopped myself from picking daintily at a stray cuticle. "Huh?"

Alden hoisted himself up on the foot rung of the bar and reached for the soda hose, helping himself to a refill. "Well, I think JT's dude-bro friends and his Wellbridge cousins put him up to it like a dare. His cousin Redmond," he sneered, sitting back down, "is the worst Wellbridge of them all."

I reached across and took the soda hose back before knuckle-punching Alden in the shoulder. "Thanks a lot. You make it sound like JT was never really interested in me."

Alden lifted a skeptical brow, which made me clench my teeth.

"He was interested," I ground out. "Plenty interested."

Alden sat back down on his stool and nursed his soda through a straw morosely while rubbing the spot I'd punched. "If you say so."

I closed my eyes and tried desperately not to replay that Thanksgiving night again in my head. The memory tapes were old and ragged from overuse.

Firecracker, you've always been mine.

My stomach flipped with a sickening swoop. I seriously did not have time for this. It was yet one more way the Wellbridge family was going to try fucking over the Honeycutts, and it damned sure wasn't happening on my watch.

"Moving on!" I said with a cheerful energy that I didn't

feel in the slightest. "Honeybridge Mead is going to be selected as the official exclusive mead supplier to the largest Ren Faire organizer in the country. And it's going to happen after we blow them away with our mead selection at Brew Fest, which is in only *five weeks*. Meanwhile, we have a tavern to run during the busiest season of the year and continue to be Honeybridge's largest tourism draw for the fourth summer in a row, thanks to Frankie and her Instagram followers. That means staying focused on our goals, people. Frog Wellbridge is none of my business, and I'm not going to let him and his beautiful fa— uh, beautiful *Porsche* —distract me."

Dan blinked. "Wait, what's Frog?"

Instead of screaming my frustration into the entire crowded tavern around me, I simply ignored the question. I grabbed my tablet and headed around the bar to the host stand, where some new people seemed to be waiting for a table. Over my shoulder, I heard Alden snort.

"A frog is a slimy, warty little—"

"Hush," Castor chided. "Frog's a nickname, Dan. You know how Pop Honeycutt calls our sister Georgia Moonflower, and Flynn is Firecracker, and McLean is Moose? He gives all the Honeybridge kids these strange nicknames, and nobody really knows where he comes up with them, but somehow, they stick. And JT is... he's Frog."

"The kind who *doesn't* turn into a handsome prince," Alden added sourly. "No matter how much Flynn wanted to think so back in the day."

I didn't stick around to hear more. After seating the new customers, I made my way through the arched doorway to the meadery section of the Tavern and shut the door, relishing the relative hush of the room.

The pristine craft room was divided from the tavern by a huge glass wall. Customers loved sitting for a meal where they could watch the tanks, fermenters, and barrels in fascination. But for me... it was like my very own playroom.

I closed my eyes and inhaled the clean, yeasty, and slightly honey-scented air. This was my happy place. I'd never set out to become a mead maker. In fact, I'd never set out to own a tavern. To be honest, I'd never imagined myself staying in Honeybridge at all.

But things changed, didn't they? Sometimes a child's dream of what he wanted to be when he grew up didn't pan out, and that was okay. Things happened that kept us from taking our original path, but that didn't mean we were on a worse path, per se, only different. And there was joy to be found in the new path, too.

I loved my new path. I'd forged it myself when I'd badly needed to start something just for fun, just for me, and I'd worked my ass off. I'd convinced my Grandpa Horace to let me make some of his home-brew mead on-site at the Tavern as a way of livening up our offerings at a time when the business wasn't doing very well.

"We'll use local honey and make a big deal of honey wine at Honeybridge Tavern," I'd suggested, with the kind of excitement and optimism that had come naturally to me back then.

Now five years and who-knew how many failed batches later, the meadery I'd founded on a lark had finally gained a reputation all over New England and beyond. It had helped breathe fresh life into the Tavern that Grandpa Horace had passed down to me, too, making it a destination for good food and excellent company. Hell, we'd even been featured by an Instagram influencer.

"It's your legacy now, Firecracker," Grandpa had said the night before he'd died. "Keep making me proud."

I rested my hand on the side of a tank and breathed deeply for a moment. Grandpa had been my rock—the person I'd leaned on when the weight of everyone leaning on *me* had gotten too heavy—and the loss of him still hurt sometimes.

Was it any wonder I'd practically thrown myself at JT Fucking Wellbridge when he'd come home for Thanksgiving a few short days later?

Now, I was finally on the cusp of turning our mead into something bigger than me, bigger than Honeybridge. The Ren Faire contract was only one step in my plan to turn Honeybridge Mead into a worldwide phenomenon.

I had big plans. And I wasn't about to let a hot pair of Brooks Brothers suit pants distract me from them.

This was the summer of Flynn Honeycutt's triumph. I was finally going to come into my own nickname and light this town on fire with an explosive new contract for Honeybridge Mead.

And JT Wellbridge needed to stand clear of the fireworks.

Chapter Three

JT

As I drove down the hill from Wellbridge House to town later that week, I told myself I was not nervous about meeting with Flynn Honeycutt.

Heck, no.

Getting nervous about meeting a guy I'd known since he'd stolen my dump truck on the first day of Blueberry Hill Pre-K would be the height of ridiculousness, right? Especially when you considered how many important people I'd met without breaking a sweat.

For example, the Italian ambassador, who was a lovely woman with an excellent nose for wine. Or Espen Bakker from those action movies, who had less charisma than my toaster when he wasn't onscreen but was hot shit at promoting pale ale. Or Korbin Burdoe and Donte Cameron from the Lakers, who were better at making tequila than they were at basketball last season, just saying. I once even spent time with royal family members—who would remain nameless due to their unexpected behavior—on a friend of a friend's Mediterranean yacht, which was not at all related to business but which I still filed under the heading of "Important Conversations I'd Had Un-Nervously."

So walking into the Honeybridge Tavern in the middle of the day should have been small potatoes in comparison.

Of course, to be fair, I wasn't acquainted with any of the people on that list quite as intimately as I was with Flynn Honeycutt.

For instance, I was not aware if any of them tended to fake right before darting left when stealing bases during overly competitive softball games. I hadn't seen any of them wrap a scarf around their fractured wrist rather than abandon their team during an ice hockey game out at Wellbridge Lake when we were eleven or seen the dull gleam of respect in any of their eyes when the Wellbridges had still gotten the hard-fought win.

I didn't know whether any of them had ever flushed to the roots when they were asked out on a date back in high school or whether any of them had ever left that date waiting in the freezing cold for hours with no mittens when they didn't show up after agreeing.

I for sure didn't hear the precise pitch of their orgasm moans in my head when I jerked off, and I'd never held the bittersweet tang of their pleasure in my mouth.

I had also not fucked shit up with any of them three years ago on Thanksgiving by kissing them when I should have insisted on talking or, later on, by talking when we probably should have kept kissing.

So, okay, maybe this meeting wasn't *entirely* the same as the others.

But, I assured myself as I stared through the windshield of the Porsche at the homey white building where a crowd of people milled outside as if waiting to be seated, none of that history mattered anymore, just like that tiny, incidental, *accidental* mud bath the other day didn't matter.

Flynn and I were adults. Able to let bygones be bygones.

And Flynn was smart—arguably smarter than me. The contract I was about to offer him was extremely fair—I'd spent the past two days poring over the numbers and research packet Alice had sent me, then studying comparable marketplace deals to make damn sure of it.

Surely a logical businessman would focus on the contract and ignore the fact that the messenger had once rimmed and sucked him until he'd sobbed brokenly and pleaded for release... Right?

As I slammed my car door shut, I conveniently ignored the fact that while Wellbridges might be known for employing ruthless logic, Honeycutts were better known for exacting bloodthirsty revenge.

A crowd of laughing people clutching bags from the nearby souvenir shop pulled open the door to the Tavern and bustled inside, and I nearly turned back to the car.

It was probably awfully crowded in there during the lunch rush. I could maybe regroup and come back later...

My phone buzzed, and I slid it from my pocket.

Alice: *How'd the meeting go?*

I rolled my eyes and dismissed the notification, but another popped up immediately.

Alice: *Because I KNOW you didn't decide to postpone it AGAIN because you feel like you still need to "get your ducks in a row" over the contract you had me draft TUESDAY, did you?*

Damn it. I was so firing her, no matter how disgustingly competent she was. It was bad enough that I was fucking around on this, which was highly, *highly* unlike me; I didn't need her to point it out, for god's sake.

Me: *I'm about to have the meeting now. As I told you, I've been busy for the past two days with family obligations.*

Obligations that included lunching at my mother's club,

teaching my mother's dog—a highly anxious Bichon named Katharine Hepburn—that my shoes were not chew toys and, for one horrifying hour that would be burned into my memory until death claimed me, exchanging horrified looks with Reagan as my mother attempted to convert us into yogaerobics enthusiasts.

Jesus, I hated myself.

More to the point, I hated the person I became when I was in Honeybridge.

Which was why I needed to get shit done and get the hell out.

I gripped my leather folder more tightly and stalked into the Tavern with a purpose... but when I got inside, I stopped dead and gawked just as much as any one of the tourists because Frankie Hilo's selfies hadn't done the place justice.

The outside of the Tavern had looked shockingly nice the other day, but the footprint had been the same as when Flynn's Grandpa Horace had been running the place. I'd had no clue that the inside would be so entirely changed.

Gone were the tobacco-stained walls and the wood paneling pockmarked with a million dart holes. Instead, the walls were now whitewashed shiplap that looked like it had been there for centuries, though it hadn't. The whole back wall was made of glass, and beyond it was the pristine, white-painted meadery with its shiny fermentation barrels, making patrons feel like they were part of the action.

Gone were the low ceilings and the red tiled floor, too. Now, a metal staircase along one side of the rustic wooden bar led up to a loft-style seating area, with deep couches and comfortable chairs in what had once been a tiny studio apartment and a storage space. A storage space where Flynn and I had spent that one memorable night...

"Just one?" a friendly voice asked.

"Huh?" I turned around, searching for the mind reader... and found a slender dude with a Tavern T-shirt and a hipster haircut standing behind the host's desk.

"Just one for lunch today?" he asked again.

Oh. "Ah, no. I'd actually like to see Flynn Honeycutt." I smiled and nodded down at my leather folio. "On a business matter."

"Okay. Well, it's the tail end of the lunch rush, and he's working the bar, but you can go wait for him if you'd like." He nodded toward the bar along the left side of the room.

Flynn moved around behind the counter, all broad shoulders and bubble-butt perfection, chatting to a customer here, filling a drink order there. His beard was scruffier than I remembered it being the other day, and he wore a shirt that was either a size too small or absolutely perfect, depending on whether you liked your bartender's nipples to be visible from a distance... which I did.

A lot.

"Great," I managed to say in a strangled voice, already moving across the floor like a moth to a motherfucking flame. "I'll just take a seat over there, then—"

"Oh. My. Gosh!" Castor Honeycutt stopped directly in front of me, clutching an empty tray in one hand, then threw himself at me with a happy little squeal, hugging me around the shoulders.

"Heya, Sunshine," I said, his old nickname coming to my lips without conscious thought as I patted his back fondly.

"I'm, like, so, *so* glad you're here," he whispered. "Flynn's been waiting for you, even if he doesn't know it."

Castor had heard about the contract I was going to offer Flynn? How the heck had that happened?

"Oh, he definitely doesn't know it," I confirmed when he pulled back. I cast a glance over his shoulder at the man in question, who worked the register with one hand while filling a soda with the other. "I had a hunch that surprising him might work better than attempting to schedule an appointment." Especially after what had gone down the other day with the puddle.

Castor grinned broadly, and his eyes, which were a dark blue-green that made me think of the deepest part of Wellbridge Lake, went all warm and gooey. He linked his arm with mine to draw me toward the bar. "It's like the stars aligned just perfectly."

"You think?" I was happy for the vote of confidence, even if I didn't get what had inspired it.

"Aw, hells yeah! It's Frog!" A man jumped off his barstool to grab me in a one-armed hug. "Heard you were back in town, man. Maria Thorpe told Becky Honeycutt, who works with my wife at Wicker Insurance." He hooked a thumb out the window.

My mind struggled to place the broad, freckled face and thinning red-blond hair.

"Ernie!" I said a fraction of a second late. "Ernie McLeroy. I didn't know you were married. Congrats."

"Yeah." Ernie blushed comprehensively. "Going on two years now. Yvonne's got a bun in the oven, too." He shoved my shoulder. "How about you, man? Word is you're here for the whole summer? You gonna put that arm to work for us in the tournament?"

My mother's gossip elves had clearly been hard at work. "Oh, no. I'm afraid I—"

"Jing, you remember Froggy's arm?" Ernie called to a dark-haired man at a nearby booth. "Holy shizoley, huh? Just a couple innings and we'd decimate the Honeycutts."

"You could try!" Brittany Merchant, one of Flynn's cousins, came bouncing up, auburn ponytail swinging. She was nearly as tall as me, though I would have sworn that the last time I was home, she'd been a gap-toothed preteen who'd tried to sell me Girl Scout cookies.

"Nice ride out there, JT." She leaned in and whispered quickly, "I heard from Wilma at the Green Quarry farm that you were back in town for the whole summer. That true? Any chance you could take me for a spin?" She batted her eyelashes.

I wasn't sure if she was more into me or the car, but either way, I would not be asking Brittany for Thin Mints.

I shook my head apologetically. "I'm only here for a couple days." I darted a look at Flynn, who was filling a drink order halfway down the bar. "Maybe less. And I'm gonna be working the whole time." And though I was pretty sure everyone in town knew I was gay, just to be sure, I added, "Gotta get back to the city, you know? Massimo gets temperamental if I have to cancel a date at the last minute."

This was not a lie, technically. Lord knew the man had been blowing up my phone with angry messages, despite flooding his Instagram with porn-tastic Speedo pics from Cabo.

"Oh," she said dejectedly. "Well, what if—?"

"Excuse me," a familiar voice said. "Is there a reason everyone is congregating and clogging the aisle for my customers?"

Ernie darted a glance over his shoulder, and his arm fell away from my shoulders. "Oops. My bad, Flynn."

"And Cas, since when do you stand around chitchatting during lunch rush?"

Castor rolled his lips together but stepped away from me, too. "Sorry, Flynn."

Crap. I turned around slowly and summoned my most charming smile. "Um. Hey, Flynn! Sorry for the... kerfuffle."

Kerfuffle? Who the hell said *kerfuffle*?

Flynn gave me a long, slow up and down, then pursed his lips and turned away.

"I'd love a moment of your time!" I called to his back. "I have a business proposition you really want to hear—"

That got his attention. "You?" he demanded, turning back toward me. "Have a business proposition for *me*? Really."

"Uh. Yes? I mean, we're both in the wine and spirits business, right? You're manufacturing, I'm distribution. You might say we're kissing cousins, in a way."

I forced a laugh.

Flynn didn't.

Jesus. I cleared my throat. "Anyway, you might know I've been working for Fortress Holdings CPG in New York for three years now—"

Flynn's eyes flared for a second like he recognized the name, which was a great sign, but then his expression shuttered, and when another memory from three years ago assaulted me—*"Just leave, Frog. Go back to your job in New York and pretend this night never happened."*—I realized that reminding him of New York just now might have been a critical error.

"How in the world would I know that, Wellbridge? And why the heck would I care? Believe it or not, I don't spend my time pondering the day-to-day lives of former Honeybridgers." He gave a pointed glance at my leather folio. "Not interested."

"But—"

"I'm busy."

"You haven't even heard the terms of the—"

"What part of not interested are you not getting?"

My nervousness evaporated under a flare of annoyance. "I'm asking for ten minutes of your time, Flynn. As a professional courtesy."

His expression turned from frosty to glacial. "And I'm telling you, *Wellbridge*, that I don't have ten minutes. You're not the only one with an important job. I have a business to run."

Never had anyone said my name with such utter disdain... which was really saying something when you remembered that I'd grown up in a town half-full of Honeycutts.

But I had a job to do here. A contract to get signed. A vice presidency to obtain.

I straightened my spine. "Then I'll sit here and wait," I said obstinately.

Ernie pulled out his wallet and dropped some bills on the counter. "I've gotta get going anyway. JT, you can take my seat."

"No, he can't." Flynn shot Ernie a dirty look. "Seats are for paying customers."

"Great!" I enthused, taking Ernie's stool. "I'm starving. Can I see a menu?"

Flynn rolled his eyes and pointed to the two enormous chalkboard menus over his head—one for drinks and the other for food—which were artfully decorated with leafy green vines and swirls... and which anyone could have seen if they hadn't been utterly distracted by the man standing beneath them.

"Oh. Right. Okay. I'll have—" I glanced at the food menu and tried to ignore the heat of my cheeks, which suggested that my face was probably pulsing red like the siren on a fire engine.

"*Ennhhh.*" Flynn made a noise like a game show buzzer. "Never mind. Too slow. You'll get what I give you." He slapped open the swinging door beneath the chalkboard and disappeared into the kitchen.

Well. That went stunningly.

The host from the front—Dan, according to his name tag—lifted the pass-through so he could take over the bar. He glanced at the kitchen door, which was still swinging, then turned his accusing glare on me.

I smiled winningly. "So, could I try some of your amazing mead?"

"Are you... Frog? Frog Wellbridge?"

"Yeah. I, uh... I guess that's me," I agreed.

Dan narrowed his eyes and *hmphed*, then turned and followed Flynn to the kitchen.

What the heck was his problem? I'd hardly met the guy, and he had no reason to dislike me unless... unless he and Flynn were together and Flynn had told him about us?

Why did that idea piss me off?

"I can get you a drink," Castor offered, taking up the empty spot behind the bar. "What kind of mead would you like?"

He gestured toward the other chalkboard above us.

Honeybridge Runway - Stylish and never dull! Raw wildflower back-sweetened with a hint of caramel and finished cool.

Honeybridge Moonflower - Bold and complex! Blueberry honey and California Pinot Noir pyment that's not too sweet and not too rich.

Honeybridge Moose Call - Mysterious and woodsy! Spicy clove and dark maple acerglyn.

Honeybridge Daydreamer - Artistic and daring! Bright notes of orange mixed with tangy mesquite.

Honeybridge Sunshine - Warm as a summer day! Sweet strawberry and vanilla melomel with resonant floral notes.

"Wow," I breathed. Despite knowing what Flynn had accomplished here—despite being in town to *acquire* it, for heaven's sake—the sight still hit me like a solid punch to the gut, filling me with nostalgia, and regret, and no small amount of pride for Flynn, too.

Not that I'd ever tell him so since I liked my testicles exactly where they were.

Castor followed my gaze up to the board also, like he wasn't sure what I was seeing, and then his sweet face flushed happily. "Oh, yeah. Guess I've gotten used to it."

"It's... *you*. All of you Honeycutt kids. Alden, Georgia, Mac, PJ, and you."

"Yup. Based on the nicknames Pop Honeycutt gave us," he agreed. "One of the first things Flynn did after Grandpa Horace died and left him this place was to get new equipment and start creating varietals. Taking things to the next level, you know?"

I nodded. That tracked with everything I knew about Flynn Honeycutt. He'd had big dreams, just like I had, but something had always held him back from leaving this town and making them a reality.

Castor frowned and tapped his lip thoughtfully. "Actually, I lie. That was the second thing he did. First, he tore out the upstairs storage area." He glanced at the loft area above us, then darted a glance at me and shrugged. "Weirdest thing. The day after Grandpa's funeral, Alden and I came in, and the place was all torn up. Flynn had done it with his own two hands, spur of the moment-like. Not sure what got into him. But it looks pretty awesome, so I guess he knew what he was doing, huh? He usually does."

My chest tightened. I was uncomfortably certain I knew what had prompted Flynn to get rid of the storage area in such a hurry.

This did not bode well for the contract I needed signed, damn it.

Flynn barged back into the bar area, smacking the

swinging door so hard it crashed into the wall and made Castor flinch.

"Lunch," he said, setting a steaming plate in front of me with a smirk. "Bon appétit."

My nose recognized the food before my eyes did, and I clapped a hand to my mouth to stop myself from retching. "Is that...?"

"Uh-huh. Fish sticks. Your favorite. Eat up."

They weren't my favorite. Not at all.

There'd been a horrible incident in the cafeteria back in third grade when my cousin Redmond had dared me to eat twenty-two of them... and I had. But then my stomach had revolted, and the ensuing carnage had earned me a nickname that made "Frog" seem elegant in comparison.

"What the hell?" I scanned the menu above his head and tried breathing through my mouth. "You don't even serve fish sticks."

"I ran down to Teddy's All-Nite to get those from the freezer section and microwaved 'em up for you specially to thank you for the mud bath you gave me the other day..." Flynn leaned in and delivered the coup de grâce. "...*Sir Spewsalot*." Then he dusted his hands together and strode off down the hall by the bathrooms.

I was pretty sure he wasn't shaking his ass in those tight jeans purposely, but his intention didn't matter.

Castor covered his mouth to stifle his laugh, but I stared after Flynn in outrage.

He'd gone too damn far. I was simultaneously annoyed and aroused when I very much wanted to be neither.

I jumped off my stool, grabbed my folder, and stalked down the hall after him. He threw open the door to the manager's office, but I managed to catch it before he could slam it behind him.

"You're going to listen to me, Flynn Honeycutt—" I began.

Flynn rounded on me, arms crossed over his chest. "It's so like a Wellbridge to try to tell me what I can and can't do," he sneered. "This is *my* bar. Hell, this is my *town*. So take your business proposals and your fancy-ass mud-mobile and leave."

"Why are you being like this?" I demanded. "Jesus, Flynn. This can't be about the puddle. That was an accident! You saw that dog run into the street and the little boy chasing him—"

"It's not about the fucking puddle!"

"Then it's gotta be about that night three years ago—"

"Fuck you. We're not discussing that night."

"You told me to leave! You said—"

"I *said* we're not discussing it," Flynn whisper-hissed, his hand slicing through the air like a knife blade. "That night was a colossal mistake."

I swallowed hard and reminded myself this was no more or less than the truth—no more than what I believed myself—and therefore, it didn't hurt to hear him confirm it.

"Give me fifteen minutes of your time to look through this contract. I promise you'll be glad you did. And once our business is done, I'll be out of your hair."

He exhaled once through his nose and rolled his eyes, maybe more at himself than me. "Fine, then. Sit. Clock is ticking."

I sat down in front of his desk, which was cluttered with all sorts of knickknacks and Honeybridge memorabilia. Black-and-white framed pictures of his Grandpa Horace and some Honeybridgers long past mixed with more current shots of his brothers and his parents out at the Retreat, their family campground. The walls behind the desk were decorated with various awards arranged chronologically, as well as a painting and a pastel portrait of Grandpa Horace that were both clearly done by Castor's twin brother, PJ, who'd always been the painter in the family. There was also the map that Horace used to have out over the bar—a map with a pin for every state and country he'd ever visited.

Flynn used to say he was going to fill up the whole map with pins when he got older, but I was pretty sure not a single other pin had been added since the last time I saw it. Flynn's whole life was in this office. His entire world was this town.

"Time's a'wastin," Flynn said.

"Right, yes. Okay." I opened my folio and turned it to face him. "Fortress is interested in acquiring exclusive distribution rights to Honeybridge Mead." I beamed like a fairytale hero, offering the prince the keys to his tower prison. "We want to place Honeybridge in high-end restaurants, resorts, and wine shops. And as you can see, we're willing to be pretty generous with our terms. You'll keep the Tavern, obviously, and the operation here. I love what you've done with the place. It's incredible, Flynn. Truly. And when you sign this deal, you'll be able to do even more with it. Hire more people. Test more varietals. I noticed there's no Honeybridge Firecracker on the menu, and you really need to fix that. Or you could take a sabbatical and travel a bit like you always wanted." I gestured toward the map. "Savor your life."

Flynn looked over the documents, seeming to ignore me as he read. He looked up with a frown. "This says the location of the manufacturing facility will be at Fortress's discretion."

I nodded. "Standard procedure. They put the factories in the places where the infrastructure is best suited to—"

"The label on the mead bottles says Honeybridge, Maine," he interrupted.

"Sure, and it'll continue to," I agreed, not sure what he was getting at.

"But it won't be *from* here if the factory is in freakin' Mississippi."

"Well, no, but the idea will be. I mean, you don't get all your honey locally, do you? You don't source the yeast here. You don't forge the fermenters. So when you think about it, it's already imported—"

"No."

"Pardon?" I shook my head, my smile wavering. "No, what?"

"No dice." He shut the folio and pushed it back at me. "You have absolutely no clue what this company is about. There is no way on this Earth that I'm letting you have any part of it."

I sighed in frustration. "It's not about *me*, Flynn. I'm just the messenger. It's *Fortress*'s offer. It's *Fortress* that can make you seriously rich—"

Flynn snorted. "Because being rich is the most important thing, right?"

"Maybe not, but it sure as fuck helps! Look, can't you put aside what happened between us and—"

"Nothing happened between us," he countered. He stood up from his chair and raised an eyebrow. "Don't let me keep you from Massimo."

Damn it. It figured he'd overheard that.

"Massimo is... He's... It's not..." I winced. How did I explain that we were friends with benefits, except not really friends and the benefits weren't very beneficial, without sounding like an asshole?

I was pretty sure the answer was in the question.

"Save it, Wellbridge. Your time is up. And in case you

had any doubt in the back of your mind—" He leaned over the desk and glared at me from close range. "—Firecracker will never be on the menu for you again."

Then he strode out of the office, leaving me behind.

I sat and stared at the awards on the wall, at first blankly, absorbing the blow of Flynn's rejection, and then more carefully, reading each one. "Best Debut Brewer" at a regional festival had led to "Best Local Brew," then to varietal awards for Moose Call and Daydream. There was a national award for Honeybridge Moose Call as "Best Acerglyn," and finally, an award last year as overall second place at Brew Fest.

A-ha. A smile spread across my face as I figured out another clue to the mystery that was Flynn Honeycutt.

Flynn did still have big dreams… he just needed to be convinced that Fortress was the way to achieve them.

Game. On.

I grabbed a sticky note from his desktop and affixed it to the top of the leather folio. "Reconsider," I wrote. Then I added my phone number below, just in case.

Flynn was a man who wouldn't back down until he'd gotten what he wanted…

But he didn't seem to realize that I wouldn't either.

Chapter Four

Flynn

As I bumped over the rutted road leading into my parents' place, I noticed the sign out front needed repainting and added it to my mental to-do list.

The Quick Lake Artists Retreat and Chakra-Centering Center—which was more like a campground with a collection of rustic cottages and one main house where my parents lived, all arranged in a horseshoe shape around a large inlet on the western end of Quick Lake—sometimes seemed like it was nothing *but* a giant to-do list, and I hated the anvil-like amount of burden it brought with it.

Still, every time I pulled back onto the property, I heaved a sigh of relief. Burden or not, it was *home*.

The Honeycutts had owned this part of Maine ever since the Honeycutts and Wellbridges had settled here and divided the area into *ours* and *theirs*, with them taking the giant hilly area and the river on the far side of the lake, closer to town, and us getting this pristine, forested area with the best views and best fishing spots. Personally, I'd always thought we'd gotten the better part of that deal... and judging by Patricia Wellbridge's constant-simmering anger at my family, it seemed I wasn't the only one.

It was no wonder. Huge fir trees ringed the open area in front of the main house, where my family was currently grilling veggie burgers and tossing beanbags into a makeshift cornhole set. Lake water lapped gently on the pebbled shore nearby, and thick, green grass led from the small beach up to my parents' house.

I'd always thought the old rambling house with its wide, covered porch looked like it had its arms thrown wide, as if to embrace the entirety of the enormous lake. Its right arm pointed toward the maintenance path that led to the campground itself, and the left arm pointed toward the footpath that led to the "artists' cottages." Each of the small cottages featured its own stretch of lake frontage, which was honestly the feature that kept them booked up so well during the summer. A peaceful lake view from your own small porch while having your morning coffee was worth its weight in gold, especially to city folk who needed a break before stroking out.

People like, say, JT Wellbridge, with his tightly tailored pants and perfectly styled city hair and "I will not be denied" attitude.

Not that I was thinking of JT, or his attitude, or the way that attitude had sunk its claws into my belly and led to me having some incredibly explicit dreams the night before, because I had solemnly vowed that I was not going to do that, so I wouldn't.

I stopped the truck and threw it into Park, pretending not to notice the sickening rattle it made every time I turned the ignition off. Other people noticed, though, because the first thing my dad said when I got out of the car was "When are you going to admit you need the Spider?"

"I don't need the Spider," I assured him. "My truck is doing just fine."

This was a total lie. The twenty-year-old pickup was

begging to be put out to pasture. But I couldn't afford to replace it just yet. I needed a little more time and hopefully a lucrative Ren Faire contract to cover the down payment.

"The Spider has never let anyone down, son," he continued, waving a beer around as he spoke. "It's as reliable as the sunrise and sunset."

Alden stepped closer to me and muttered under his breath, "Way less colorful, though."

I snorted. It was true. Our father, who we called Huck because "Honeycutts don't believe in parental power dynamics," had dubbed his old car "Spider," not because it was a cool convertible like a Fiat or MG Spider. No, this land yacht had gotten its nickname after my brother PJ had said it looked like a spider because it was brown with pitted black spots on it. The 1971 Lincoln Continental had been a million years old before any of us were even born, and now it resembled something from a horror movie.

"I'll keep that option in my back pocket, though. Thanks, Huck."

My father nodded sagely, his scraggly gray beard brushing the front of his V-neck hemp shirt where it met the vegan leather cord that held his green aventurine stone. It was a heart chakra crystal meant to attract abundance, and Huck had always looked at us kids with the kind of affection that told me exactly what he considered abundance to mean.

My mother, on the other hand, wore moonstone to bring luck and joy to her adventures. It was for the crown chakra —the center of transformation—which basically summed up Willow Honeycutt's deepest desire. Sometimes I thought she didn't much care what she transformed into, so long as it didn't happen here.

My father gave me a knowing grin. "The Spider has

plenty of room for nookie, Flynn. Don't knock it till you try it."

Willow looked over from where she was tending the burgers on the grill. "But bring some anti-negativity spray if you're going to do that. Huck and I had a disagreement the last time we drove it. You'll want to clean that out before trying to create amorous vibes."

Castor looked up from his phone with a frown. "What did you fight about?"

My little brother was always the peacemaker, worried about harmony and family unity. I loved him for it, though I often worried about his tender heart.

Huck broke in. "Not a fight, son. More of a slight—" He coughed a bit guiltily. "—disagreement."

"Huck wanted to go back to Morocco," Willow said as if it was the worst thing anyone could suggest. "In the winter."

"How dare he want to take you back to one of your favorite places," Alden said with obvious sarcasm.

Our mother waved this off. "I liked Morocco fine, but right now, my heart is set on going to Sri Lanka. Yoga on the sea in the morning and a mangrove safari on the Madu river after lunch. And the weather in midsummer is so perfect you can sleep right out under the stars." She sighed happily.

Midsummer.

I shot my father a look, and Huck shrugged in a familiar "you know your mother" way before nudging her aside and taking over the grill.

"Sri Lanka?" I pinned my mother with a glare. "When are you leaving?"

"Well." She fiddled with the little silver bells on her bracelet. "You know, August is the inter-monsoon season, but the least crowded time to travel is just a little before that—"

"When?" I insisted.

"Three weeks. We booked our tickets last night."

I clamped my teeth together and nodded. "Brew Fest is in five weeks. You promised you'd help me prepare for it since it's also my busiest season at the Tavern."

I wasn't sure why I bothered restating the facts when Willow was perfectly aware of them. She'd done what she always did—made all kinds of promises about being here for us and then flitting away on another adventure without a second thought. The wanderlust, the incessant need for *more* and *different,* was part of who she was, and I'd tried to stop fighting it long ago.

It hadn't worked.

Willow's warm brown eyes flashed up to me with a hint of apology. "I know, darling, and I meant it. I did! But Dr. Vindhya can only see us at that time, and I've been following her for ages and ages. She's the one who does the pulse diagnosis to balance the doshas—remember me mentioning it? You have no idea how out of balance your father's vata is."

I could honestly say I didn't, but I also wasn't about to justify the remark with a response, so I simply nodded again and walked off.

I kicked off my shoes and wandered down to the lake's edge, dipping my toes in the cool water and daring the insects to try me. Suddenly, I was in a slapping mood.

A few moments later, steady footsteps followed behind me, and my grandfather appeared at my side. "Huck and Willow told you about their next adventure?"

I nodded, keeping my gaze on the water, even when the golden sunshine reflecting off the water seared my eyes. "Don't know why I'm surprised. They've stuck around for five months this time. Not sure they've been here for that many months together since Castor and PJ graduated high school."

Pop sighed and shifted his hands into the pockets of his khaki pants. "Don't worry, Firecracker. The work'll get done in time for your festival. Your brothers and I will make sure of it. And plenty of other Honeybridgers will pitch in, too, if you ask 'em. You know how this town works."

I let out a breath. "Yeah, I know. It's just frustrating, Pop." I huffed out a laugh. "You'd think I'd be used to it by now, right? I mean, how old was I when they first started traveling? Eleven?" I shook my head at myself. "Twenty years, and it still pisses me off. I think I'm more angry at myself for caring than I am at them for leaving."

"Your parents love you, you know. More than anything."

I folded my arms over my chest. "Yeah."

"Love don't always look the same to different people, that's all, kiddo. Sometimes love looks like not holding yourself back from doing the things you want to do, 'cause you know the resentment would poison the relationships you have with the people who matter most."

Even if it means you're leaving those people behind to pick up the pieces?

I didn't say that out loud, though. There was no point to it.

Pop contemplated the lake in front of us. His hands lay casually ensconced in his pockets, and the curled edges of his white hair lifted a bit in the evening breeze off the water. "You know, Kiss Me Quick Lake got its name because—" he began.

"I know," I said, trying to cut him off because I knew exactly where this was going. "I know all about the damned lake, Pop."

I knew *too* fucking much.

He ignored me. "Legend has it—"

"That when a Wellbridge and a Honeycutt who 'love

true' kiss in the lake, magic happens. Curses lift, feuds end, fireworks explode, tiny baby angels descend from above, milk and honey flow, peace fills the land, the Beatles get back together... take your pick." I turned to give him a hard look. "No one really knows because it hasn't happened in a dozen generations, and it's not gonna happen in this one either. Wellbridge egos are too heavy to float."

"*Hmph*. Sounds much more legend-ish when I tell it."

I scowled. "Can we just enjoy a moment of peace and quiet, please?"

Pop made a big production of peering around at our family, as if questioning my definition of peace and quiet, and I snorted because, okay, maybe peace meant something different to my boisterous family.

Willow had dropped a burger on the ground and was giggling as my father scrambled to save it from the drooling jaws of my brother McLean's black Lab, Lily. Castor was laughing at his phone, where he was FaceTiming the evening's events to our sister, Georgia, in LA. And Alden was screaming at Dan to avoid parking on the "smushy" spot in the makeshift overflow parking area next to my parents' driveway.

I caught sight of McLean standing well away from the action at the edge of the trees, smiling slightly at our family's antics. As the middle child of the family, Mac had been born with several extra helpings of social anxiety, making him quieter and more serious than the rest of us, at least until you got him talking one-on-one.

Thankfully, Willow and Huck had "let Mac be Mac," as they referred to it. So Mac had created his own little world here on Honeycutt land, living in a cabin he'd built himself far away from the others, where he could be closer to the animals he loved.

This situation might have been ideal, except that Mac

also ended up being the one who handled bookings and maintenance on the property while my parents were gone, which I hated for him. Still, the man was only twenty-five. He had plenty of time to figure out a better situation, and I had no plans to rush him.

Mac watched silently for a long moment before meeting my eye. I brought my hand up to pull my lower eyelid down.

I see you.

His smile widened, and he plucked his shirt over his shoulder before dragging his thumb down the side of his jaw.

I'm uncomfortable. I'm sorry.

Pop grumbled. "I never did understand that stuff you boys do with the hand signals."

I laughed and patted the center of my chest twice.

I love you.

"There's a reason for that, Pop. Secret bro code is only for bros. You're not one of the Honeycutt bros. You're the Honeycutt Pop."

"Moose talks with his hands more than his mouth these days."

"Nah. McLean talks plenty. You just have to catch him one-on-one."

McLean lifted a hand in salute, then turned and disappeared back into the woods. Lily let out a faint woof under her breath and took off after him at a slow jog. Nobody seemed to notice, and if they did, they were used to it.

"We gonna talk about Frog?" Pop asked after a moment, giving me the side-eye.

"Nothing to talk about." I gave him a half-smile and bumped his shoulder with mine. "Now, let's get some food before they eat it all."

I murmured hello to Dan and one of Alden's stylist friends before making my way over to the long picnic table where our potluck had been assembled. Dan had brought a tray of appetizers from the Tavern, and Castor had made one of his enormous salads. Alden, as usual, had brought the drinks.

"Here," Castor said in a low voice, shoving a full insulated tumbler of wine in my hand. "You're probably going to need this."

"Am I?" I said, amused. "What for?"

"Oh..." He waved a hand. "You know."

I shrugged and took a hearty gulp, then began fixing myself a plate. When I had a heaping selection of food, I found a camp chair beside Castor and plunked myself into it, content to dig in.

After three bites of salad and another twelve swallows of wine, it began.

Alden leaned forward from his seat across the fire pit from me. "Oh my god, those Wellbridges. I swear. I had Patricia in my chair today, and she couldn't stop waxing poetic about JT."

My head shot up like it had been yanked by some sort of invisible string.

Willow walked over and handed me another insulated tumbler, forcing me to set down my plate so I could hold both beverages. "I couldn't help but make you a special brew, honey," she said sympathetically. "It's good for destressing. And also constipation."

"I don't like tea," I said, repeating a familiar mantra from my childhood.

She narrowed her eyes at me. "You don't have to like it, you just have to drink it."

"Anyway," Alden continued, "Patricia said JT is all but engaged to some asshat named Brantleigh. I mean, I haven't met the guy, so I don't know for sure that he's an asshat, but if Patricia approves of him—"

Engaged?

I choked on my constipation tea, and Cas helpfully patted my back too gently to accomplish much of anything besides making me feel comforted and loved.

Like I needed any of that shit right now.

"Don't want to hear about JT," I grumbled before shoving more food in my salad hole.

Willow sighed and gave me one of her concerned looks. "I was afraid this might happen. Huck, get out the talking stick. Also, boys, where is your brother? Alden, get out the drums and summon McLean."

"What? No." I shook my head firmly. "No drums. McLean knows we're eating. He'll come if he feels like it. And *definitely* no talking stick. No talking stick needed."

My father leaned forward with his own concerned look. "We always use the talking stick when emotions are high. You know that."

"Emotions aren't high," I assured him. "They're low. Like, super-duper low."

Pop pursed his lips across the fire at me. Cas's face crinkled in concern.

I shot Alden a look. If he so much as gave one hint of worry, I was leaving.

He laughed. "What kind of ritzy jackass name is Brantleigh? I'll bet twenty bucks the guy knows how to do that valet money-pass-handshake thing."

I couldn't help but snort at the idea this was a special skill a rich country club guy would have. "He probably also knows how to tie a real bow tie," I suggested.

Cas joined in. "Ten bucks says the man has cufflinks with his initials engraved on them."

The three of us met each other's eyes and said at the same time, "And uses them."

We broke out laughing enough for McLean to finally make his way back out of the woods and help himself to some food. He ended up taking a seat by Pop, well away from the non-Honeycutt members of the group. Even though he was a very tall, broad-shouldered man, McLean tried not to take up much space in the world. He hunched over and began eating, stopping periodically to hand a nibble to Lily, who sat patiently at his knee.

The conversation—*thank fuck*—turned to PJ's art show down in Boston in a couple of months and then to the Box Day display my mother had crafted outside the General Store—a floral arrangement that "captured the essence of divine feminine energy" or some shit and had mostly come from her own cutting garden.

But Alden eventually brought the discussion back around to Patricia Wellbridge.

For someone who disliked the Wellbridges arguably more than I did, the man could not stop talking about them.

"And *then* she bragged about how Brantleigh was going to inherit a bunch of family money, which didn't really matter since JT was so perfect at his job. He apparently never fails to land a client he wants, and his nickname is the Rainmaker." He snorted.

I rolled my eyes. "His nickname is Frog."

Pop's eyes were on me. I could tell he wanted to say something about why he'd given JT that nickname, but I didn't want to hear it. "Anyway," I continued quickly, "he won't have that name for long since I'm not giving him my business."

Dan was the one who made a disgruntled sound. "He wants your business? What do you mean?"

I glanced at my head bartender in surprise. "Didn't I tell you about the Fortress offer?"

"I knew it!" Alden said. "That rat bastard. How dare he."

"How dare he what?" asked Cas in confusion. "I thought he worked for some liquor distribu... oh."

I set down the tea and returned to wine-glugging. Somehow my tumbler had been refilled already, and the wine was cool and crisp, easy going down. "He wants exclusive distribution rights to my life's work." I snorted. "As if."

Willow was clueless. "Oh honey, that's fantastic!"

"Fuck him," Alden said. "Fuck him and his stupid tattoo and the really sweet Porsche he rode in on."

My father shot him a look. "The f-word is a sign of low blood sugar."

We ignored him, especially because Alden had already scarfed down a portobello burger, two black bean burgers, and a heaping stack of the Tavern's bacon-topped potato skins. Low blood sugar was definitely not his problem.

"You're not doing it," Alden proclaimed.

"Agreed," McLean said softly. "It's never good to go into business with a—"

"*BupBupBup!*" I said quickly, cutting him off before he could say "a man you've been in love with since the dawn of time" or some variation thereof. Thanks to a hexed bottle of Balvenie Caribbean Cask Scotch, Moose was the only person in the world who knew my true and extremely complicated feelings for JT Wellbridge... though I was pretty sure Pop suspected it, too, because he was psychic like that.

McLean lifted an eyebrow, and the edge of his mouth quirked up. "A Wellbridge. What did you think I was going to say, Flynn?"

I ran my middle finger up the bridge of my nose while Alden muttered a "damned right."

Pop squinted his eyes and rubbed his chin. It was his thinking pose. "Wouldn't you want to see Honeybridge Mead in restaurants and shops all over the country? I thought that was your dream. I thought that was why you were doing the Brew Fest thing—so you could get selected for the Ren Faire and then find yourself a distribution deal."

"It is," I snapped. "Of course it is. But not if the mead's going to be bulk manufactured in some sterile... okay, well, it needs to be sterile. Obvs. But not in some giant corporate, generic... shitty factory located in... in... Hoboken or whatever. Honeybridge Mead is manufactured in Honeybridge. Period."

It seemed like everyone was staring at me now. I sank deeper into my chair and comfort-gulped my wine.

Cas, ever the peacemaker, attempted to find a solution that made everyone happy. "What if JT could find a way to make that happen?"

"He can't," I said. "Besides, if Fortress took over manufacturing Honeybridge Mead, then what would I do? Lie in a fucking hammock all day staring out at the lake?"

Cas tilted his head at me. "Maybe, yeah. For a little while, at least. Remember in high school when that was actually your dream? Every summer, you'd set up a hammock over on—"

"I had a lot of dreams, Sunshine," I interrupted. "But I grew up and remembered we live in the real world."

A world where someone had to fucking stick around and manage things, damn it.

"Firecracker wouldn't want to give him the satisfaction," Alden said. "Especially after Patricia was all, 'JT's the best,' and 'JT always seals the deal.' She even said JT is up for a promotion to VP." He rolled his eyes. "Which, like, you'd think would bother her since she's constantly sighing about how he's too busy to come home, but Wellbridges always gotta brag about something. Right, Flynn?"

I made a noncommittal noise.

Patricia had been plenty happy when JT had been offered his impressive new job. She'd talked about it nonstop for months at a time when I'd really wanted to forget JT existed.

"Can we just take a minute to remember his nickname is Frog?" I said, feeling the effects of the wine-guzzling already. "It's not Rainman or Meadmaker or whatever. I'm the mead maker. Me. *Me.*" I thumbed myself in the chest a little too hard. That was going to leave a mark.

Dan glanced at me with an affectionate grin. "The best mead maker. Frog should be so lucky as to sign your mead to his roster."

"And he's called Frog because he's the kind of asshole that puts frogs in people's sleeping bags. *That* is the kind of asshole who wants to steal my life's work away," I continued a bit more loudly.

"That's not—" Pop began.

Cas shook his head. "I don't think he wants to—"

"Furthermore," I said, on a roll now, "I don't need a *frog* to be happy. No one needs a frog. They're not actually princes." I lifted my wine tumbler to Alden in a salute for reminding me of that fact. "And I am perfectly capable of obtaining my own happily ever after. Right now, all I need is for JT to return back under the rock he crawled out of—" I paused. "The lake he crawled out of? Where do frogs live, Mac?"

McLean blinked like a deer in headlights. "I... I mean... they can thrive in many habitats depending on—"

"Never mind. Doesn't matter. He can crawl right back to whatever habitat he belongs in—" I swung my hand wildly, spilling out an arc of constipation tea that hit the fire and made it sizzle. "—and leave me the hell alone. I'm going to get this Ren Faire deal and make my own happily-ever-ending without... without..." I kind of forgot what else I was going to say.

Castor reached over and patted me on the knee. He didn't say, "There, there," out loud, but I could tell he was thinking it.

Alden heaved himself out of the camp chair and threw away both of our paper plates before hauling me out of my chair too. "Let me drive you home before you light your bra on fire, princess."

"I don't need to go home," I said defiantly. "I'm fine. I'm *great*."

Dan seemed reluctant to speak but did so anyway. "Did you want me to check on the batch for you? I'm happy to head back to work if..."

The mead. Fuck.

"No!" I pressed the heel of my hand to my forehead. "No, I've got it. Forgot about that. A mead maker's job is never done. See? Another reason JT could never be a mead maker. What was he thinking?"

Thankfully, Alden got me out of there before I could pontificate any longer, though my mother wouldn't let me leave without another one of her special brews, this one designed to help purge toxins.

We rode in companionable silence for a while until the lights of the town's decorative streetlamps illuminated the clusters of people walking to and from restaurants and shops.

A hot-as-fuck runner caught my eye, and I settled deeper into Alden's passenger seat with a sigh as I enjoyed the eye candy. The man had his shirt off and a tiny pair of jogging shorts that hugged his delectably tight ass. Curved muscles in his legs flexed and bunched, and his ass bounced with every footfall. Sweat poured down the man's back and up into his... hair.

Wait. I knew that hair. I knew that back.

I knew that *body.* Intimately.

That motherfucker.

"Mpfh," I grunted. "Find a mud puddle."

Alden turned to stare at me. "What the fuck are you talking about?"

"Nothing."

"Flynn... are you okay?" he demanded. "This JT thing seems to have really gotten under your skin. Normally, you're the unflappable one. What's going on?"

I loved my brothers. All of them. I'd lay down my life for any one of them. But Alden was as much of a gossip as any other stylist at any salon on Earth. I wasn't about to confide in him that I was having mixed feelings about JT.

Besides, they weren't mixed feelings. They were *no* feelings. None whatsoever.

Which was why I didn't watch JT as he rounded the corner and jogged out of sight. And I didn't think about him as I checked on the mead and made the necessary adjustments before heading out back to the tiny house I lived in behind the Tavern.

I loved my little house. After demolishing the storage room and studio apartment over the Tavern in a fit of rage and grief after that foolish night I'd spent with JT, I'd had to move back home to the Retreat and live at my parents' house. I'd only been there a month when Pop had come into the Tavern for lunch one day and casually mentioned a tiny house he'd seen for sale on a flyer at the grocery store.

It had been abandoned mid-build out on a large property near Shapleigh. With my brothers' help, we'd towed it to Honeybridge and installed it in the back lot of the

Tavern property. It had taken a month to finish the build, another four months to sort out the utilities, and about ten seconds to feel at home once I'd moved in and made it my own.

I loved having a place of my own, and I loved being close enough to the Tavern to babysit my batches of mead when necessary and fill in for missing employees when needed. My work was everything to me, so living on-site worked perfectly.

After locking the door behind me, I began pulling off my clothes. I'd splurged on the shower, upgrading it from the original plastic stall to a tiled enclosure with a giant rainfall showerhead, powerful side jets, and an on-demand water heater. I'd never been much of a bath person, but I loved lingering in the shower, especially in winter when I was trying to warm up from an icy January walk across the lot.

I threw the faucet handle on and waited for the hot water. As soon as the spray was just the right temperature, I stepped into the shower and closed the glass door.

My eyes slid closed, and I let out a groan as the hard spray pummeled my tight muscles. As soon as I began to relax, my brain helpfully supplied a mini slideshow of images for my viewing pleasure.

JT sweaty and jiggly in his tiny running shorts.

JT perfectly primped as he grinned at me with that cocky face across my office desk as he handed over his company's offer.

Fuck.

I groaned and slid my hand down. There was no reason not to use JT's image for a little tension release. The man owed me that much. And I had the memories, after all. Why not make use of them?

I cued up twenty years' worth of JT images. JT in swim

trunks, flying off the end of the rope swing into the lake with a whoop.

JT catching my eye across the chemistry lab and making a face about how boring Mr. Blinney's class was.

JT showing up to the prom in a designer tuxedo that had reminded me he'd always been meant for bigger and better things.

JT's tuxedo shirt plastered to his back with sweat as he danced his feet off later that night with Callahan Whitney.

My balls tingled as I remembered how it had felt to go home that night and jerk off to the memory of that sweaty back and his muscular ass in those tux pants.

"Fuck," I groaned, out loud this time.

JT Wellbridge was a selfish asshole, but he was a sexy one.

I ran a hand up my stomach to my chest and then my throat, remembering how it had felt when he'd pinned me to the door in the high school locker room one time to get in my face about my attitude during a basketball game in PE class.

He'd clasped my throat with his large hand, but as he'd yelled at me for getting away with foul after foul, I'd felt the tiniest stroke of his thumb along the skin under my ear as if he'd been exploring the feel of me.

"Oh god." I was going to come. I was going to come to the memory of JT Wellbridge yelling at me when we were sixteen.

My hand shuttled over my cock as I reached for my hole with the other. My hands were slick with soap, and steam coated my skin as I finally let myself remember our one and only time together.

JT looking up at me like I was god's gift as his lush mouth worked the length of my hard dick.

JT sucking me and rimming me until I saw stars.

You've always been mine.
Give it up. Give it to me.
Just once, Firecracker.

His voice had sounded hoarse and broken that night. More real and vulnerable than he'd ever been with me before. With his hands on my body and his scent in my nose, I'd pictured him standing across from me at Grandpa Horace's graveside service, all windblown and messy, and remembered how his sad eyes had met mine.

I'd thought, in that moment, *JT Wellbridge knows me. JT Wellbridge could be my anchor.* And I'd been so, so close to giving in and letting him fuck me.

Something had held me back, though, even after he'd swallowed my cum and held me for hours while I'd sobbed. Some instinct had made me hesitate, knowing that my dick and my grief were not reliable decision-makers. And in the end, I'd been right. Because mere hours later, he'd walked right out the fucking door to resume his real life, and he hadn't come back until now.

This was why I usually refused to get off on the memory of JT Wellbridge. Because the movie always ended the same stupid way.

But just when I was about to give up and take my tired self to bed, my finger brushed over my sensitive rim, and my mind spun, spitting out two brand-new images—the way JT's blue eyes had gone hot and stormy the moment they'd met mine across the bar the day before... and the arrogant note he'd left on top of his prissy leather folio, right in the center of my desk.

Reconsider.

And all the refusals and hesitations in the world couldn't keep me from coming hard against the shower wall screaming out the fucker's name.

Chapter Five

JT

Breakfast in Wellbridge House was a special kind of torture.

Sometimes a man just wanted to sleep late on a Saturday, then hit the kitchen in his boxers, drink a mug of black coffee, and eat sugared cereal while standing at the counter. That sort of impropriety would never be tolerated in Patricia Wellbridge's home, though.

My mother believed the only civilized way to begin the day was at precisely 8:00 a.m., *en famille*, at a table set with Royal Doulton and covered with food that she, herself, would never eat.

"Reagan? Darling, I had Rosalia prepare those eggs especially for you. Nice and runny, just the way you like them. You really must eat something. You're looking so peaky," she fretted, pushing away her own half-eaten plate of melon spears and fat-free cottage cheese. "And your pallor will be memorialized in our family photos for the Honeybridge Ledger later today. Isn't that right, Senator?"

My father grunted from behind his newspaper.

I glanced up from my tablet, where I was triple-checking the new and even more generous offer for Honeybridge Mead that Alice and I had hurriedly pulled together, just in case Flynn stuck by his refusal, and glanced across the table at my brother in amusement.

Reagan's normally perfect blond hair hung in a hank over one bloodshot eye, his jaw was covered in stubble, and judging by the way he rubbed his forehead when he thought no one was looking, his peakiness was almost definitely the result of too much champagne at Ashley Waitrose's party down at the marina the night before.

No wonder the discussion of runny eggs made him look "peaky."

"Don't want any," he mumbled. He took a cautious sip of black coffee before staring back down at his phone.

"Of course you do," Mother countered. "You love eggs, Reagan! Remember when you used to dunk your bread soldiers in your soft-boiled eggs as a child and joke that you'd eaten a whole army?"

"That was you as a child, Mother."

"Oh." Mother seemed startled for a second that *her* childhood experiences were not *our* experiences, almost as though we were wholly distinct human beings. "In any case, nothing could be better than a nice gooey egg for perking you up! And Rosalia made a special stop at the farm stand to get them, so we know they were laid just this morning by hardworking Honeybridge hens."

Reagan shook his head and went a shade paler, the idea of hens laying gooey eggs not helping him in the slightest.

"How do we know they're hardworking?" I asked, drawing my mother's attention because I was the best big brother and not at all because I enjoyed baiting her.

"I..." She blinked. "Well... because. They're from Honeybridge."

"Sound reasoning." I nodded thoughtfully. Then I added, "And kudos to you for letting go of the Honeycutt-Wellbridge rivalry, at least as it pertains to breakfast food."

Mother snorted delicately. "Rivalry? Pfft. Honestly, Jonathan, it's hardly a rivalry. A rivalry would imply that the Honeycutts are our competition, when it's quite apparent to even the most casual observer that Wellbridges exist in a social strata that's far above—" She stopped and narrowed her eyes. "Wait. What does that have to do with our breakfast?"

"Oh, only that when I ran past the farm stand the other morning, I happened to see Willow Honeycutt delivering some eggs." I sipped my coffee and shrugged, innocent as a tiny baby. "You remember she's kept chickens out at the Retreat for years, right?"

In point of fact, my mother was not only aware of Willow Honeycutt's chickens, but she'd campaigned for a town ordinance against what she called "nuisance birds."

Mother's jaw dropped. "On second thought, don't eat those eggs, Reagan," she said firmly. "I feel like a buttered croissant would be more restorative. The croissants are from Natalie Trowbridge's bakery, and even though her grandfather was a Honeycutt, her sister married a Wellbridge, which shows the evolution of good sense." She nodded once, in total agreement with herself.

"And couldn't we all use a little more good sense, really?" I asked no one in particular. I snatched one of the pastries from the basket in the center of the table, then added, "Just out of curiosity, where do we get our butter?"

Mother opened her mouth, then pinched it shut again, and I made a mental note to apologize to Rosalia for the conversation she was going to be subjected to sometime soon.

Reagan flashed me the barest hint of a smile.

"Maybe you should just go back to bed, Rea," I suggested, earning myself what I considered serious brother points. "Sleep off your, ah... peakiness."

My mother stared at me like I'd suggested Reagan jog through the neighborhood naked and quacking. "He couldn't possibly! Honestly, Jonathan, what are you thinking? Today is Saturday. Box Day Saturday! A day of redemption I've been toiling toward since last year's..." She paused and touched a lock of her perfect ice-blonde bob. "... setback." The doorbell chimed, and she sat forward excitedly. "Trudy and Louise agreed that I'm a shoo-in. In fact, I'm certain that doorbell is a delivery from the florist to celebrate my win in advance."

I hid my grimace behind my coffee cup. It would take far greater capacity for willful ignorance than I currently possessed for me not to have heard my mother talk about Box Day all day, every day since my arrival, but I'd really expected to be back in the city before I had to experience it. Sadly for me, Flynn Honeycutt hadn't fallen in line with my plans.

Not only had the stubborn ass turned down Fortress's proposal in his office on Wednesday, but he'd also ignored all three messages I'd left him yesterday, too, asking him to get in touch with me.

Clearly, the only way to pin the man down was to do it in person... and if I'd gotten nothing else from our brief meeting Thursday, I'd for sure been reminded of just how much I wanted to pin Flynn down.

Preferably against a bed.

With ropes to bind him there, if necessary.

"Jonathan? Jonathan, now *you're* looking flushed!" Mother complained. "Are you ill also?"

"Er, no." I blinked away my thoughts. "I'm fine. But I won't be able to make it to the Box Day presentation, I'm afraid." I shrugged apologetically. "Duty calls. I need to talk to Flynn about the Fortress contract. I'm sorry I'll miss seeing what you and long-lost Cousin Henrietta"—but let's be honest, mostly Henrietta—"came up with."

Mother gaped. "You can't work on a Saturday, Jonathan! Not when your family needs you. Tell him, Senator," she implored my father. "Tell him Conrad wouldn't expect him to be distracted by work on the day the Wellbridges regain our Box Day glory."

When my father didn't respond quickly enough, she narrowed her eyes, and suddenly, my father jumped in his seat and fumbled his *New York Times*, almost like someone had kicked him in the shin with her pointy-toed shoe. His round face and ruthlessly gelled grayish-blond hair appeared for the first time all morning. "What? Oh. Yes, boys, do as your mother says." He lifted his newspaper again.

"Also, the Penningtons arrive today," Mother went on excitedly. For some reason, she addressed this comment to me, though Brantleigh Pennington had been Reagan's classmate in high school. I barely knew the kid, and from what little I remembered, he was an entitled ass. "Poor Brantleigh has been having a very hard year. His parents are *divorcing*." She said this last word in a whisper.

"They're not his parents." Reagan rolled his eyes. "Brantleigh's mom's married to some Hollywood producer and lives in Calabasas. You mean Brantleigh's father is divorcing his second wife because she's been cheating on him with her tennis instructor. I say good riddance." He shrugged. "Mr. Pennington is hot. He could do way better."

"Reagan Ford Wellbridge!" Mother's cheeks turned red. "I thought you were dating Mary-Lillian McLeroy."

"That ended weeks ago." Reagan waved a casual hand. "And even if it hadn't, I'm a man with eyes in my head. Hot is hot."

I held back a snort. Our mother assumed Reagan was

straight, but in reality, my brother was a bit of a try-sexual—as in, he'd *try* to sleep with just about anyone but never stuck with anyone for long.

"I beg your pardon!" Mother's blush deepened to a near-purple color. "My son will not be *any* sort of sexual about Thatcher Pennington, thank you very much. Not at *my* breakfast table. Thatcher's a friend of your father's, for heaven's sake."

"Not really," my father interjected without moving his paper. "He's a good fifteen years younger than me. Smart man, though. Waited to divorce Heather until after she inherited her own money from her grandfather, so there's no chance of her getting spousal support. Not that she would've gotten much anyway, what with the ironclad prenup they signed."

I shook my head in disgust. I knew better than anyone that not every marriage was a love story. My own parents' relationship had begun more like a business deal, with my father agreeing to marry a woman seven years his senior in order to get her name, money, and social clout to further his political ambitions. And, to give them credit, they'd not only managed to make it work, but they were really devoted to one another, in their own way. But I couldn't imagine a life like that for myself.

Hearing them talk about it made me even more grateful that I'd left town before I'd started to view this as normal.

"*In any case,*" Mother went on, undeterred. "We need to take pity on poor Brantleigh. He's known Heather his whole life—"

"Five years," Reagan corrected. "Maybe six."

"—and she's been like a mother figure to him—"

"Only in the most Kardashian sort of way."

"—so naturally, I offered to host Brantleigh for the rest

of the summer so he'd have someone his own age to spend time with—"

Reagan sobered up for the first time all morning. "You what? Oh, god, please no. You said they were coming for the *weekend*—"

I shoved a croissant in my mouth to stop myself from laughing.

"—and he'll also give Jonathan an appropriate young man to settle his romantic affections on!"

I aspirated my croissant. "No," I managed to choke out with the last of my air. "Not happening. Do not matchmake for me."

"We'll see," she said airily, spearing a tiny sliver of cantaloupe. "These things blossom and take on a life of their own!"

Not if I stomped them dead and salted the fields.

"Brantleigh's going to be so impressed to see you win the softball game, too, Jonathan. You and Reagan both." My mother patted her hair and sniffed.

"Not me," Reagan said firmly. "Last time I played, I was medevaced to Portland because Aunt Margot threw a bat and broke my clavicle."

"Accidents happen! And everyone knows Margot has terrible aim."

"Thank god she does since she threw the damn thing at my head."

Mother threw her hands in the air. "Fine, then. Jonathan will lead Team Wellbridge to victory himself—"

"I'll be too busy," I objected, but she pretended not to hear me.

"And if the heady tang of victory in the air happens to stir up some amorous feelings between you and Brantleigh on the softball field, darling, wouldn't that be wonderful?"

I pushed up from my seat, unable to bear it a moment

longer. This whole thing was getting entirely out of hand. I needed to get the contract signed and get the fuck out of Honeybridge. Immediately.

"I'll see you all later. Rea, feel better. Mother, best of luck to you and Henrietta." I kissed my mother's cheek and ignored her pout.

When I reached the front hall, Rosalia stopped me. "Mr. Jonathan. I was just about to come get you. You got a package." She gestured to a plain wooden box about the size of a wine bottle on the front hall table.

The box had no shipping label, only a white tag that said "Jonathan Turner Wellbridge, III."

Odd.

I opened the lid and found a bottle of Honeybridge mead nestled on a bed of confetti.

Holy shit. My heart beat faster. Flynn must've reconsidered and decided to accept my offer after all, and I could be out of town by sunset. My stomach flipped with a mixture of excitement and something that I refused to believe was disappointment.

I lifted the bottle out of the box to examine it and only then noticed the strange confetti sprinkled around the bottle: irregular specks of black-and-white paper and—was that brown leather?—that looked like it had been run through a woodchipper.

Beneath the bottle was a folded slip of paper I hurriedly opened.

"Dear FROG," Flynn had written in his bold, looping scrawl. "I already savor my life. Hope *you* savor *this*, since it's as close to distributing Honeybridge mead as you're going to get. Get used to losing, Rainmaker.—F.H."

I closed my eyes, torn between pissed off and amused.

Say what you wanted about Flynn Honeycutt—and I could think of a few choice things to say, for sure—he said what he meant, and he stuck to his word. I admired that, even if it made me want to shake him.

The man was being an obstinate fool, ignoring all that Fortress was offering.

But damn if the fucker hadn't also packed the bottle with the shredded remains of Fortress's contract, leather folio and all, which was so perfectly vindictive I had to bite my tongue to stop myself from laughing.

Round 1: Flynn Honeycutt.

But if he thought I was going to back down, he had another think coming.

I traced my thumb over the last sentence of his note. *Get used to losing?* I didn't think so. I was just getting warmed up.

"Mother," I called, striding back toward the dining room. "What time did you say that softball game was?"

Game on, Flynn Honeycutt. May the best *Wellbridge* win.

―――

"Score is tied, two to two! Bottom of the ninth. Bases loaded. Frog Wellbridge is up to bat!" Pop Honeycutt yelled into his microphone near the Honeycutt bleachers, clearly not understanding—or maybe not caring—how microphones worked. "Back in high school, Frog had great aim but tended to be a little overconfident, and he wasn't the greatest at tracking the pitch before the hit. Let's see what he can do against the Honeycutts' star pitcher!"

I shook my head and exchanged a wry look with Kurt "Righty" Honeycutt, the Honeycutts' left-handed catcher. "I don't know if I appreciate Pop's version of color commentary."

"No shit." Kurt grinned and rubbed at the collar of his

orange Honeycutt T-shirt. "He's the only person in town impartial enough to be a fair referee, but he insists on calling the game, too, and his memory is annoyingly long. Every time I'm up to bat, he tells the story about when I whiffed the ball twelve years ago. Gets in my head and throws me off."

At least I wasn't the only one.

I tapped the bat against my toes, right-left-left-right, the way I used to back in high school, tugged my Wellbridge-blue shirt down firmly over my tight pants, and settled down into a batting stance. The man on the mound flexed his broad shoulders, wiped his palm against his luscious bubble butt, and adjusted his baseball hat like *he* used to do in high school... and somehow, I just knew, like I knew my own name, that he was gonna pitch low.

Flynn nodded at some signal Kurt threw him, reared back, and sent the ball arcing over the plate—low but way faster than I'd anticipated.

"Oooh, and Frog gets a strike! Is it just me, or is Firecracker... *on fire?*" Pop laughed at his own joke.

The man on the mound smirked, and I rolled my eyes, like the sight of that smirk didn't instinctively make my stomach swoop.

Meanwhile, the Wellbridge fans in the bleachers and even the Wellbridge players on the bases erupted into loud cheers of "JT, JT, JT!" and "Close the deal, Rainmaker!" which was incredibly cringy... but I had to admit, it was a nice change to be well known. Back in New York, my own doorman occasionally asked me for ID.

On the next pitch, I was ready. Flynn tilted his head to the right—a sure sign he was gonna throw a curve. Seriously, how did everyone in town not know this by now?—and I managed to get behind it. I hit a line drive between second and third, where Castor Honeycutt was daydreaming in the outfield, then darted to first base and parked myself there, watching in triumph as Marta Wellbridge and then Hank Croucher were able to score.

The crowd—at least the Wellbridge side—went wild, screaming and chanting my name. And for one way-too-brief second, Flynn's eyes met mine. I grinned at him wildly, and his lips quirked with wry humor. He lifted his chin just the tiniest fraction in acknowledgment, and *that* was when I felt like I had won.

I took a single step toward him... but then a scream from third base made both of us turn our heads.

My cousin Redmond, who'd flown in from DC for the weekend, looked like he was still trying to cross home plate, but somehow, Alden Honeycutt had gotten the ball and was refusing to let him pass.

"Game's over, kids," Pop called through the PA system.

But Alden didn't seem to hear him, or else he didn't care. His eyes were practically glowing as he and Redmond faced off. Redmond looked left, then darted right, trying to make a run around him, at which point Alden let out an unholy screech and tackled Redmond to the dirt.

Flynn and I shared a single concerned glance before running in that direction.

Alden jumped to his feet. "You. Are. Out!" He pointed an accusing finger down at Redmond, who was twice as tall and broad as Alden but fortunately way calmer. Alden threw both hands in the air victoriously. "Out, out, out!"

Flynn jogged over and wrapped a restraining arm around his brother just as I hurried over to help Redmond up.

"Not sure what you're celebrating. We lost, Alden," Flynn said.

"Don't care," Alden said cheerfully, eyes still on Redmond. "*I* won."

Alden Honeycutt reminded me of my mother sometimes, though I was pretty sure neither of them would appreciate that comparison.

Redmond snorted and began dusting himself off.

"So, Firecracker..." I rolled up and down on the balls of my feet. "I got your message this morning. Thanks so much for the mead, by the way. I hadn't been planning to play today, but you inspired me."

Flynn tightened his arm around Alden. "Not now, JT."

"What message?" Alden demanded, eyes stormy. He looked from me to Flynn and back. "What mead?"

"Don't worry about it," Flynn soothed.

"I'm thinking you might have been wrong about which of us needed to get used to losing, though," I mused, rubbing my chin thoughtfully. "Because as far as I can tell..."

"*Not. Now. JT*," Flynn insisted, this time meeting my eyes. "Didn't your mother ever tell you that no one likes a gloater?"

I wasn't sure anyone had ever told Patricia that, so she for sure had not taught me.

"If not now, when?" I persisted. "No bullshit, Flynn, I want to talk to you about this. Find terms that will work for you. Please."

Flynn opened his mouth, then shut it again.

"Flynn said *no*." Alden was shorter and thinner than Flynn but didn't hesitate to step in front of him defensively. "Leave him alone." He shot a scathing up-down glance at Redmond. "*All* of you Wellbridges, just leave us alone."

Flynn draped an arm over Alden's shoulder again. "Come on, Runway. Let's go."

Flynn shot me a look that was ninety percent annoyance and ten percent apology before dragging Alden off, saying something about walking to the Tavern to cool down.

I may have stood and watched them walk away.

Belatedly, I turned toward Redmond. He was staring after the Honeycutt brothers also. "You okay?"

"Yeah." Redmond ruffled his hair, shaking off the dust. "Fine."

"Did you do something to piss Alden off?"

"Other than being a Wellbridge?" He shrugged.

But before I could question him further, Redmond spotted his girlfriend and his mother waving from the sidelines and lifted his hand in a wave.

He clapped me on the shoulder. "Awesome game, JT. We have to catch up soon, okay?" He began walking away backward and shot me the warm, charming heartbreaker smile that my aunt Louise used to claim made Redmond a natural politician. "Take the train down from New York to DC or something. I'll show you around."

"Yeah, okay. Call me—"

"Jonathan! *Jonnnnnathannnn!*" my mother cried from the stands behind me.

Every instinct cried out for me to ignore her and follow Flynn back to the Tavern, to push the tiny bit of headway I felt like I'd made. Instead, I sighed and turned around.

My mother was on her feet, waving like I might not see her in her lime-green designer short set, while my father was head down in his phone, and Reagan sat forlornly beside a chattering, Gucci-clad Brantleigh Pennington. Poor Reagan looked like he wished he were anywhere else on Earth.

"Darling!" Mother rushed over to kiss my cheek and take both my hands in hers. "Thank you, Jonathan, for restoring our family honor when I couldn't," she said solemnly.

My mother had lost Box Day. Again. And she was being even more melodramatic than usual about it. So I nodded seriously and accepted her thanks and did not roll my eyes, no matter how badly I wanted to.

"We'll have a victory party to celebrate once we win the entire softball tournament, of course," she mused. "Late August or perhaps September. We'll have to see when we can get a permit for some fireworks—"

Before I could ask what the hell she was talking about, my cousin Marta came over with her wife, Holly. Though Marta was technically my mother's cousin, she was closer to my age. She was also one of the only Wellbridges in town who didn't let my mother steamroll her, which meant she was one of my favorite people.

"Good game, JT!" Marta offered me her hand to shake while Holly went up on her tiptoes to kiss my cheek. "Well played."

"Thanks to you scoring the winning run!" I said with a grin.

Marta laughed. "Thanks to you managing to get a hit off Firecracker. Glad to hear you'll be sticking around for the summer. Our team might stand a fighting chance."

I gave my mother a side-eyed glance, but she was suddenly very, very busy adjusting the clasp on her bracelet and didn't meet my eyes. "Not the whole summer, I'm afraid. Only another day or two. I'll need to get back to the city."

"I've always thought it would be so fun to live somewhere exciting like New York." Holly's smile was kind. "But then I remember I'm an introvert and a homebody who likes having a support system around. Do you love it there?"

I hesitated. *Love* was a strong word.

"Some parts are great, some aren't." I shrugged. "I really enjoy my job, though."

"Fortress would be lost without him," Mother interjected. "He's going to be a vice president, you know."

Marta looked suitably impressed by this, but I felt like an asshole.

"It's not a done deal yet," I hurried to say. "I'm actually in town trying to work with Flynn Honeycutt to acquire distribution rights for Honeybridge Mead."

"Good," Marta said firmly. "Flynn needs a backer who believes in him. You know I lent him the money he needed to renovate the Tavern after Horace died—I mean, Honeybridge Savings and Loan did, but I was the underwriter—and Flynn has impressed the heck out of me with how well he's done. He repaid the entire loan early. And with the increased business he's had since that singer posted a picture from the Tavern on her Instagram—"

"Frankie Hilo," Holly supplied. "The woman who sings that song about love on a velvet lounger or whatever. You know the one. She's a huge fan of Honeybridge Mead."

"Luck," my mother scoffed. "Nothing but luck."

"Not true!" Holly's pretty face creased in a frown. "Luck might have made Frankie wander in there, but the quality of her experience is what made her post what she did. Flynn's got a half-dozen mead varietals, plus seasonal offerings. A bottling operation. A mailing list." She ticked off on her fingers. "Six full-time employees. Plus, he's single-handedly reinvigorated the local honey market, and he's not shy about promoting his suppliers."

I blinked. This had not come up in the research Alice and I had done.

I remembered taunting Flynn that his mead was practically imported already, and I winced. I'd underestimated him.

"And Flynn's mead is truly excellent," Marta confirmed. "That's what makes visitors flock to the Meadery for tours."

There were tours, too?

Suddenly, Fortress's "generous" offer didn't feel so generous. Flynn had said that I had no clue what his business was about, and I'd been so sure that was just an excuse for him making decisions based on our past history.

Apparently, I'd been wrong.

Mother made a dismissive noise, and Marta rolled her eyes impatiently. "It's true, Patricia. With some careful expansion, Flynn's mead is going to gain a worldwide following, which is probably why Fortress is so eager to sign him. There's nothing the man can't do." To me, she added, "Did you know Flynn taught himself all about mead varietals in just the past couple years?"

I shook my head. I'd had no idea, which was basically the running theme of this conversation. "I thought his Grandpa Horace taught him back when we were still in high school. I thought that's why Horace left him the place."

"Horace made a decent home-brew mead and taught Flynn as much as he knew," Marta agreed. "But even back then, Flynn wanted to turn the Tavern into something more. As soon as he helped Alden go to cosmetology school and it became clear that PJ would get his art scholarship, Flynn saved up enough money to attend a special mead-making school out in California—one that would have taught him about the business management aspect as well as the craft. But then, of course, Horace died so unexpectedly that November." She shrugged, and Holly sighed sadly. "Flynn didn't get to go."

I felt like I'd been sucker punched. "I didn't know."

How many times could a man say that in one day? But now I wasn't thinking about the contract negotiation; I was thinking back to Thanksgiving weekend three years ago.

Flynn hadn't only been grieving the loss of his grandfather back then; he'd also been grieving the loss of his dream... after making sure his brothers would realize theirs.

Snippets of our postorgasm conversation that night drifted through my brain.

"Come to the city," I'd said into the darkness, hoping I sounded casual.

Flynn's back had immediately stiffened. "What?"

"I've gotta go in a minute. I've got an early flight in the morning 'cause I'm starting my new job the day after, but... I'd like to do this again," I'd blurted awkwardly. "See you again. So maybe you could come down sometime. I could take you out or..."

Flynn had pulled away immediately. "No. I have a business to run. I can't afford distractions."

I'd blinked, stung by his words. "I have a job, too—my freakin' dream job—but I'd still be willing to—"

To... what? Have a long-distance friends-with-benefits thing?

Flynn was right. I couldn't afford the distraction either.

Flynn had snorted like I'd just confirmed what he'd been thinking. "Just leave, Frog. Go back to your job in New York and pretend this night never happened."

I hadn't thought it was possible to regret that stupid, impulsive night more than I already did—Flynn had been at his most vulnerable, and I never should have let things go as far as they had, no matter how long or how badly I'd wanted him.

But now, replaying my own words, hearing myself gloat about my *dream job* and try to ease the sting of rejection by rubbing Flynn's face in the fact that I was leaving town... *god*. No wonder Flynn thought I was an asshole.

I *had* been.

I hadn't just mishandled this contract negotiation; I'd mishandled everything between us.

"Couldn't someone else have stepped up to take care of the Tavern while he did his courses?" I demanded hoarsely. "His brothers? His parents?"

She shook her head. "Alden and PJ were at school. McLean was taking care of the Retreat. Georgia was out in California. And Castor's a sweetheart, but..."

"But he'd be giving away the mead to anyone who looked thirsty," I finished, frustrated. "What about Huck and Willow?"

Marta hesitated. "They're sweet, too, in their way, but not exactly... reliable."

"Not to mention blue-ribbon thieving wastrels," my mother interjected with a sniff.

"Mother, honestly," I said, more harshly than strictly necessary, thanks to my guilt. "Willow Honeycutt is a very nice woman, and she didn't *steal* anything."

"A very nice—?" Mother inhaled sharply through her nose and drew her entire body up straight. "Jonathan, I do believe all the excitement of the afternoon has taken its toll on you. I'll expect you back at the house directly to help plan our Late-Summer Victory Extravaganza." She put her nose in the air, turned on her heel, and left.

Holly sighed after her. "Poor Patricia. That woman is so unhappy."

"Delusional," I corrected.

Marta watched my mother stomp away. "Childish. Patty had her shot at Huck Honeycutt back in the day, and she chose not to take it. This whole thing with Willow is sour grapes."

"What?" I gasped, every bit as melodramatically as my mother ever had.

Marta snorted. "Figures Patricia never told you this story. All very innocent, of course—they were only fifteen or so at the time—but some folks talked about Huck and Patty being the pair who'd fulfill the legend. You know, the legend of the lake?"

"Yes, of course," I said impatiently. "More or less." Everyone in Honeybridge knew *of* the legend of the lake. Nobody actually knew what was supposed to happen when it came true. "What happened?"

Marta shrugged. "For all that Huck's easygoing, he's never been one to back down or roll over about anything important. And you know your mother sure as hell doesn't. Unstoppable force, meet immovable object." She slammed her two fists together. "They had a falling-out over something, and your mother never apologized. She cared more about winning than she did about Huck. And you reap what you sow."

"Marta," Holly scolded. "Be kind."

Marta grinned warmly at her wife. "Storytime's over anyway. Let's get going, babe. I need a shower. JT, if we don't see you before you leave, kiddo, safe travels."

I nodded and said goodbye distractedly, but as I walked to my car, my mind reeled. My mother... and sweet, shaggy Huck Honeycutt? I couldn't think too hard about that without gagging.

I reached the Porsche and fished out my keys, then blinked as thoughts rearranged themselves in my brain. My mother's mistakes. My own. Being wrong... and actually *saying so*. How winning really looked a lot like Flynn Honeycutt's smile. Then I turned on my heel and walked back across the field in the other direction, breaking into a jog when I got close to the Tavern.

I wanted the contract. I wanted my damn promotion. That hadn't changed. But in that moment, it was just as important for Flynn to know there was someone out there who recognized his sacrifices and incredible achievements. Who wanted him to be free to achieve his dreams without worrying about his family or his town or his business.

Who wanted him *happy*... even if it meant upping the Fortress offer so high Conrad's bushy white eyebrows disappeared into his receding hairline and Alice wondered whether I'd been abducted by aliens.

When I got to the Tavern, I took a chance and detoured around back to the little house I'd spotted before, then pounded on the door.

"Flynn," I began the second the door cracked open. Then I stopped and, in fact, forgot how to speak entirely because Flynn Honeycutt stood there wearing nothing but a scowl and the tiniest scrap of a towel wrapped around his waist.

"What?" he demanded, one arm braced on the edge of the door. One large, very lucky droplet of water dripped from Flynn's hair and down his pec to his nipple. "Come to gloat some more, Rainmaker?"

I lifted my gaze to his. "I... no. I'm here about the contract."

"I shredded your contract," Flynn growled.

"I know. The confetti was hard to miss. I want to make you a better offer." I took a deep breath. "I'm increasing the original compensation by twenty percent, and you can choose suppliers for the honey and the fruits or whatever," I said in a rush.

Flynn stared at me like I'd lost my mind, and not without reason. "You can't do that."

"I can," I confirmed. "I just did. Take the deal, Flynn," I pleaded. "You can use this money to take mead-making classes. You can live your dream."

"Mead-making classes." He scowled. "Are you drunk? I already know how to make mead, asshole."

"No, I know. I..." *Fuck*. I wasn't saying this right, and I was messing things up again. "Could you maybe put a shirt on?" I asked in a strangled voice. "While we talk about this?"

Flynn pushed the door open, rolled his eyes, and took two steps deeper into the little house. Part of me wanted to look around the space—Flynn's space—but the rest of me was way too focused on how the towel stretched across his round ass as he walked.

He grabbed a T-shirt from a basket of folded laundry sitting on the back of the sofa near the door and threw it on. "Better? Your delicate Wellbridge sensibilities all protected, Frog?"

No. "Yes. Thank you. As I was saying, I want you to have a chance to do the things you've always wanted—"

"Stop," Flynn said. He crossed his arms over his chest. "You are never gonna convince me you're doing this for my benefit, okay? So don't even go down that road. You only want my mead recipes. You still want to steal Honeybridge Mead away from me. Away from Honeybridge."

I pushed a frustrated hand through my hair, which was still damp and dusty from the game. He sounded like my mother, talking about her damn blue ribbon.

"I'm not trying to *steal* it, Flynn. I'm trying to pay you so Fortress can use your recipe, distribute your product, and get you billions of dollars. You get to keep everything you have, and you get to have more besides. I don't want to take anything from you. I'm trying to *give* you something."

I was trying to make things right, damn it.

Flynn dropped his arms to his sides and took a step toward me, putting us right up against each other. "You're not fucking hearing me, Wellbridge. I don't want anything from you."

But his chest heaved as he said it, his eyes sparked green fire, and I knew the same way I'd known all his pitches before he threw them that Flynn Honeycutt was a damn liar because there was definitely *something* he wanted from me.

And I... well, I was an idiot who failed to learn lessons because, just as I had on that stupid November night, I felt my body respond to his in a way that made my common sense and good intentions fly out the window.

I spun him in a half turn, braced an arm across the top of his chest, and pressed his back against the wall beside the door. "Nothing, Flynn? You sure about that?"

I couldn't say for sure who moved first or if maybe the two of us were in sync for once. All I could say for sure was that a second later, his mouth was on mine, and holy fuck, it was even more glorious than I remembered.

I grabbed his face in both my hands, holding him in place so I could plunder his mouth with my tongue. He tasted like cinnamon and temptation, and I leaned my body against his with a groan. I sucked and bit at his lips, feasting on the addictive and familiar taste of him, then ran my tongue down the taut cord of his neck until he shuddered.

Flynn grabbed the blue baseball shirt at my waist, yanking it out of my uniform pants until his calloused fingertips found skin at the small of my back. He spread his fingers wide, a man claiming territory, before pulling me in even closer so the hard ridge of his cock pressed against mine.

I shuddered. "Yes," I whispered. "*Yes*. Fuck, Flynn, I want—"

"Hey, Flynn!" a male voice called before a knock vibrated the door inches from our heads. "We need you out here, babe. The after-game crowd's getting rowdy, and Kendall's out sick, so it's just me, Alden, and Cas." He paused, then knocked again. "Flynn?"

Flynn stared up at me, breathless and wanting, for a

long moment. Then his eyes shuttered, and he cleared his throat. "Hang on, Dan."

I stared at Flynn in shock. "I... I'm so sorry. This shouldn't have happened."

Flynn's eyes widened.

"No! *Shit.*" I clenched my hands on his shoulders. "I mean I... I *wanted* it to. Obviously. But I didn't mean to muddy the waters with—" I huffed out a breath. "I came here to discuss the contract. You're just so hot that I—"

"JT," Flynn said calmly.

"Yeah?"

"Back your person away from my person."

I squeezed my eyes shut. "Fuck."

"Now."

I took a large step away. "But—"

"No buts. You're right. This should not have happened. Add it to the stack of mistakes I've made where you're concerned." Flynn sidestepped away, grabbed a pair of shorts from the laundry basket, and pulled them on, tucking away his erection.

He's going commando? To work? In front of who knows how many drunken ballplayers and hot tourists?

My mouth went dry, and my nostrils flared.

"Come in, Dan!" Flynn called with fake cheer.

"No, wait," I pleaded in a low voice. "First, let me explain what I—"

"Hey!" Dan pushed the door open but stopped dead when he saw me standing there. He looked back and forth from Flynn to me suspiciously. "What's going on?"

"Not a damn thing," Flynn said. "Wellbridge here came by to renegotiate. He thought he could throw me a little *added incentive*," he said bitterly.

I gaped. "Oh, for the love of— Firecracker, that's *not* what I was trying—"

"You arrived just in time to hear me tell him that I'm not interested in his contract *or* his incentives, and I never will be." He snagged his sneakers from a spot next to the laundry bin and pulled those on, too. "And now, Wellbridge is going to leave..." He threw the door open and unceremoniously shouldered me out. "...so we can get back to our fucking work."

Flynn clapped Dan on the shoulder, steering him toward the back entrance of the Tavern, and I watched them go.

How the hell had I messed this up yet again? Where was the confident competence that had helped me close dozens of Fortress contracts and lead Team Wellbridge to softball victory? I was offering Flynn *everything*... and I still couldn't get him to agree. I was so frustrated—with him, with myself, with the whole fucking situation—that I was almost tempted to just get in my car and drive back to New York, damn the consequences.

But as Dan disappeared inside the building, Flynn paused with his hand on the door and darted a look over his shoulder at me, almost like he was checking to see if I was still there. The molten heat of his gaze—angry, confused, and wanting—burned through me like a lit fuse, and I knew in that moment I was not going to leave. Not this time. Flynn and I had unfinished business.

Conrad had said winning the contract for Honeybridge Mead would be the most important deal I made all year...

But something told me that winning over Flynn Honeycutt might be the most important deal of my life.

I just had to figure out how to stop it from slipping through my fingers again.

Chapter Six

Flynn

JT Wellbridge was fucking *everywhere*.

The man was a brain worm, dedicated to making me as crazy as possible when I could least afford the distraction. The human equivalent of hearing "Manic Monday" on the radio and then not being able to get it out of your head.

JT was Manic Monday.

"You'll never guess who came by the Retreat yesterday evening to congratulate me on my Box Day win," my mother said, plunking herself down on a stool at the bar Sunday morning. "JT Wellbridge! Such a sweet boy."

"He did what?" I glanced up from the beer tap I'd been working on behind the bar and narrowed my eyes. "I told him I'm not doing business with him. If that kiss-ass thinks he can get to me through my family—"

Willow *tsked* disapprovingly. "He didn't mention a thing about your business. He wanted to offer a sincere compliment..."

I grunted, unconvinced.

"Then he sat and drank some tea with me—don't you give me that look, Flynn Honeycutt. Some people *adore* my teas—and he was so grateful that I made him a special brew to increase his fortitude and conviction."

Great. Exactly what JT did *not* need.

Why didn't *he* get constipation tea?

"And when he was done, he harvested the first crop of my tomatoes," she finished with a happy sigh. "I brought them by in case Kendall wants to make fresh bruschetta for your customers."

I glanced toward the tavern kitchen, where my chef was making hateful eyeballs at me.

"I'm sure she appreciated that," I muttered while I continued tugging on the wrench to get a stubborn tank valve to open. "Now all she has to do is source about a hundred more tomatoes, and she'll be able to serve more than two tables with it."

"After he harvested the tomatoes, he made plans to take Pop fishing this morning," she went on, still singing the praises of our erstwhile hero, Jonathan "Suckup" Wellbridge. "Honestly, Flynn, the way you boys talk about him, you'd think he was an ogre, but I've always said Frog has a particularly bright aura, especially for a Wellbridge."

"Oh, he's bright alright. More like crafty as a—*fuck!*" My wrench slipped and banged my other hand. *Hard.*

"Language, sweetheart," she murmured, looking around at the half-full tavern. "You wouldn't want to offend your customers, would you?"

I ignored her and rubbed at the sore spot on my hand. I held JT responsible for that injury.

Castor dropped off a tray of appetizers at a nearby table before swinging over to drop a kiss on Willow's cheek. "You hungry? Want me to put in an order for you? We just got a huge to-go order, but I can get Kendall to make you something first."

"Aren't you the sweetest boy? No, thank you. I'm on a cleanse."

"Who called in the to-go order?" I asked. Most people who needed larger orders placed them well in advance.

"JT did." Castor's eyes went all liquid and dreamy. "I'm guessing his family must've told him good things."

"Patricia? Tell him good things about the Tavern?" I shook my head. "Never. Besides, Trent always lunches at the club, and Reagan probably drinks his lunch if the other night was any indication, so that just leaves JT himself. Give him fish sticks. There are still some in the freezer."

Castor thought about it for a minute. "They're hosting that other guy and his family, don't forget. What's his name? The pretty one. Ashley... Farnley... something-ly?"

"Brantleigh," I grumbled, remembering the engagement rumor with a sour twist in my gut. Frog certainly hadn't seemed engaged when he'd had his tongue down my throat yesterday, I thought with a vicious surge of something that absolutely wasn't jealousy. "What did JT order? No, you know what? Never mind. I don't care." I shook out my throbbing hand and put my attention back on the stuck valve. "I'm working."

Willow didn't take the hint. "Anyway, I wanted to make sure you're coming for dinner tonight, sweetheart. It's Lily's birthday, and we're making something special."

"Lily's birthday?" It took me a minute to process the fact my mother had just invited me to a dog's birthday dinner.

"Yes. And don't bother getting her a deer antler because your brothers already went in together on one. Your father and I got her a hemp rope bone. Maybe stop by Paws and Claws and check out their new Pride line of collars and leashes. Moose would love that."

Moose would love to be left alone was what Moose

would love, but that was not the way the Honeycutt family rolled.

"I'll figure something out," I said. "I really need to get back to work now, if you don't mind."

"'Course not, baby. I'm off to parade my Box Day medallion in front of Patricia Wellbridge. Alden said she's getting her nails done at the salon. I'm sure she's brimming with excitement over my win." She turned away with a bounce to her step, setting off the little bells on her wrist and ankles. Her colorful peasant skirt swung in an arc against the doorframe.

"Smug satisfaction doesn't become you," I called after her with a laugh. "There's probably a tea blend for that!"

She swung her hips extra wide in response.

But after she left, I didn't immediately get back to work. Instead, I found myself tapping the wrench against my palm and thinking about the man I'd been actively trying *not* to think about.

Strangely enough, I wasn't worried that JT had been cheating on some society fiancé when he kissed me. I didn't know JT that well anymore—and maybe not ever—but I didn't believe he would have gotten engaged to another man and then kissed me savagely against the wall of my living room.

And it *had* been savage.

Beautifully so.

He'd manhandled me, shoving me with his arm and then clasping my face to hold it where he wanted it. His lips had been rough and hungry, and god... I'd wanted so fucking much. So much more from him.

Sometimes I thought I'd never get enough of him, even though I knew full well he wasn't for me, and last night was the last time I'd be getting any of him at all.

When I found myself touching my own lips while I

replayed the scene on a loop, I bit out a curse under my breath and forced myself to focus.

I worked on the stuck valve until it finally came loose. After fixing the tap, mead-making tasks kept me busy until the lunch rush picked up, and then I was on my feet nonstop until it was time to head out to the Retreat for the... *shit*. The dog birthday dinner.

Since the pet store was already closed, I swung by Nat's Sweet Buns to pick up a cake instead, where my cousin Kurt was doing the same thing.

"You'd better not be getting a pupcake," Kurt warned with a grin. "I got here first, and I'm going to get all the credit."

I nudged him to the side so I could see what was left in the display case. "Fine, I'll get a..." I spotted my absolute favorite thing. "The Oreo cheesecake," I told Natalie with a smile of thanks when she came out of the back with Kurt's order already boxed up.

"Oh, shoot." Her eyes widened. "That's the last one—lots of folks having Fourth of July barbecues this weekend, you know? And JT Wellbridge just called and put it on hold. He'll be by to pick it up soon." She gave me an apologetic shrug. "I guess maybe Brantleigh Pennington's as much of a sucker for them as you are."

Brantleigh? Was going to eat *my* cheesecake? Fuck no.

The smile from earlier froze on my face. My teeth felt weird and too big for my mouth. I slowly covered them up and nodded. "'Course. 'Course he is. Who... who wouldn't be? That cake is... great. Simply... wonderful. Obviously."

Poor Nat felt bad. "I have your second favorite here. The red-velvet cake. Want me to box it up?"

Irrational rage overtook me like a flash flood. "No, actually. I really *need* the Oreo cheesecake. Nothing else will do. I'll give you a hundred dollars for it."

Nat blinked at me before looking at Kurt to see if this was a joke, but Kurt didn't notice because *he* was busy looking at me like I'd sprouted two extra heads. Needless to say, I'd never done something as... as... *Wellbridge* as throwing down over a bakery cheesecake, but apparently, there was a first time for everything.

"Ah... but..." Natalie began.

I put on my best Honeycutt smile. "I know JT asked you to hold it, but today is my brother's..." I said the word "dog's" too softly for her to hear, "birthday, and, well... we really need that cake."

She bit her lip. Clearly, she didn't want to upset a Sweet Buns regular like the Wellbridge family, but she also didn't want to upset *me*. I tried a different tactic.

"JT will understand, I promise. Just tell him I needed it for Moose, okay? If he gets mad, he can get mad at me. He owes me one."

In fact, by my accounting, he owed me a lot more than that.

"Oh, right." Natalie's face cleared. "I forgot the two of you were tight." She reached into the case for the cheesecake.

"What?" I squeaked. JT and me? *Tight*? Was there a dog whistle in here, or was that high-pitched noise coming from me? "No, no, no. We weren't... We never... We didn't... I barely know the guy!" I blurted.

Okay, that was just plain dumb. Fortunately, Natalie had already disappeared into the back to box up my ill-gotten gains.

Kurt shuffled next to me. "So. That's interesting."

"Shut up."

"You don't know JT Wellbridge? The guy you played an absolutely cutthroat game of softball against yesterday? The guy who'd buy up all of those little chocolate caramel candy things you liked, back when we were kids, just so you couldn't have any? The guy you almost went out on a date with in high—"

"No," I gritted out with a glare. "We do not talk about that."

Kurt held up his hands. "Okay. Alright." He mimed zipping his mouth shut. "Just saying, you *were* tight in a way, weren't you? Even if you weren't exactly friends."

I frowned. "No. Just... hush. Look, I needed the cake, and I'm not going to let JT Fucking Wellbridge serve it to—"

The bell over the door tinkled.

Please don't let it be JT. Please don't let it be JT.

"Hi, Natalie, I'm here to pick up an Oreo cheesecake."

I let out a relieved breath. It was *not* JT.

Trent Wellbridge came in looking harried and sunburned. He wore plaid Bermuda shorts and a golf shirt. His gray-blond hair stuck up through the opening of the hot-pink visor on his head, and the sunglasses hanging from his collar gave his portly frame the false appearance of a little cleavage.

Before Natalie could stammer an apology, I reached out my hand for a shake and plastered on the Honeycutt smile again. "Hi, Senator Wellbridge. I've already got the cake. I told JT I'd pick it up for him. Have a great day!"

I quickly tossed some cash on the counter and grabbed the box, bolting out of the shop while Trent Wellbridge's jaw still hung open in surprise.

On the drive out to the Retreat, I almost, *almost*, opened the box and started eating the cheesecake with my hand out of spite. But it was my offering to Lily's celebration, and I was determined not to reveal myself as the immature asshole I apparently was.

Even if it was JT's fault I'd sunk this low.

When I arrived, the cookout was in full swing, with not

only my family but lots of their friends. Someone had hung strings of colorful lanterns across the outdoor eating area, and there were already tiki torches down by the dock ready to be lit as well. My mother had even pulled out the fabric birthday pennant she used to hang up for our birthdays when we were small.

The guest of honor was decked out in a giant purple neck bow and was clearly enjoying all the attention. Meanwhile, her owner sat quietly off to the side on a split-log bench. I plonked the cheesecake box on the food table and sat down next to him.

"Happy Lily Day," I said, nudging him with my shoulder.

McLean gave me a half-smile. "She's a good girl. Can't believe she's already five."

We stared out at the lake in companionable silence for a while as the sun dipped closer to the trees and turned the water into molten gold, all the way out to the horizon. I tried to take some deep breaths and absorb the chakra-centering power surrounding us, hoping it would ease the nervous agitation I'd been feeling since yesterday afternoon.

It didn't work.

"Oh my god, listen to the latest Wellbridge bullshit," Alden said, un-centering the shit out of my chakras.

I held up a hand as he approached our bench with Pop. "Nope. No thanks. This is a non-Wellbridge space. I don't care what terrible thing Patricia said or did. I don't care if Redmond has stolen a hundred bases or kicked a million puppies. And I for sure don't want to hear about JT. No frog parking." I waved a hand to indicate the entire area around us. "All frogs parked here will be toad."

McLean snorted softly, and Alden rolled his eyes. "No, but seriously. Listen—"

I met his eyes. "I'm *being* serious. JT came back to town,

and suddenly, that's all anyone is talking and thinking about." Myself included. "I need *one* minute of this day, here in the bosom of my family, on Honeycutt land, where I'm not being bombarded by all things JT. Okay? Can you do that for me? Please?"

Pop and Alden exchanged a look, and I caught Pop's wince. "What?"

"Er... nothing," Pop said, shoving his hands in his pockets and looking out at the lake in a totally fake pose of nonchalance.

I narrowed my eyes. "Spill, old man."

He sighed. "Well, it might be hard to avoid JT since he's... here."

I spun around on the bench and scanned the guests for the familiar head of too-gorgeous hair. No luck. "Where? I don't see him."

Pop inclined his head out at the water. In the near distance, I could see Milk Bottle Island, the little jut of land in the middle of the lake that my brothers and I had spent hours and hours exploring as kids. The bright red kayak was obvious, pulled on the rocky shore.

How dare that motherfucker trespass on our island?

I hadn't realized I'd said this out loud until McLean cleared his throat softly. "Well... it's not technically our island, though, is it? The lake belongs to the town, and so do the little islands in it. We just own this big piece of shoreline. So, really, even if Willow hadn't invited Frog to Lily's party when he was helping in her garden, he wouldn't be..." He darted a look at my face and cleared his throat again. "I mean, yeah. Trespassing. *Grr*. Infuriating."

I nodded once. "Fuck him," I said, standing up and striding over to the wooden rack of kayaks. I yanked a yellow one down and shoved it to the edge of the water.

"Is he... is he going to angry-kayak right now?" Alden asked nobody in particular.

Pop sighed. "Firecracker..."

"Save me some cheesecake," I called over my shoulder, stripping off my jeans so I was clad only in my swim trunks and sweatshirt. I'd be damned if I was going to miss the Oreo cheesecake I'd rightfully stolen just because Jonathan Island-Trespassing Wellbridge couldn't stay where he belonged.

I pulled the paddle hard through the still water, enjoying the cool air against my hot skin and the faint lapping sounds of the water against the hull. Water drops slid down the paddle as I raised one end to cut the other through the surface of the lake.

Once I was out on the water and halfway to the island, I realized I actually felt more centered. I stopped paddling and took a few deep breaths, closing my eyes and concentrating on filling my lungs with the clean evening air.

A mosquito went up my nose and down my throat.

God fucking dammit.

I angry-kayaked the rest of the way to the island while choking on mosquito guts. This was all JT's fault—just like every other damn distracting thing that day—and he needed to hear about it.

I pulled my kayak up on the rocky shore and only stepped two paces into the tree line before I noticed JT swinging in a portable hammock between two trees—the same trees where I used to hang my hammock, back when I had time for hammock-hanging—looking like the dictionary definition of relaxation. He wore a pair of faded cargo shorts Patricia would never have authorized if she'd seen them and a T-shirt that had ridden up over his lean stomach. His tanned legs were crossed at the ankles, and one lean, tanned hand—the one with the pretentious crown tattoo peeking out from under his fancy watchband—held a paperback book.

It was utterly infuriating that anyone so annoying should be so sexy.

"Stop it right now," I yelled. "This is harassment!"

He lifted an eyebrow at me as he looked me up and down. Then he went back to his book. "I agree. Beat it."

My arms flapped out to my sides in outrage. "I mean *you* harassing *me*. I'm not going to stand for it."

He kept his gaze on his book. "I'm on an isolated island, Firecracker. And I was here first."

I stared at him, my mouth opening and closing like a fish. A very outraged fish. *How. Dare. He.*

JT glanced at me again, then looked away in dismissal. "Leave me alone, Flynn. It's clear that you're not capable of having a productive conversation with me right now."

Something in my gut twisted. "Me? No way. It's *you*—"

He sighed and cast his eyes toward the sky, looking suddenly weary. "It's a Sunday. Can't we just take one day off from the whole JT-is-the-root-of-all-evil thing? I already know. And you can start back up tomorrow, okay?"

I gasped, partly in shock—how did he know I'd been blaming him for things? Was the Rainmaker a mind reader now, too?—and partly because I couldn't believe one human being could contain so much *wrong*.

"Maybe *you* could take a day off," I shot back, "from trying to... to... to take what's mine. *As always*."

"What?" JT glanced at me in surprise. "What have I ever taken from you?"

My peace. My sanity. My self-control. My affection, every time I'd been foolish enough to give him a chance.

I was smart enough not to say any of that.

"The... the... the science fair in ninth grade!" I flapped my arms again. "The blue ribbon was gonna be *mine*. I made that whole potato battery experiment showing the voltage from different types of potatoes, and *you* let your stupid trained rat out of his cage the night before the presentation, and he ruined my project before I could even present it."

JT sat up and turned toward me, throwing his book aside and propping himself with his feet on the ground to keep the hammock from swinging. He watched me for a long moment, his jaw tight, and he twisted his watch strap like the action might calm him down.

"No comeback," I said smugly. "As I thought. When a Wellbridge wants something—"

He threw up his arms, giving up all pretense of calm. "Fine. *Fine.* You want to do this now after all this time? Let's do it."

"Do what?"

He stood up, tossed his book onto the hammock, and crossed his arms over his broad chest. "You wanna know what really happened during the ninth-grade science fair? Gwen Dunbar gave you the idea for that project, didn't she?"

"I..."

"Don't bother lying about it. Gwen told a bunch of us that she was trying to help you because she wanted you to ask her to Homecoming." He rolled his eyes. "But I'm guessing she *didn't* mention that the reason she had this amazing idea and research just kicking around was because her brother Lonny had already won the fair with that project a few years before... or that for a little while there, Lonny had a side business selling his old projects for cash."

My mind raced to process this. "Hold up, I didn't give Gwen one cent for that—"

"Doesn't matter. My cousin Turner *did* fork over cash for an AP English Comp paper from him once, and he got caught immediately. All the teachers were very aware of Lonny's scam. Turner probably would have gotten expelled if my mother hadn't intervened—because it would never do for the Senator's nephew to be branded a cheater." He gave me a hard look. "Who would have intervened for you when you got caught, Firecracker?"

"I..." I lifted my chin stubbornly. "That's irrelevant." Though I couldn't help realizing that the answer was *no one*. Certainly not my parents, who'd probably been off exploring some far-flung destination. Not Pop or Horace, who would have been busy running their businesses, or my mother's brothers, who could barely keep their own kids in line.

"And let me state for the record," JT added hotly, "that by damaging your project, I disqualified myself from the fair, too. And poor Julius Cheeser had been training to run that maze for *months*."

I was not going to laugh. I wasn't.

"You're claiming you destroyed my project to keep me from being expelled?" I demanded incredulously. "Why not just *tell* me—"

"Because you never would have listened. You would have blown me off, and you know it."

I swallowed hard. This... was hard to refute since it was the absolute truth.

Still, I refused to yield. "Great. Fine. You're incredibly noble. So what about sophomore year in Spanish class? When I was top of the class until *some* asshole decided to switch from French to Spanish *and* get a private tutor just so he could become Señora's teacher's pet? What noble, self-less act was that about?"

He rolled his eyes and set his hands on his hips. "That wasn't selfless. That was my mother deciding that having a son fluent in Spanish would be helpful for the Senator's career. She made me study with a tutor all summer long so I could get up to speed. So, *lo siento* that I stole your crown, Flynn, but it was definitely not done on purpose. Jeez."

I was losing momentum, my anger burning off as quickly as the warmth of the day now that the sun was going down. So I searched my memory banks and grabbed onto something even larger. Something guaranteed to stoke my wrath.

"You know what *was* on purpose?" I jabbed a finger in the air between us. "The time I applied for a part-time server job at the country club, and you made sure I didn't get it."

For the first time in this whole conversation, JT appeared caught on the back foot. He rubbed at the nape of his neck. "Shit. How'd you know that was me?"

His admission of guilt surprised me, but I tried not to show it. "There was no one else it could have been. I hadn't told a single other person I was applying. But then that day you helped me change my tire, I—" I'd let myself trust him like a fucking idiot who willfully refused to learn his lesson. "—I thought maybe you could help me get the job, so I spilled my guts. But a week later, after I beat you in that debate, you got all pissy—"

"What? I did not!"

"—and then Olivia Symons gave *me* that prom-posal when everyone assumed she'd be asking you, and you were jealous—"

"Do you hear yourself? I'm *gay*, Flynn. I was never—"

"—so you decided I wasn't good enough to serve the precious elites at Honeybridge Golf and Country Club."

"Are you insane?" JT grabbed his hair with both hands, making the fine, dark blond strands stand on end. Somehow, this made him look even sexier, which only made me madder.

"Tell me I'm wrong," I demanded. "Go on."

"You *are* wrong. Dead wrong."

"Oh, really? Then why would you—"

"Because I didn't want you there!" he snapped like a man pushed beyond his limits. "I didn't want you working your ass off the way you always have—always *do*—while the rest of us fucked off all summer playing stupid *golf* and going sailing, okay? I wouldn't have been able to stand it. Not because I didn't think you were good enough—because I thought you were *too* fucking good."

The minute the words were out, JT's eyes widened like he couldn't believe he'd said them. Neither could I. But it was the very fact that he looked so alarmed, like he'd give anything to be able to suck those words back, that convinced me of his honesty.

We stared at each other for a long minute, both of us breathing hard.

"Instead, I had to work my ass off all summer at the Tavern," I said quietly. "Because someone had to put food on the table while my parents were in New Zealand or wherever, doing fuck-all to help me raise my brothers and sister and look after my grandfathers. And believe me, the patrons there did *not* tip as well."

JT's head went back. He closed his eyes and shook his head minutely. "Okay. You're right. I... hadn't considered that." When he opened his eyes again, the look in them was strangely soft and tender. Regret tinged with something horrifyingly like sympathy.

Utterly unacceptable.

"Yeah, well. Whatever," I said gruffly. "It worked out. But it's just another example of how you've fucked with me our whole lives. And that's not getting into the whole business of—"

I broke off, literally biting my tongue to keep the words

back. Had I really been about to bring up that fucking date he'd asked me on? A moment so humiliating that just remembering it fifteen years later made me want to curl up like one of McLean's injured hedgehogs?

"Never mind." I turned to go. The trip back to the Retreat side of the lake would be less of an angry-kayak and more of a pity party.

"I'm tired of fighting with you, Flynn," JT said from behind me.

I paused without turning around. "Then stop."

"You think I've always had it out for you, but that's just not true. I don't get what this thing is between us. Why it feels like the universe always seems to pit us against each other, as if only one of us can win. Because in some ways, it feels like you and I..."

He hesitated, and I was suddenly sure I didn't want to know what he was going to say next. Like it or not—and I very much didn't—I was way too vulnerable around him. I always had been.

"It's like we're tied together or something," he went on softly. "Always pushing and pulling on each other. Like magnets, maybe. Or tides. I wouldn't be *me* if it hadn't been for you. And I..." He blew out a breath. "I need you to know I'm not your enemy, Flynn."

The sincerity and sadness in his voice called to something inside me in a way that was almost irresistible. I was really glad I couldn't see his face, otherwise I might have dropped to my knees for him, right there on the beach, and begged him to forgive me for my accusations. To let me be close to him.

And then I'd be right back where I'd been all those times before.

Because Kurt had been right at the bakery earlier. JT and I *had* been "tight," even though we weren't friends. Our lives had been entwined since forever... just not always for the better.

In fact, not *ever* for the better, as far as I was concerned.

I let out a breath. "Fine, then. We're not enemies. But..." I thought about what I needed from him. What I wanted out of this weird dynamic between the two of us.

What I *wanted* was out of the question.

What I *needed,* though... that was easy.

"Just stay out of my way, JT. That's all I ask."

I climbed into the kayak and used the paddle to shove myself away from shore. It was nearly a clean getaway.

But before I got more than a kayak's-length from the island, my mouth overrode my brain, and I couldn't resist calling over my shoulder, "By the way, there was a weird mix-up with your Oreo cheesecake. Nat sold the last one to *me* mere seconds before your dad arrived. *Lo siento*, Frog. Next time, try harder."

Chapter Seven

JT

I had never wished so fervently to find out I was adopted as I did after spending Honeybridge Regatta Day on the water with my family and their guests.

This was Flynn Honeycutt's fault. And I had *evidence*.

Exhibit one: If the man wasn't so damn desirable and hadn't kissed me senseless after the softball game last Saturday, maybe I wouldn't have tossed and turned my way through enough sex dreams to start my own subscription service this week, and I would've been alert enough to invent an excuse when my mother voluntold me I'd be manning one of the Wellbridge family's sailboats for the festivities.

Exhibit two: If Flynn hadn't called out that taunt about the cheesecake at the birthday party, I'd have taken him at his word and stayed out of his way. The raw emotion in his voice that day had clawed at my insides, and I truly didn't want to hurt him... even if it meant finding Conrad another craft mead account to earn my promotion. Instead, though, Flynn had deliberately provoked me, knowing full well that not a single cell of my body knew how to back down from a challenge, especially from him. The fact that I'd actually ordered the cake specifically because it was Flynn's favorite and asked my father to hand it off to Marta, who was coming to the party, didn't change that in the slightest.

And exhibit three: If Flynn had simply agreed to the damn deal, like any sane person would, I'd have already taken my sexually frustrated ass back to New York in triumph the way I'd initially planned instead of repeatedly messaging Alice to reschedule my meetings with other prospective clients so I could extend my stay in Honeybridge and having to suffer through her snarky replies.

Case. Closed.

But despite Flynn being the obvious guilty party in this situation, the man did not seem to be suffering in the slightest. In fact, he'd managed to avoid speaking to me for days. I'd haunted the Tavern so much that I'd learned the names of every employee, tried every dish and mead varietal on the menu, and chatted with nearly every person in town as they passed through for lunch or dinner, but the most I caught was a glimpse of Firecracker's fine ass as he strode through the bar on his way to the meadery or a smirky eyebrow lift as he sashayed from the meadery back to the bar.

Meanwhile, the longer I stayed in my mother's orbit, the more I was subjected to cruel and unusual torture, like—

"Oh my god, that was so, *so* fun! And you drove the boat like, so, *so* well, Jonny!" a high-pitched voice behind me cried as I clomped up the dock from the boat to the marina. "You were giving us, like, serious, *serious* Christopher Columbus vibes. Am I right, ReaBae? And, like, it doesn't even matter that we didn't win the race thing, because, like, we totally had the prettiest, *prettiest* boat! I am so here for that cerulean blue you picked for the cushions, Patty!"

"I feel physically ill," Reagan said in a low voice as he trudged along beside me. "I think it might be too much sun. Or possibly a bug I picked up."

"That bug has a name, ReaBae," I reminded him in a harsh whisper. "And it's Dysen. One would think you'd remember it because it's the name of a fucking vacuum cleaner. And since you were the one who invited Dysen to join us today, you'd better make a miraculous recovery in the next ten seconds because if you attempt to ditch me with her, I will murder you and post the pictures from the time Mother made you golf in plaid knickers all over social media. It's bad enough Mother's stuck me with Brantleigh."

Regan sighed and rubbed at the back of his neck. "I swear, Dysen seemed normal last week at Ashley's party."

"Pretty sure you were too impaired to make that determination."

"I guess," he admitted. "But, like... her dad's a politician, so she knows what it's like to have to deal with that. She's not a local—she's only in town because her mother wanted to do a family yoga cleanse out at the Retreat—so she doesn't give a shit about rivalries and childhood nicknames. She's thirty-one. Has a full-time job. Mother was thrilled to hear about her *advantageous connections*." Regan ticked these attributes off on his fingers. "And I thought dating someone older would be... different. Like she'd be a bit more mature. Looking for more than sex. Capable of having intelligent conversation on a variety of topics."

"Reagan," I said with exaggerated patience. "She's an underwear model, man. Which doesn't mean she's not brilliant but also doesn't scream 'I enjoy intelligent conversation on a variety of topics.' She makes Brantleigh look like a Rhodes scholar."

Dysen's voice drifted forward again. "And then I was like, 'Okay, like, noooo, there is no way Fredrika Larsson deserves that Calvin Klein contract more than I do! Because my ass is sculpted.' And I mean, like, it's literally sculpted, Patty. By Dr. Nasim Kasman in Beverly Hills. And it looks like a... a... shoot, what do you call that thing a sculptor guy makes?"

"A... a sculpture?" Brantleigh sounded understandably confused.

"Yes!" Dysen cried. "Oh my god! You're so, *so* smart, Brantleigh." She paused for a second. "Are you *sure* you're gay?"

Reagan made a haunted, whining noise, but I hardened my heart. I loved Reagan, and maybe the silver lining of these summer shenanigans was that I got to spend more time with him—he'd hung out with me at the Tavern three afternoons this week already—but he needed to grow up a little.

"Break it off," I advised in a low voice as I pushed open the coded gate at the end of the dock and stepped out onto the boardwalk. "Today. Mother will get over her disappointment, just like she will when I finally convince her Brantleigh and I won't be having spoiled, disgruntled babies together."

"Okay." Reagan nodded firmly. "I will."

"So, like, where's the after-party, hotties?" Dysen threw an arm around each of our shoulders.

"Oh, uh." Reagan glanced at me, then took a deep breath. "The thing is, Dysen—"

"I do believe most of the young people are heading over to the Honeybridge Tavern," my mother offered brightly from behind us. "A primitive sort of eatery, owned by *those Honeycutts*, and not our usual fare, but I've heard they have an adequate drinks menu. And isn't it fun to soak up a bit of the rough-and-tumble local flavor?"

I turned my head. Even after a day on the water, my mother's blonde hair was still firmly in place. Clearly, so was her attitude. "The whole Tavern is renovated and gorgeous. Reagan and I both thought so. You should come and see for yourself."

"Oh, heavens no." She let out an exaggerated yawn. "No, the Senator and I will be heading home to get our beauty sleep before golf tomorrow. But Reagan and Jonathan would love to take you and Brantleigh over, Dysen. Wouldn't you, boys?"

Dysen must've been related to a Rockefeller for my mother to be pushing this connection so hard. If anyone else in Honeybridge had attempted to call her Patty to her face, she'd have razed the town.

"I'd rather not," I said tightly. By which I meant there was no force in the universe that could compel me to bring Dysen and Brantleigh to Flynn Honeycutt's bar, where Flynn would see them—and, worse, *hear* them—and give me that smirky smirk of his. "Beauty sleep is kinda sounding good right now."

"Oh my *godddddd!*" Dysen squealed. She shook Reagan's shoulder excitedly. "ReaBae! Do you mean *the* Honeybridge Tavern? The one that went viral after Frankie Hilo posted a picture there last year? Oh, my god. I so, *so* need pics, like *right now*, and I'm saving them to my highlights. Did you know all three Cassidy sisters went there last fall and took duck-face selfies in the bathroom? It was *iconic*! I. Con. Ic. And one of them got a picture with the Tavern's owner, and the man is, like, *gorgeous*. I mean, not like *gorgeous* gorgeous, more like power-tool gorgeous. You know?"

"No," I said coldly. "I have no idea what you're talking about." Anyone who could look at Flynn Honeycutt and think he was not gorgeous—full stop—was dangerously absurd.

"Alright, then," Brantleigh sighed, as though he were the final decider-er of plans. He batted his eyelashes up at me. "Jonathan and I will go, too. We'll stay just long enough to take a selfie, then bounce to a club or something."

Bounce to a *club*? Where did the man think a place like Honeybridge was hiding its nightlife?

"Oh, I think Jonathan would love that more than anything!" Mother cried.

I opened my mouth to argue with her—vehemently—when Reagan spoke up.

"I think the Tavern sounds amazing," he said. "Flynn sells the best mead ever. We should totally go."

I shot him a glare, but Reagan gave me puppy dog eyes that clearly screamed *"Please don't leave me alone with them!"*

Ugh. Apparently, there *was* a force that could compel me to bring this crew to the Tavern, and it was brotherly love. Was it too late for me to jump in the water and swim for shore? Ideally, a foreign shore, without extradition?

"Fine." I extricated my arm from Brantleigh's. "But we're only staying for one drink."

I was very afraid that was going to be one drink too many.

When we got to the Tavern, the place was packed with a combination of locals and wide-eyed tourists who'd come to town for the regatta and to attend what Willow called a Yoga in Nature Spiritual Awakening out at the Retreat. Every table was full, and the bar area was standing-room only, which meant we were able to blend in with the crowd. For once, I didn't want Flynn to notice me, let alone speak to me.

Dysen went off to the restroom immediately upon entering so she could "hashtag remix" the selfie she'd referenced earlier, while Reagan, Brantleigh, and I threaded our way to the bar.

"Evening, Frog!" Pop Honeycutt called from a high-top

table toward the back as we passed. "And Mr. Important. Lookin' good, kiddo." He held out his gnarled hand, and Reagan shook it politely.

We found an empty spot at the back corner of the bar and squeezed into it.

"Frog Wellbridge! Awesome game last week," Tori Honeycutt called from a nearby table where she and her husband, Rob, were sitting. "You gonna be around for the next one?"

Before I could answer, Brittany Merchant rushed over and threw her arms around my brother. "Holy crap, now it's officially hot guy night at the Tavern! Eye candy for days! We've got you, and JT, and Flynn, and Redmond, and these guys Brooks and Mal who are staying in one of the cottages out at the Retreat—and I think they're a couple because *oh my god* the way they eye-fuck each other!—and Alden, even though he's in a shit mood, and Cas, and this haw-aw-awt silver fox who was chatting up Redmond earlier…"

"And me." Brantleigh smiled ingratiatingly. "I'm Brantleigh Pennington, remember?"

"Oh." Brittany blinked, then glanced Brantleigh over, from his highlighted hair to his spray tan, to his preppy outfit and boat shoes. She smiled kindly. "Right. Sure. You too."

Brantleigh seemed nonplussed. I rubbed a hand over my mouth to hide my smile.

"What about me, Britt?" Rob Honeycutt interjected.

Brittany rolled her eyes. "Not you. You're taken." She winked at Tori.

"Jonathan is taken, too." Brantleigh locked elbows with me.

I really wished he'd stop doing that.

"Wait." Brittany's eyebrows lifted. "You're together? Well, hot damn. Plot twist."

"No," I said firmly, taking back my arm. But as annoying as he was, Brantleigh didn't deserve to be shot down completely in a public venue, so I softened my statement by adding, "He's a friend of the family. It's... complicated."

"Seems pretty simple to me, Frog," Flynn said from directly behind me, because *of course* he was standing right there, right then, and of course *this* was the one moment all week he deigned to speak to me. "Don't be shy. Who's the lucky guy?"

I groaned under my breath. I hadn't been exaggerating the other day on the island when I said the universe had it out for me and Flynn. There was a particularly savage kind of Murphy's Law that governed our interactions, where any misunderstanding or misinterpretation that could arise *would*... and always at the moment when it was least possible to explain myself.

I turned to face him, all broad-shouldered, hot-tempered, green-eyed, grumpy-assed perfection, and it settled in my bones that I'd probably never find another man half as compelling as I found him.

I also noticed that he looked more frazzled than I'd ever seen him, with his cheeks flushed pink, his Tavern T-shirt rumpled, and his dark hair standing on end like he'd been running his hands through it.

"Brantleigh's father knows my parents," I explained. "They've been visiting this week, and Brantleigh's very... nice." Sort of. Not really. Brantleigh smiled up at me adoringly, and it made me a little nauseous, so I followed this with "But we're not together."

"Yet," Brantleigh sing-songed.

"Wait." Brittany narrowed her eyes at Brantleigh. "Pennington, as in Thatcher Pennington, the silver-fox hottie at the bar who makes all the ladies gasp every time he smiles? The guy Marta Wellbridge said was gonna be investing in

Patricia's Downtown Revitalization Plan, which suddenly got at least six women in town dreaming up business plans just so he'd *invest a stake* in them?" She nudged Reagan in the side, but Reagan didn't react. "That guy's your *dad*, Brantleigh?"

"Ew." Brantleigh shuddered. "No. Thatcher Pennington, as in the old-as-fuck know-it-all who's got a stick up his ass at all times. *That's* my dad. *Brantleigh, when are you going to get a job? Brantleigh, your clothing budget could feed a small nation.* Fucking killjoy. I'm going to Turks the second he says forced family bonding time is over. Oooh!" Brantleigh seemed to startle himself by having an actual idea. "JT can come with!"

"Great plan," Flynn told Brantleigh enthusiastically, his eyes on mine. "JT should totes go with."

"No," I said firmly, shooting him a glare. "He shouldn't."

"Go where?" Dysen returned from the ladies' room and draped herself dramatically against my other side. "Did you find us a club where we can get our dance on, Jonny?"

Flynn's tired eyes lit up like he'd been given a gift, and he mouthed, "*Jonny,*" before pinching his lips together like he was saving the word up to tease me with later.

"Flynn, everyone, this is Dysen." I took a step back, extracting myself from her clutches. "She's Reagan's... guest."

Brantleigh groan-sighed. "We introduce ourselves to the waitstaff here? The charms of this town never cease." He pulled a twenty-dollar bill from his pocket and leaned over to tuck it in the front pocket of Flynn's shirt with a wink. "Vodka cranberry, please, cutie. I'm parched."

Rage seared through my gut like a flash fire.

This, I tried to tell Flynn with my eyes. *This* is why I didn't want you waiting on my asshole friends back in high school.

"Flynn is not the waitstaff," I said hotly. "He owns Honeybridge Tavern." *You insufferable buffoon.* "And he's my..."

I hesitated. We weren't friends, no matter how much I wanted to be, and we'd agreed we weren't enemies. But anything in the middle seemed to be way too tame for the way that Flynn provoked me, fascinated me, infuriated and humbled me.

Flynn tilted his head to the side and watched me across the table with a little smile playing around his mouth. He seemed just as curious about how I'd finish that statement as the others were.

"He's my Flynn," I said firmly. Then I lifted my chin and glared around the table, channeling Patricia Wellbridge for all I was worth, daring anyone to contradict me, especially Flynn himself.

Flynn looked away. "Vodka cranberry," he told Brantleigh smoothly. "Sure thing. Anything else for you guys?"

After taking our order, Flynn walked off, and I clenched my fists at my sides, trying to remember why it would not be good to assault Brantleigh for being an asshole.

In the end, I didn't have to.

"I cannot *believe* you said that to Flynn," Reagan said hotly, shoving Brantleigh's shoulder. "That was rude and disgusting."

"ReaBae's right," Dysen said solemnly. "So, *so* uncool. You need to get woke."

"But... the man's a Honeycutt." Brantleigh spread his hands helplessly, like this was in any way an excuse. "Patricia said *those Honeycutts* were rude and uncivilized. She said they're cheating social climbers. Who cares if I was rude?"

"I do. Because my mother is wrong." I seethed, moving

my reckoning with my mother up to the top spot on my priority list. "And you'd better fucking apologize when Flynn comes back, do you understand?"

Except Flynn didn't come back. He sent Castor over with our order, while Flynn stayed behind the bar making drinks with a precise sort of choreography that spoke of how good he was at his job and how much practice he'd had at it. He didn't glance in my direction even once.

"Cas," I asked in a low voice as he set my Honeybridge Sunshine in front of me. "Can you get me into Flynn's office so I can wait for him? Please? I just want to talk to him." Again.

Cas shook his head, but his eyes were kind. "Eh. Probably better if you don't, JT," he answered in the same hushed tone. "Not right now. He's in a grouchy mood. He's been run off his feet all day with the regatta folks, and he's closing by himself in a few hours because Alden and I have to head out to the Retreat to help my mom. It's the first night of the waning moon," he explained when I frowned at him. "You know, the most potent time to harvest valerian root?"

I sighed.

I insisted on leaving after one round of drinks, and though Brantleigh maintained that I was still upset over nothing, he didn't protest. This was fortunate for him because I was officially out of patience, and if I heard one more ignorant word out of his ignorant mouth, he was going to find out exactly how rude and uncivilized a *Wellbridge* could get.

When we got back to the house, I turned down Brantleigh's suggestions of an impromptu house party and/or a private massage and shook my head when Reagan asked if I wanted to help him light the fire pit. My brotherly affection had been exhausted, so I telegraphed him an apology with my eyes before excusing myself to my room and throwing myself on my bed.

Being back in Honeybridge had caused me to regress into a moody teenager—one who lusted over Flynn Honeycutt from afar because the gulf of misunderstandings between us seemed too wide to bridge, and who did my parents' bidding while dreaming of a future where I could leave this town and my family behind.

I'd left that child in the dust when I left Honeybridge. I'd made my own life. Learned my own lessons through countless triumphs and painful mistakes. There were some things I didn't like about life in the city—namely, being expected to rearrange my life at the whim of my boss—but I liked the man I'd become there. I didn't know why I couldn't reconcile the new me with my old hometown.

Part of me wanted to say *fuck it* and head back to New York just so I could feel like myself again... but I couldn't do that either.

Flynn Honeycutt held me here, just as surely as if he'd tied me to that hammock on Milk Bottle Island and kept me prisoner.

And it wasn't *only* about needing him to sign the contract so I could earn my promotion either. Not anymore. As important as that was, I also wanted to ease his burden somehow. To make him smile. To fix this star-crossed-whatever-the-fuck between us, at least a little bit, and leave him a couple of positive thoughts of me to replace the decades of misunderstandings.

I didn't want Flynn Honeycutt to hate me.

A light tap landed on my door a few moments later, and Reagan stuck his head in. "You busy?"

"Busy planning how to tell Mother that if she wants to cement our connection to the Penningtons, she can date Brantleigh her own damn self."

He snorted. "I would pay to see that." He hesitated, then came inside and shut the door behind him. "Uh... are you okay?"

I shrugged. "Sure. Just tired."

Reagan nodded slowly, his hair flopping down over his forehead. "Look, I know it's been a while since we were close or whatever. But... if you want to talk about you and Flynn, you can talk to me. I'll probably understand better than you think."

"Me and Flynn... what?" I demanded, my heart rate kicking up though I tried not to show it. Had I actually been obvious enough that even someone as self-absorbed as *Reagan* recognized it? "I need him to sign the contract so I—"

"You give him *sex eyes*," Reagan interrupted. He lifted an eyebrow. "You give him *broody* sex eyes."

"What? *Pfft*. I do not. I'm not a brooder, Reagan," I said... broodily. Damn it.

"Your whole body lights up when he's around." Reagan crossed his arms stubbornly. "Your eyes follow Flynn around the bar like a dog at its dinnertime."

I pursed my lips, simultaneously offended and amused. "Gassy and disgruntled?"

"Like you're hungry as fuck," Reagan said matter-of-factly. "And Flynn's the juiciest bone in town."

"Ohhhkay. That's enough." I sat up. "Flynn's an attractive man. I've never denied that. But we're not... it's not like that between us."

As far as anyone in town was concerned, it never had been.

Reagan rolled his eyes. "You're not subtle. I saw what I saw, not just today but every time I was at the Tavern with you this week. I kept waiting for you to make a move, but you didn't, and I was like, *since when is JT so lame?*"

Reagan examined his perfectly buffed nails. "But it occurred to me that you might not have realized Flynn looks at you the same way."

I frowned. "Rea, I appreciate you trying to... comfort me in your uniquely insulting way—"

He snickered.

"—but I know for a fact you're wrong. Flynn's been ignoring me for a week."

"Oh, I know." Reagan leaned against the door. "But it's impossible to ignore someone that completely unless he's thinking of you constantly. Here's what I know: Flynn is aware of exactly where you are at every moment. He looks everywhere *but* at you. Talks to everyone *except* you." Reagan ticked the items off on his fingers. "But as soon as someone makes you laugh—like when Marta told everyone that story about her homicidal rabbit the other day, remember?—Flynn gets distracted from the not-looking for a second. And when he *does* look at you, JT..." His voice trailed off into a small smile, and he shook his head.

"What?" I demanded, sitting forward and no longer pretending I wasn't invested. "What happens?"

Reagan sighed. "I have never seen someone crave another person so deeply before. It's, like, this tangible, electric *thing* that stretches out between you whenever you're in the same room. I'd give a lot to have someone look at me like that."

I sucked in a breath, trying to imagine Flynn looking at me like that... before reason asserted itself, and I scowled. "No. Flynn doesn't like me."

"Craving and dislike are not mutually exclusive. If you think that, you really need to follow more celebrity gossip pages. But Flynn doesn't dislike you, JT, even if maybe he wishes he did. You can see it on his face. And okay." Reagan held up a hand to cut off my protest. "He probably doesn't trust you. You have history. He doesn't want your contract. Blah, blah. But you need to stop ignoring the giant horny elephant in the room, if not for yourself, then for the sake of the rest of us who are caught in your pheromone backwash. Besides, how can you two build trust when you're both being dishonest about this huge, important thing? And for fuck's sake, why are you letting him push you away? How is that gonna help anything?"

Whoa. When had my *little brother* started being so mature and observant? Since when did he make so much damn sense? But he was missing one crucial fact.

"I've tried talking to him. Repeatedly. Flynn refuses to listen."

"Who said anything about talking?" Reagan demanded, exasperated. "Take action. *Show* him how you feel. Show him how things can be different."

I blinked at Reagan, stunned.

I'd been waiting for Flynn to give me a signal that he wanted me, either in business or in bed. To recognize that he could trust me.

But what had I done to *show* him that I was trustworthy? That things between us didn't have to follow the same pattern they always had?

And since when did I wait around for shit to happen? That was the old, immature JT Wellbridge's process, not mine.

How fucking ironic that it had taken a conversation with Reagan, a guy who seemed as stuck in his life as I'd ever been, to point it out.

"So, you're suggesting... what?" I asked eagerly. "That I go over there and..."

"Let him take out his frustrations on your ass, then see where you are? Yes. Yes, I am."

I shook my head. "Such a way with words."

"It's a gift." He flashed a grin. "I'd better get back downstairs before Dysen and Brantleigh burn the house down for funsies. What are *you* gonna do?"

Good question. I thought of Flynn, all worn down and frazzled from dealing with a bunch of snobby assholes all evening and then closing the bar by himself. I wanted to help him, right? So... why wasn't I helping? Why was I leaving him to do things alone?

I threw myself off the bed and shoved my feet into my sneakers. "I'm going out for a run."

He ducked his chin. "A run... past the Tavern?"

"I might head in that direction, yes."

"*Iconic*," Reagan said in a spot-on imitation of Dysen's voice.

I chuckled. "Thank you, Rea. I owe you one."

He gave me a soft smile. "You're welcome. I hope you stick around long enough for me to collect."

Honeybridge's town center was nearly deserted by the time I jogged down there. Technically, bars could continue serving until 1:00 a.m., but Horace had always closed the Tavern by 11:00 p.m. sharp, and I was glad to see that Flynn kept to that tradition.

The door to the Tavern was locked, but I knocked on it repeatedly until a tired voice from inside called, "We're closed. Come back tomorrow."

I banged again with the side of my fist this time.

"Seriously? We're closed for the night!"

I banged some more, using both hands this time.

From inside, I heard the scrape of a chair, a dull thump, and then the snick of the door lock before Flynn cracked the door open just a few inches.

"Are you fucking for real? We're— Oh. It's you. What do you want, *Jonny*?"

As loving welcomes went, this was... neither loving nor welcoming, but still I drank him in—his eyes, his broad shoulders, those thick legs. He was so exhausted it was practically coming off him in waves, but he still looked determined.

How could anyone not want Flynn Honeycutt on their team for... basically anything? The man was relentless.

"It's me," I confirmed, a beat too late. "And I really dislike that name."

Flynn sighed and leaned against the doorframe. "What do you want, JT? I'm warning you, I do not have the patience for your shit right now. You could hand me a contract paying me the moon and all the planets, and I'd run it through Pop's paper shredder just the same."

"I'm here to help you."

"By having Fortress pay me all the money ever printed so I can hire a floor mopper while I sip mango martinis in Belize?"

"No. By mopping the floor while you sit and have a cold drink."

Flynn blinked, clearly startled, then narrowed his eyes.

It was my turn to sigh. "You're trying to figure out my angle, but there *is* no angle. I'm just trying to show you that I meant what I said last weekend. I want to help. I'm not your enemy, and—" I hesitated. *Open and honest, right?* "And I also maybe felt like shit about Brantleigh being an elitist asshat earlier, and even shittier when Cas said you'd be closing alone, and I've been thinking about you. A lot." When Flynn remained silent, I persisted. "Forget about the contract with Fortress for right now. I just want to help mop your floor or whatever else you need. Okay?"

Flynn expelled a breath and pushed the door wide,

rolling his eyes. "Fine, then. You wanna spend your evening mopping, knock yourself out. I've got a billion glasses to wash, plus setup to do for tomorrow."

I stepped inside. Music played softly over the speakers—probably had been playing all day, but I hadn't been able to hear it until all the other noise was gone—and I smiled to myself as I noticed it was an oldies tune, the kind Horace used to play.

It wasn't my first time being in the Tavern after hours, but the last time, Flynn hadn't hesitated to let me in, bowed with grief and tipsy on mead as he had been.

Flynn locked the door and looked at me strangely. I wondered if he was thinking of that night, too. He cleared his throat and pointed to the kitchen. "Mop and bucket are over there. You'll need to flip the rest of the chairs onto the tables and sweep first, then mop."

I saluted him and got to work.

We worked in silence for a long while, me cleaning the floor while humming along to an old John Denver ballad and Flynn doing whatever he was doing behind the bar while making occasional trips to the kitchen. It was comfortable. Cozy, even. I liked it.

I felt Flynn's eyes linger on me from time to time, and I liked that even better.

When the floor was done, I emptied the bucket and stacked all the cleaning supplies neatly in the back closet. Then I ducked back into the bar area. Flynn was bent over, adjusting some nozzle on the floor, and I valiantly tried not to ogle his ass. *This is about helping Flynn, not yourself.*

"What else do you need?" I asked softly.

Flynn startled and whirled around like maybe he'd forgotten I was there. "Uh. I don't know. Nothing, I guess." He swallowed and looked me up and down like he was noticing for the first time what I wore—a T-shirt, running shorts, and sneakers. "Were you... exercising earlier?"

"Kinda. I ran here. Flynn, I—" I began.

"JT, we should—" Flynn said at the same time. He swallowed. "You go ahead."

Fuck, why was this so hard? I had all the convincing words and smiles in the world when talking to other people, but never with him.

In the end, though, I didn't have to say anything because the song on the speaker changed at that moment, *exactly* like it had that night three years ago, to one of Horace's favorite '70s songs, "Just the Way You Are."

I sucked in a shocked breath and stared across the small space at Flynn, who was staring back at me the same way—like lightning had struck us for the second time.

Maybe the universe did have it out for us. Maybe these sweet, stolen moments were all we were ever supposed to have. If that was the case, I was going to make the most of them... by *showing* Flynn how I felt since words were our kryptonite.

Slowly, like I was approaching one of McLean Honeycutt's beautiful untamed creatures, I held out my hand just as I had on that other fateful night. "Dance with me?"

Flynn watched my hand warily for one beat. Two. Then just as I thought he was going to hiss and claw or maybe punch me, he released the breath he was holding and took my hand in his, pulling me into his body. I set my free hand just above his hip, and he wrapped his free arm around my back as we swayed to the music.

Fuck, it felt good to let him hold me. I'd forgotten just how good. His fingers were warm and strong on the small of my back, and the sway of his hips never faltered. He smelled like leather and honey, sweet and biting and real.

I clasped his hand tightly and stepped back, spinning him away for just a second in time to the music.

"For the record, this is a terrible idea," Flynn growled, his voice so heavy with want that I shivered.

"This is a fucking fantastic idea," I breathed, and then I reeled him right back into my arms. "Trust me."

Chapter Eight

Flynn

Could I trust him? Thirty years of past experience suggested no.

Did I want to? I pressed my nose to JT's neck and inhaled a breath of him—clean summer sweat layered over a fragrance that was smoky and no doubt expensive—and felt my gut tighten with need.

Yeah. Yeah, I definitely wanted to.

"Let me take you to bed, Firecracker." His voice was low and easy, as if he had no reservations or stress about the decision.

How nice for him.

"We shouldn't." Those two whispered words were as close to a denial as I could muster, and even as I said them, my fingers dug into the muscles beneath his T-shirt, and my hand clenched his more tightly, begging him silently not to listen.

All hail Flynn Honeycutt, the king of mixed signals.

But JT only chuckled lightly, like he understood my struggle. "Flynn, baby, stop thinking so hard." His lips moved against my temple, and I fought a full-body shudder.

"Not your baby," I insisted, dragging my nose up the

tendon in his neck. His muscles tightened around me, clasping me against him as he shuddered, too.

"But you could be," he murmured, his hand moving lower until it hovered just over the curve of my ass. "For tonight."

Christ, the man was temptation incarnate. Always had been. Regardless of how much he provoked me, he also turned me on more than any other man had in my life. He was at the very top of Flynn Honeycutt's Personal List of Sexy Humans, far above any celebrity or local guy I'd dated.

The last thing I wanted was a repeat of what had happened three years ago, but I was a different person now. Stronger. No matter how good it was between us, I wouldn't delude myself into thinking it could be anything more than physical or anything longer than one night.

I closed my eyes and took another deep breath of him, stalling for time. I hoped like hell he hadn't put on that cologne for the spoiled asshole who'd been here with him earlier. The very idea was absolutely infuriating... and fury made me reckless.

I licked a broad, claiming stripe up his neck and bit lightly on his earlobe.

"*Fuck*," he whimpered. JT dropped all pretense of dancing, and the hand that wasn't on my ass immediately moved to the nape of my neck, holding my mouth exactly where it was.

"This is just sex. I don't want you to think it means anything," I murmured, my breath coasting over his ear.

"I know," he whispered.

"Because it doesn't. And it never will."

"Okay."

"And you'd better not feel smug because you—"

With a frustrated, needy growl, JT grabbed my head

with both hands and smashed his mouth against mine, shutting me up very effectively.

I made a *mpfh* sound against his lips and then let it turn into a drawn-out groan.

God, he felt good. Water-in-the desert good. Coffee-in-the-morning good. Sun-on-your-face good. The kind of good that could make a man ignore a whole lot of past wrongs, at least temporarily, because it felt so damn right.

His warm hands moved down to span my back as he held me close. One of his legs shifted between mine, and he used it to rock us back and forth to the music, though we both knew it was just an excuse to stay pressed close against each other.

We kissed and kissed and kissed as the songs changed one after the other. I lost myself in the feel of his hands, the smell of his skin, and the taste of his mouth. JT Wellbridge was overwhelming to the senses. Without even trying, the man had me on total overload. Complete meltdown.

"Where's the music player?" he asked.

I blinked at him in confusion until he smiled softly. Affectionately.

"The music. I want to turn it off." His voice went low and rough. "We're going to your bed."

I bristled at his bossy tone, but my dick betrayed me. It liked the tone just fine, and since it was leading the charge right now, I kept my biting back talk to myself. Instead, I mumbled something about high-handed Wellbridges as I moved to turn off the music.

The low rumble of his laughter didn't make my dick harder, but only because it wasn't possible for my dick to get any harder.

When I finished turning everything off, I looked up to find him watching me with patient intensity. He held out his hand to me for the second time that night, and my eyes caught on the tattooed skin peeking out from under his watch strap, stark black against his honey-gold tan.

This is just sex, I reminded myself, gritting my teeth. *Just sex. Use him for tension release. You deserve one night to let off steam.*

I ignored the hand he offered and grabbed his wrist instead, towing him toward the back door. I didn't want affection or tenderness. Not patience and polite manners. If we were doing this—and we sure the fuck were—someone needed to set the right tone from the outset.

Once I'd made sure the back door to the Tavern was locked, I grabbed his wrist again and marched him across the back lot to my little house. If my hands shook a little while typing in the code for my door, it was only because I was so horny. It had nothing to do with nerves. It was *not* because I cared.

But when I locked the door behind us, flipped on the lamp, and turned to JT, time went wonky, and the air around us felt strange. All the urgency of a moment ago seemed to dissipate as we stared at each other.

He was so damned perfect. The beautiful heir to the Wellbridge family dynasty. The golden boy Patricia and Trent had lorded over our community for decades as if there'd been such a thing as Honeybridge royalty and JT was the future king.

At times, I'd suspected JT himself didn't feel that way, but he'd gone all-in with it anyway to make his parents proud—fancy schools and designer clothes, rich friends and elitist hobbies, his move to New York after college to carve out a high-powered job in the corporate world, and even the ridiculously pretentious, ridiculously sexy tattoo of a crown on his wrist. I'd told myself that going along with his parents' idea of him as royalty was just as bad as believing it himself.

Now, in the muted lamplight, I looked at him more closely, and I couldn't help but see the things that didn't add up. One of his tidy fingernails was ragged and bitten, like his week hanging around Honeybridge hadn't been particularly relaxing. The faded T-shirt he wore boasted of a New York City Parks volunteer event instead of some highbrow sailing race. A small scar at the edge of his jaw reminded me of the time he'd fallen on the corner of a display rack while helping Pop sweep up the General Store back in elementary school.

I frowned, staring at that scar. Why had a Wellbridge been helping out at Pop's store in the first place?

"Why did you work at the General Store in fourth grade?" I blurted.

JT's perfectly smooth forehead creased in confusion. "Is this a test? Or some kind of strange Honeybridge foreplay?"

I ignored him. "You didn't need the money. And Pop sure as heck didn't need a random kid when he had all of us Honeycutts. So... why?"

And why had I never thought to ask before? Not about this. Not about the science fair. Not about the mortifying not-a-date. I was suddenly afraid I'd made a serious error somewhere along the way. Or maybe I was making one now.

JT firmed his stubbled jaw. "Because Pop asked me to. That's why."

"But—"

"Did you want to spend tonight talking?" he interrupted. "Because you said just sex. And discussing your grandfather while I'm trying to get us off is kind of a deal breaker."

"Yeah, but—" He was right, of course, but the inconsistencies still bugged me. Now that I'd noticed them, I couldn't unnotice them.

"But nothing." JT took a big step forward until his chest brushed against mine. His hands gripped my hips. "Tonight, my plan is to figure out where you keep a bed in this shoebox." He glanced around my tiny house, his eyes glowing with amusement and lust, the headiest combination in the world. "Then, I'm going to shove you down on it, strip you bare, and pound your hole until we don't remember our own names, let alone anything that happened in fourth grade."

I was dizzy from his words. I sucked in a breath to try and steady myself and licked my lips before replying. "Who said I was bottoming?"

JT's eyes darkened. The intensity almost made me drop to my knees right then and there. "I say it."

Oh fuck.

My legs wobbled a little, and JT's hands tightened on my hips. I could argue with him and pretend I didn't want his fat dick inside of me, or I could take him up to my bed and let him fulfill years' worth of fantasies.

There was no choice to be made here.

"Y-yeah," I breathed, trying and failing to sound casual. "Fine." I turned and stepped to the slim ladder that functioned as a staircase. "Follow me."

As I began to climb, JT took the opportunity to run a hand up the inside of my thigh and into my shorts. My heart thumped harder as my lungs struggled to take in enough oxygen. When his fingers brushed my sac, I almost fell off the damned stairs.

"Steady," he murmured, moving his hands up to my hips. One of his thumbs snuck under my shirt to rub a gentle circle on the skin above my waistband. Why was he such a magical fucking sex master? The man could touch me lightly with one finger, and I already wanted to come all over myself.

"Yeah, fine," I said again. Because I was on fire with the words.

When I got up to my bedroom loft, I was relieved to see I'd left it fairly tidy that morning. The bedding was thrown into place, and there weren't any dirty clothes on the floor.

Not that I cared. Not that I was trying to impress anyone.

Liar.

I cleared my throat to cover my nerves. "So. We've found the bed. When do we get to the shoving and the pounding?"

JT didn't answer. I glanced over my shoulder, half expecting to find him giving my personal space judgy eyeballs, but he wasn't. He was staring at a large black-and-white framed photo hanging on the wall at the top of the stairs with his jaw hanging open.

Ah, fuck. How had I forgotten?

My stomach twisted. "That's a photo of the Retreat that McLean took when he was little—"

JT shook his head wonderingly. "That's a photo of *me*."

"What? No. It's some random kid jumping off a rope swing into Quick Lake at the Summer Picnic. Alden maybe. Or Castor." Alden had never been that tall in his life, and Castor was scared of the rope swing to this day.

"It's me. You have a picture of me hanging in your bedroom."

"Whoa, whoa, whoa. Egotistical much?" My voice sounded reedy to my own ears. "I like the composition. And McLean was so proud of capturing that perfect moment. The light coming off the water droplets, the pattern of the ripples on the surface of the water. He'd saved up for months to buy that camera."

"I remember," JT said, turning to look again. His eyes

locked back on the photo, and he brought his finger up to point. "And that's you in the water. Right here."

I stopped breathing. "How did you—? I mean... is it?"

But I was bullshitting him, and we both knew it. Because of the reflection of the sun on the surface, anyone looking at the photo couldn't see under the water. The only way to know I was under the water was to remember, to have been there.

The air inside the little loft felt hotter. Alive, suddenly, with the scent of coconut sunblock and the ghost of long-ago laughter.

"You were lying in wait to drag me under," he said with a faint smile. "I remember you could hold your breath forever. And I would fight you off again and again, but you wouldn't let go of me until I yelled, '*I yield to Flynn Honeycutt, king of this lake.*'"

I didn't want to do this anymore. Memories swarmed over me like a horde of angry bees looking for places to sting, and I felt stripped raw. Vulnerable, in a way I'd only ever been with him.

"I thought this was *sex*," I said angrily.

He turned to face me, his blue eyes troubled. "Me too," he said softly.

I swallowed hard. I opened my mouth to tell him to leave, but that wasn't what came out.

"I want you to wreck me." My voice didn't sound right. It sounded hoarse and ragged, desperate and too... something.

JT's breathing became audible as he turned to face me. "You have no idea what you do to me," he said, almost to himself. "Take your clothes off, Firecracker."

I was naked in seconds, climbing onto my bed when JT's hands grabbed my hips and pulled my ass back. His teeth bit into the flesh of one of my ass cheeks before his tongue soothed it. I closed my eyes and dropped my face into the bedding.

"Why do you taste like soap?" he said against my skin as he nibbled his way up to my lower back.

"A customer knocked a pitcher of beer all over me. I had to run home and shower a couple hours ago."

He made a deep humming sound. "Thank god for drunken customers," he murmured before moving his mouth back down to my ass and making free with my hole, licking and sucking until I pushed back against him needily.

"Oh fuck," I squeaked. "Fuck, fuck."

JT pulled his wet mouth away from my tender skin just long enough to ask, "This okay?"

"You know it is," I whimpered in response. "More."

Jonathan Magic-Tongue Wellbridge was rimming me. I felt like a puddle of drool, warm and sated, oozing down onto the bed on jelly legs.

I would have lectured the stupid me from earlier, the one who'd thought this was a bad idea, if only I had the brain cells to do something other than lie there and beg.

His strong hands gripped my ass like he owned it, and in that moment, he definitely did. JT could do whatever the hell he wanted to me as long as it made my dick this hard.

"Your ass." His voice was muffled. "So good. Want to do so much to this ass."

I wanted that too, but I didn't have words to articulate it. And I didn't have to, really. Not when JT seemed to know exactly what I wanted. Not when my throat kept making embarrassing keening noises the way it did.

I would have been embarrassed at how needy I was, but I was too overwhelmed with sensation. This was the best thing that had happened to my body in as long as I could remember, and I wasn't going to fuck it up by thinking overmuch about the repercussions.

Nope. I was in this for a mind-blowing orgasm. And I was going to have it without guilt. JT and I were supposed to be not-enemies, which was almost close to *friends*. So he could be a friend with benefits for just one night, and it didn't need to mean anything.

Not a single thing.

"Shut off your fucking head," JT growled, smacking my ass with a sting. "It's just sex. Lay there and fucking take what I'm giving to you. Let go."

I hated that he could read my mind after all this time. "I am," I managed to say, lying through my drool.

"You're not. But you will."

He flipped me onto my back and crawled over the top of me until we were nose to nose. His eyes were so fucking pretty they made my chest ache. A hank of hair flopped down from its perfect style and fell into his eyes.

I reached out to run the strands through my fingers.

"I don't want to do something you don't want," he said in a much softer voice. He lifted one hand to caress my cheek. "But I'd be lying if I said I didn't want to fuck you so badly right now I'm literally in pain."

I blinked up at him. "I want that too," I admitted in a breathy voice.

He looked uncertain, and I knew why. My heart began to beat erratically as the memory of last time finally came flooding in.

"This isn't... I'm not... Last time, I..." I fixed my teeth together in defiance. "This is just sex."

I winced. Did that make it sound like last time wasn't?

JT searched my eyes before sighing and moving off me. He settled against the headboard and ran his fingers through his hair, slipping the wayward hank back into its proper position. "About that night... I need to explain—"

Oh dear god.

I pushed myself up and sat next to him, leaving enough space between us to keep from touching. "No, you really don't. It's fine."

He turned to face me. "It's obviously not."

I looked down at my rapidly deflating dick and reached for the throw blanket at the foot of the bed to cover us with. This wasn't a naked-cock conversation.

"The things I said," he began. "I shouldn't have pressured you to—"

"You didn't," I interrupted.

"For fuck's sake, Flynn." JT leaned forward, filling the space I'd tried to put between us. "For once in our damn lives, can we just have a whole conversation? You were sad that night. You'd just lost your grandfather. You were vulnerable, and I..." He shook his head. "I wanted you so damn badly that I didn't think. I took advantage. And I'm sorry."

"You're sorry." I was suddenly, irrationally angry. "Sorry it happened? Sorry we fucked around? Sorry you wanted me?"

Temper lit his eyes. "Sorry I *hurt* you, asshole!"

"You didn't hurt me," I shot back, appalled. "You couldn't."

I was pretty sure we both knew that was the biggest lie I'd ever told.

I threw up my hands. I was mortified... and angry that I was mortified. Miserably afraid... and royally pissed off that he could make me afraid. I was ruining my one no-strings night of Frog-sex, and I hated that, but I couldn't stop it.

"I get it, okay?" I yelled. "I get it. You're sorry. I'm sorry. You're sorry that I'm sorry. This is why we don't talk about the past. We *suck* at talking. And it doesn't fucking matter anymore. So can we just move on? Are we going to do the sex?" I gestured to the bed. "Or are you leaving again?"

The last word of my diatribe landed like a rock in a lake, sending rippling currents through the suddenly quiet room.

JT tilted his head to one side and stared at me for a long moment, and I was certain that he was going to get dressed and go. It would serve me right, too. For once, I couldn't even find a way to blame him for it because I'd have driven him out with my vitriol.

Then, miraculously, one side of his lips quirked up. "*Do the sex*," he mused. "It's like poetry when you speak, Flynn Honeycutt. So *seductive*. So alluring. This must be what keeps all the Honeybridge boys coming 'round."

My face flamed, and I pushed feebly at his shoulder. "Fuck off," I said without heat.

He tilted my chin up with one finger, forcing me to look at him. "Do you want me to leave?"

I swallowed and grasped the blanket in my lap like a lifeline. "No," I managed to whisper. But I knew he needed more. *Deserved* more. So I forced myself to go on. "I wanted you then. I want you now. Please. Don't... don't leave."

JT reached over and clasped the back of my neck, pulling me close enough for a sweet kiss. I let myself go, let myself simply enjoy the moment in case it was the last time I felt his lips on mine.

When he pulled back, his face was serious enough to set my heart stuttering again.

"Okay... but we need some rules."

I rolled my eyes, but JT yanked me down the bed, pressing my back onto the mattress and climbing on top of me until his weight pressed me down and reinvigorated my cock.

His grin was sexy enough to make me frown.

"Fine," I huffed. "What are your rules?" Because now that JT's bare dick was sliding against mine, I was ready to agree to almost anything... as long as it wasn't more talking.

"You need to let go. And I want you to shut the fuck up. I want your head and your mouth to just stop. Do you think that's at all possible?"

This was exactly what I wanted, what I needed, so even though it was on the tip of my tongue to say, *make me*, just out of habit, I bit it back and nodded instead.

JT's grin widened, and he dropped a lingering kiss to my mouth. "Good. If you want me to stop, pinch me, but don't say a word. Promise me."

His suggestion made me harder, and I had to work to get enough oxygen into my lungs. "Promise," I mouthed before shooting him a smug look. I could be silent. Just watch me.

He shook his head before looking around. "Condoms and lube. Where are they?"

I thumbed in the direction of the bedside table.

Once he had what he needed, he kneeled on the bed and looked down at me, tapping one finger to his kiss-swollen lips like he was formulating a plan.

I wanted to tell him to hurry, to put his hands on my dick or shove his fucking cock into my hole already, but there were rules. And the rules said I couldn't talk.

I had to lie there and take it.

JT's eyes lit up, and he gave me a patented Wellbridge smirk, like he knew exactly what I was thinking and was getting off on it. My dick swelled at the sight, twitching against my belly. Then he leaned down and proceeded to kiss me so thoroughly, I forgot the events of the previous half-hour.

JT's hands were everywhere on my body, lighting me up like I had a million tiny sparklers sizzling along my skin. I groaned, deep and needy, into the thick air of my loft. JT's lips dipped into the curve of my hip, and the tip of his tongue left behind wet trails that turned cool when he blew air against them.

My body sank into the mattress as I reminded myself to calm down and enjoy every minute of JT's ministrations. He was nothing if not diligent in his attention to every square inch of my body.

I wanted to taste him and touch him, give him back a fraction of the pleasure he was giving me, but I couldn't move. And anytime I tried to, a low growl of warning would escape his throat.

My cock made a puddle in my happy trail, and I wondered how it was possible for the man to kiss absolutely every speck of my body but not put his mouth on my dick.

The sound of my heavy breathing surrounded us. JT's humming noises as he sucked on a particularly enjoyable part of me made me light-headed.

This was nothing like the hookups I'd had in the past or even the relationship sex I'd had the few times I'd tried dating someone more seriously.

It was different. Of course it was.

It was JT. My Frog. And whether I wanted to or not, whether it was *wise* or not, deep down, I knew he'd take care of me.

"Do you know how much this happy trail turns me on?" he growled hoarsely, rubbing his nose into the coarse hair on my stomach. "Always has. It's amazing I didn't trip over my own feet anytime we were in the locker room together."

I threaded my fingers through his hair, lightly scratching his scalp the way my brother Alden had advised me years ago.

"The way to a man's heart is through his stomach, but the way to his dick is through his scalp. Do you have any idea how many shampoo boners I see on a daily basis?"

I lifted my knees and arched up in hopes of sending JT the dick-sucking message.

"Stop being bossy," he mumbled before dipping his tongue into my belly button. "Patience, baby."

I opened my mouth to tell him to fuck off when I happened to catch his eye. He winked at me, clearly baiting me deliberately. I groaned again and looked at the ceiling before covering my face with both hands and screaming my frustration into them.

But my screams cut off abruptly when JT's mouth took hot, wet hold of my cock and sucked it down.

"Fucking fuck!" I broke the no-talking rule, but just for a second. As soon as his tongue joined the party, all I had left in my vocal cords were little mewling sounds.

He was talented enough to make me regret the years I'd let pass. Why hadn't I kept him here, chained to Honeybridge, Maine, if for no other reason than to fellate me on a regular basis?

He sucked me to the brink of release and then promptly pulled off, shoving my thighs in the air to move his hot mouth down to my hole again.

I bit the back of my hand to keep from swallowing my tongue. The scrape of his scruff against my thighs felt incredible. I wanted every part of him, everywhere. On me, around me, *inside of me*.

My head buzzed with the knowledge I wasn't going to last. I was going to come before JT even got the condom on, and I'd have yet another experience of what it was like to come without JT's dick in my ass.

No fucking way.

I reached down and palmed his forehead, shoving it away from me and giving his glassy eyes the most desperate puppy-dog face I could manage.

He lunged up and smashed my mouth with his, bringing with him the taste of my precum and everything else he'd had his mouth on. It was dirty as fuck, and it made me even more light-headed. JT was covered in the scent of sex with me.

The thought made me heady. It would have made me harder if that had been possible.

"You're so fucking sexy," he murmured in my ear, nipping at the lobe and then the tender skin below. "Let me have you. Please. I've waited so long for this."

Hadn't I already told him yes like a million times? Hadn't I begged him with my voice and my body? Hadn't I —*ohmyfuckinggod...*

JT's fingers found my hole and brushed it firmly with slick lube before plunging one inside. I sputtered out something that wasn't even a word but meant some kind of combination of *oh hell yes* and *will your finger please marry my ass* but probably sounded more like *murpfh*, because I was suave like that.

My body was covered in sweat as I writhed beneath him. His lips stayed close enough to my ear to murmur words of reassurance and encouragement. *Shh, you're doing so good, you're so fucking tight, so hot, you drive me insane, that's it, my Firecracker, just like that...*

"Please," I finally croaked. If he made me wait any longer, I was going to actually cry.

When he finally knelt back on his heels to suit up, I examined his beautiful body. His chest hair was plastered to his skin with sweat, the previously well-styled hair on his head was all over the place from my grasping fingers, and his abs were flexed into faint squares as he struggled to get the condom on.

JT met my eyes, and his face morphed into a killer grin, the kind that made my heart literally fling itself against the front of my rib cage.

You are everything I've ever wanted and can never have.

When he leaned back down to line himself up at the

entrance to my body, I watched his face, trying to imprint this fleeting moment into my permanent mental hard drive. As soon as he began pressing inside of me, I hissed in welcome, but he misinterpreted the sound.

"Baby? Too much?"

I shook my head frantically and grabbed at his hips to pull him closer, faster, harder. Not enough. Never ever enough.

He continued more carefully, taking his sweet damned time and watching my eyes to make sure I was okay. When he was finally fully seated inside me, I wrapped my arms and legs around him and held him tight.

"Flynn," he breathed against the side of my face. "Holy fuck."

He pulled out, resisting my hold and lighting up my channel until I threw my head back and arched my body toward him with a cry. From the moment my voice hit the air, he was almost out of control, pounding me into the bed the way he'd originally promised, grunting commands for me to *take it*, to *like it*, to *hold on* and *not come yet*.

His words made me crazy, made me want to explode. Made me want to cry with the rightness of them... and run from their overwhelming intensity. But it was what he said after we both came in a screaming rush that terrified me most.

We lay in a sweaty, panting heap while trying to catch our breaths. When he finally grabbed the condom to pull out of me, I winced.

He shot me a look of apology that turned tender the minute his eyes landed on my face. And then he reached out and brushed the damp hair off my forehead with his fingertips.

"Wait here, sweetheart. Let me take care of you."

He didn't stick around for a response... which was good because I didn't have one.

Sweetheart?

Let me take care of you?

He shuttled down the staircase ladder and found the bathroom, turning on faucets and moving around to clean himself up while he whistled a low tune.

I stared at the top of the stairs with an open mouth. What the fuck had just happened? I was still processing when JT returned to the loft with a damp cloth.

"Uh... thanks," I said, reaching for it.

He batted my hand away and cleaned me with gentle, efficient movements, then flung the cloth toward the stairs and pressed an affectionate kiss to my nose.

"So." I cleared my throat. "You probably need to..."

He moved his lips down and shut me up with a soft kiss, then moved me under the sheet and slid in next to me.

"Flynn?"

"Y-yeah?"

"What did I say about thinking?" he muttered. "Cut that shit out. You promised. Now, go to sleep."

He arranged me into a spoon position against him and tucked his face into the curve of my shoulder.

I let out a deep breath.

Sleep? With Frog Wellbridge in my bed? Ha. Easy for him to say. JT made me feel many things, but relaxed had never been one.

I yawned hugely. *He'll probably get bored soon and go home.*

My tired eyes slid shut, and I allowed myself to relax into him, too worn out to do anything else. *Might as well enjoy his arms around me for a few minutes.*

It was the last thought I had until morning.

Chapter Nine

JT

Spending the night in Flynn Honeycutt's bed was one revelation after another.

Revelation number one: Flynn was a snuggler.

The man was pricklier than a cactus and spent way too many hours of the day killing his own joy by overthinking, so I never would have imagined that he'd tolerate being held for long. But two minutes after I'd wrapped my arms around him, he'd dropped into sleep like a stone into a pond. He'd rolled with me in the night, too, keeping our connection, like once his body was sated and pliant and his brain shut off, he could finally let himself have what he needed.

Which led me to my second revelation.

Carly from the Premiere Sleep Shoppe at Lexington and Twenty-Third had steered me wrong. The secret to a good night's sleep was not, in fact, the plush topper and premium king-sized mattress she'd talked me into. It turned out, squeezing onto a smallish mattress filled with organic oat hulls in an un-airconditioned loft in the height of a humid Maine summer while a gorgeous man nearly as large, broad, and hot-blooded as me drooled into my chest hair and made my left arm go numb was the true key to a good night's sleep...

As long as the drooler was Flynn Honeycutt.

I brushed back a lock of his dark hair with the back of my finger and stared down at his face. The pinkish dawn light highlighted a faint spray of freckles on his cheeks and gilded his morning scruff. The acres of his smooth skin—paler across his back and shoulders, deeper gold where the sun had tanned him—were slightly bruised from my mouth and fingers and reddened from beard burn, and every mark felt like a victory. A visible reminder that Flynn wanted me, too.

He should always look this way.

I traced my finger down his hairline and over the curve of his ear, and Flynn's forehead scrunched. His arm wrapped around my chest more firmly, and he burrowed into me like I was his own personal pillow before going boneless once more.

I pressed my lips together, trying not to laugh as I imagined what Flynn would do if he ever learned of his own behavior. The outraged horror. The immediate denial. The walls building.

And suddenly, I didn't feel like laughing anymore.

To say that last night had not gone according to my expectation would be a massive understatement. *Just sex*, I'd told myself as we'd slow danced around the bar. *Keep it simple. Keep it light.*

I was pretty sure I'd failed on all counts.

Memories littered the ground between us like land mines, exploding at the slightest touch. Flynn attacked with hurricane intensity, all vicious thunder and lightning, whenever he felt threatened. And I'd nearly walked out the door at least three times, thinking my attempt to get us on firmer ground was doing more harm than good.

Thank fuck I hadn't left. I would have missed out on the sweet satisfaction of having Flynn yielding and undone beneath me. Missed out on giving him the pleasure and relief he deserved. Missed out on the most mind-shattering, earth-shaking orgasm of my entire life.

Which brought me to a third revelation. Flynn was brilliant. He was valiant. He was witty and challenging and loyal and passionate. But he was also skittish as a deer and stubborn as a mule. He was determined to fight anything I proposed, whether it was a night of hot sex or a deal with Fortress, no matter how good those things could be for him.

So if I wanted him to be happy in the long-term—and I fucking did—I couldn't wait around for him to decide he could trust me and come to the negotiating table... I needed to *show* him how great it could be and blow through all of his objections.

In short, I needed to figure out a way for Fortress to keep the manufacturing and distribution of Honeybridge Mead in Honeybridge.

The idea was simple, but the execution of it... I blew out a breath, and my arms tightened around Flynn involuntarily as I imagined the complexity of it. It would be unlike any deal I'd negotiated before.

Working things this way would increase up-front costs exponentially. But if I adjusted the terms so the majority of Flynn's compensation came on the back end, trusting that Honeybridge Mead's star would continue to rise the way I now knew it would, I could make this a profitable acquisition for Fortress... and an absolutely killer deal for Flynn.

The hardest part would be convincing Conrad Schaeffer that we wanted to set up a manufacturing operation in the backwoods of Maine in order to sign one small-town meadery to Fortress's roster. I'd need to have bulletproof numbers and projections. Every i dotted and t crossed.

"I'm gonna make this happen, Firecracker," I whisper-vowed in his ear as the first rays of morning sun peeked through the skylight above us. "You'll see."

"*Nnkay*," Flynn replied eloquently. He gave my hip a fond pat... then shoved me away and rolled over, tugging the sheet over his head.

I grinned. Thunder and lightning and *sweetness*.

A man like that was worth all kinds of complexity.

I climbed out of bed and dressed, then hurried downstairs as quietly as I could so as not to wake Flynn. I quickly looked up contact information for Hayden Lewis, Honeybridge's local real estate agent, and sent him an email asking to set up a meeting to check out available properties. Then I emailed Alice a request to pull and examine every contract with nontraditional manufacturing terms that Fortress had ever signed.

By the time I sent off Alice's email, Hayden was already calling me back. I'd forgotten that this was how Honeybridge rolled.

"Shit," I muttered, darting a glance up the stairs. There was nowhere soundproofed in his closet of a house, and Firecracker needed his rest after being worked off his feet yesterday. Probably better to handle my calls on the walk home, even if it meant I wouldn't be able to say good morning.

I slid my shoes on and stepped out to the porch, shutting the door behind me.

"Hayden. Hey. Thanks for calling me back. I know it's early—"

"Frog!" Hayden interrupted. "Holy sh-*shoot* am I glad to hear from you."

A giggling voice in the background repeated, "*Holy shoot!*" then demanded, "More Cocomelon, Daddy!" and

Hayden excused himself for a moment before his voice came back on the line.

"Sorry about that, Frog. The early thing doesn't faze me —some of us have been watching cartoons for hours—but getting your call sure did! You're moving home to Honeybridge?"

"What? No. Of course not," I said, honestly baffled about why he would think that. What in the world would I do around here?

"But you said you needed property..."

"Oh! Not property for *me*. Property for a manufacturing operation. I'm in the early planning stages of... something."

"Ah, too bad. I told Fabienne it was too good to be true when we heard your message, but I couldn't help hoping. It was so much fun talking to you at the Tavern the other afternoon. You had a lot of insights on consumer trends we wanted to pick your brain about for Fabienne's new catering business."

"Oh." It *had* been fun talking with them, and not just about business. We'd chatted about wine and the best spots in Portland for live music, and when I'd mentioned my favorite Caribbean restaurant in New York, Hayden's wife had offered to make me her mother's recipe for Haitian griot and pikliz one night. "I mean, we're still friends, even if I don't live here, right? You can call me when I'm in New York, too. Always happy to chat."

"Yeah. Sure," he said a bit doubtfully. After a brief hesitation, he went on. "Jonas Wellbridge-Littlefield was thinking of asking you to join our pickup band since you mentioned you'd played piano in that jazz group in college. Sometimes we play at the Tavern and that kind of thing. But... you probably wouldn't've been interested in that, anyway."

Natalie, who was setting up tables outside Sweet Buns, grinned and waved as I walked past, and I lifted my hand in return. "I mean, no, I would, Hayden. That would be totally my thing, but..."

"But yeah. You can't do that from a distance. I get it. Same problem joining Jace Honeycutt's relay team for the Lake Run this fall."

"Jace *Honeycutt*?" I repeated. "Wants me on *his* team?"

"It's for charity, Frog." Hayden's pause was rife with disapproval. "There's such a thing as too much Honeycutt-Wellbridge competition."

"No, of course! I wasn't... I didn't mean..." Realization dawned. "Is that why he asked me to his dinner party?"

"It's a potluck," Hayden corrected patiently. "You know, where everyone brings a dish?"

I'd never been to a potluck in my life. The people I socialized with preferred to show off their private chefs at elegant dinner parties. What were you supposed to bring to a potluck?

"Yeah, obviously," I agreed. "A potluck."

"Anyway. Tell me more about the property you're looking for."

By the time I'd completed the slow walk up the hill to Wellbridge House, I'd outlined my wish list—industrial space inside the town limits, with the right zoning and environmental clearances, ideally available for a long-term lease to minimize Fortress's cash outlay—and Hayden had given me a few other factors to consider.

"You're asking for a lot," Hayden said finally, blowing out a breath. "That's a lot of space in a pretty central location, and we don't usually have a lot of inventory. Remember that most Honeybridgers don't relocate unless they absolutely have to."

I scuffed my toe against the stone path that led to my parents' door and frowned. "Don't they?"

I'd spent my childhood anticipating my departure. I'd jumped at the chance to escape the narrow confines of this place. Hearing that other people didn't feel that way was my second revelation of the morning.

Hayden chuckled. "Okay, maybe some of the guys you were friends with did. Davis and Baker. Cosmo. Thad Feldmann. Your cousin Redmond—and honestly, I can't blame him because if your aunt Louise were my mom, I'd've had a hard time staying, myself. A few others, too." He chuckled. "But no. Most of the rest of us have bloomed where we were planted. New folks have moved in and made us more diverse than ever. We've even birthed a whole new generation."

As if on cue, his daughter giggled in the background and called, "*Holy shoot!*"

I huffed out something like a laugh. "Right. Well. Good luck with that. So, uh... nothing you can think of, property-wise, huh?"

"Oh, I didn't say *that*," Hayden said slyly. "I just needed to give you a little background information so you'd understand why it's a miracle that the Hornrath Chair facility is up for sale *and* that Rachel Cho is giving up her lease on her commercial kitchen space since she's outsourced her candy manufacturing to a company down in Portland."

I swallowed hard. "The Hornrath Chair Company? Hayden, I could kiss you. With tongue."

"Wow. I mean, usually I work on commission," he said dryly, "but... I think Fabienne would be down with that if she could watch."

I laughed fully this time. "How soon can I see the space?"

"Hmm... Little Marie and I could meet you outside Sweet Buns in, say, an hour?"

"Perfect! I just need to go home and change," I said without thinking.

"Go *home*? You're out already?" His voice lowered. "Do tell."

"Nothing to tell," I lied as I jogged up the stairs and opened the front door. "I've been out jogging. See you in an hour." I disconnected before he could ask me any follow-up questions.

I wasn't going to say a word about anything Flynn-and-Frog related. I imagined one of the Honeycutts—or, worse, one of the Wellbridges—teasing Flynn about it and shuddered. Flynn would retreat behind a wall so high I'd never see him again. And I very much wanted to see him again... as soon as possible.

The way he'd given himself to me, responded to me with such perfect vulnerability, and begged me, "Please don't leave," was everything I'd wanted from him three years ago. Hell, everything I'd wanted from him even back in high school. In fact, it was all I could do not to run back down the hill to the Tavern and wrap him back in my arms.

One night had not been enough.

"Jonathan!" my mother called from the doorway to the dining room when I stepped into the front hall. She was already neatly dressed in a pair of crisp white cropped pants and a sporty sleeveless blouse. "Darling, why aren't you dressed for golf?"

"Uh." I frowned down at my running shoes. "Why *would* I be dressed for golf? I hate golf."

She blinked, bewildered. "Of course you don't. You've golfed since you were tiny."

"And I've hated it since I was tiny," I agreed. "Probably

had to do with the plaid knickers you used to make us wear."

"But... the Wellbridge family always golfs the day after the regatta." She patted my chest lovingly. "Go and get changed."

"Not this Wellbridge," I said firmly. "Oh, hey. Do you know what to bring to a potluck?"

Mother's eyes widened. "A *potluck*."

"Yeah. Jace Honeycutt is having one, and everyone is supposed to bring—"

She shook her head so fiercely her blonde bob swayed. "I *know* what a potluck is. Since when are you going to potlucks at Jace Honeycutt's house?"

I shrugged. "Since he invited me, and it seems fun."

"Darling," she said with strained patience. "We don't—"

"But *I* do," I said, my temper building. Or at least I wanted to start.

For the first time in a long time, my mother looked at me —*really* looked—like maybe she heard what I was saying and understood the boundary I was drawing. She nodded slowly.

Then she completely ruined it by saying, "Do you suppose *Brantleigh* would enjoy the potluck? If that's what you young people are—"

I closed my eyes and shook my head. "No. No, I do not think Brantleigh would enjoy a potluck. Brantleigh doesn't enjoy *anything* because he's an entitled ass."

"Jonathan!" She glanced around the front hall as though Brantleigh—or his father—could appear at any moment... which I supposed they could.

"And while we're on the subject..." I drew her into the dining room for a modicum of privacy and lowered my voice. "I have several things I've been meaning to say to you. Number one: I will *not* be sent on any more dates. No." I held up a hand when she opened her mouth to interrupt. "If you and Dad want Thatcher Pennington's support, one of you can date Brantleigh."

She pursed her lips. "That wasn't my only reason for hoping you two would hit it off. Brantleigh is... *young*," she said diplomatically. "But he comes from a good family. He's socially adept and can be quite charming when he tries to be, which could help you with your career. He could be a support for you. A real partner, like your father is to me."

Had she never had a conversation with Brantleigh?

Not delusional, just Patricia Wellbridge, I reminded myself.

"Mother, I don't want to date someone because they're socially adept and charming. I want..." Prickles. *Thunder*. I cleared my throat. "I don't know what I want or if I even want anything. I never really imagined myself with a life partner. But I do know that I'll find him for myself. And," I added, "he will *not* be a person you've trained to be rude to the Honeycutts."

"Rude? I would never—"

"You told Brantleigh they were uncivilized social climbers." Just saying the words made my anger from last night surge again. "For someone who claims there's no rivalry with the Honeycutts because they're not worthy of being our rivals, you spend an inordinate amount of time scheming to undermine them, and it needs to stop."

"Scheming?" Mother clasped a hand to her chest. "Jonathan Turner Wellbridge, you take that back. I would never!"

"And yet you did. Not only with Box Day but by spreading false rumors about the Honeycutts to Brantleigh. One would think you'd see how poorly it reflects on the Wellbridge name when your guests are rude to half the residents of Honeybridge on *your* say-so." I raised an eyebrow.

Her mouth opened, then shut again, like she'd honestly never thought of this. She put her nose in the air. "I don't know what else could possess you to say such a thing. I assume it's all that *jogging*. Perhaps if you try some yogaerobics instead."

I didn't reply, but I felt the corners of my mouth lift in a smile without conscious thought. *Possessed* was a good word for the way I felt. Something about Flynn Honeycutt had sunk claws deep inside me, making me feel more grounded and confident than I had since... well, since I'd gotten back to Honeybridge.

"However, because I do care about the Wellbridge reputation, I'll have a word with Brantleigh," Mother allowed.

"Good. I'd hate for this to be a subject that's discussed at next week's softball game." I raised an eyebrow threateningly.

"Wait." Her eyes widened. "Will *you* be at next week's game?"

"I... I might. It's looking that way." After a brief hesitation, I admitted, "My work for Fortress has hit a snag, and I need to figure out my next steps. It might take some time. And I'm going to stay here while I do." Because I wanted as much time with Flynn as possible.

"Oh, Jonathan. That's... that's *wonderful*." She bit her lip, and it was my turn to stare at her in bewilderment.

"Okay. Uh... if you'll excuse me, I'm going to have coffee with Hayden Lewis."

"The Realtor?" Mother gasped. "You're looking at Honeybridge real estate?"

Shit.

"No. We're just having coffee," I lied. "Don't get excited. I already have a home, and it's in New York."

"Of course!" she agreed. "Of course you do!" But I could tell by her satisfied smile as she assured me she understood that she did *not* understand and did not *wish* to understand either.

As I went upstairs to take a shower, I rolled my eyes. Some people just got an idea in their head and ran with it without consulting any of the other parties involved.

She was headed straight for disappointment.

I met Hayden outside Sweet Buns a little while later with a coffee for each of us and one of Nat's cookies for little Marie.

Other than a giant keyring dangling from his wrist, a substantial-looking toddler strapped to his chest, and a pronounced receding hairline, Hayden looked the same as he had back in high school.

The first space he showed me, the former candy factory, was a strong contender. The short term of the lease would allow for some flexibility down the road, but the space would require a ton of renovation that made it a not-so-great investment.

The Hornrath Chair Company, though, was perfect. More perfect than perfect. It was located kitty-corner behind the Tavern, literally a stone's throw from Flynn's place, and it had plenty of room for whatever equipment Flynn might need plus storage, plus office space. More than that, there was something about the exposed wood in the building—rough-hewn timber that had stood there for a hundred years—that spoke of history and permanence. I knew without knowing how I knew that Flynn would love it, and the fact that it was a purchase—a commitment—felt like a good thing, even though I was fairly certain Conrad Shaeffer would take some convincing.

"You ready to make a deal?" Hayden wiggled his sandy

eyebrows as we stood in the center of the dusty first floor. The air smelled like woodchips and memories.

I shook my head sadly. "Not today, unfortunately. I need to put together a bunch of numbers and get buy-in from a couple people at Fortress first. Any other potential buyers lined up?"

"Not sure. I'll check with the other guys at the office and let you know."

"Please," I agreed. "It's really important." This plan would only work if the location was right.

Hayden pursed his lips. "You gonna tell me what this is for?"

I hesitated. "I don't suppose there's such a thing as real estate agent/client confidentiality?"

"Not officially. But there's such a thing as 'the guy who drove you home after you shot too much Jägermeister junior year and never told a soul' confidentiality, and I owe you that much." He elbowed me lightly. "What gives?"

I told him about Fortress and Honeybridge Mead, the offer Flynn had rejected, and my plan to keep the manufacturing in Honeybridge.

"Whoa." Hayden grinned. "That would be phenomenal for Flynn. What did he say when you told him?"

"I haven't talked to him about it yet. That's where the confidentiality comes in. See, Flynn and I have... history."

Hayden snorted. "That's putting it mildly." When I shot him a look, he spread his hands. "Dude, you once bought out every pack of Cocoa-Caramel Bits at Pop's store just so Flynn couldn't have any. When they hung your team shirt on the wall after Honeybridge High won the championship sophomore year, he crossed out the *W* in your name and changed it to Smellbridge."

I snorted fondly. "I fucking *knew* that was him. But okay, so you agree that he's automatically going to reject anything I suggest without considering it, right? That's why I don't want to even bring the contract up again until my bosses approve it and I can make him an offer he can't refuse." I grinned. "This deal is going to be life-changing for him."

Hayden's brow puckered. "But... what if he likes his life the way it is?"

"Being run off his feet every night at the Tavern, while also running the Meadery on the side, plus having to help his family at the Retreat, and take care of his grandfather, too?" I shook my head. "The man is exhausted. He *needs* this, even if he doesn't know it."

"Right." Hayden smiled gently. "Well, I hope it all works out. Let me know if you have any questions. I'm here. And I'm gonna tell Jonas to ask you about coming to jam with our band some night, too."

I nodded. But after Hayden locked up and walked off, I felt... restless. After talking to Hayden about Flynn, I wanted nothing more than to find the man, wrap my arms around him, and reassure myself that we were on the same page now. *Finally.* Unfortunately, it was nearly noon, which meant the Tavern would be open and packed with regatta visitors again. Flynn would be way too busy to sneak away even for a moment.

I walked aimlessly down Fruit Street in the sunshine, past the art gallery and the Honeybridge Historical Society's log cabin museum, and found myself climbing the three steps to the General Store before I'd consciously decided to go there.

The white clapboard building that housed the General Store was a large square with a wraparound porch. It looked nearly as old as the log cabin across the street, and probably was, which was why the store was a unique blend of a modern convenience store where local Honeybridgers came to buy bread and canned veggies and a touristy penny candy heaven. Flanking the three front steps were a pair of Rose of Sharon bushes that Pop Honeycutt tended like children.

I pushed open the front door, and the jangling of the bell transported me back to childhood. The air smelled like candy and Popsicles and the lavender sachets Willow Honeycutt made, and I felt myself calm immediately.

Pop was behind the long wooden counter, handing a messy-haired little boy some change and a wax paper bag. "You share nicely with your sister, Oak."

The boy scowled. "No way. Lorna's mean."

Pop gave the boy a conspiratorial wink. "Remember, a mighty oak stands tall and shares its shade with everyone."

The boy huffed. "I guess you're right." He snagged his bag off the counter and headed for the door. "Thanks, Pop."

Pop laughed and shook his head fondly at the boy's retreating form.

"Does it get old, teaching the kiddos how to get along?" I joked.

Pop looked up at me, and his smile widened, making the creases at his eyes deepen further. "I keep hoping one of you'll actually listen. Until then, I keep trying."

I laughed and walked closer, past the displays of souvenir candles and postcards and the low freezer of Popsicles, so I could lean my crossed arms against the counter.

Pop frowned. "You look tired, Frog. Up early fishing again?"

I smiled, thinking of the reason I hadn't gotten more hours of sleep, and shook my head. "Nah. I wouldn't go fishing without you. You're my good-luck charm. Just... at loose ends, I guess. For a little while."

"Hmm. Your mom doesn't have anything she wants you to do to fill up your time?" Pop grinned like he knew better, and since he'd been greeting Honeybridgers in his store since the dawn of time, he probably did.

"Oh, plenty," I confirmed wryly. "If I wanted to golf, or play tour guide for her guests, or lunch at the club... which I don't."

"Lots of other stuff you could do in Honeybridge that you'd like better." He scratched his cheek with one blunt finger. "Lots of folks who'd love to see you, too. Your time's what you make of it, whether you're here in town or..." He waved a hand. "...wherever else you might go. But then, deciding what you really want to do is the tricky part, isn't it?"

I blinked. "Are you... trying to give me some kind of life lesson here?" I demanded, amused. "Because I'm not little Oak. That stuff won't work on me anymore."

"Heck no. You're grown and mature now. The way your mom talks, you're about to be a vice president of your company." He nodded toward a worn straw broom propped in the corner behind the counter. "But since you're here and you've got nothing better to do, maybe you wouldn't mind helping me out with a little sweeping."

I raised one eyebrow, but his expression was all innocence. "Sweeping's good for the soul, Frog."

With a sigh, I went behind the counter and grabbed the broom.

"Heard you were here in town to acquire distribution rights to the Meadery."

I glanced up from my work. "Flynn told you that?"

"He did."

"Did he tell you he turned it down?"

Pop smiled gently. "Oh, yes. Very vocally. My ears are still ringing."

I snorted and continued sweeping. "He barely listened to the proposal I gave him. I don't even think he read the terms. He just... flat out decided he couldn't do business with me because he didn't trust me."

"Is that what he said?"

I thought back. "I don't remember exactly what he said." I'd been a little distracted by my own reaction to the sight of him after so long. By how badly I'd wanted him. By how much I hated him being angry at me. "But the gist was pretty clear." I took a deep breath and let it out. "I'm going to fix it, though. Flynn'll see that I'm not out to take anything from him, and I never have been. I'm gonna make it so this deal will give him everything he wants."

"Will it, though?" He pointed to the area I'd just swept. "Think you missed something."

I ran the broom over that area again and nodded. "Oh yeah. Flynn'll have plenty of money and plenty of freedom. He can live his life exactly the way he wants, and he won't be tied down by responsibility to his family or his business." Thinking of what Hayden had said, I paused what I was doing to run my fingers over my watch strap, tracing the tattoo beneath, and remembered why I'd gotten the ink in the first place. "Anyone would want that, wouldn't they?"

"Ah, Frog," Pop chuckled. "Your heart's always been in the right place."

I wasn't sure how he could make a compliment sound like a criticism. "You think I'm wrong?"

"You ever tell anyone the story of why I call you Frog?" he asked, apropos of nothing.

"Huh? God, no. Definitely not." My face heated.

"You know folks think it's because you put a frog in a sleeping bag on a campout?"

"Yes." I knew because I'd invented that story myself.

Pop chuckled again. "Nothing to be ashamed of in caring for other living creatures."

I pursed my lips. "I was an eight-year-old idiot with no understanding of amphibian biology."

"You were a sweet boy who wanted to make sure the frogs out at the lake stayed happy and warm for the winter, even if you had to dig each one up all by yourself and find it a home. You just didn't realize they could take care of that for themselves."

"What's that got to do with anything?" I rolled my eyes and answered my own question. "More life advice disguised as casual conversation."

"Just an old man's reflections," Pop said, his eyes twinkling like a person half his age. "But if you're looking for advice, I'll tell you this: Firecrackers can light up your whole world, but if you underestimate 'em, they're dangerous as all heck. You gotta treat 'em with care."

This, at least, was self-explanatory.

"I know that," I promised solemnly. "I maybe haven't always been careful, but I will be."

Pop snorted. "You'll learn to be anyway. Ah, you and that grandson of mine." He sighed with fond exasperation and shook his head. "Some people gotta do everything the hard way."

I scowled. "What's that supposed to mean?"

"Means maybe you can head out to Quick Lake later on. Huck and Willow are leaving town in a couple weeks, so we're having another cookout at the Retreat. Gotta make the most of the time they're here."

"Oh. I shouldn't intrude. Flynn would be annoyed if I went while he was at the Tavern working—"

"Flynn'll be there," he said with amusement clear on his face.

I cleared my throat. "I'll bring dessert."

Chapter Ten

Flynn

Waking up with no sexy Frog next to me was totally fine. It wasn't like I was expecting him to stay over, obviously. It had only been a one-time thing. If he'd still been there when I'd woken up, I would have kicked his ass out anyway.

So when I found myself snapping at Dan for the tenth time since opening the Tavern, I decided it was because he was incompetent.

"The Daydream Brew bottles get the orange caps, not the blue," I hissed. "Jesus, Dan. Fucking pay attention to what you're doing."

I didn't look back up from the temperature gauges again until I realized he hadn't acknowledged my correction. When I glanced up, I saw anger simmering on his face. His jaw ticked, and his nostrils flared.

"What's the problem?" I asked, politely leaving off additional judgy commentary.

"The problem is my boss. He's a total asshat. What the hell has gotten into you today? I know the Daydream gets orange caps. Know how I know? I designed them." He turned the ID card on the bottling tank toward me. Moose Call. The brew that used the blue caps. Fuck.

"Carry on," I muttered, going back to noting the temperature of the batch of must I was working on.

"No. You need to tell me what's up because if you're stressing about Brew Fest, we're in good shape. We're even ahead of schedule."

"We need to have those bottled and stored and still do setup before the dinner rush," I said, nodding to the racks of bottles he had lined up.

"No shit. You're acting like we haven't done afternoon bottling three times a week since the day you hired me. Besides, Kendall's coming in to help with the dinner shift. What's going on?"

I bit my tongue to keep from telling him there was absolutely nothing going on. Nothing involving anyone who gave a shit about anything, least of all me.

God. I fucking hated JT Wellbridge. Every damn time I let the man in...

"I'm fine. It's fine. Let's just get this done."

He stared at me for a few more beats before sighing and returning to his task. I went back to work and tried to calm down. It didn't work. Within minutes, I'd ruined the batch of must and had to start over. I cursed and kicked the wall to keep from kicking or punching my beloved equipment.

"Ow, fuck. My foot. Shit." I hobbled over to a nearby bench and dropped my face into my hands. Dan joined me and placed a tentative hand on my back.

"Want to talk about it? I know a lot is riding on this Ren Faire contract, but I think our chances are really good. You've done an incredible job preparing, and whatever supply we don't end up using can be sold off at the fall festival here in town. Is that what you're worried about? Leftover inventory? Because I really think we'll get the contract."

I straightened back up and tried to give him a smile.

"Thanks, I appreciate it. Sorry for biting your head off earlier. It's not really Brew Fest. It's just... other stuff."

He kept his hand on my back and began to rub soothing circles across it. "You did the right thing turning that Wellbridge guy down."

I turned to him, shifting so his hand couldn't reach my back anymore. For some reason, the comment rankled, even though he was right. "Why do you say that?"

Dan shrugged. "Who knows if that company would even do right by Honeybridge Mead? What if they decided to sell it into discount stores and change the entire image of the brand?"

"They wouldn't do that," I said automatically. "Surely things like that would be covered in the contract."

Dan shrugged. "Maybe. But then you'd have to get a really good lawyer to make sure you were protected. And I can't even imagine how much that would cost. They'd be going up against some fancy New York firm, probably. How would you even find the right attorney? It's not like you could use Taft and Hobbs here in town. They've probably never even seen a corporate contract like that."

Considering I'd smoked up with Lela Taft in high school, I wasn't sure she'd be my first pick anyway, but I didn't say it out loud. Dan was right. I'd have to protect myself. Not that I was considering it, of course. Because I wasn't. All my prior objections were still in place. Honeybridge Mead belonged in Honeybridge, and I didn't trust JT Wellbridge's fine ass as far as I could throw it.

"Then let's make sure we get that Ren Faire contract so we don't need a company like Fortress to make it to the next level, okay?" I patted his knee and stood up. "Let's finish up here so you can get back behind the bar and I can get a few invoices paid."

We worked for another hour before things started

picking up on the Tavern side. Dan got to work at the bar, and I moved to my office to get some bookkeeping done. After half an hour, Alden popped his head in. "Close it down. Cookout time."

I sighed. "Changed my mind. I'm not going. I've had enough family time for a while."

He threw himself in the chair across from my desk. I caught a familiar whiff of the high-end styling products he used at the salon. "This is the last one before Willow and Huck leave, and I promised Moose we'd come."

Alden knew McLean was my Kryptonite. I glared at him. "Stop using Moose to get what you want. You could have just told me it was important to you."

"It's not important to me. But it's important to Pop. Come on, I told him we'd pick him up at the General Store."

I sighed and finished up a few things on my financial app before closing down the laptop and following Alden out of my office. After stopping to tell Dan where I was going, he waved me off with a wink. "Go, have fun. You clearly need some time away from here. I've got this."

"Thanks," I said, giving him a sincere smile. He didn't need to take my shit, but I was glad he did. I couldn't do half of what I did at the Tavern and Meadery without his help.

As soon as we arrived at the salon's parking lot, where Alden's Mini Cooper sat waiting for us, Alden shot me an evil grin. "Guess what I heard?"

"No," I said, holding up a hand as soon as I slid into the little car. "No salon gossip about JT. Please."

"Who said it was about JT?" he asked innocently. But I knew my brother better than that.

"I did. And I don't want to know."

"Suit yourself," he said with a sniff. We rode in silence for a minute before pulling up in front of the General

Store, where Pop was already waiting on the bench outside.

I moved to the back seat so Pop could take the front. Once he was settled, Alden turned toward the Retreat. "Pop, you'll never guess what I heard at work today."

Shit.

"If it was about Redmond Wellbridge, save your breath," Pop said. "I already heard the news."

Alden got really quiet and glanced over at Pop, opening his mouth and then closing it before looking back at the road ahead. It was clear he didn't know what Pop was talking about. If he wasn't going to ask, then I was.

"What about Redmond?"

Pop shrugged. "Not important. The real hot gossip is the one about a certain *Frog* sneaking down the alley behind the Tavern very early this morning. Might you happen to know anything about that?"

Heat flooded my face while warmth flooded my heart.

He'd stayed. JT had slept in my bed all night. My throat suddenly felt tight, so I cleared my throat. "What? Who? No. What?"

"Smooth," Alden muttered. "It couldn't have been that early because Prissy Newton was out for her chai latte when *she* saw him, and she never leaves the house before seven."

I needed a change of subject ASAP. "Have either of you heard from PJ? He's been awfully quiet lately about how art school is going. I'm starting to worry."

Castor's twin brother had always had wings on his feet, so I'd done everything I could to help him fly. PJ was a talented painter, and he wanted to see the art of the world— Florence, Paris, Berlin, London, Vienna... His bucket list was never-ending, and I hoped his education would give him the start he needed.

But my brothers and Georgia and I had been a unit for so many years it was strange to go more than a week without at least getting a funny text or picture from each of them.

Alden flapped a hand over his shoulder. "I'm sure he's fine. He's been dreaming about going to MassArt for years. Now thanks to you, he's living the dream, and he's having too much fun to call home. Stop worrying already."

Pop was conspicuously silent.

"Pop, what do you think? Have you talked to him?" I asked.

"I don't like the kids he lives with," Pop grumbled. "It's not a good environment for studying."

Alden laughed. "I'm not sure it's called studying in art school. Maybe he just needs a nice place to splatter paints against a canvas."

Pop gave Alden a harsh look, which wasn't like him. Alden immediately made a sound of apology.

"I just wish there'd been room in the dorms, that's all," Pop said finally. "I'm sure he'll find his way."

I didn't tell him there'd been plenty of room in the dorms. That hadn't been the problem. The problem had been the fourteen grand price tag in addition to the three grand needed for his health insurance. It wouldn't have left him enough money to buy art supplies. Thankfully, he'd found a group of students to live with off campus. It meant sharing a tiny room with three other kids in bunks, but it also included a kitchen where he could save money by cooking at home.

Before I could worry too much about another one of my brothers, Alden pulled into the Retreat and parked the Mini next to a familiar convertible sports car.

"Fucking Christ," I muttered. "Why is Frog here? I swear to god, if Willow invited him again..."

"Hush." Pop opened the door to climb out. "I asked him. Huck wanted his thoughts on sustainable packaging."

"Packaging for what?" I blurted, hopping out and turning to scan the family group for the familiar stylish head of hair. Sure enough, he was standing there yucking it up with my father, who was looking at him like he was the messiah. I walked over to eavesdrop.

Huck was as eager as a puppy. "That's what I told him. The bag-in-box setup will actually give additional shelf life to the mead itself. It provides a—"

"Are you kidding me?" I asked, not bothering to interrupt politely. "What the hell do you know about the shelf life of mead?"

"Firecracker! Hey, buddy," Huck said, beaming and throwing an arm over my shoulder. "I read an article about different ways beverage companies can reduce their carbon footprint. I think it's important for Honeybridge Mead to set an example for—"

I interrupted him again because that was the kind of mood I was in. "Since when do you care about my business?"

Like a record scratch, my heated tone made everyone stop talking and turn to see what was going on. Huck's eyes looked like saucers, and I immediately regretted my words.

JT's forehead crinkled in concern, but he kept his mouth shut, thank god.

"I'm sorry, I didn't mean..." I began, trying to figure out a way to un-asshole myself.

Huck shook his head sadly. "No. I get why you might feel that way, Flynn. Your mom and I aren't always around to help out the way you'd probably like. But that doesn't mean we don't care about the Meadery. Or that we're not proud of what you've done with it."

"I know. I'm sorry," I said again. "It's just been a long..." I glanced at JT against my better judgment. Heat raced up my neck to my face. "Day."

Castor, ever the peacemaker, shoved a cold mason jar holding some kind of fruit drink into my hand. "Rum punch. Chuck it down."

I took a giant gulp, already knowing Cas's special recipe would hit the spot. Instead of apologizing yet again, I wandered over to the water's edge and focused on downing the alcohol in hopes it would chill me the hell out.

While I brooded, I overheard snippets of conversation. JT telling Willow about a vegan restaurant she should try the next time she and Huck were in New York. JT asking Pop if he needed more help in the shop tomorrow. JT laughing with Castor about something.

When Castor's laughter turned to uncontrollable giggling, I turned to see what was going on. JT had his phone out and was showing something to Cas. Maybe a meme or video. Whatever it was, it was bringing such joy to my little brother's face I couldn't help but smile, too.

Damn JT Wellbridge and his charming personality. Damn him straight to hell.

I turned back to the water and tried not to think about him, but it was impossible. He was the kind of person who took up room in a crowd. People gathered around him and wanted to hear what he had to say. He had the innate ability to connect with individuals by finding common ground.

No wonder he was so good at his job. Everyone loved him. And he made people believe in possibilities.

The man sold dreams. And it was dangerous because there was a huge part of me that wanted to buy what he was selling.

When I went back to the food table to refill my punch

from the large pitcher, Alden sidled up to me. "So... you and the froggie, huh?"

"Hush." I glanced around to make sure JT wasn't nearby. "It's not... it wasn't... I didn't plan it." Understatement of the millennium.

"I bet. But it was hot as fuck, right?"

My head whipped back toward Alden.

Whatever he saw in my face made him laugh like a hyena before taking another deep sip of his punch. "Yeah, I figured. That's good, Flynn. Real good."

I stared at my brother in shock. He was the only one of us Honeycutts who disliked the Wellbridges as much as—or more than—I did. "It is?"

"Hell yeah! Frog's gorgeous. And yeah, okay, so a Machiavellian Wellbridge mind hides beneath those Wellbridge blue eyes. But that doesn't mean you shouldn't enjoy his big Wellbridge dick while you can."

What?

I glanced down at Alden's nearly empty cup. "How much have you had to drink?" He had to have been drinking a lot more than me to have outpaced me so quickly.

"Who remembers?" He snort-chuckled to himself. "Remembering shit," he said seriously, "is a liability."

"Did something happen?" I demanded. "You were fine in the car until Pop mentioned..."

Alden shook his head firmly. "I'm blowing off steam." He poked me in the chest with his index finger. "Which is exactly what you should be doing. You can use the Frog for stress relief—which you seriously need, bee tee dubs—and then wave him a hearty godspeed whenever he fucks back off to New York. The perfect summer fling!"

While his words should have excited me at the idea of having a fling with JT, they made me nervous and jittery instead. The idea of JT leaving Honeybridge at the end of the summer should have brought me a sense of relief. A known end point for a casual, temporary thing should have made the idea of a summer fling perfect.

But it didn't. It felt like not enough.

And that scared the shit out of me.

"I don't know if that's a good idea," I said to Alden. "I need to focus on Brew Fest."

"You need to get your dick sucked is what you need. And I find I quite like the idea of you using a Wellbridge for just that purpose." He threw back the last sip of his drink and grabbed my full cup to replace it. "At least they're good for something."

He wandered away, and I frowned after him until McLean nudged me aside to grab himself an organic ginger ale, and I turned my attention to my taciturn middle brother. "Wow. Three family dinners in a row. You must be feeling sociable these days."

He shrugged. "Not really. But it'll be quiet after they leave." He glanced at Willow and Huck.

"When do they fly out exactly?"

Before he could answer, JT approached and handed something to McLean. "Hey, Moose. I meant to give this to you the other night when I came by."

McLean inspected the little leather pouch before unsnapping it and pulling out what was inside. It looked like a nice pocketknife with wood inlay on the handle. My brother whittled in his spare time, but he already had a pocketknife.

I opened my mouth to say so when McLean gasped.

"It's a carving jack," he said in wonder. "Holy cow."

JT looked beyond pleased at the awe in McLean's reaction. "I saw it in a specialty shop in the city, and it made me think of you. The blades are high-carbon steel. The shop didn't have the left-handed one, so I special-ordered it online, and it arrived last week. I was gonna send it to you, but, well..." He shrugged. "Here I am."

Yes, here he was. *But not for long.*

"He's not left-handed," I said, more sharply than I intended.

McLean looked up at me, a soft rebuke in his gaze. "No, but I carve away from me, which means I use left-handed whittling tools." He looked back at JT. "How did you know?"

"I didn't. But the guy in the store mentioned it mattered which hand you used and which way you carved. I remembered you carving at one of the Scout campouts when we were younger and hitting PJ with the chips because you carved away from yourself instead of toward yourself." He grinned. "The guy at the store said that meant you needed the left-handed jack. I took a chance. Glad I was right."

McLean let out a soft laugh. "Grandpa Horace said I was too young to carve toward me. He was afraid I'd cut myself. By the time he trusted me to change, it was too late." He looked back up at JT. "Thank you so much for this. I'll... I'll make you something with it."

JT nodded seriously. "I'd like that. It would be nice to have a touch of Honeybridge on my desk at work."

McLean smiled shyly and wandered off to inspect his new tool on his own, away from prying eyes.

"That was nice of you," I admitted grudgingly, my eyes on the lake. "Thinking of Mac."

"I'm a nice guy, Flynn." JT's eyes begged me to believe him. "Or I try to be, anyway."

I made a noncommittal noise. There were many more examples of not-niceness on the tip of my tongue, just waiting for me to call them forward the way I had every other time JT and I talked. Dozens of hurts and misunderstandings I could have used to reinforce my own anger. But I was tired of fighting the pull of JT.

I was tired of being so damn scared.

I really wished Alden hadn't stolen my drink. At least then I'd have something to focus on besides the man beside me. Seeing him here, interacting with my family, being kind and generous to my beloved brother, was doing things to me.

Dangerous things.

I stuck my hands in the back pockets of my shorts and tilted my chin toward the lake path that ran past the artists' cottages, asking a silent question. *Come with me?* JT nodded eagerly and fell into step at my side.

For a moment, we walked the path in silence as my family's voices faded behind us. The silence wasn't tense, but it wasn't easy either. Years' worth of things we'd never talked about seemed to walk alongside us.

"It's funny, you know?" he said as we passed into the tree line at the edge of the clearing. "I would've told you that I didn't think about Honeybridge much when I wasn't here, but I guess I did. I mean, I texted Pop pictures from the Andy Warhol exhibit at the MoMA last month, 'cause I knew he'd like 'em. And when I was out west last spring, I sent your mom some seeds so she could grow—"

"California poppies," I finished, turning to stare at him. "That was you?"

He nodded. "They're supposed to be good for sleep tinctures. And then last month I wandered into this hobby store one day. I sometimes feel like all I do is work, and maybe I need a hobby. And I thought of McLean and how whittling was comforting to him."

And me? I wanted to ask but couldn't. *Did you think about me?*

"What about, um, squash? Do you still play?" I asked instead. He'd been an avid sportsman growing up: golfing, swimming, and sailing in the summer, playing squash and basketball, and skiing in the winter.

"Yeah, actually," he said brightly. "The building I live in has squash courts. That's one of the reasons I chose it. I have a few folks I play with from time to time. I ski, too, when I can manage a few days off. And run, obviously. Sometimes on the High Line."

I nodded. I hated that he knew everything about me—every street in my town, the bakery I frequented, which freaking *hand* my brother whittled with—but I couldn't picture anything about his real life with his high-rise apartment building and his fancy corporate job.

"Well. If you're up for a swimming competition, I could probably make that happen," I offered.

He laughed and let his shoulder knock into mine. "And that wouldn't be because you're an amazing swimmer and I'm terrible in comparison, would it?"

"You're not... *terrible*," I argued.

JT grabbed at his chest and turned toward me, sending a lock of his perfect hair into his eyes. "Oh my god," he gasped. "Oh, *shit*. Was that... was that a compliment? Coming from you? Warn a guy before you rock his foundations to the core like that, Honeycutt."

I knocked my shoulder into his, harder this time. "I take it back. You're an asshole and a terrible swimmer. In fact, you have no redeeming qualities whatsoever."

JT hooked his finger into my pocket, tugging me to a stop. "Interesting." His voice dropped an octave to something huskier and far more promising. "You seemed pretty convinced I had some redeeming qualities last night when I had my—"

I turned to face him fully and clapped a hand over his mouth. "I don't recall any such thing."

I felt JT's smile beneath my palm, and his expression was warm and affectionate. But the look in his eyes... *Hoo, boy.* The naked longing there hit my bloodstream harder than Castor's punch drink.

I had the sudden realization, standing there in the fading summer sunshine, that Jonathan Turner Wellbridge III was *flirting with me*. How unbelievable was that?

More unbelievable still, I was... enjoying it.

JT grabbed my wrist to hold my hand more firmly against his lips. Then he opened his mouth and ran his tongue along my palm.

It was a little-kid maneuver, but there was nothing childish about the way I reacted. I sucked in a stuttering, shocked breath as my dick went from interested to seriously fucking aroused. When had my palm become an erogenous zone? How did JT know this about me when I didn't?

Without taking his eyes off mine, JT turned my hand and took the tip of my index finger between his plush lips, sucking slightly. "I could remind you, Firecracker. I'd really like to remind you."

What the fuck were we talking about? What was my name? All the oxygen in my lungs deserted me at once. My knees trembled, and my cock pulsed against my fly.

"I..." I licked my lips and tried again. "I..."

"Yes?"

"No." I shook my head instinctively, forcing my mind out of my pants and back to the conversation. "You could've reminded me this morning," I shot back, though the words came out way breathier than I'd hoped. "But you were too busy sneaking out."

JT bit lightly at my fingertip. "I didn't want to wake you."

"Oh, yeah?" I swallowed. "You knew I was at the Tavern all day. But this was the *one* day you never came by to claim a barstool."

"You knew I was there all those days last week." He grinned, satisfied. "You noticed me."

Noticed him? Was he insane? That would be like not noticing a tornado carrying your house to Oz. Or not noticing that time had stopped. It was amazing I'd managed to get any work done at all.

JT sucked my finger into the wet heat of his mouth just long enough for me to forget what gravity was, then pulled off with a pop and a cocky little smirk that should have been off-putting. *Was* off-putting. Definitely did not make me want to throw him down on the ground right here at my—

Fuck.

I took a step back and stared at him, panting. "Well, you picked the wrong time to remind me because now we're at my parents' house, surrounded by my family."

JT made a show of glancing around us at the empty woods, but I shook my head firmly. "I can't, Frog. Really. Not now. Any of the guests from the cottages could walk this way. And Alden's drunk off his ass, and he'll need me to drive him and Pop home. And then I have to close up the Tavern since Dan pulled a double today."

"Okay." JT ran a hand through his hair. He squeezed his eyes shut and blew out a long breath. "No, you're right. Not now."

I nodded and told myself my disappointment was irrational.

Then his eyes opened, and the piercing intensity of his blue gaze froze me in place. "So when?"

"P-pardon?" I squeaked.

"Not now, so when?" He stepped toward me again, and his hand cupped the back of my neck. "I'm not gonna wait around while you overthink things anymore. Especially since you tend to overthink things *wrong*."

I scowled. "I do not!" I paused. "What's that even supposed to mean?"

"It means earlier, back there—" He gestured toward the clearing by the lake where my family congregated. "—I was hoping you'd come talk to me, but you didn't."

"That's because I... I..." *Fuck*. I *had* been overthinking. "I was busy."

"So I decided... I was done waiting for you to come to me." His hands smoothed up my hips and settled just above my waistband. The heat of his skin against mine felt incredible. And incredibly distracting.

"Oh. Well. Yes. That's... good."

"Mmhmm. And I'm done waiting for you to accept the offer Fortress sent me here to make," he whispered, leaning in to nuzzle at the curve of my neck.

"Y-you are?" I narrowed my eyes. "Wait, so... you're not gonna try offering me three billion percent profits? You're not even going to throw in your Porsche? Dan says it's a sweet ride."

His laughter coasted over my skin like warm honey. "It definitely is. Would that have worked?" Then he answered his own question before I could. "I know you better than that, Firecracker. It might work if your cousin Brittany was in charge, but you have standards you won't compromise. I respect that. I promise I do."

"Oh. Yes. Well. Good." I tamped down another flare of that same irrational disappointment that he'd given up already.

JT was doing precisely what I wanted by backing off.

Obviously. It would be ridiculous to be unhappy that the man respected my standards.

And this made things much, much simpler. No conflict of interest. No worrying about what he really wanted from me.

It was all for the best. Definitely.

"I mean, you laid out your terms for me on the first day, and shredding the contract was kind of a clue that you weren't happy with the offer."

I huffed. He made me sound unreasonable and cranky when I hadn't been. Had I?

"You were so upset you even shredded the *folder*." JT's voice caught with amusement. "And returned it to me as confetti."

Great. I officially sounded like a serial killer. Just what every boy longs to hear. "Yes, I know. I was there. And I'm the one with the ruined paper shredder. Can we not talk about this anymore?" I demanded.

I made a half-hearted attempt to get away, but JT tightened his hold on my waist and sank his teeth into the tendon at the join of my shoulder, holding me in place.

Shit, that felt good.

"Stay," he muttered after a long, teasing moment, and to my chagrin, my body locked in place like a dog following a command.

He inhaled deeply and groaned, as though the scent and flavor of my skin was getting him off, and I suddenly stopped worrying about how embarrassing I was being. Was there anything more arousing than having the sexiest man in the world want you as badly as you wanted him? I was pretty sure I'd reached some kind of personal lust pinnacle right there against that tree.

"I'm for sure not going to wait," JT growled in my ear, "for you to decide whether last night was explosive enough for us to repeat it. Because it was." He sucked lightly on my neck, and I gasped as my dick started to get very, extremely excited again. "It *will be*."

So arrogant. So bossy. I was going to tell him so. Any minute now.

"O-okay," I breathed shakily instead. I cleared my throat and tried to redeem myself. "I mean, I suppose there are worse ways to spend an evening."

JT chuckled. "You just keep tempting me to remind you, huh?" With gentle force, he backed me up a pace, and then another, and another, until my shoulders knocked against a tree trunk. His grin was feral... and gorgeous. "Being inside you was one of my top five ways to spend an evening."

"Top *five*?" I gasped, torn between outrage and laughter.

Damn but I liked sparring with him.

I was starting to think I'd *always* liked it. That maybe being at odds with JT Wellbridge was more satisfying than being perfectly peaceful and content with anyone else.

"Yep. The list also includes having your cock down my throat." His teeth scraped across my jaw, then down to the point of my chin. His scruff—which was more like an actual beard these days, and I was not complaining—dragged against my skin, setting every nerve ending alight. "Having my tongue in your ass. And, ah..."

He stepped back just slightly, pulling me far enough away from the tree that he could wrap his arm around my waist while his other hand clasped mine. He grinned at me triumphantly. "And slow dancing with you in the Tavern."

Oh.

I was light-headed. Caught in his eyes and the inescapable rightness of this moment. I tried to force myself to think of a reply, of anything that would get us back on firmer footing, but the best I could do was "That's only four things."

He let go of my waist and twirled me before reeling me back in. "Sure. I'm saving the last spot. I'm sure you'll find some way to fill it."

"Well... I do have ideas."

JT threw back his head and laughed. From this close, I couldn't help but notice the way his eyes crinkled at the corners, just a little, and how one of his bottom teeth was just the slightest, endearing-est bit crooked.

JT Wellbridge was far from perfect, no one knew that better than me, but standing there in his arms, watching him happy... it was a perfect *moment*. Maybe the most perfect of my life.

My heart, which was already racing a mile a minute, skipped a beat in pure terror.

"You can tell me all about those ideas," JT promised. "Starting... tonight." He phrased it like a statement, but I knew that he was asking me permission. That somehow he wasn't sure I was going to grant it.

Neither was I. For a long beat, I simply stared at him while warring factions battled between my heart and head. Eventually, one of them won.

"Yeah." I nodded slowly. "Okay."

"Really?" He smiled brilliantly and, for the first time all day, pressed his lips to mine. A contract sealed. "Look at the two of us, having actual conversations and getting along. Who even are we right now?"

I huffed out a breath and pushed him back lightly because if I didn't do it then, I wouldn't do it at all. "I'm Flynn Honeycutt, and I'm fucking starving, so let's go back and get some food."

"After you, Mr. Honeycutt." JT spread out a hand toward the path like a game show host.

I shook my head. "You're such a dork," I sighed. But as I passed him, I may have grabbed his hand and swung it as we walked for a pace or two... or a quarter of a mile. And when I finally let go of it, just before we passed out of the trees into the clearing, I may have whispered under my breath, "The Tavern closes at eleven."

Chapter Eleven

JT

"Put your hand on my dick, for fuck's sake," Flynn growled. "Or I'll do it myself."

"I'm getting there." I tweaked his nipple and rutted my aching cock against his left ass cheek, partly because I needed it and partly because I knew it would drive him insane. More insane. "Patience, baby."

"Fuck you... and fuck your patience... and fuck your *babies*. I should not..." Flynn panted, "have let... you in tonight. Your smile when you got here... was pure fucking trouble."

That was probably true. The only way I'd gotten through the rest of the cookout, followed by a very frustrating call with Alice where she insistently reminded me about the meetings she'd scheduled me in New York this week, was by fantasizing about how I was going to get Flynn off.

Needless to say, by the time I'd arrived at the Tavern, I'd already been half-hard and a hundred percent focused.

God knew my smile at that precise moment was probably pure fucking smugness, but it was entirely justified because I'd gotten Flynn exactly where I wanted him—bent over his own bar top, his thick, muscled forearms braced on the wood while I held him down with one hand on his nape and teased his wet, open hole with the other.

I was literally living the fantasy.

He turned his head to the side to glare at me over his freckled shoulder with one green eye, and my gaze caught on his kiss-swollen, spit-shiny lips. Fuck. That image instantly imprinted itself in my permanent spank bank.

If you'd asked me two months ago what the most beautiful sight on Earth was, I'd have told you about the sunset views from the Alexander Vineyard in Napa, where the hills and trees seemed to roll on into infinity. But I'd have been wrong.

At that moment, I knew categorically that *this* was the most beautiful sight—Flynn Honeycutt, stone sober and wild with lust, laid out before me like a banquet, trusting me with his body. I wanted to see him like this always, over and over again. I wanted Flynn to lay out the terms for *that* deal.

Despite all the progress we'd made with using our words out at the Retreat earlier, though, I knew better than to say any of this out loud unless I wanted him to panic and bolt, leaving a Flynn-shaped hole in the Tavern wall behind him.

Instead, just like last night, I was determined to show him how I felt without words. To make him even half as crazy for me as I was for him.

"That's some bold talk from a man who was so eager to be fucked that he announced last call fifteen minutes early, just so all the customers would be gone by the time I got here," I teased, my voice nearly as hoarse and wrecked as his. I trailed my fingers lower to fondle his balls, and Flynn's hips jerked.

He swore ripely. "I hate you, Frog. Loathe. Abhor. And I was not eager to be fucked. For all you know, I was eager to do the fucking."

I felt my lips twitch despite how desperately aroused I was. "Oh, god. How embarrassing. I totally misinterpreted. See, when I squeezed your ass while we were making out, and you moaned like a porn star, flipped around, laid yourself down, and commanded that I rim you, I immediately thought you wanted me to fill this hole." I ran my fingers over his opening again, letting them catch on his rim, and his breath caught. "When you begged for my fingers and said, 'More, JT. Fill me, JT,' I thought this was what you wanted." I stuffed two fingers back inside of him, tagging his prostate.

Flynn made a keening noise.

Christ. *Perfect*.

I lifted his chin in my other hand and twisted his head further so I could nip his jaw and run my teeth over the freckles on his shoulder. "Because otherwise, I would have been really fucking thrilled to take your dick," I whispered, rutting against him again. "Remember that for next time."

"Fucking *fuck*," Flynn said eloquently through gritted teeth. He pounded one fist against the countertop. "Get inside me now and make me come, or there won't be a next time. I don't fuck around with jerks who get off on edging."

"*Tsk, tsk*. Someone's telling lies, Honeycutt." But I opened a condom packet with my teeth and rolled it on before dragging my cock down the cleft of his ass. His high-pitched whimper made my blood sizzle. "You fucking love it. You love when I tell you you have to lay there and take it. You love when I make you lose control."

I didn't give him a chance to make another snarky comment. I slid my cock inside him slowly, letting the warm, silken heat of him surround me.

Flynn's entire body shivered, from head to foot. His eyes clamped shut, and his mouth opened wide, but no sound came out. I wasn't even sure he was breathing.

Me, on the other hand? I couldn't shut up.

"Oh, fuck. Flynn Honeycutt, you are... incredible." I ran my hands up his smooth back, caressing his shoulders, before smoothing them back down to grab his ass cheeks and spread him wider so I could watch him take me. "Love seeing you like this. I love that you let me inside you this way. Love how tight you are and how well I fill you."

I pulled out of him just a little so I could admire how his hole looked stretched around me, all obscene pink perfection. Then I dug my fingertips into the firm muscle as I thrust back inside, wanting to mark him all over.

"Fuck, baby." I ran a hand up into his hair and tugged lightly. "You take me so perfectly. This was exactly what you wanted tonight, wasn't it?"

Flynn's breath sawed in and out, filling the air with needy whimpers. "Oh, fuck. I wanna come. JT. Frog. I want—"

"Tell me."

"I want you to fuck me harder. I want you to come all over me. I... I want..." He broke off as I pulled all the way out of him and slammed back inside.

I pounded into him over and over, like if I could just fuck him hard enough, seat myself deep enough inside him, maybe I could convince him how good we could be together.

"J-Jon," he cried brokenly. "Please, Jon. Touch me. I'll do anything. I'll give you anything you want. I—"

Ah, shit. I swallowed hard. I was a lot of things to a lot of people. Jonathan. Mr. Wellbridge. Frog. The stupid fucking *Rainmaker*. No one had ever simply called me Jon, and to say I liked it—liked that Flynn had come up with it—was a serious understatement.

I reached around and grasped his dick, which was bobbing against his stomach, leaking precum like a fucking faucet.

"I want you to come for me, Firecracker," I commanded. "I want you to say my name when you do."

I jerked him in time to my strokes as best I could. It was a weird angle, and the rhythm wasn't a hundred percent perfect because I was losing concentration, losing myself in Flynn.

Flynn didn't seem to mind. His breath whooshed in and out of him, and his channel clenched around my cock.

"Fuh—gahd," he wailed. "Yeah. Yes! I'm so close. Don't stop. Don't you fucking stop!"

Like there was any chance of that happening. I wouldn't—couldn't—stop, even if the damn Tavern collapsed around us. "I'm right here, Flynn," I vowed. "Right here."

Flynn's fingertips turned white, like he was trying to dig his fingers into the wood, and he widened his stance, bracing himself for the onslaught. Only a few strokes later, he cried out, his voice ringing through the empty bar as he spurted against my hand... and probably the cabinets. "Jon! Oh, Jesus fuck, Jon!" He sounded relieved. Bewildered. Undone.

Hearing him that way, knowing I'd caused it, was all it took for me to follow him over the edge.

I rested my forehead against his shoulder blade, with my arm still wrapped around him and my hand still awkwardly holding his dick. I was incredibly reluctant to let go. Having sex in the Tavern sounded amazing and was, but now I was going to have to convince Flynn to let me stay over when all I really wanted to do was fall asleep with him in my arms and not think about the coming week.

"What got into you tonight?" Flynn slurred. "Did Willow give you one of her teas or tinctures after I left the Retreat?"

I blinked, struggling to recall anything that had happened between the time Flynn had left the Retreat with Alden and Pop and the time he'd opened the Tavern door, hauled me inside, and kissed all the thoughts out of my head. "Uh. No? She served up the strawberry shortcake I brought from Nat's. Why?"

Flynn twisted a little, pushing up from the counter, and I let go of him so I could withdraw without making a mess.

Here we go, I thought, removing the condom and tying it off. *Time to be convincing.*

But Flynn didn't move away; he only twisted far enough to wrap his arm behind my neck and peck a kiss to the corner of my mouth. "'Cause I'm gonna buy you strawberry shortcake for the rest of the damn summer if this is what it gets me."

"Oh. Well, that's..."

Shocking.

Thrilling.

Both.

As I stood there, stunned, he grinned and reached around to slap my ass. "Now, back off and let me finish cleaning this place up. Having a summer fling with you is one thing; fucking up my business is another. And throw that condom away when we get back to my place, 'cause if Dan spots it in the trash here, I'll never hear the damn end of it."

I blinked and moved aside. "Yeah. Okay." So... we were having a summer fling? I was invited back to his place? Just like that? No convincing needed?

Part of me didn't want to question my good fortune, but the other part wanted my attorney to look over the fine print so I didn't mess this up.

Flynn hauled up his jeans and looked at me curiously as he did up the button. "What's up with you?"

You surprise the hell out of me constantly. I crave you the way plants crave sunshine. I already know the summer isn't going to be enough. I'm afraid I'm gonna fuck this up if I push too hard.

"I, uh, got a call from my assistant, Alice, after you left the Retreat," I said instead, searching out my own clothes. "Her aunt took a bad fall and dislocated her shoulder."

"Ah, damn." Flynn's forehead crinkled. "She gonna be okay?"

"Yeah, no, she'll be fine. But Alice needs to take a couple days off to take care of her, and she won't be able to help me much on the, um... time-sensitive project I'm trying to bring together, so I'll have to do it myself."

I stared at Flynn, thinking about three years ago and a similar conversation I'd tried to have and praying this one had a different ending.

I swallowed and lowered the boom. "I have to go back to the city in the morning. Just temporarily. I'll be there until..." I winced. "Probably Thursday. And then I'll be back."

Flynn nodded slowly. "I see."

"I wouldn't leave if I didn't have to," I blurted, tugging up my pants and leaving my shirt off.

When the words were out, I was surprised to find they were true.

For more time with Flynn, I would gladly stay in town, even if it meant postponing my important meetings and spending my days avoiding my mother's social events. Especially because it meant more softball games (which meant more softball *victories*) and a chance to make Willow's family recipe for wheatberry salad to bring to Jace's potluck.

This thing between us was temporary, so I wanted to hoard every minute that I could spend teasing and laughing and fighting and fucking with him.

"Believe me," I added.

Flynn nodded again but didn't seem entirely convinced. He turned away to grab a bottle of cleaner and a rag, then busied himself washing the countertop. The muscles of his naked back bunched and flexed in a really compelling way.

"You could come if you wanted." Once the offer was out of my mouth, I realized exactly how much I wanted him to accept it.

Flynn paused but didn't turn around. "Leave the Tavern during the summer rush so I can flit off to New York? *Please.* I haven't even been able to get to Ogunquit in years, much less out of state."

Damn. He sounded so resigned when he said that. I thought back to the map in his office and the dreams he'd stowed away. It made me doubly determined to make the Fortress deal happen for him... which meant I really fucking needed to get to New York.

The irony was thick.

Flynn finished his job. He moved around me to the kitchen door and reached out a hand to turn off the fairy lights around the chalkboard menus. The tiny lights gave the space a romantic golden glow bright enough to have gotten us arrested for indecency by any passing police officer, if Flynn hadn't already prepared by closing the blinds before I arrived.

He paused with his hand on the switch, then turned to face me, his earlier satisfaction replaced with defiance.

"Listen. I don't know what your rules are for... for summer flings, Wellbridge, but I am a person who only flings with one person at a time."

Wellbridge. Not JT. Not Frog. Definitely not Jon.

I sighed and lifted one eyebrow. "One person at a time, as opposed to... having orgies?"

His jaw hardened. "As opposed to me fucking around with anyone else while you're in New York."

I inhaled sharply. "Good." The very thought made my stomach burn and my fists clench. *Mine. Mine, mine, mine.*

Flynn stared at me expectantly for a moment, like maybe he wanted more than a one-word answer, but I had nothing else to give him unless I wanted to admit just how territorial I was suddenly feeling. And I didn't.

"What?" I finally demanded.

Flynn huffed out a breath and stared at a spot just over my shoulder. "What I'm trying to say is, are you're gonna see your... Massimo while you're down in the city?"

I peered at him for a second, trying to make sense of his words. Who the hell was—

"Oh, *Massimo*! Shit." I sighed. "Yeah. I guess I will." I bit my lip a trifle guiltily. Massimo was a nice enough guy, and he hadn't been pleased that I'd sent him to Mexico alone. I probably owed him more of an apology for changing plans at the last minute.

Flynn's nostrils flared, and he smiled a brittle smile. "Good. Great. Best of luck with... everything. No hard feelings." He strode past me to the Tavern's front door lock, unlocked it, and swung it wide. "Drive safe."

Drive safe? Crickets chirped in the darkness outside the door as Flynn and I stared at each other. Or, more like, I stared at him while he resolutely stared at not-me.

Reagan was right. When Flynn ignored me that

profoundly, it meant he was hyperaware of me... and probably overthinking something.

"Did I...? No." I shook my head. "Please tell me what's going on? What did I do? Because I could guess, but I'd guess wrong, and then you wouldn't speak to me for *five* years this time."

"You didn't do anything wrong." Flynn put his chin in the air. "I just assume that you want to save your energy for Massimo."

"Whaaaat?" *Why would I—?*

The frustrated, embarrassed sound that escaped Flynn's mouth made me want to wrap my arms around him. He ground his teeth together and finally bit out, "Look. You can... you can have a man in every port. Hell, you probably do. And most guys would be fine with that. But I'm not... I'm not down with being your man in this port. Okay?"

I blinked at him. At his stiff posture and carefully neutral face. At the blush that suffused his cheeks.

And when the light finally dawned, my jaw literally dropped.

"Oh, Flynn," I breathed. I stepped toward him. Into him. Pushed the door closed behind him with one hand and then pushed him against it. "You idiot. I'm not going to have sex with Massimo." I made a face at the very idea. "God, no."

He grabbed at my shoulders and tried to shove me away. "Get off. Seriously, JT. *You're* the idiot. I tried to bring this up and have a rational conversation. If you're not going to fuck him, then why did you say—"

"I wanted to see him because I need to apologize to him. Though I'm thinking I can probably do that by text," I added quickly. "And I agree. I'm a total fucking idiot. But in my defense, it never crossed my mind for a single second that you could be jealous."

"I'm not—!" he began.

"I thought I was the only jealous one around here."

Flynn shut his mouth with a clack, his gaze pinging from one of my eyes to the other. Cautious. Hopeful.

I rubbed my thumb over his bottom lip before tilting my forehead against his. "I don't know how two people can speak the same language and not hear each other," I said softly. "Maybe one of these days, we can start to believe that we don't secretly want to hurt each other. That we're something better than not-enemies."

Flynn huffed out a breath.

I leaned back so I could look into his eyes. "But in the meantime, let me make this perfectly clear: you are the only person I want to be with, Flynn Honeycutt. The only person who's getting my attention. The only man I think about. Okay?"

His fingers flexed into my shoulders. "For the summer, you mean. Since it's a... a summer fling."

If that was as much as he would give me, that's what I would take. And if I already suspected that the summer was going to go by much too fast, well... we could renegotiate when the time came.

"Yeah," I agreed. "That works for me. And in the meantime, there's no one but the two of us. Deal?"

Flynn's green eyes looked into mine warily. "Yeah, okay," he agreed softly. "Deal."

———

I threw my keys on the sideboard table in my apartment entryway and threw myself down on the sofa, heedless of my silk suit and all the wrinkles I was crushing into it. I felt like I'd lived six lives from the time I'd kissed Flynn goodbye just before dawn that morning.

Being back in my real life after so long away felt like the first workout after a long vacation from the gym. I'd lost all my stamina for polite elevator chitchat. I couldn't bring myself to care about Jeff Namath's big contract, even when he'd leaned against my office doorway and told me about it in annoying detail. The traffic and crowds that used to make me feel like part of something huge and vibrant were annoying. And when I'd walked into my building a few moments ago, the doorman had once again asked me for ID because he didn't recognize me.

I needed to get my head back in the game, and I knew it... but it was really hard when my mind kept veering north. I wondered what Flynn was doing, which customers at the Tavern were making him laugh and scream in frustration, how stressed he was over his preparation for Brew Fest, whether Alden was teasing him over the way we'd disappeared into the woods yesterday, and whether Flynn could possibly be feeling like the whole world was a little flatter today, like I did.

I finally gave in and shimmied up on the sofa so I could pull my phone out of my pants pocket. I'd forced myself not to text Flynn all day—I didn't want to seem weird or needy, and both of us needed to concentrate on our work—but I was missing our connection.

Me: *Hey, I know you're working right now, but did I leave my AirPods on your nightstand last night?*

The reply was immediate.

Firecracker: *Sorry, who's this?*

I grinned, the fatigue of the day falling away instantly. Christ, the man made life fun.

Me: *Are there many people who could have left their shit on your nightstand last night? Were you entertaining in there while I was asleep?*

Firecracker: *See, I would have told you Frog Wellbridge was the only one...*

Firecracker: *But Frog promised this morning that he'd text me when his flight landed. I can only assume he got lost somewhere between Honeybridge and New York.*

Firecracker: *Too bad. I was just getting used to having him around.*

My stomach lurched sideways and landed in a puddle of goo. I liked the idea of him being used to me. I liked it a lot.

Me: *Shit. I didn't remember I was supposed to message. I got to the office at noon and it was go go go all afternoon. Sorry.*

Firecracker: *Hmph. I'll forgive you just this once since you were under the influence of a morning blowjob orgasm when you promised. But you'll owe me. Big time.*

I snorted.

Me: *Seems fair.*

The bubbles by his name floated for a long moment before his reply came through.

Firecracker: *Damn. Bad day?*

I frowned at the screen. It *had* been a long, shitty day, especially without Alice to brainstorm and share my workload. I wasn't sure how Flynn could know that, though.

Me: *???*

Firecracker: *Dude. You, JT Wellbridge, just agreed that you owe me, no negotiations, no demanding to know my terms. You must've had a bad day to be so far off your game.*

Firecracker: *Or else maybe you really missed freeloading on my bar stool while every person in Honeybridge stops by and gets all up in your business. *laugh emoji**

Firecracker: *Be honest. It's that one, isn't it? You just can't get enough stories about Jalissa's daughter's drama* *club rehearsal and how Ernie McLeroy's arthritic knee proves climate change is real. LOL!*

Yeah. Strangely enough, that was exactly it. And it was no laughing matter.

I sat staring at the phone for a long moment, stunned by the truth of this. I didn't just miss Flynn; I missed... Honeybridge. At least the kind of Honeybridge I'd experienced the last two weeks, with potluck invitations and cookouts at the Retreat and no golfing whatsoever. I missed *Flynn's* Honeybridge.

Jesus. How had that happened?

Firecracker: *Seriously. You okay? Don't make me come down there.*

God. If only. I wanted him sitting beside me on the couch, calling me Frog and giving me shit.

Me: *I definitely would have preferred to be at the Tavern instead of returning emails all day. And my boss called a quarterly meeting for Wednesday morning, which means tons of work for me to get done tomorrow.*

Firecracker: *If it makes you feel better, you wouldn't have wanted to be here today either. The air conditioner in the country club's dining room broke and they had to shut down.*

Me: *So?*

Firecracker: *Sooooo I had the entire Honeybridge Gentlepeople's Society at the Tavern all afternoon discussing whether Queen Anne's Lace is a wildflower or an invasive species and whether it needed to be eradicated from the roadsides in our fair city.*

Me: *Dear god. Please tell me my mother wasn't involved.*

Firecracker: *Oooh. I could, but I'd be lying.*

Firecracker: *It got really heated at the end there. Willow has passionate feelings about the sanctity of wildflowers. She kept saying things like, "Well, Patricia, as an HERBALIST..."*

Firecracker: *And YOUR mother has strong opinions about weeds. She kept saying things like, "Well, Willow, as a person with EYES..."*

I snorted.

Me: *Was there a bar fight? Did you have to call Sheriff Bliss? Is there video evidence???*

Firecracker: *Nope. Because then Tam Wickram—they're the person opening the bike shop on Smith Lane, out near the border of McGillicuddy, you know?—stood up and suggested that Honeybridge should just pave over the roadsides and create a dedicated bicycle lane, and BOTH our mothers lost their minds.*

Firecracker: *I think Tam might be regretting their decision to move here.*

I laughed out loud, feeling way lighter than I had all day.

Me: *You're right. That sounds awful. How did you ever survive?*

Firecracker: *Funnily enough, I found a brand-new pair of AirPods just sitting on my nightstand this morning, so I cranked up my music and tuned them out. :) It was fate, I think.*

Yeah. I was starting to think it was.

———

Firecracker: *Whatcha doin?*

I glanced over at my phone and smiled, then pushed my

chair back from my desk, stretching my neck from side to side.

My Tuesday had gotten off to a rough start. It seemed I'd gotten a little too used to Nat at Sweet Buns having my usual coffee order ready when I walked in the door, so when the barista at my usual coffeehouse—a guy I'd spent arguably more minutes of my life with than half the guys I'd fucked—had spelled my name wrong, it had made me question my life choices.

Who the hell spelled JT wrong?

But the real trouble had started when Ginny from Baby Virginia Winery had called early this morning to accept the contract I'd presented the day before.

Ordinarily, signing a contract would have been cause for celebration, but Ginny had been so damn trusting and excited about what this meant for her employees that I'd strongly suspected she hadn't really understood the part of the contract that said we'd move a large part of her operation away from her facility in Christiansburg.

There'd been a long silence on the line while I wrestled with my conscience—the deal was *not* sneaky or underhanded in any way. Those contract terms were industry standard, and Fortress was offering very attractive compensation that Ginny needed in order to keep Baby Virginia competitive. After all, not everyone was like Flynn, willing to turn down big money to keep their operation local.

But then a familiar, scathing voice had sounded in my head—*"Is being rich the most important thing, Rainmaker?"* —and I'd caved. I'd told a very bewildered Ginny to have her attorney go over everything with her one more time before she signed... and then I'd spent five full minutes banging my head against my desk after hanging up, wondering what the fuck was wrong with me.

I still wasn't entirely sure, but the way that my heart

leaped at a simple two-word text from Flynn was probably a pretty good clue.

Me: *Drowning slowly under a mountain of contract research. This message is my dying gasp. You?*

Firecracker: *Drowning slowly under vats of mead that need to be bottled. Working on a new varietal.*

Me: *Well, shit. I feel like you get the better end of this deal.*

Firecracker: *Yeah? Well whenever you're ready to trade in your high-profile, extremely profitable career for backbreaking labor with no job security and no 401k, come see me.*

I snorted. After a day like today, he had no clue how tempting that was.

Me: *Question—Would the job benefits include unlimited access to the mead?*

Firecracker: *Fuck no. You can't drink my profits, Frog.*

Me: *Damn. What about unlimited access to the meadmaker?*

Bubbles swirled next to his name for a long moment, and I bit my lip, imagining him blushing as he worked out a reply.

Firecracker: *Not at this time, but I'll ask Kendall and Dan what they think of that employee benefit at the next team meeting.*

A bark of laughter burst out of me, so startling in the quiet office that one of the PAs passing my open door fumbled her coffee.

God, I really *liked* Flynn Honeycutt.

Me: *On second thought, maybe better to reconsider the free mead.*

Firecracker: *lol. Is that your professional advice? I*

mean, if you're sure...

Me: *Very. I'll negotiate my access to the meadmaker separately.*

Firecracker: *Oh, will you now? Hmm. You can try, Rainmaker. But I only handle that type of negotiation in person.*

Me: *I promise you, Honeycutt, it'll be a VERY personal negotiation.*

The bubbles swirled next to his name once again, for longer this time.

He was blushing. He was so definitely blushing.

Firecracker: *Stop distracting me when I'm working, JT.*

Uh-huh. I laughed out loud again, then sighed as I tucked my phone away and got back to work.

Me: *Pumpkin pie and mead are two things that should not be together. I refuse to believe that's your new varietal. It's still mid-summer for god's sake.*

Firecracker: *But summer won't last forever.*

I scowled down at my phone. I'd asked a single, innocent question about the new type of mead Flynn was dreaming up, and the man was being annoyingly tight-lipped about it, teasing me with nonanswers and stupid remarks.

Me: *Stop the lies and spill some actual details, Honeycutt.*

Firecracker: *Ohhh, I see. You're still drowning in paperwork, aren't you?*

Yes. Yes, I was. And ready for the weekend, despite it only being Tuesday night.

Me: *So what if I am?*

Firecracker: *Sooooo, your work makes you bitter, Jon. The only people who don't adore pumpkin pie flavored ANYTHING are bitter people.*

I huffed. So annoying.

Since I read "Jon" in Flynn's deep voice, I also may have chubbed up a little beneath my suit pants, and that was annoying, too.

Firecracker: *How late are you working?*

I blew out a breath. The time at the top of the phone read 10:30.

I had three contract renewals to finish up, two of which were urgent. I also had a metric shit-ton of research Alice had emailed, which I needed to review. Working until 1:00 a.m. (or 2:00 a.m. or later) was something I did once or twice a week, and since there were at least two other people still working on the floor, I knew I wasn't alone. In a competitive field like this, not only did I have to work long hours to make deals, but I also had to make sure it didn't seem like I was slacking off amongst my peers.

Me: *Another couple hours probably. Why?*

Firecracker: *No reason. You should get back to it. Goodnight.*

My shoulders slumped. Right. Yeah. I *should* get back to work. I would.

But I didn't immediately put the phone down, which meant I saw the next text pop up a few moments later.

Firecracker: *Fuck it. I was just thinking it's nearly closing time, and if you wanted to FaceTime, you could keep me company while I did setup for tomorrow. That's all.*

Firecracker: *But it's NOT a big deal.*

Firecracker: *In fact, the more I think about it, the stupider it sounds.*

Firecracker: *The work would take ten times as long with you distracting me and trying to pump me for info on the new varietal.*

Firecracker: *Forget I mentioned it. Bye.*

Firecracker was always prickliest when he wanted something most.

I loved that I *knew* that about him. I loved what it meant even more.

I stood, unplugged my laptop, and grabbed my suit jacket from the back of my chair.

Me: *Leaving now. Call you in 30.*

"Arnold Findlay is looking at our contract very favorably." Jasmine Reyes casually smoothed the cuff of her purple jacket. "He'll sign within the week."

"And Gemstone Distillery will join the Fortress family." Conrad Schaeffer slapped the conference table exuberantly with his palm. "Excellent news, Jasmine. Great work. Keep me posted. So, Jeff, how's it going with Archdale?"

Had quarterly update meetings always been this monotonous? Or was it just that I hadn't closed my eyes until four o'clock and I had to fight the urge to sleep with every blink?

When my phone buzzed, I surreptitiously extracted it from my pocket and held it under the table.

Firecracker: *Pretty sure I'm dead. Killed. I'm typing this from beyond the grave so the police know that you're the top suspect and that death by orgasm is real.*

I pressed my lips together and pretended to be fascinated by Jeff's report for a moment until my heart quit hammering.

Me: *I won't let you pin this on me, Honeycutt. If the police wanna find the real culprit, they need to look at the impressive toy collection in your top drawer. I witnessed the whole thing.*

As in, I'd watched with my hand on my cock and my tongue hanging out of my mouth as he worked himself for a fucking hour until I'd given him permission to come.

Turned out, FaceTiming with Flynn while he did setup *was* pretty distracting. For both of us. And very, very rewarding.

Firecracker: *I've had all those toys for years and I've never had this issue because I've also never been with anyone who got off on edging me like you do. It's annoying as fuck.*

Me: *Mmmm. You sure seemed annoyed. So annoyed you were dripping and whining, begging for it, LETTING me edge you. Christ, the way you looked when I finally let you jerk yourself, Firecracker. Hngh.*

Firecracker: *Fuck off. You were just as bad. WORSE. You were practically drooling, ready to jump through the screen. You were out of your mind for me.*

Oh yeah. I'd been right there, dancing along the path to insanity alongside him. I'd never dreamed that video sex could be so fucking thrilling.

"Wellbridge? Jonathan, are you with us?" Conrad demanded, leaning toward me and waving a hand in front of my face.

I jerked to awareness to find every eye in the conference room on me. *Shit.* I slid my phone back in my pocket guiltily. "Yes, sir. I apologize. I was just texting a, um, business contact."

"Excellent. But Jeff, here, is having a little problem with Archdale Vineyards. Maybe he could use a little advice."

"Archdale?" I frowned at my coworker. "I talked to Harrison Yang for three months before I... passed that lead off to you." I'd been about to say *before Conrad redistributed my leads so I could spend the summer in Honeybridge*, but I refrained. "He was ready to sign on the dotted line."

Jeff's mouth tightened, and his fingers tapped the table. "Any idiot would sign at the percentage you were offering."

Not anyone, I thought with a strange flare of pride. *Flynn hadn't.*

"Most people would," I allowed. "Because it's a fair deal that would be profitable for everyone involved. So what happened?"

"Archdale's earnings declined last month—"

"We knew they would," I agreed. "It's a ramp-up year for them, after a stellar performance last year—"

"So I renegotiated."

I stared at him, waiting for his words to make sense. "You... changed the terms of the offer they were considering?"

Jeff jutted his chin obstinately. "That offer expired, so I made them a new offer based on the most current information, yes. A deal that will ensure that Fortress doesn't lose money." He flung out a hand toward our boss. "Conrad agreed."

Of all the ridiculous, shortsighted...

"Even if Archdale weren't poised to absolutely skyrocket in another year or two," I said as patiently as I could, "had you considered how it would look to Harrison for you to change the offer before he'd formally decided? What that might make him think about Fortress as a company?"

"It says that we back *winners*," Jeff insisted. "And that Harrison should sign this current offer quickly before his next earnings report comes out."

"Alright, Jeff, no need to get hot under the collar." Conrad chuckled. "Maybe we need to rethink our offer based on our Rainmaker's insight, hmm?" He smiled. "Speaking of which... Jonathan, how's the Honeyharvest Mead contract coming?"

"Honeybridge."

"Yes." Conrad nodded. "I'm eager to hear how our offer was received."

"Er, actually..." I definitely was not going to mention the status of my leather folio. "There was a snag, and I decided to rework our offer. Did you get the report I emailed you?" The one I'd been expecting a response to for an annoyingly long time.

"I received it." Conrad leaned back in his chair and studied me. "I'm not sure what to make of it. It's definitely not what we discussed initially."

"It's not," I agreed. "But I think it's exactly what we need in this case. A huge portion of Honeybridge Mead's cachet is due to its quaint, small-town branding. Moving the manufacturing operation elsewhere might save us money initially, but we'd lose money in sales by losing the narrative. You can't make Honeybridge Mead in Portland or Boston," I said, quoting Flynn shamelessly. "It wouldn't be the same."

Conrad nodded slowly. "Well, I admit you've intrigued me. And I appreciate the amount of work you've done, laying the groundwork. How many contracts did you go through to check for precedent before you wrote this up?"

"Hundreds, sir."

"And you've spent two weeks up in the middle of nowhere, schmoozing the owner, too." He grinned and looked around the conference table. "I hope you're all seeing how the Rainmaker got his name, ladies and gentlemen. The man does whatever the heck it takes to close a deal."

Jeff looked nauseated by the way Conrad praised me, and for once, I agreed with him. Conrad made me sound ruthless when I prided myself on being fair.

"It wasn't exactly a chore to spend time with him," I protested, which was a massive understatement. "And I think this deal will be a true win-win for all parties."

"That's the spirit, Jonathan," Conrad said with an approving nod. "And I'm willing to consider your plan. Pending budgetary review."

I grinned, letting relief wash through me. But my smile froze when he continued. "But son, let's get the lead out. I want the deal locked up by the end of the month."

"The end of... of July, sir?" That was only two and a half weeks away. "I thought you said..." I darted a glance around the table. I didn't want to make it public that Conrad had encouraged me to devote my entire summer to securing this one contract—it smacked of favoritism, not to mention my mother's interference, two things I loathed—but he was changing the rules in the middle of the game, taking my six remaining weeks of summer with Flynn down to three.

I was nowhere near ready.

"I know what I said." Conrad's mouth tilted in an approximation of a fond smile. "But I've been brainstorming strategies for Brew Fest with the marketing folks, and we've decided to make a big to-do about signing Phillip's Cider—that company from Montpelier. We're thinking banners made up linking our company names, a Fortress presence at their booth, the whole nine. We want to give Honeytown Mead the same treatment."

"Honey*bridge*," I corrected, more snappish than I'd intended. "It's Honeybridge Mead, from Honeybridge, Maine."

"That's what I said," Conrad assured me. "We figure Fortress will look even more attractive to other Brew Fest competitors if they see we've already signed *two* powerhouse local companies. They'll be clamoring to do business with us. So go ahead and send your proposal to Jane in Operations to work out the specs today with my conditional approval, if that's what it'll take to bring this mead maker to the table," he went on. "We haven't done a contract like this in a while. We're gonna need to move carefully."

"I respect that." I nodded. "But, sir, I can hardly present the offer to the client until it's approved. And we'll be getting close to Brew Fest. Honeybridge Mead's owner has pinned a lot of hopes on winning the mead contest. He'll be too distracted to commit before then."

Conrad stared at me for a beat, two. Then a slow smile spread over his face. "And you're thinking if he doesn't win best mead and get that Ren Faire contract, he'll be willing to settle for a contract with better terms! Atta boy, Jonathan."

"What?" My jaw dropped. "No! No, that's not—"

"Alright, Rainmaker," he chuckled. "I'll let you have your way on this one. But I'm still going to need you working with Liz intensively on the preparations for the festival and with Jeff to get Archdale signed. I see lots of opportunities to expand our reach." He winked. "Not that I need to tell you about maximizing opportunities." He clapped his hands and faced the table again. "Alright, who's next? Jacobs, tell me where we are with Migueyes Tequila?"

By the time I walked back to my office a half hour later, I was irritated without really knowing why. My phone had buzzed with incoming texts several times, but I'd ignored them.

I sat down heavily at my desk, wishing there was someone I could talk to, but Alice was working from home, and I knew my other friends and work colleagues wouldn't understand why I was upset.

Hell, *I* wasn't really sure why I was upset.

Conrad had tentatively approved of my plan for Honeybridge Mead, and he'd changed his mind about wanting it done quickly.

And yes, the thought process that had made Conrad agree to the delayed timeline was cringy—as cringy as Jeff Namath's entire update had been—but signing contracts at the most profitable terms for the company wasn't a bad thing. Not if both parties agreed.

So why did hearing Conrad talk about *opportunities* make me feel like I needed a shower?

I wondered if it would be weird for me to call Hayden to talk about this. Or maybe Marta. Or Pop Honeycutt, with his weird life advice. *Sweep the floor while I tell you a story about the Honeybridge Fish Fry back in 2010 that will make this whole problem make sense, Frog. Ah, ah! Be careful with that broom, son. You missed something. Now, what was I saying? Oh, right...*

I ran my hand over my face. I hadn't missed the fact that all the people I thought might help were people in Honeybridge, the town where I'd been so sure no one knew me anymore. Maybe folks there knew more than I gave them credit for.

My phone buzzed again, and I took it out to find a whole wall of texts that I'd missed.

Firecracker: *No comeback?*

Firecracker: *Jeez, fine. Don't be prissy about it. It was a mutual thing. We were out of our minds for EACH OTHER, okay?*

Firecracker: *And I wouldn't be opposed to doing it*

again. Speaking of which, I'm off tonight. I can pencil you in after 6. But no more edging.

Firecracker: *Or at least LESS edging.*

Firecracker: *Okay, whatever. Edge me as much as you like. Is that what you want to hear?*

Firecracker: *JT?*

Firecracker: *Blink once for fine or twice if you need to be rescued or avenged.*

Firecracker: *K. I'm guessing you're off conquering the world. I'm gonna go back to enjoying my corner of it. Later.*

And just like that, I knew exactly what I needed to make me feel better.

My fingers flew over the screen.

Me: *<wink emoji> <wink emoji>*

Flynn replied instantly.

Firecracker: *Well, okay then. Whose house are we toilet papering?*

Damn. One word from Flynn Honeycutt—*we*—and suddenly, I didn't feel pissed off or alone anymore. And wasn't that scary as fuck?

Fortunately, I thrived on adrenaline.

Me: *No one's. I don't need avenging, I need a rescue.*

Me: *I'm done with work for the week as of this minute, and I want to take you away, Flynn. Tonight.*

He didn't reply, but I'd bet every designer suit in my closet that he was standing in the Tavern, holding the phone in his hand, scowling at the screen.

Me: *We can go to Ogunquit, just you and me... and maybe a friend from your drawer if you want?*

Me: *I know how much you love it there, and you said you haven't gotten to go in years.*

Me: *And I figure you need a break from reality. Fuck knows I do. So what if we just did something spontaneous?*

Still nothing. I swallowed hard.

Me: *I know you're gonna say that you and me being spontaneous is nearly as disastrous as us talking, but we've gotten better at communicating, haven't we? We communicated REALLY effectively last night.*

Me: *Say yes.*

Me: *Please, Firecracker.*

Three dots appeared beside Flynn's name, then disappeared.

I held my breath.

They reappeared... and then disappeared again... before reappearing once more.

Firecracker: *I have a bunch of bottling to do for Brew Fest, remember?*

Shit. I dropped my chin to my chest as an icy bucket of reality poured all over me. Of course he did. And that was his priority, like finalizing the contracts I'd left undone the night before was supposed to be mine.

Just because I was craving his presence badly enough to disregard everything important didn't mean he felt the same impulse.

Me: *Right. I knew that. I just got overly excited for a second there. lol.*

Me: *I'll slink back to my extremely profitable career now.*

Me: *Unless that job offer you mentioned is still open. I could help, if you needed it.*

Firecracker: *Not necessary.*

Wow.

Okay.

Well, I couldn't ask for anything clearer than that, could I? Flynn got an A+ in communication. Sadly, I got a D- in setting reasonable expectations.

Me: *The offer stands if you change your mind. I'll stop distracting you now. Back to work for both of us!*

Firecracker: *Fuck. Okay, look, if we do this, you need to PROMISE we won't talk about work or anything stressful for the next twenty-four hours.*

I sucked in a breath and forced myself to read the text twice. I couldn't believe Flynn was going to let himself have this. Let *us* have this.

Then I closed my eyes and exhaled. *He was.*

Me: *Yes. I agree. Hard agree.*

Firecracker: *I'm serious. Or I'll hold you down and take my revenge. It'll make my little victory at Quick Lake all those summers ago seem like nothing and prove to you I truly am the King of the Lake once and for all.*

In that moment, I couldn't remember what the fuck he was talking about, and I didn't care. My brain had short-circuited at the idea of him holding me down.

Me: *Right. Anything you say.*

Firecracker: *Okay. Then I'll pack a bag. You can pick me up at 7.*

Firecracker: *And I need to be home Friday morning at the latest.*

Me: *No problem.*

My hands might have shaken just slightly as I clicked over to my browser and pulled up the phone number for my favorite bed-and-breakfast in Ogunquit—a little place not far from the scenic beauty of the Marginal Way and all the shops and restaurants downtown.

I really wanted to share that place with Flynn. And for once in my life, I would have no qualms about name-dropping my father in order to secure the best room in the house.

My coworkers were wrong if they thought I'd do

anything to close a business deal. But when it came to being with Flynn Honeycutt, clearly, there wasn't much I wouldn't do.

I wanted this, wanted *him*, for as long as he'd agree to let me have him...

And maybe even longer than that.

Me: *I'm on my way.*

Chapter Twelve

Flynn

I spent the entire drive to Ogunquit alternating between relishing the feel of the cool breeze and sunshine on my skin in JT's fancy convertible and convincing myself I'd made an irreversible mistake in accepting his invitation.

What the hell had I been thinking? A romantic trip away to a bed-and-breakfast in Ogunquit with JT? *Jesus.* I was asking for heartbreak on a silver platter. Why not go ahead and confess the deepest feelings of my heart and have him laugh in my face? Might as well do that while I was at it.

But then I saw the place, and I couldn't for the life of me regret coming here.

I'd seen the inn from the outside many times before. Situated on a rocky outcropping right over the water, with flowers spilling out of hanging baskets everywhere and a rainbow flag flapping lazily in the breeze coming off the ocean, it was the picture-postcard sort of place I'd daydreamed about staying... before hiking my ass to someplace more budget-friendly down the street.

Now, I was enjoying the view from the inside. And, I

realized, for once, I was the guest and not the host. I could relax.

Of course, that was easier said than done.

"Do you need a quickie beej before dinner?" JT asked with a knowing grin after the host left us alone in our room. Somehow, we'd lucked out and gotten one of the rooms with a stunning view of the ocean. "It might pull your shoulders down from around your ears."

I tossed my bag on the big bed and wandered over to the open windows. In the distance, I could hear waves crashing and seagulls squawking. The sinking sun was chasing shadows across the lawn leading down to the beach.

"It's beautiful," I murmured.

"Mm," he said, coming up behind me and slipping his arms around my front. "Sure is."

He smelled like coffee and a long day at the office despite his flight to Honeybridge and the drive to Ogunquit. He must have been exhausted.

"Do you need a rest?" I asked without looking back at him. The warmth from his solid body felt good behind me. "Sounded like you had a crazy day."

"You're not getting me to crack that easily, Honeycutt." JT tucked his nose in my neck and pressed a kiss there. "You made me promise no talk about work or anything stressful, remember? So we're not talking about work. Or thinking about work. Work? Who's work? Don't know her. Never met her."

I snorted.

"Besides, being with you *is* a rest. I don't care what we do as long as we do it together."

He was so fucking sweet.

But I needed him to stop acting like we were together like a real couple. We weren't. We were temporary. A summer fling. It was the only way I could keep from completely flipping the fuck out about the two of us being together like this.

"Okay, that's it. Get naked and lie facedown. I'm going to spank the shit out of you," he growled.

I turned around and stared at him. "Like hell you are."

He looked pissed. "You were threatening me over text, but now *you're* the one breaking the promise. I can tell by the look on your face that you're overthinking things. Your brain is spinning so fast I can see smoke. When are you going to just let yourself enjoy something for once?"

I brought my hands up and scrubbed my face. "Look, I'm sorry. But I don't know how to do this."

"Do what, exactly?" JT's voice was casual, but his Adam's apple bobbed nervously when he swallowed. A couple of weeks ago, I'd have said JT Wellbridge didn't know how to be vulnerable, but now I knew better... and that knowledge did not make it any easier to navigate this situation. "What can I do or say that will put you at ease and help you enjoy our time here? Do you want me to promise this means something? Or that it... *doesn't*? Whatever you need, I'll do."

He seemed to wince when he said he could tell me it didn't mean anything. The idea of hurting him only made me more tense.

"You have to understand, I've never had a vacation. I almost never even have days off. I don't really know how to..." I motioned vaguely with my hands to indicate the entire strange concept of purposefully doing nothing.

"How to *vacation*? Really?"

I shook my head, feeling my face heat in embarrassment. Normal people took vacations even if they stayed home and did some projects around the house. But I'd never been able to afford it. With the inconsistent income from the Retreat, my parents couldn't be counted on to support my siblings' education, so I'd done it. At least... I'd done it to the best of my ability. In fact, I was still doing it since PJ had finally started art school.

JT's hands came up to frame my face. "Take a deep breath and hold it."

"Don't Willow me," I warned. "I was doing meditation breathing in the womb. It doesn't work for me."

"Not like this." He leaned in and ghosted his lips across my cheek, over my forehead, down my nose. His lips almost touched my skin but not quite. I didn't realize I was holding my breath, but I knew every molecule of my skin was begging for him. "Close your eyes," he whispered against my neck. "And guess where my lips are going to go next."

I did as he said. Goose bumps prickled on my skin in anticipation of his movement. He took his sweet-ass time moving down into my collar, and then he pulled my shirt off and continued teasing my chest and shoulders, my diamond-hard nipples, and my back.

His fingertips skated lightly over my skin as he moved me, undressed me, explored me. By the time I sensed him shifting to his knees, I was already rock hard and leaking.

JT's warm breath hit the sensitive skin of my cock and made it jump. *Please, please suck me...*

He moved lower down and teased my balls, my inner thighs, even my ankles. He ran his lips lightly over every part of me until I was shaking so hard I thought I was going to pitch forward and crash both of us to the floor in an awkward heap.

"Jon," I breathed. "Please."

He moved up and took me into his hot mouth, suddenly anything but light with his lips. He sucked hard and fast, wet and dirty, until I came with a choking whimper-grunt while clasping his hair in a death grip.

"Fuck," I managed to sputter. "*Fuck*, fuck. Christ."

He stood up quickly and took my mouth with a hard kiss, one hand gripping the back of my head to hold me there while his other hand jerked his own dick fast and with zero rhythm. Within seconds, I felt his hot release hit my stomach. The salty taste of my own still lingered on his tongue, and I chased it as he stopped kissing long enough to groan through his orgasm.

His chest and neck were streaked with red, and I noticed his hands shaking too. He was wrecked from the simple act of sucking me off.

As if it had been simple.

We needed a joke to break the tension because it was either that or blurt that I was pretty sure I was in love with him.

Way to keep your summer fling casual, Flynn Honeycutt, you giant fraud.

"I like your method of meditation breathing more than my mom's," I said lightly, patting him on the shoulder before stepping around him and heading toward the bathroom. When I got to the cool tiles of the bathroom, I turned to look back at him. His grin was almost enough to make my knees wobble again. "Get your ass in here, and let me scrub it. I have plans for it later."

He made quick work of pulling off the rest of his clothes and joining me in the shower, where both of us happily acted like everything was fine and this was simply a summer fling.

We were a pair of lying liars.

———

"You seemed upset that your parents were leaving town," JT said later at dinner. The candlelight made him even more attractive, which didn't seem fair to me. His skin glowed, and his eyes shone. The table was in a premium spot, nestled in the corner between two huge picture windows with a view of the water. The clinking of silverware and glasses gave the restaurant enough background noise to lend a sense of privacy to our conversation. "Wait. Is that a stressful topic?"

"Nah. I'm used to it. They're always off someplace," I said. "I just wish..." I bit my lip to stop myself from turning into a whiner. It was none of my business where my parents traveled. Or when.

"Don't do that. Don't censor yourself with me," he said softly. "I want to know how you really feel. I get the sense you don't complain very often."

JT's words surprised me. "Are you kidding? I complain all the time. All I do is complain. I gripe at Alden for gossiping. I complain to Dan about annoying customers at work. I bitch to Castor about Dan fucking up simple things in the Meadery. I even complained to Pop the other night because..." I stopped when I realized I was going to say *because you were at the cookout.*

JT's chuckle was easy and relaxed. "You're doing it again. Censoring yourself. Can't you see I'm a dead end? Who am I going to tell? My mother? Hardly. My father wouldn't listen even if I threw scotch on his face while I was confessing murder, as long as the scotch was top-shelf. And my brother Reagan, despite appearances, is actually a pretty upstanding guy. So... *talk.*"

"I don't want to ruin our nice time by unloading the salt truck all over my parents."

JT leaned forward and squeezed my hand on top of the table. "Every dinner is better with a little salt. I'd kick us off by telling you some Patricia stories, but I think that falls under the *stressful* heading, and I don't want to break our deal."

I snorted, then quickly took another sip of my wine and savored it, grateful for the distraction. JT had started to order a bottle of champagne, but he must have seen the panic on my face because he'd quickly changed it to a chardonnay instead. I didn't need this to be more romantic and special than it already was. We weren't boyfriends, for god's sake, and we certainly weren't celebrating anything.

But if the man wanted to know what was on my mind, I could tell him. At least some of it.

"Fine, then. You've been warned." I set down my glass with a little *click*. "I'm annoyed and hurt that my parents are leaving the country while I'm working my ass off preparing for Brew Fest, which is in a couple of weeks—"

"Three weeks from Saturday," JT agreed mildly.

I gave a clipped nod at this reminder that *of course* he knew exactly when Brew Fest was, and not because I'd mentioned it but because he was no doubt going with Fortress. It was only dumb luck that we hadn't run into each other there in the past.

I clenched my napkin in my fist below the edge of the table, where he couldn't see. "Right. Well. I haven't been able to expand my operation as much as I'd like yet, and I could have really used their help preparing, that's all. Willow had promised to be here for it, and I counted on her." I shrugged like it was no big deal. "It's my own fault, really. I shouldn't have trusted her. She always does this."

I took another sip of the wine, pointedly not looking at him. The crisp chardonnay suddenly tasted bitter in my mouth.

JT's foot nudged mine under the table. "I'll help. I told you I would."

I almost choked on the wine. "You were serious? Why would you do that? Brew Fest is my shot at getting the Ren Faire contract, which means getting a whole bunch of distributors vying for my attention. You'd be helping me get an even better deal than the Fortress contract I turned down."

JT sat back in the chair as emotions passed across his face unchecked. Surprised. Sad. Offended. Annoyed. *Hurt.*

Panic surged through my brain, making my stomach twist and my breathing wonky. I reached for my wineglass with fumbling fingers and nearly knocked it over before snatching my hand back awkwardly.

"I would help because you asked, and I... We're friends, Flynn. Aren't we?" JT paused and pressed his lips together for a moment like he wasn't sure he should finish his sentence, then finally blurted, "I care about you, for fuck's sake."

Sudden, horrifying tears rushed to my eyes for no reason whatsoever, and I stood abruptly, shoving my chair back with a horrible screeching sound. "Sorry. I can't... I need to... One second."

I rushed out of the main part of the restaurant in search of the men's room. When I found it—empty, thank fuck—I leaned back against the door and took a great, heaving breath of the artificially flowery air, trying to calm myself, but once again, the meditation breathing let me down. Then again, this was a pretty extreme situation. The most extreme.

I wasn't just "pretty sure" I loved Jonathan Turner Wellbridge III; I was one hundred percent, without a doubt in love with the man... and it was a disaster beyond anything I'd imagined.

I'd known from the moment Frog swaggered into my office with his sexy smile and his stupid, prissy leather folder that if I let this happen—if I let myself fall for him again—I'd be merrily flinging my own heart straight into a woodchipper. And that was plenty bad enough.

But tonight, seeing the sweetness and patience in JT's eyes, knowing how much trouble he'd gone to just to give me a night of rest and make the guy he was hooking up with happy, I was suddenly afraid this disaster was going to cut both ways and JT might get hurt, too.

What kind of dumbass heard the man he loved say "I care about you" and bolted from the table like a gazelle from a lion? Me. Only me.

And why? Because the man I loved was offering me friendship and kindness and sexual release, just as he had when Grandpa Horace had died... and I couldn't handle it. I wanted so much more from JT Wellbridge that settling for less was impossible.

The truth was, there could be no comfortable, lukewarm halfways for me when it came to Frog Wellbridge. There never had been. It was either full-on love, or it was hate. Heart eyes or daggers drawn. This summer fling had been me balancing on the pivot point of a seesaw—a state I couldn't possibly sustain for long—and sure enough, I'd tipped.

So what the hell was I supposed to do now?

I didn't want to be in love with JT, that was for damn sure. The man was leaving again in a few weeks, and who knew how many years it would be until he came back next time? Unrequited love was the sad, emo shit my sister, Georgia, sang about, and I wanted no part of it.

I still wasn't sure I could trust him—certainly not with this giant, aching love bruise in the center of my chest that made me extra vulnerable.

And though I really, really wished I could hate him again and go back to blaming every hurt and misunderstanding on his arrogant, scheming *Wellbridgeness* like I had in the past, I couldn't manage to get there either.

In short, I was screwed.

"Why? Why did I let this happen again?" I leaned over the sink and looked at myself in the mirror. I was wide-eyed and manic, like only a man in the throes of an anxiety attack could be. "I'm a fucking idiot. Since when have I ever been able to guard my heart from this man? Since never."

The door opened, letting in a rush of noise from the restaurant along with my date. JT's face was creased with concern, and I had no idea how I was going to explain my erratic behavior... let alone my hyperventilation.

But it turned out I didn't have to.

"C'mere," he murmured, reaching for the front of my button-down shirt and fisting it to haul me close. He wrapped his arms around me in a crushing hug and simply held me without saying a word.

"Sorry," I managed to choke out. "For—"

"Don't. It's my fault for pushing you to talk about stressful things when you didn't want to."

That was not the reason I'd been upset. Not remotely. But I let it stand.

I tried to pull away, but JT's arms held firm. "Two more minutes," he murmured. "Just breathe."

Two minutes?

I was not a hugger by nature. I wasn't sure I'd ever hugged anyone for such a long stretch, not even Willow when I was a tiny baby. And given the swirling vortex of emotions happening inside me, it would have felt less dangerous for JT to suggest bungee jumping without a cord or skydiving without a parachute.

But after several beats, the tension in my shoulders began to ease as my body melted against his. His broad palm smoothed up and down my back comfortingly, and I shuddered out a breath as I let my arms come around him, too.

He was warm and strong, familiar and... mine. At least

for the time being. For the duration of this hug. Of this dinner. For tonight. I wasn't going to think further than that.

"You okay now?"

I took a deep breath, surprised to find that my lungs were working normally again. "Oh, yeah. Totally over it," I lied. I cleared my throat. "And you're right. This was definitely all your fault. Which means I get to collect my forfeit."

JT did exactly what I needed. He pulled back just far enough to shoot me a teasing glare that made the world firm beneath my feet once more. "Pffft. Eating cold lobster is my forfeit, Firecracker."

"Pffft, yourself. If you'd ordered the shrimp like I suggested, they'd still taste okay cold." I pulled away from his embrace, grabbed his hand, and led him out to the dining area. "Besides, just have them heat up your melted butter, and you'll never notice the lobster is cold. Better yet, just throw back the ramekin of butter, and don't even worry about the lobster."

JT's bright grin helped release the last of my tension and embarrassment. "Such a *philistine*," he said in a perfect imitation of his mother's haughty accent. "Just what I'd expect from a *Honeycutt*."

I laughed out loud and squeezed his fingers tighter. God, the man was everything kind and attentive, and so damn easy to be with when I wasn't expending all my energy hating his guts.

I bit my lip and darted a glance at his profile. Okay, so this was going to end in disaster. That was a given. But I'd survived disasters before, and I would do it again.

What I *wasn't* going to do was continue freaking out and holding JT at arm's length, especially when I'd agreed to a temporary thing in the first place. It wasn't fair to him.

To either of us. For once, I was going to enjoy every minute of the calm before the storm.

Stick to easy, nondramatic topics, Honeycutt.

Usually this was easier said than done, at least for me.

But when we sat back down and I saw the candlelight do its magic on his face again, I remembered something Willow had said once about gargling salt water for "centering halotherapy" when crystals and other items were unavailable. So, apropos of nothing, I told him the story of how, at the age of six, my brother PJ had taken her advice and dumped a saltshaker into his ice water at a restaurant in Bar Harbor before gargling his little butt off in front of everyone.

JT didn't seem to mind this abrupt right turn in conversation topic. In fact, he seemed downright thrilled that I was sharing a silly story.

He followed that up with a hilarious story about the time Reagan had done Beyoncé's "Single Ladies" dance in the Senator's box at a Red Sox game on a dare, not realizing that "The Star-Spangled Banner" had already begun playing down on the field. When the cameras had panned to the box to get the Senator's reaction to the national anthem being played, Reagan's prank had been broadcast nationally. "It looked *exactly* like Reagan was shaking his ass to the music," JT gasped through his laughter, which set me off laughing, too. "My dad had to make a statement to the press later about how Reagan was just really, *really* patriotic."

I laughed so hard I grabbed his hand on the tabletop, and JT twined our fingers together.

By the time our food came, I felt centered, as if I'd gargled the magical salt water myself. It was a potent reminder that not everything between us had to be scary or fraught with emotion. When I let myself stop thinking about the past or worrying about the future, the two of us could simply... *be*. And it was wonderful.

As we ate, he told me about his life in the city, the people he sometimes played squash with, the restaurants he preferred, the sights he saw when he jogged. He mentioned a sales incentive trip he'd taken with his coworkers to a swanky resort in Puerto Rico.

"I was there with every salesperson and their hetero spouse. It took about ten seconds before I was everyone's gay best friend." He shrugged as I grinned at him. I could picture his gorgeous ass in a swimsuit, surrounded by all the ladies tittering over him. "It wasn't that bad. I ended up with some great skincare tips and quite a few phone numbers of various cousins and coworkers. You know how it is. They know one gay guy, and suddenly, he's your perfect match." He winked at me before popping another bite of lobster in his mouth.

"And were any of them your perfect match? Did you actually get set up?"

He looked smug. "I did actually get set up, and one of them was quite good at—"

I held up my hand to stop him. "Don't."

"Squash," he said with a cheeky grin. "We would have never been compatible in bed, but Carl's a damned fine squash player. In fact, we had a game set up for this weekend, but I canceled it so I could head up here."

"Sorry," I said, flashing him my own smug grin.

"No, you're not."

"No. I'm not. Not one single bit." JT was mine for as long as I could have him. "Cousin Carl can suck it." I met his eyes and lowered my voice. "While I suck you."

The flush that came up his neck and onto his cheeks was sexy as fuck. I wanted to take him to bed right then and there. "Your mouth is making promises, Firecracker," he murmured. His eyes bored into me, heating me up from the inside.

I focused on my dinner. If all went to plan, I'd need the calories for the night of gymnastic fucking ahead of us. The conversation returned to benign topics, and I finally found enough maturity to ask him about his job. "I hear you're really good at what you do. What do you like most about it?"

He lifted one eyebrow flirtatiously. "Are you trying to make me talk about work after you made me promise not to, Honeycutt?"

I laughed and shook my head. "I already won the forfeit, remember? And I'm genuinely curious."

"Okay, then." His eyes lit up, which made my stomach drop. As much as I wanted him to be happy, I didn't necessarily want to hear about him being happy in New York.

"I like the challenge of it. The connection of it. I started off selling our distribution services to retailers, bars, restaurants, and shops. I didn't switch to the supply side until recently. I loved visiting the retailers and talking to them about their clientele, their brand, their goals. Figuring out what we had to offer that would improve their business and then helping make it happen. I wasn't sure it would be that way on the supply side, but it is. It's actually even better. I'm helping small businesses grow. Helping people achieve their dreams."

I could see that. JT was a very outgoing person who could make friends with a potted plant. He was like Alden in that way. Alden thrived in a busy hair salon because he was happy talking all day long to anyone and everyone. I wasn't quite the same. I enjoyed talking to my customers, but I also needed time alone either in my office, out at the lake, or even in the Meadery, where a glass wall separated me from the rest of the Tavern.

But I loved watching him talk about the people he'd connected with and seeing the happiness he got from their success. "I can tell you love it," I said, finally admitting the truth. It seemed like he was exactly where he was supposed to be, even if Fortress was located in New York.

"I do," he said. He hesitated for a second before admitting, "Mostly. But I guess there are some not-great parts of every career."

"Totally. I don't *enjoy* dealing with tricky customers, or negotiating with suppliers, or managing employees. But the rest makes it worthwhile."

JT laughed. "You've just listed all the parts I like best about my job. For me, though, the problem is that..." He gnawed on his lip. "I used to think everyone I worked with had the same motivations as me. Like I was part of something worthwhile. Now, I'm not so sure. And then there's the whole promotion thing..." He darted a look at me and fell silent.

"Your promotion to VP?" He looked surprised that I'd heard about it, and I smiled. "Come on. It's Honeybridge. And you know how your mother talks."

"Right." He paused for a second, then leaned closer like he was imparting a secret. "The thing is, I earned that promotion twice over," he said fiercely. "I worked my ass off."

I nodded. I had no trouble believing that. "That's why they called you Rainmaker. Because you were their closer."

He dipped his head in acknowledgment. "But just when I thought my boss was ready to finally make the announcement, he told me I needed to make one more deal. It didn't seem fair at the time." He toyed with his fork for a moment, not looking at me. "It still doesn't."

I sucked in a breath. I told myself it wasn't a hundred percent clear whether he was talking about the Honeybridge Mead deal, but my stomach squirmed a bit with guilt anyway. Maybe if I reminded him of the happy side effect of us not being in business together, it would help.

"That sucks. But I mean, there is a definite upside to you dinging your unbroken deal-closing record with me, isn't there?" I teased. "If I thought you were still out to woo me to Fortress, I never would have slept with you."

He frowned. "You... wouldn't?"

"Come on, Frog, this can't be a shock. Given our past, it's possible that I might have a, uh... trust issue or two... when it comes to you."

"I noticed," JT agreed faintly.

I rolled my eyes. "Anyway. I'm not saying nothing would have happened that first night because... well, it kinda took me off guard."

"Same," he whispered.

I nodded. "But after that? This whole..." I waved my hand. "Summer fling? And the texts? And being here with you now?" I shook my head confidently. "No. It would be a huge conflict of interest for both of us."

"Would it?" JT ran a hand over his mouth.

"Heck yeah. If you hadn't told me in the woods the other day that you'd given up on trying to convince me to take Fortress's offer, I'd probably always wonder if this whole thing wasn't just part of some kind of giant sales pitch."

His eyes widened.

I winked. "You might not know this about me, but *some* people have suggested that I'm an overthinker."

"You? Never," he joked, but his smile seemed a little forced... and no wonder, really.

I winced internally. I hated that I'd nearly ruined our date earlier. The last thing I wanted was for him to dwell on it.

"That would be a real shame, too," I purred. I pushed back my plate and locked eyes with him across the table. "Because I have big plans for you tonight."

He let out a strange chuckle—not at all what I'd been expecting.

"Flynn," he began. "The thing is..." He glanced away and faltered.

Oh. Oh, shit.

"I mean, unless you changed your mind." I made myself laugh lightly. "No, that's... it's... whatever. Tonight's been a lot." *I'd* been a lot. "Not exactly restful. It's probably not too late for you to un-cancel your squash date." I tore my napkin off my lap and set it on the table. "I can get a ride back to—"

"No!" he blurted. "Fuck no. You're... that's not..." He blew out a breath, and when his blue eyes met mine, the panicked longing in them froze me in place. "Flynn Honeycutt, I have never wanted any man as much as I want you," he said baldly. "Not ever."

"Oh." I blinked, trying to summon the ability to speak clearly, though his words had tilted my world on its axis. "I see. So..."

"So I'm good with your big plans," he said hoarsely. "I'm good with you being naked in any scenario."

"Right. Okay. Then..." I swallowed. "I guess we should pay the check."

I told myself to let the strange moment go. Maybe JT was low-key upset about the loss of his promotion, especially since I was the cause of it. Maybe it had nothing to do with me at all. Hadn't I *just* promised myself that I was going to stop holding JT at arm's length and enjoy this while I could?

JT was here with me tonight. Wanting me. For now, nothing else mattered.

After he paid the bill and pulled me by the hand toward the car, I decided to tease him, hoping to reset the mood between us. To make things light and casual.

I waited until he pulled the car out of the well-lit parking lot and onto the dark road before I reached over and ran my hand across his dick and down between his legs. He made a sound of surprise and quickly tightened his grip on the steering wheel.

"You're going to get us killed," JT hissed, as if anyone could hear us on the quiet road.

"You'll keep us safe," I whispered. He hardened quickly under my hand, and I continued to stroke him lazily through the fabric of his trousers. "Besides, I want you to be desperate by the time I take your ass."

This time, the sound was a choking cough. "You want me to bottom for you this time, huh?"

I watched his reaction. "Problem?"

JT glanced at me before looking back at the road, but when his dick jerked in my hand, I could tell what his response would be before he said it. "Hell no, it's not a problem. I'm up for pretty much anything that will make you feel good."

His words made my stomach pitch and roll in the best way.

He's not an asshole, I realized.

The fact that these thoughts kept coming to me like revelations was a sign of just how effectively I'd built my walls up against JT over the years, only letting in the facts that confirmed my opinion of him.

JT had always been a giver, from the time he'd passed over his favorite pudding cup to Samuel Horner at lunch after some asshole kid had tripped Samuel on the playground, to the time he'd raced out of our biology final early to take Krissy Tan to her swim meet championship when her car wouldn't start.

It had hurt that he'd always been destined for bigger and better things than Honeybridge. It had hurt that he'd always been one more thing I couldn't have. But that was no excuse for the way I'd deliberately, repeatedly misjudged him.

I glanced across the darkness toward him. His face was partially lit by the light from the dash, and the angle of his jaw begged for my lips. I bit back the urge to kiss him.

"You're a good man," I admitted softly.

JT glanced in my direction and bounced his eyebrows at me. "Mmmhmm. I'm gonna be *real* good for you."

I knew a deflection when I heard one, and it made my breath catch. He was doing it again, trying to keep things light and casual for my sake. Trying to calm me down and give me *rest*.

But what I really needed was to be brave. To do what I'd already told myself I'd do and stop flip-flopping between hot and cold with him.

As soon as he pulled the car into the small lot behind the bed-and-breakfast, I grabbed his hand and practically yanked him through the large house and up to our room. Then I closed the door and nudged him toward one of the chairs by the windows.

"Sit there."

He obeyed immediately. I cued up a certain playlist on my phone and set it down on a nearby table. As soon as JT's eyes landed on me, I began a slow striptease.

"Patsy Cline? Really?" he teased, even though his eyes were blue fire, plenty hot enough to tell me he was just fine with my music selection.

"'Crazy for You' was the song playing at the General Store when you bought me a pack of candy cigarettes in fourth grade," I said, pulling the hem of my shirt up enough for him to see my happy trail, a sight I knew turned him on more than almost any other part of me.

His eyes darkened. "Was it?"

I nodded and pulled my shirt the rest of the way off. "And the next song was the one that was playing at the lake when you kissed Jackson Irving senior year."

JT's knuckles turned white where he gripped the arms of the chair. "He kissed me."

"You let him." I moved my hands to my belt as I did a slow, sensuous turn and shook my ass. JT's breathing hitched. These were really nice pants, perfectly fit in the rear to show off my assets.

"I only let him because I was too busy staring at your dick print in those yellow board shorts you wore to notice when he came at me for the kiss."

I completed the turn and met his eyes. They were hungry enough to make my stomach tighten. "Really?"

He nodded and slumped down in his chair so he could spread his legs to make room for his own tightening pants. His hand came down to rub himself, which only made me hotter. "Firecracker, when we were in high school, I couldn't keep my eyes off you. I used to jack off every fucking chance I got. I was late to fourth period English nearly every day because the sight of your happy trail in the locker room would make me pop wood. And one time, the summer between junior and senior year, I saw your ass in your tight softball pants and had to run into the men's room at the ballpark to get relief."

I opened my pants and turned around again, lowering them enough to reveal the snug briefs I wore. "This ass?" I wiggled it for him until he groaned.

"Get over here," he growled, "and sit on my dick."

I faced him again as the song changed to "It Wasn't Me"

by Shaggy. JT barked out a laugh. "Oh, shit, I remember this," he said. "Jackson tried to jerk me off in the water later that night. Didn't want to take no for an answer. I told him to try it on with your cousin Len."

"Len's straight."

"No shit. But Jackson deserved the prudish set-down Len gave him."

Now it was my turn to laugh. Len had never been homophobic, but he'd been the leader of the purity brigade back in high school. The very idea of someone hitting on him would have sent him into a tailspin of pearl-clutching.

"Know who's not straight?" JT demanded. "*Me*. Hurry up with the naked-making."

I let the pants slide to the floor and ran my hand over my junk, squeezing and stroking through the red cotton before running my hand up my stomach to my nipples. "Where's the fun in that?" I asked.

JT sat up and began pulling his own shirt off with a muffled "Fuck this."

I continued playing with myself while he stripped. Once he was completely naked in the chair, I continued the tease by sliding my thumbs into the waistband of my briefs. "I'm hard as fuck for you," I said. "Going to fuck you against the back of that chair."

JT closed his eyes and threw his head back, letting out a groan and squeezing the base of his hard cock. "Killing me, Firecracker."

When his eyes opened and landed on me again, I finally pulled my underwear off and let him see how hard I was for him. I walked slowly toward him and climbed into his lap, straddling his naked cock until it ran between my ass cheeks.

"Would you believe," I gasped, moving just enough to

tease both of us, "that some people get off on edging? That they could do it for hours?"

He threaded his fingers into my hair and yanked my head back with just the right amount of roughness. "No more. If this is the revenge you talked about earlier, you've made your point."

I chuckled darkly, then dragged my cock against his hard abs, shivering at the friction. I hadn't been thinking of that at all, but now that he'd reminded me...

"Hmmm. I'm not sure I have. I believe I said I was going to hold you down and make you admit defeat, just like that day at Quick Lake." I pressed a line of teasing kisses along the bristly edge of his jaw and hovered my lips over his for a moment, so close to kissing... but not. "And you still seem pretty bossy, Frog."

I removed his hands from my head and placed them firmly against the arms of the chair in unspoken command. Then I slid down his lap so I could nip at his collarbone and nuzzle his armpit. I ran my tongue over the crook of his elbow and even pressed a kiss to the part of his ridiculous tattoo that peeked out over his watch band. He groaned but didn't move.

"Not bossy," he choked out. "*So* not bossy. You win. See?"

I snickered and gave in to the temptation to run my fingernails over his nipples. His cock jerked, so I did it again... and then *again*... until his hips jerked up rhythmically, searching for the friction I was denying him.

"Flynn. *Fuck*. Please!" His eyes were hazy with lust, and his mouth hung slack. He looked so undone I had to climb back onto his lap just so I could kiss him properly, savoring the flavor of him. I rocked my ass back against him again, so close to exactly where I wanted him to be, and he let out a long, low whine.

I wasn't exactly sure who was being punished in this scenario any longer.

I leaned in and whispered in his ear. "What do you want tonight?"

JT's warm hands moved around my back and up to grip my shoulders. "You," he said, voice cracking. "Only you. Always you. *I yield to Flynn Honeycutt, king of this lake.*"

His words were sharp-tipped arrows piercing deep and leaving rivulets of vulnerability seeping out everywhere. I was bludgeoned by him, and I couldn't care. Not now, not while I had him in my arms and at my mercy. Instead, I gave myself over to it, let him have my body, broken pieces and all.

"I'm yours," I said simply. "Take me."

JT held me tight and stood up, striding two steps to the bed, where he laid me down gently and climbed on top of me. Somehow, he knew I'd changed my mind about topping him. That wasn't at all what I wanted. I wanted him to own me, inside and out. I wanted him as close as he could get to my heart.

He kissed me first for a long time, his hands roaming all over me with tender exploration and affection. I wrapped my legs around him to hold him there as if terrified he might get up and walk away.

JT's hands brushed hair off my face and replaced it with soft kisses and murmurs of how sexy I was, how hot I made him, how lucky he was to be with me tonight, and how grateful he was that I'd said yes to going away with him.

He rocked our cocks together agonizingly slowly, just enough to keep me on the edge but nowhere close to tumbling over it. I wanted to beg, but I didn't dare. I didn't want to do anything to make our time together pass more quickly.

When JT finally produced lube and a condom and slid

inside of me, a wave of overwhelming relief washed over me.

This. This is where I'm meant to be. This is whose body should be rocking into mine. This is the person I want to hold on to, now and forever.

I closed my eyes and let myself have it, let myself feel all of it, deserve all of it.

For tonight at least, Jonathan Wellbridge was mine. And I wasn't letting him go.

Chapter Thirteen

JT

Firecracker: *Missing: one smooth-talking Frog. Last seen in my bed. If found, please return to Honeybridge Tavern. Generous reward offered.*

I pulled into the driveway of my parents' house the following weekend, slammed the door of my Porsche closed, then leaned my ass back against the car so I could grin down at my phone like a total sap.

Me: *How generous are we talking, baby?*

Firecracker: *I'm feeling VERY generous.*

My grin widened.

Me: *Wow. You must really have a thing for this frog.*

Me: *He must be your favorite frog ever.*

Me: *The handsomest, smartest, sexiest frog in all the land.*

Firecracker: *Changed my mind. You can keep him.*

I laughed out loud.

Me: *What are you doing awake? You were so tired when you got back from taking your parents to the airport last night, and you looked so peaceful when I left, I didn't want to wake you.*

Firecracker: *It's 9AM. Can't lay in bed all day, especially not all alone. Got a tiny little thing called Brew Fest on my calendar. You've maybe heard of it?*

Me: *But we knocked out half the Daydream you need for Brew Fest last night. And, BTW, whoever put the labels on those bottles and packed them for transport did a five-star job. Hope that's going in my annual review.*

Firecracker: *I think what I like best about you is your humility, Jon.*

I snort-laughed. I loved riling Flynn up, partly because I knew he enjoyed it, too. At least, he did these days.

Something had changed between us that night at the inn in Ogunquit a little over a week ago. Flynn had stopped erecting walls between us and had allowed himself to be vulnerable with me—at least when we were in bed together. And I'd stopped trying to delude myself that anything besides Flynn's happiness was my top priority.

Me: *Want me to come by again tonight and help out?*

Three dots appeared and disappeared on Flynn's side of the conversation, and I rolled my eyes. Clearly, not *everything* had changed.

Me: *Let me rephrase. I'm coming over tonight. You can decide whether you want me to sit there shirtless while you bottle the mead so my abs can inspire you to greatness, or if you'd actually like me to do work.*

Firecracker: *You helped out nearly every night last week. Dan was gonna stay and help tonight.*

I huffed out a breath.

Me: *You'll let DAN help, but not me? Come on.*

Firecracker: *I pay him, JT.*

JT, I noted wryly. Not Frog. Not Jon. Someone's hackles were up.

Me: *You can pay me, too. Just not in cash. *Smiley emoji**

Firecracker: *You don't have to help me all the damn time, you know. That's not what this is about. Summer fling, remember?*

My heart beat thickly in the hazy, humid morning air.

Yes. I definitely remembered. I also knew the summer was not going to be long enough for me... and that, after what Flynn had said the other night at dinner, I wasn't sure I was even going to get that long.

I didn't know how Flynn had gotten the idea that I'd given up on signing Honeybridge Mead to the Fortress portfolio. It was true that I hadn't mentioned it for a couple of weeks. There were so many moving parts involved in my new plan that I hadn't wanted to get Flynn's hopes up until Fortress gave final approval and Hayden was able to lock down the real estate we'd need. I couldn't remember the exact words I'd said to Flynn that day in the woods—something about respecting his standards and understanding why he'd rejected the initial contract, maybe? But he'd clearly taken that to mean that I was walking away from the deal entirely. I wondered if maybe Flynn was just used to people walking away from him.

I'd opened my mouth to explain things right then and there, but the look on his face across that table—skittish, vulnerable, heartbreakingly defensive—had stopped me. That was the look of a man who was waiting for the other shoe to drop. Who was so scared of happiness that he was ready to build up a wall to push me out at the slightest provocation. Admitting that Fortress still considered Honeybridge Mead an active lead—especially when I couldn't say for sure what contract terms I'd be able to offer—would be exactly the spark Flynn needed to set him off.

So I was stuck keeping a giant secret from him... for his own good.

It sounded terrible and felt even worse, but Flynn and I had so much history and hurt between us that this utterly illogical option was the only one that made sense for us.

And it had made this past week hell.

The only thing I could think of that might improve the situation was to help Flynn with Brew Fest prep. The more time I spent with him, the more chances I had of convincing him that I truly cared for him. And the more prepared he was for the festival, the more likely he'd be to win the whole damn thing, and the more choices he'd have.

I was *not* Conrad Schaeffer. I didn't want Flynn to take the deal because he had no other offers. I wanted him to choose Fortress—choose *me*—because he saw how good it could be.

Me: *I WANT to help, Flynn.*

Me: *Besides, when we work together, it goes so much faster, which means I get to take you to bed sooner.*

Me: *And I told you I have to be in the office Monday morning for strategy meetings with the head of marketing about one of our other clients. I have to leave tomorrow night. I want to see you as much as I can.*

Flynn didn't reply for so long that I sighed and typed out something that would guarantee a response.

Me: *AND the boss-and-naughty-employee vibe really works for me... Mr. Honeycutt.*

Flynn's rolling dots took days off my life.

Firecracker: *You make a compelling argument.*

Firecracker: *I have a whole to-do list I need you to take care of for me before you leave for the day, Jonathan.*

Firecracker: *I want you to rim me. At least twice. I want you to fuck me over the bar. I want to ride your dick* *while you sit at the chair in my office. I want you to do that nipple thing you do, because it never feels as good when I try to do it to myself.*

Oh, shit. Just like that, I was sporting a semi in my basketball shorts, right on the circular stone driveway in front of Wellbridge House. Generations of Wellbridges were no doubt turning in their graves over the mental images I was getting of me worshipping Flynn Honeycutt's nipples.

Not that I gave one single damn.

Me: *That's funny, Mr. Honeycutt, because the list of things you want to do to me is more like a list of things you want me to do to you. And that's a very ambitious list for one evening.*

Firecracker: *Tsk, tsk. Are you a complaining, naughty employee to ALL your bosses?*

The idea of being like this with Conrad Schaeffer was physically revolting, and I knew Flynn knew it, too, the asshole. I imagined him grinning down at his phone like the cat that ate the canary, and I chuckled.

Me: *No, sir. Eager to get started, sir.*

Firecracker: *Excellent. Then I'll expect you to report for duty right after the softball game. Oh, and Jonathan?*

Me: *Yes, sir?*

Firecracker: *Don't bother showering. I'll only get you sweaty again.*

I clutched the phone to my chest and grinned like a lovesick teenager.

I wanted Flynn to trust me completely. With everything. But knowing he at least trusted me with his body and his desire, his humor and his sweetness, felt like a rare and precious gift from this man who hated relying on anyone for anything.

And that was why this past week had also been absolute *heaven*.

I didn't take it for granted.

"Jonathan! Jonathan, darling!"

I closed my eyes and stifled a groan as my mother's voice sounded from way too close behind me. My dick deflated instantly.

My mother had backed off after our little chat a couple of weeks ago. She hadn't contacted me while I was in New York, hadn't asked questions when I picked up my car last week, and hadn't asked where I'd been when I came back from Ogunquit on Friday. I knew Brantleigh was still staying in the house because I'd seen him at breakfast a couple of times, but she hadn't attempted to arrange any further dates between us. She'd even asked Rosalia to make me a salad to bring to Jace Honeycutt's potluck... which seemed like cheating, but what did I know? And when I'd met her on the front lawn early last Wednesday morning—she'd been on her way to do yogaerobics with Madeline Pond while I was coming back from Flynn's to shower and jump on a video call—she'd compressed her lips firmly but hadn't asked where I'd been.

I'd hoped we'd turned a corner in our relationship, but I could tell by the tone of her voice now that my reprieve was at an end.

"Mother!" I pasted on a smile as I turned to face her. "Aren't you looking lov— Uh." I blinked and frowned as I caught sight of her ensemble. "Very Edwardian?"

She beamed from beneath the brim of an enormous feathered hat, and when she clasped her large shallow basket in both hands, the rows and rows of lace on her long yellow dress quivered.

"Thank you, sweetheart. I've come out to collect some roses. You can walk with me." She threaded her arm through mine and led me along the crushed-seashell path toward the side garden, where roses grew along lattice archways and topiary trees as tall as me flanked an enormous stone fountain. "You remember that I'm hosting the Honeybridge Botanical Society Luncheon today, of course."

I was positive she'd never mentioned it, but I nodded warily. "Alright."

"Amita Laghari has hosted it in recent years, but this year, it was decided that since Amita has had that terrible, terrible luck with her ankle ever since the tennis tournament at the country club—and honestly, any woman our age who tries to do a diving volley should consider herself lucky when she only sprains an ankle!—the luncheon would be here at Wellbridge House." Mother's smile widened a fraction, clearly not particularly torn up over poor Mrs. Laghari's injury.

When we reached a large stand of yellow lollipop-shaped rosebushes that precisely matched her dress, she took a pair of shears from her basket and attacked the flowers with more enthusiasm than mercy.

"Well. That's... great," I said, because really, what else was there to say? "I hope it goes swimmingly." I hesitated. I didn't want to get involved any more than I had to be, but my curiosity was overwhelming. "Do the Botanical Society women always wear—" I bit my tongue and swallowed the word costumes. "—these dresses?"

"Of course not, Jonathan." She frowned at me reproachfully, one hand on her hip. "Honeybridge exists in the twenty-first century, you know. These days, we encourage all attendees to wear whatever they choose as long as it's family-friendly!" She pursed her lips and leaned in like she was telling me a secret. "Unlike the monstrosity of a dress George Chang wore two years ago. All bust and no bustle if you know what I mean."

I had no idea what she meant, and I was equally sure I didn't want to know.

"In any case," she went on, turning her attention back to her flowers, "we finalized the luncheon menus last weekend, and Rosalia has been working on the tablescape all week. It's going to be the talk of Honeybridge!"

"Excellent! I'm happy for you."

"Hmm. You'd know all about the arrangements, of course," she said primly, "if you'd been home at all this week."

Oh, lord. Here it was.

"We've talked about this. I've spent this week attempting to work, which is nearly impossible to do remotely. And it's worth mentioning that in the past three weeks, I've attended both the Honeybridge Diversity Committee's Quarterly Fundraising Planning Tea and the Friends of the Honeybridge Arts Council's Preprandial Cocktail and Lemonade Reception, captained a boat for Team Wellbridge in the regatta, and played in two softball games in addition to accompanying you to yogaerobics, which I warned you would be a one-time-only event. That's more than enough."

She sniffed. "You haven't seen your brother."

"I ate lunch with him once last week and three times the week before." I folded my arms over my chest.

"And Brantleigh—"

"Is a useless, spoiled child with a terrible attitude. I try to avoid him as much as possible," I said impatiently. "Why are we rehashing all this when I've made it perfectly clear that my priority is—"

"Work. Yes, you've made that very clear." She straightened. "But you're not too busy with work to spend every night at the Tavern." I sighed resignedly, and she nodded in triumph like I'd confessed to a terrible secret. "Oh, yes. I've heard all about it, beginning practically the moment you arrived! Imagine how I felt having to hear from *Prissy Newton* that you've been spending time with that... that..."

"Careful—" I warned.

"*Honeycutt*," she choked out.

Well, damn. So much for trying to keep things quiet to protect Flynn from gossip. Not that we'd tried very hard in the past week. The whole town knew where I ate my lunch every afternoon, and they had to notice the distinct lack of animosity between me and Flynn recently. Alden and Castor had helped us with the bottling most evenings this past week, and Alden had given Flynn eyeballs at least twice over some flirty comment we'd made.

I stared down at my feet for a beat, hoping the crushed seashells would grant me patience. "I understand that you're upset that I didn't tell you. But I won't hear a single negative word about Flynn, Mother. Not one. You know my feelings on the Wellbridge-Honeycutt feud. If we live in an era where anyone in town can dress like the Dowager Countess from *Downton Abbey*, then we sure as heck live in an era when I can... spend time with a Honeycutt without you turning it into a Shakespearean tragedy."

"Hmph." She lifted her chin. "Even if I had no opposition to you dating one of those Honeycutts, darling, how would you ever make it work? You live in New York, as you remind me endlessly, and Flynn does not. You're only here for the summer."

The way she so matter-of-factly hit on the elephant I'd been trying to ignore only served to make me more impatient.

"I'm trying to work a deal between Fortress and Honeybridge Mead that would give Flynn choices—"

Mother frowned. "Nonsense. Flynn rejected Fortress's generous offer weeks ago."

The gossip in this town was ridiculous. "Yes. He did. But I—" I clamped my lips together.

She narrowed her eyes. "But you're still trying to make it work?" Her eyes widened. "You *are*. You still want your promotion."

"That's not why!" I shut my teeth with a *clack*. The stupidest thing I could do in this situation was to spill my secret directly to the biggest gossip in Honeybridge, the one person who wouldn't hesitate to use it to sabotage my relationship with Flynn. "I care about Flynn, okay? I want him to be happy." I nodded firmly, hoping that would put an end to the conversation.

But my mother was not simply political arm candy. She was the brilliant strategist who'd helped elevate my father from a poor, ambitious unknown attorney into a state senator being considered for governor. And now that she'd gotten this idea in her head, I could practically see the wheels of her brain turning.

"That's why you met with Hayden Lewis," she accused. When my mouth fell open in surprise, she waved a hand airily. "Oh, darling. Fabienne Lewis and I are on the library board together. Of course I asked her exactly which properties you and Hayden discussed. I couldn't imagine why you were looking into commercial property, but now I see. Flynn Honeycutt is making demands."

"No. He isn't." I rolled my eyes heavenward. "Look. This *needs* to stay between us, Mother. And when I say *us*, I do not mean you, me, and the entire Botanical Society. I do not mean you, me, and Aunt Louise. No one, and I mean no one, can know about my meeting with Hayden, especially Flynn. Okay?"

"For heaven's sake, why? Is it because you're dating a potential client? Is that..." She lowered her voice and widened her eyes. "...taboo?"

I snorted. "No. At least, I don't believe so. I don't think the rest of the world would think so either, but Flynn..." I sighed and reached out a finger to touch a single velvety rose petal. "Flynn would take it the wrong way." I felt my lips pull up into a wry, affectionate smile. "He usually does."

My mother blinked, then sat down on a wrought-iron bench and set her shears beside her, still frowning. After a moment, she shook her head. "I don't understand, Jonathan. I'm trying, but I don't."

"Flynn's not making demands, Mother. I wish he would. But he's determined to be self-reliant. Everything he has, he's achieved for himself. Expanding Honeybridge Mead, restoring the Tavern, learning to run a business... even keeping his family together. He's had no one to help him, except maybe Pop. Still, when I came to him with Fortress's offer, he rejected it, even though it's exactly what his business needs. He said he was committed to keeping the manufacturing in Honeybridge. He cares more about his business, his family legacy, than he does about himself. And he cares about this town."

My mother pressed her lips together but remained quiet.

"So I came up with an idea that would let him have both. The distribution with Fortress, which will give him enough money for him to travel and expand and help his family, *and* the ability to keep the meadery in town. I want him to have choices, you know? To know someone has his back. I want him to have..." My voice came out clogged with emotion, despite my best efforts. "...whatever he wants most." *And I want that to be me.*

"Oh, my darling." Mother's eyes were round and shining with some emotion I'd never seen in her before. "You... you really do care about him, don't you?"

I nodded once.

"But if you and he are together for the long haul..."

My mouth twisted up. "I don't think Flynn's ready to commit to that."

"Yes, but once he is," she insisted, and I had to smile at her assumption that the world would always spin exactly the way a Wellbridge wanted it to. "Would you move here? Would you give up your job?"

"Of course not," I said immediately. "I'm about to get promoted."

She nodded in agreement. "So, then?"

I rubbed my chin and let myself think about it. A future where Flynn had agreed to the Fortress contract and fallen head over heels for me... what would that even look like, practically speaking?

I rubbed my chin. "I couldn't move here full-time, no. The hours are long—longer once I make vice president—and I can't work from home. It's a competitive industry, and I need to be in the office so I can stay in the loop. Plus, I need to travel. A lot."

"Is it possible Flynn would leave with you, then?" Mother asked. "Follow you to New York?"

I shook my head instantly. "Not a chance. Hell, I can barely get the man to take a vacation. He'd never leave his family or Honeybridge."

It would have to be a long-distance relationship for the time being. A relationship filled with goodbyes. Knowing what life with Flynn's parents had been like, I could only imagine how rough that would be on him. And hell, I wasn't much better. Thinking about leaving him tomorrow was already killing me.

"That's one thing Flynn and I have in common."

I frowned distractedly. "Hmm?"

Mother lifted a shoulder, looking almost... embarrassed.

"Your father and I have had many chances to leave Honeybridge over the years. Your father would say, 'But Patricia, there's so much more diversity in New York, more museums in Boston, more political opportunity in Washington.' But I could never understand running off to find something better when I could simply improve what was already here."

I blinked at her in surprise. "The Honeybridge Diversity Committee? The Friends of the Arts Council? That's what those things are all about?" I'd assumed that all of those organizations were simply excuses for my mother to chair another committee.

She inclined her head regally, and the feathers on her hat dipped and swayed in the breeze.

I grinned at her—a real, full-on grin—for the first time in years. "That's... truly impressive, Mother."

"Hmph." I caught sight of a tiny smile playing about her lips before she ruthlessly suppressed it. "When a Wellbridge wants something, Jonathan, we don't allow ourselves to be limited by circumstances," she said imperiously. She gave me a significant look. "We make our own."

I nodded slowly. It turned out Pop Honeycutt wasn't the only one in Honeybridge who could turn a conversation into a life lesson.

"Now." She folded her hands in her lap. "What can I do to help you with your endeavor?"

I shook my head. "Nothing. Truly. Just... Keep it under your hat." I tweaked one of her feather plumes. "I'll figure it out. Somehow."

She nodded solemnly. "Of course you will."

I tilted my head. "And you're really willing to accept me dating a Honeycutt? Really?"

Mother sighed. "Obviously, it wouldn't be... an *ideal* connection. But I want you to be happy and to do the Wellbridge name proud, Jonathan. In that order. So if dating one of those Honeycutts helps you achieve that purpose and helps you to be in Honeybridge more, too... well, I suppose there are stranger things in the world." She shrugged like she couldn't imagine any of them.

Then her brow lowered as if a thought had just occurred to her. "Just to be clear, though... at the softball game this afternoon, will you and Flynn be playing on opposite teams, or..."

"Oh, heck yeah. I'm gonna make him eat dirt," I said cheerfully. "The town sign is gonna say 'Home of the Ultimate Softball Champion Wellbridge Family' by the end of the season. Flynn wouldn't have it any other way."

Mother smiled and reached out a hand to cup my cheek. "You'll make me proud." She pulled away a second later and wrinkled her nose. "You smell like honey and oranges," she said. "And something decidedly... earthy."

I pressed my lips together to hide my smile. "Flynn's mead."

"Ah." My mother sighed gustily. "Well. I'll get used to it, I'm sure." She patted my chest. "Go get dressed, darling. I need to finish my centerpieces, and the ladies will be arriving shortly. You know your Aunt Louise believes in being fashionably early. So gauche."

I laughed as I bent to press a kiss to her cheek.

As I headed back to the house, I began brainstorming ways that I could make everything work out. Ways that would give me the job I wanted... and the man I was coming to believe I couldn't live without.

"Jonathan," a voice said from the shadow of a latticed archway.

I jumped two feet in the air and made a very unmanly *eep* sound. "Jesus Christ, Brantleigh!" I yelled. "Warn a person. What the fuck are you doing out here?"

"Waiting for something fun to happen. And now it has."

He smiled and stepped into the sunshine wearing a tennis outfit so white it seared my eyes. "I was hoping you'd walk by."

I wrinkled my nose. "Oh?"

"I need a doubles partner, and your brother's terrible at it. No killer instinct." He winked and gave me a flirty grin that put all his very white teeth on display. "Come play with me. Please?" He pouted prettily and fluttered his eyelashes. "I don't handle rejection well."

I let out a breath. I hadn't been very patient with Brantleigh over the past few weeks. He was spoiled and entitled, yes, but he was young. And if I'd learned nothing else from my time in Honeybridge, it was that people sometimes could surprise you.

"Look, Brantleigh, you're very... handsome," I said. It was the truth. Sort of. "And it really sucks that you're having a rough time right now. I sincerely hope that gets better. But you and I..." I blew out a breath. "Look, my mother had an idea that you and I would be a great match, but I'm sure you're as aware as I am that we don't have anything in common, so—"

Brantleigh's smile didn't dim. "That's not true. We travel in the same circles. We know all the same people. I have a trust fund, you have a trust fund. You're ambitious, I'm ambitious." He laid a smooth, thin hand on my arm and leaned closer to whisper in my ear. "I like sucking cock, and I'm willing to bet you like having your —"

I pulled away with an uncomfortable laugh. "Ohhh, whoa whoa whoa. No, see, I have a trust fund, but I never use it. And I'm not interested in... *that*."

He quirked an eyebrow. "Blowjobs?"

"Not with you," I said flatly, my patience dwindling rapidly. "I'm seeing someone."

"That's not a problem." He closed the distance between

us again and coasted a hand over my chest. "Keeping secrets makes things spicier, don't you think?"

"No. I don't." I removed his hand from my person. "Hear the words I'm saying: I'm not interested."

Brantleigh's nostrils flared. "You'll change your mind." His smile turned into something more calculating.

Okay, so maybe some people were exactly as they appeared on the surface.

"I really won't. Not ever," I said firmly. "There are lots of other great guys in town, though. I'm sure one of them would be *thrilled* to take you up on your offer."

I said a silent apology to the gay population of Honeybridge.

Brantleigh tilted his head to an Instagram-perfect angle. "Maybe you're right," he said slowly. "Since I'm stuck in this town for *weeks*, maybe I should get out and chat up some other men."

I nodded. "That's the spirit."

"Maybe keeping secrets *is* overrated." He tapped his lower lip thoughtfully. "So perhaps I'll hit up the Tavern. Get to know the locals. That's where *those* Honeycutts hang out, right?"

A flare of apprehension gripped me, and my eyes narrowed. If this guy hit on Castor or Alden, Flynn was going to need bail money.

If he hit on Flynn, *I* would.

"Don't make trouble," I warned.

"Please. I'm not a *child*, Jonathan." Brantleigh curled his lip. "People always underestimate me. You. My father." He rolled his eyes. "I promise you, I'm not as useless as you think."

"I didn't say you were useless," I protested. Wait, *had* I?

"Later," he called over his shoulder, flouncing toward the house.

"Yeesh," I said under my breath as I watched him go. I stood in the bright sunshine for a long moment after he'd let himself in through the french doors, letting him get to wherever he was going so I wouldn't run into him again.

I didn't know Thatcher Pennington well—we'd barely spoken more than a few words here and there over the years—but I could not imagine dealing with Brantleigh long-term. I really hoped karma had something good in store for him.

Firecracker: *Guess who's gonna be pitching for Team Honeycutt today? You're going down, baby.*

I glanced down at my phone and smiled.

Me: *Wait, are you talking about what's gonna happen DURING the softball game? Or AFTER?*

Firecracker: *lol. You're gonna have to wait and see, Frog.*

Fuck, I thought as I tucked my phone back in my pocket. I really hoped karma had something good in store for me and Flynn, too.

But in the meantime, I had a softball game to win.

———

"Bases loaded," Pop Honeycutt warned. "The Wellbridges are up by two, the Honeycutts have two outs and two strikes! Flynn Honeycutt is at bat, and the Honeycutts need a run, but Frog Wellbridge's been awful stingy out there on the pitcher's mound for Team Wellbridge. Everyone knows Firecracker's got a temper and a half on him. Can he stay focused long enough to make the play?"

Flynn tapped his bat on the ground and shot his grandfather a glare at his color commentary.

Pop smiled complacently back at him.

From the pitcher's mound, I laughed out loud.

"Just throw the damn ball, pitcher!" Flynn called. "I feel myself aging over here. FYI, this is not what they mean by a slow ball!"

From second base, Alden Honeycutt hooted.

"You're not gonna score on me, Honeycutt," I yelled, loud enough to carry. "Doesn't matter how fast or slow I go."

"I've already scored on you, Frog. Several times, in fact." Flynn's grin was a feral, gorgeous thing, entirely inappropriate for an occasion when I was wearing tight softball pants, damn it.

"Nuh-uh," my teenage cousin Nadia yelled from the stands. "You only scored one run. The score's 3-1, Flynn!"

Flynn's grin widened as he shifted his stance beside the plate. He and I both knew he wasn't talking about the game.

"I'm trying to decide how I wanna pitch it to you," I called, pursing my lips. "Fast or slow? Faaaast? Or slooooow."

Flynn huffed impatiently. He knew I wasn't talking about the game either. "If you don't decide real quick, I'm gonna come over there and pitch it to *you*. Hard."

I bit my lip. "I might let you."

"Pretty sure that's not how innings work, though, is it?" Castor called from third base. "You can't just—"

"I know, Cas!" Flynn said impatiently. I snorted, and Flynn's hot gaze flew back to mine.

"I think this is a delay of game," he shouted. "Ref? Ref! Is this a delay of game?"

Pop grabbed his mic and wrinkled his nose. "How the heck should I know? Just move it along, Frog."

"But Flynn!" I clasped a hand to my chest and smiled sunnily. "I thought you liked it when I... delayed your game. Makes it more fun for everyone that way."

"More fun for you," Flynn shot back. "Pitch the dang—"

I wound up and threw the ball unexpectedly, landing it square in the middle of Marta's glove.

"Strike three," Pop called sadly. "That's all she wrote!"

Flynn closed his eyes and grimaced as the Wellbridge dugout went wild.

"That's our Frog!" my cousin Marta yelled, straightening up and pulling off her mask.

A few other spectators took up the chant. "That's our Frog! That's our Frog!"

I shook my head and grinned as I jogged over to home plate.

"Oooh," I taunted in a low voice. "Looks like your bat just couldn't get a piece of my ball today, baby! Looks like Firecracker's... fizzled. Whomp, whomp." I rocked back and forth on the balls of my feet smugly.

Flynn ran his tongue over his teeth and glanced up at me. His hair was a damp mess that curled against his neck and forehead where it peeked out of his ballcap, his cheeks were covered in dark scruff, and his orange T-shirt was molded to his lean muscles with a combination of sweat and dirt.

In short, he was the sexiest man who'd ever lived, and I wanted to throw him down right there and kiss him until the entire town understood our double entendres.

"You cheated," he said in his deep voice.

"*Moi*? I did exactly what you asked me to do," I said innocently. "You said—"

"I know what I said," Flynn interrupted. His eyes flashed a gorgeous, dangerous bright green. "You have exactly thirty seconds to say goodbye to everyone in your family."

"Oooh. Threats? You gonna kill me, slugger?" I arched an eyebrow. "Ditch my body where they'll never find it?"

"Nothing that easy." He stepped closer, getting all up in

my personal space, mashing his Honeycutt T-shirt right against my Wellbridge one. "I am going to get my bat all over your balls and delay your game until you're begging me to pitch. There will be absolutely no fizzling until we have done every single thing I texted you earlier."

"We have work to do tonight," I reminded him.

He gritted out a single word. "After." Then he shoved me away from him with two hands. "Fifteen seconds now, Frog."

I swallowed my smile and ran off to say my goodbyes, thinking Bossy Flynn might be my favorite Flynn.

Later that night as I lay in his loft bed staring up at the rafters through the darkness, with Flynn's head on my shoulder and my hand threaded through his overlong hair, my entire body thrumming with the aftereffects of our mind-blowing lovemaking, I thought that this—being with Flynn—was the real win of the day. And I was going to figure out a way to keep it.

But as I found out the following week, there were certain circumstances even a Wellbridge couldn't control.

Chapter Fourteen

Flynn

The days were flying by. As busy as the Tavern was with tourist season in full swing and as crazy as I was prepping for Brew Fest, it was actually a good thing JT wasn't around during the week. If he'd stayed in Honeybridge instead of going back to the city, I probably would have let him distract me right into bankruptcy.

The man didn't realize what a compelling argument against work he made when he was standing naked in my home, asking if he could suck me off. Or rim me. Or fuck me hard over the kitchen counter.

"Blue caps, Flynn, Jesus," Dan said before muttering, "And you think I'm the one not paying attention?"

I blinked down at the bottles in front of me. Sure enough, I'd put the wrong caps on nine bottles already. I cursed and reached for the bottle opener so I could start over.

"Why are you rushing?" Dan asked. "The dinner crowd won't pick up for another hour, and we've already gotten a ton of prep done today. The T-shirts are packed and ready. The extra brochures should be here Monday. And I've already confirmed the truck rental for Tuesday."

"Yeah, but JT is coming in tonight, and I don't want to be stuck finishing this later." I began placing the proper caps on the Moose Call bottles. "I have some business stuff I want to run by him tomorrow. Thatcher Pennington is back in town for a long weekend, and he stopped by to talk to me about investing—" I broke off with a headshake, not wanting to dwell on the exciting possibilities just yet. "Doesn't matter. If I can get this batch done before JT gets here, I won't feel so guilty for taking a few hours off."

Dan turned to me, resting his hip against the workbench and crossing his arms in front of his chest. "Flynn... Are you sure you know what you're doing?"

I glanced up at him. "No. I'm never sure I know what I'm doing. You think I shouldn't take time off tomorrow? You're probably right. That Red Hat tour group is coming in for lunch." I stuck another cap in the bench capper.

"That's not what I mean. When JT Wellbridge first came to town, you hated him. He tried to get you to sign distribution rights over to his company, and as soon as you said no, he started wooing you. Suddenly, you like him. Now, he's taking all of your attention during your busy season. You clock out early on Friday and Saturday nights. You're rushing Brew Fest prep because of him. You're gonna ask him for business advice. I find it suspicious, that's all. I'm worried."

I opened my mouth to argue with him, to tell him he was wrong about JT, but then his words sank in. "You think he's only hooking up with me to get me to sign a distribution deal?" I let out a laugh, but it sounded strained, even to my own ears.

Dan's fingers ran through his short hair. "No. Not exactly."

"Good, because that's pretty fucking insulting to both him and me. Besides, he accepted it when I declined the

Fortress deal. He hasn't brought it up the whole time we've been... hanging out together."

"Someone nicknamed the Rainmaker doesn't give up, Flynn. If you ask me, he's biding his time before trying again or coming at it from another angle. I'm not saying he doesn't want you. Maybe he wants you *and* the deal, but a guy like that definitely still wants the deal."

I wondered if this was Dan's jealousy talking. He'd made flirtatious comments to me a couple of times earlier in the summer, before JT started spending so much time here and it became an unstated fact that we were... hanging out. Dan had toned it down a little since but hadn't stopped completely, and I got the feeling he was biding his time until JT left town. But was he upset enough about it to think the worst of JT?

"Well, he knows he's not getting it," I said. "When I said no to the Fortress deal, I meant it."

"What happens if he sabotages Brew Fest?"

"He wouldn't do that," I snapped, almost slicing my hand open on one of the bottle cap edges. "He knows how important this is to me. Besides, he's been helping with prep." I carefully placed the bottle cap in the bench capper and moved my hands out of the way before grabbing the handle and pulling it down.

"He dropped that case of mead the other day, Flynn."

My pulse sped up just from the memory of it. Each case of mead was like precious golden nuggets right now as we hoarded as many bottles as possible. Thankfully, none of the bottles had broken in the fall, and JT had been more upset than anyone.

"It could have been any one of us," I muttered. "And one case would hardly sabotage the whole event."

Dan moved closer and lowered his voice. "Look, I didn't bring this up to upset you. I just want you to be careful.

There's a ton of pressure on you from all angles. You're exhausted. You're running yourself ragged because of this guy, and something's going to eventually have to give. And I don't want to see you also dealing with heartbreak when JT goes back to his real life in a couple of weeks."

A tight ball thickened in my throat. "I hear you. But that's why this is only a summer fling. We both made it clear from the beginning it's nothing serious."

This was the biggest joke ever, considering my feelings for JT were as serious as a heart attack... the heart attack I was getting ready to have right now since Dan had pointed out there were only a few weeks left of summer, and one of them would be spent at Brew Fest. JT's and my season together had dwindled to mere weeks.

I'd been doing pretty well at sticking to the promise I'd made myself in Ogunquit. I wasn't dwelling on the past, and I hadn't let myself overthink the future. I was living in the moment, storing up all of JT's funny texts and every night of hot-as-fuck phone sex like a squirrel preparing for winter.

But I'd be lying if I said I hadn't started scowling at my phone recently for having the gall to display the date in bright lights every time I turned it on or that I hadn't caught myself staring at a supplier invoice earlier that morning and thinking, "Due August 26th. Will JT be here then?"

Yet every time I tried to dream up a casual way to convince JT to extend our time together—"*You see, Frog, when I said a summer fling, I meant astronomical summer, which doesn't end until late September*"—I ran up against a brick wall.

A couple of extra weeks wouldn't be enough. I was pretty sure no amount of time would be.

"Think about it," Dan said. "And in the meantime, you need to stop doing... whatever it is the two of you stay up all night doing and get some sleep instead." He raised a knowing eyebrow at me that made me blush beet red. "You leave for Brew Fest in a few days to start setting up, and then it's off to the races. You need to be in fighting shape for the media events Wednesday and Thursday." He ended his lecture with a smile that reminded me he truly was speaking out of his concern for me. Regardless of his romantic feelings, Dan knew me better than most people outside of my family and cared about my well-being.

"Thanks," I said. "You're a good friend."

I stopped what I was doing long enough to step over and give him a hug. He'd gone above and beyond to help me get things ready for the festival, and I didn't know what I would have done without his help.

Dan wrapped his arms around me and hugged me tighter—too tight. "Anytime, Flynn," he whispered.

Of course, that's when JT walked in.

"Oh, uh... want me to come back later?" he asked awkwardly. I saw right through that bullshit, though, since he had to have seen us hugging through the glass wall separating the tavern from the meadery.

I shot him a knowing look and stepped away from Dan. "No. I want you to come here and finish capping these bottles so I can finish payroll. As soon as I get it done, I'm free for the rest of the night. Cas is staying to cover for me."

I didn't miss Dan's disappointed sigh.

I didn't miss JT's resigned one either, but this was stuff that needed to get done before I could take off for the day. I batted my lashes at him and said in a low voice, "I'll make it worth your while."

"Yeah, you will," he growled just as softly. He walked over to the work sink in the back of the room to wash his hands and called over his shoulder, "I'm anticipating the best annual review *ever*."

I snorted.

When Dan finished building the last of the carrier boxes and made his way out to the Tavern to finish up the dinner rush, I walked over to JT at the sink and wrapped my arms around him from behind, burying my face into his collar to inhale his scent. At some point, his expensive cologne had stopped smelling so exotic and *other*. Now it just smelled like comfort. Like rest. "Hi."

He turned around and grabbed my face with his wet hands before kissing me hard and fast. "Fuck, I missed your face," he growled against my lips before kissing me some more.

We low-key made out in the corner of the Meadery until I remembered people could see us if they looked closely enough. I pulled back and adjusted myself as discreetly as possible. "That's enough of that," I croaked before blowing out a breath and shaking my head. "God, you're dangerous to my equilibrium."

He grinned before turning back to the sink and washing his hands again. "Go finish your payroll, Firecracker. It's going to take me three minutes to finish capping these bad boys, and then your ass is mine. Literally."

"*Mpfh*," I grumbled, walking out of the Meadery toward my office without looking back. JT Wellbridge was dangerously good-looking, and I knew if I caught another peek of him, I'd pop wood right there in the bar.

I didn't know how, after a lifetime of knowing the man, I could still be surprised by the overpowering want I felt whenever he was near me, but there I was. He made me stupidly horny just by existing.

When I sat at my desk, I had a hard time concentrating on the payroll for reasons that had nothing to do with the sexy frog in my meadery. Two servers came in to ask various questions about the schedule or notify me of swapping shifts, and Kendall needed to make a last-minute change to the weekend menu due to some supplier shortages. By the time I actually submitted my files for processing, it was after six, and JT had brought two plates of burgers and fries into the office.

As we ate, JT told me about the highs of his week—signing a new craft brew label out of Rhode Island and pitching a new winery in Oregon—and the lows—helping the marketing team prepare for Brew Fest.

"I thought you'd like that part," I said, dragging a fry through some of Kendall's spicy ketchup. "Meeting the potential new clients, chatting them up, figuring out what they want and what it'll take to make them sign on the dotted line."

He swiped at some burger sauce on his chin and scowled. "You make me sound like a used car dealer."

"Do I?" I asked, startled. "I don't mean to at all. But you said you liked the challenge of it. Figuring out what people want and how you can connect them to it. And you're good at it, Rainmaker."

"Yeah, not so much recently." He threw his napkin on my desk. "The Operations team is taking forever to approve this contract I want to offer. And I had to help a coworker attempt to save a deal that went south because Jeff Namath is a greedy fucker who made the whole company look bad."

I had no idea who he was talking about, but the disgust in his voice was palpable. I winced. "Did it work?"

He made a seesaw motion with his hand. "The offer is better now. More equitable. It *might* have improved Harrison Yang's opinion of our company..." He shook his head. "But I don't know if the deal is right for him anymore, which sucks." He ran both hands into his perfect hair—which wasn't so perfect anymore since he hadn't made time to visit his fancy New York salon in a few weeks—and scrubbed hard, disordering the strands. "Sorry. I don't mean to take it out on you. It's just... a lot of work. I have two smaller clients who'll be at the festival, and I'll need to spend a lot of time at their booths. But Conrad—my boss—he wants me spending the bulk of my time with Phillip's Cider, making sure they're happy, but also walking around prospecting and closing new deals. Alice is trying to organize a schedule for me, but it's proving difficult."

"Is he going to be there? Conrad, I mean." I wondered whether I'd get to meet him.

JT made a huffing sound and shook his head. "No. That's not his job. His job is to throw up as many roadblocks as possible and make it impossible to do mine."

"Whoa." I'd never heard JT talk about his dream job that way before.

As he spoke, I began to notice traces of sleep deprivation on JT's handsome face. He'd begun to lose the golden tan he'd gotten earlier in the summer since he'd started commuting back to the city last week, and his eyes had smudges of darkness underneath them. He looked like I felt.

I stood up and stacked our plates before grabbing his hand. "Come on." I led him into the kitchen, where I thanked Kendall and deposited our dirty dishes. As soon as we left through the back door, I noticed the lights in my tiny house were on.

"I put my bag in the house already," JT explained. "Hope that's okay."

"How did you know what the code was to the door?"

His laughter rang out in the evening air, making me feel a warm, buzzy feeling in my chest. "I didn't. But I guessed and got lucky."

My face flooded with heat. "Asshole," I muttered.

"3-7-6-4," he recited in a sing-song voice. "Know what those numbers spell out on a phone keypad?"

"Shut it," I warned.

"F-R-O-G!" He skipped ahead of me and turned back, shaking his hips and wagging his finger.

"That's a coincidence," I lied.

"No, it's not. It's because you're obsessed with me. Admit it! You think about me all the time."

"If I do, they're terrible, hateful thoughts," I muttered. "Because you're annoying as fuck. And where the hell did you get enough energy to do the Dance of Smugness when a minute ago you were asleep on your—*oof*! Hey!"

JT grabbed my hand and twirled me in a circle before reeling me back in so our chests were pressed together. "I'm not sure," he whispered, keeping my arm pinned behind me. "But I think it's you."

"What?" Staring up at his eyes made me feel drunk.

"Being with you," he explained. "When you're near me, I feel... alive. I keep wondering if it always felt this way and I just never noticed. Weird, right?"

Since I'd just had a similar thought about him, I shook my head fiercely. "Not weird."

JT pressed a soft kiss to my lips, then danced us in a slow circle right there in the parking lot. The setting sun was warm on his skin, reminding me of the candlelight on his face that night in Ogunquit. And with each unhurried moment we spent swaying in the sunshine, he seemed to drop more of the stress from his workweek. His smile widened, and his eyes lit up. He teased me with made-up songs about frogs as he spun me around and tangoed me across the pavement to the front door of my little house.

Had there ever been a summer night more magical than this? This short three-minute commute from work to home with JT Wellbridge singing and dancing for me? I wasn't sure. I wanted to capture it like lightning bugs in a bottle the way Alden and Georgia and I used to do for McLean.

When we stumbled into the house and closed the door behind us, JT pulled me into an embrace and kissed me before I could give him hell for his horrible singing voice.

It took half a second before I'd forgotten about anything other than his lips on mine and the sharp press of his beard on my chin and neck. His hands grabbed my ass and kneaded it.

"Fuck, I missed you," he groaned. "Needed this. Needed you."

With JT's hands all over me and the pressure of his hard dick against my hip, I got a second wind, too. I pulled off his tie and began unbuttoning his shirt. "You wear a suit well, Rainmaker," I teased, dropping kisses at the base of his throat as I uncovered the skin there.

"Don't call me that," he grumbled. "Isn't there something better you could be doing with your mouth than teasing me?"

"Never," I said with a laugh. My phone buzzed in my pocket, but I ignored it. "Teasing you is one of my favorite things to do."

"I smell like an airplane," he said as I nuzzled into the center of his newly bared chest. I loved that spot on him.

"Maybe a little but not for long."

My phone stopped buzzing and started up again. JT sighed and stepped back. "See who's lighting you up. I'm going to take a quick shower."

I groaned and reached for the phone. "I fucking hate being a business owner sometimes."

It was Dan.

"Hey, man, sorry to do this, but Cas got sick and had to go home. We're slammed over here. I tried everyone else, but no luck."

I glanced at the open door to the bathroom, where JT had just exposed his bare white ass. I wanted to eat it. I did not want to work a Friday night shift in a very busy tavern.

"Fuck."

"I'm sorry," he said, sounding sincere. "I even called Alden to see if he'd come in, but he's up in Bar Harbor helping out at a client's wedding this weekend."

"Yeah, fine. Not your fault. Be there in five." I hung up and called Castor.

"I'm *so* sorry, Flynn," he answered in a rough voice. "My stomach is a mess. I had some sketchy leftovers for lunch, I think."

"Oh, hon. I'm sorry. Do you need anything? JT is here and can bring you anything you need. Saltines or Gatorade?"

"God, no. No, thanks. I have some stuff here, but I'm a long way away from being able to stomach anything. I think I'm just going to rest."

I ran a hand through my hair and looked around, wondering if JT would want to hang out here and wait for me or if he'd choose to head to his parents' house instead. "Well, just call or text if you need anything, and take it easy."

"Sorry again, Flynn. I know you wanted to spend some time with JT tonight."

"It's fine. Don't worry about it. Shit happens, okay?"

When I ended the call, JT was done with his quick shower, and he appeared in the doorway in nothing but a towel. I gritted my teeth and tried not to scream in frustration.

"What's going on?" he asked, using another towel to dry his hair. His chest dripped with water, and his muscles flexed as he moved. My dick started crying out in protest.

"I have to work tonight. Cas is sick, and no one else can cover for him."

"Shit, babe. Is he okay? Does he need me to do anything?"

I walked over and wrapped my arms around JT, tucking my face into his clean neck for just a second of comfort. "No, but thank you. I'm sorry about this."

JT squeezed me and then stepped back. "It's okay. I have some work I can finish. I ducked out early and didn't get everything done I was supposed to. It's fine."

I met his eyes. "Are you... can you...?" I looked around the tiny house as if my dignity was anywhere nearby.

"Spit it out, Firecracker."

"Do you want to work here? Or... or you can work in my office at the Tavern if you want? I mean... unless you wanted to head back to your parents' house, which is totally fine. Better, probably. Less distracting." I bit my lip to shut myself up.

Suddenly, JT's lips tightened like he was holding back a grin. "You're not getting rid of me that easily, Honeycutt. I'm staying here. I don't care how late you come home, I'll be naked and ready."

I blew out a breath and ducked my head. "Yeah, good. Okay. Yeah."

JT grabbed my chin and forced my head up to meet his eyes. "I know your business comes first, Flynn. And that's okay. Don't worry about me. I'm a big boy."

I reached down and stroked his dick through the towel. "Braggart."

When I turned and walked out of the house, he was still laughing. I entered the back door of the Tavern with a big goofy smile on my face.

And he was right. When I came shuffling back to the house after midnight, JT Wellbridge was naked and ready.

But I wasn't.

I was beyond exhausted. My feet hurt, my legs hurt, my

entire body smelled like spilled beer and fried food, and I had the beginnings of a headache.

"You look like ass," he said as soon as he saw me.

"You silver-tongued devil," I muttered, kicking off my shoes and yanking at my filthy clothes. JT stood up from the small sofa where he'd been lounging under a soft throw, watching videos on his computer. He helped me take off my clothes and then led me to the shower. "You're already clean," I said stupidly when he took off his own clothes and joined me under the hot spray.

"Mm-hm. But you're filthy. You'll sleep better after a shower."

"Was gonna bang you," I said, leaning into the warm strength of his body. "Bang you so hard."

"Well, when you put it so seductively..." I felt the vibration of his chuckle. "Rain check."

"Sorry."

"Nope. No sorries. Besides, I had a few guys swing by for an orgy earlier, so I'm good for now."

I barely had the energy for a laugh. JT's hands felt amazing on my body as he washed every inch of me. His touch lulled me into a kind of trance.

"Castor doing okay?" he asked.

"Yeah. He was feeling a bit better when I talked to him an hour ago. But I told him he could take tomorrow off, too, if he needed."

"Hmm. Probably good. Sucks since you need all hands on deck this week. Tough being a brother and a business owner at the same time, huh?"

"Mmm." My head lolled on my shoulders. "Sometimes, I wonder if I'm doing the right thing," I confessed in a low voice.

"How do you mean?"

I hesitated, but I was too tired to measure my words,

and they all came tumbling out. "I worry that Cas should be pursuing something bigger and better than working an hourly job as a server at a restaurant. And PJ... I haven't heard from him in weeks other than one-word answers to my texts asking how he's doing. Is that normal? Was I right to send him to Boston alone? And McLean... now that my parents are gone, he's all alone out at the Retreat having to deal with the guests by himself during the busy season. I haven't had time to help at all this week. What if it's too much for him? Too much people time? If I didn't have the Tavern, I could help them all more, except..."

"Except you couldn't because there'd be no money," he finished gently.

"Yeah."

He poured shampoo into his hand and began massaging my scalp. I let out a groan of satisfaction.

"Flynn, you're talking about adults. They need to find their own way. I'm not suggesting you stop supporting them, but you have to let them make their own choices and learn their own lessons."

"It's hard." I leaned into him and wrapped my arms around him. JT widened his stance to keep us steady and then moved me under the water to rinse the shampoo off. Suds ran down his chest to his thighs. I watched the bubbles move over the curves of his leg muscles and down to the tile floor.

Simply being here like this with him was a gift in so many ways. A gift so precious, I was scared to think too closely about it for fear it would wash away completely like the soap suds.

JT made a sound of agreement that rumbled through his chest. "Yeah. I'm sure it is. But you're giving them a firm foundation, and your commitment to the Tavern and Meadery helps them know your family will always have a home here in Honeybridge regardless of what happens with your parents' place."

"I guess." Thankfully, my parents' property—the center, artists' retreat, and campground—was owned free and clear and held in trust. It had been passed down in the Honeycutt family for generations. Even if they fucked it up, the land was still ours.

"I understand, though," JT said. "I sometimes worry if I've made the right call, too."

"You?" I snorted tiredly. "You've got your shit together. Kicking ass in New York. Confident in your path, and you're ticking off milestones along the way. It must feel good."

He didn't answer for a moment, long enough that I looked up to see his expression.

"Not always so confident. I feel a lot of family pressure, too, just in a different way. Your parents left you alone too much, too young. Mine have never left me alone, no matter how old I've gotten. I had to leave town to escape from their expectations, or who knows what I'd have become. Probably Patricia Junior, winner of the Box Day competition," he said dryly.

I chuckled a little. He was joking, but I knew that humor covered a serious truth. "Bold of you to think you'd have beaten me."

"Oh reeeeally." His fingers dug into my aching muscles, smoothing away tension, and my eyes slid shut. "You're saying that if I'd competed in Box Day, you'd have competed too?"

"Obviously. And won or died trying. But it's always been that way with us, hasn't it?" That was a truth, too, and if I'd been more awake, I'd have shut myself up, but I was so tired and comfortable I kept talking. "Someone recently told me that you and I have always been *tight*, even if we weren't friends, and I think maybe that's right. We were like... whajamacallit? Magnets." I yawned. "Action and reaction."

"That's chemistry, baby. Magnets are about attraction and repulsion."

I laughed. "There you go. We've always had that, too, haven't we?"

"We have." JT's fingers tightened on my skin. "I sometimes wonder if the path I'm on is the one I'd have taken if I'd been left to my own devices."

My eyes opened in surprise. JT, the smart and social, energetic and focused heir to the Wellbridge throne, with his killer education and contacts and hotshot career, was questioning his path?

"What else do you think you might have done? It's not too late. You could still become a male model or porn star. You'd be great at it."

His dancing eyes were framed with wet, spiky lashes. "Good to know. I'll pencil that in as a backup plan."

I ran a hand up his chest. "Sorry, I didn't mean to joke about it. I really do want to know what your dream job would be if you weren't at Fortress."

JT turned off the water and moved me aside to grab a towel from the nearby hook. "I dunno. I wanted to play baseball, I guess. But you knew that."

That didn't make any sense. I knew he loved playing, but he hadn't pursued it seriously at all. "But you quit the team after sophomore year of high school."

"Sure." He began drying me with the towel. "Because my mother said I needed volunteer hours for my college applications and a trip abroad every spring break. You can't play baseball if you're out of the country during spring break."

"Your mother. Honestly." There had never been any love lost between me and Patricia Wellbridge, but hearing this story made me imagine committing an act of violence on the woman. "Mpfh."

JT laughed softly while he moved the towel up to my hair. It felt good to be cared for this way. "I appreciate the homicidal expression on your face, Firecracker, but my mother's not *that* bad. She wants me to be happy..." He gave me a half-smile. "She just thinks she knows what will make me happy better than I do." He smoothed the towel over my forehead and kissed each of my eyebrows in turn. "Since she was the one who gave Conrad the idea of sending me to Honeybridge this summer, though, I suppose she's right occasionally."

He pressed a kiss to my lips, and I sighed dreamily. Okay, fine. For bringing JT home, I'd give Patricia a mother point or two. Maybe two and a half. But... "I'm not okay with her canceling your baseball dream."

"She didn't, baby. I was the one who made the final decision. I read about a first-round draft pick for the Astros who experienced a career-ending injury in his second major league game and ended up working for his cousin's landscaping business cutting grass." JT shrugged. "That was all it took for me to nope out of playing professionally. I knew I never wanted to rely on my parents or my trust fund for money. And I didn't want to be too far away from them either."

"Yeah, right. You wanted to stick close, but you've barely been home these last several years?" I took the towel from him and used it to dry his own body. "Why?"

JT's eyes bored into mine, but he kept his mouth shut. It took me a while to realize what he wasn't saying. "Because of me?" I gasped. "Because of that night after Grandpa Horace died?"

He sighed and grabbed the towel from me to finish drying himself. "Partly, yeah. To get away from my mother's meddling, also, but... Yes, a lot of it was because of that night." He gripped the towel tightly, and his eyes met mine. "I fucked up, and I didn't know how to fix it, so I just... let it go. I told myself it was better if I stayed away. It was selfish, and I'm sorry."

I shook my head and lifted a hand to his mouth to shush him. "You've already tried apologizing for that, remember? And I didn't accept. *No sorries*," I quoted his words from earlier. I cleared my throat. "Now, tell me more about baseball. Because you in those pants could be a—"

"Don't do that," JT pleaded. "Not now. Talk to me. Or if you can't do that, *listen*. When I left you that night, Flynn, I felt awful. I'd gone to Horace's funeral that morning, and I'd seen you standing at his graveside looking so gorgeous and strong and *alone* despite being surrounded by so many people. All I'd wanted, I swear, was to come over that night and tell you how sorry I was for your loss. Because maybe we *were* like magnets or whatever, but all I knew was that when *you* hurt, *I* hurt too."

I shut my eyes, but that didn't block out his words.

"And then we had a drink. Two. Castor locked up, but you and I stayed, and I was *giddy* because you were letting me be with you." He swallowed hard. "That Billy Joel song came on, and I don't know how we started kissing, but it was like every fantasy I'd ever had was finally coming true. I didn't stop and think about where you were emotionally." He shook his head. "I didn't stop to think about the fact that you'd never have been with me that way if you were in your right mind, since you didn't actually like me or trust me—"

"I liked you!" I broke off with a wince. "Okay, maybe I hated you a little, too..."

"Right. And then we were together, and it was... it was..." He shrugged. "Fucking phenomenal. The best I've ever had. Just like every time with you is, you know?"

My eyes widened. No, it was safe to say I didn't know that he felt that way.

"And then I had to leave. To go back to the city. And..."

"And I pushed you away," I croaked. "Because I wished you could stay *so badly*... and I knew you couldn't." I gave him a shaky smile. "Because you were building a career in New York. And I needed to stay in Honeybridge."

The world had turned a thousand times since then, and here we were... right back in essentially the same spot. But maybe there were some things I could do better this time.

"I didn't blame you, Jon. Not for what happened that night and not for leaving. But it was easier, I guess, to be angry about it than to admit the shitty, boring truth. That we weren't right for each other because we needed different things out of life."

JT crushed me against him, and I returned the hug, clinging to him a little desperately.

"I don't ever want you to think you took advantage of me," I whispered, "because you didn't. I chose you. I wanted you. I'd wanted you for a long, long time," I admitted.

"Really?" He pulled my hand away from his mouth and stared at me, almost in disbelief. "How long?"

I huffed out a laugh and tried to pull away, embarrassed despite all my earlier confessions. "Jesus, Frog, I don't know. Since high school at least." Longer. It had been longer. "I mean, I did agree to go on a date with you at one time, remember? Even though you stood me up." I fought to make the words light and not bitter. Like that I didn't still physically cringe at the memory of that night.

"Uh." JT shook his head but wouldn't let me free my hand. "Flynn, that never happened."

My stomach tightened. *Don't be a fool*, I warned myself. *Don't ruin this beautiful moment because you need to prove a point about the most traumatizing experience of your high school years.*

"Actually." I sniffed and made myself laugh lightly. "It did. You probably don't remember—"

"I remember that it took me *months* to work up the courage to ask you out. You were so damn gorgeous and funny, the best person to compete against because you always gave a thousand percent at everything, just like me. So I asked you to hang out with me at the lake to look at the stars, like the world's sappiest idiot. I made it my personal mission to get you to say yes."

"And I did," I reminded him hotly.

"Yep. But then you left me standing by the boathouse at the marina, holding an industrial-sized pack of your favorite Cocoa-Caramel Bits, for *hours*. Even though it was February, and it started to—"

"Snow!" I whispered, my breath coming faster. "I remember it distinctly. Because I was standing outside, by the *boats at my house*. You know, the kayaks *everyone* used to use when we rowed to Milk Bottle Island!" I slapped his chest lightly. "What the actual fuck, JT? Why would you think I'd meet you at the marina, like I was a damn Wellbridge with a racing sailboat?"

"Me?" His jaw dropped. "How is this *my* fault? I said *boathouse*, not kayak shed. Besides, no one in the world says *boat at your house* all fast together like that. And why would you think I'd drive out to the Retreat when you know your brothers would have hounded me as soon as they saw my car?"

Now that he mentioned it, I felt a little bit foolish. Why had it never occurred to me that he meant the freaking boathouse? Why hadn't I called him and yelled at him? Why hadn't I asked him to explain or even demanded an apology?

Because I'd spent thirty-two years knowing this guy had the capacity to break my heart, and even now, it was hard to believe he wouldn't. Because retreating from hurt and pretending I was unaffected was my best and only defense mechanism.

I stared at JT as my throat got tighter and tighter, and stupid tears pricked the backs of my eyes. I'd been so damn wrong, so damn often, that the magnitude of it overwhelmed me. But I couldn't find the words to get us past this, to explain in a way that would make him understand and make us *okay* again, without getting into a deep, emotional conversation that I couldn't handle at that moment.

I was literally swaying on my feet from fatigue, and this conversation had sapped the very last bits of my energy.

JT watched me carefully, and his eyes softened a second before he dragged me toward him and buried his face in my hair.

Do not pity me, I wanted to warn him, feeling my hackles rise. *Do not apologize again for something that was my damn fault as much as yours—*

"I had no mittens," he whispered mournfully.

"W-what?" That was the absolute last thing I'd expected to come out of his mouth.

"No mittens. I was like one of those bedraggled Oliver Twist orphans... but, you know, dressed in an L.L.Bean parka instead of rags and carrying a giant bag of candy instead of a bowl of gruel."

The image was so absurd that I snort-giggled. "You poor thing. I stood outside so long Willow was convinced I'd developed an interest in astrology. She made me read a book about the impact of planetary bodies on our chakras and drink epic quantities of hawthorn berry tea to realign my Anahata."

I felt his nod. "I had to eat the candy," he whispered in that same sad voice. "Just to survive."

My whole body shook with laughter. "You ate my candy?" I demanded. "The candy you brought for *me*? You're such a fucking Wellbridge."

Then JT was laughing, too, his arms tightening to hold me against him as we both doubled over at our utter ridiculousness. And suddenly, we *were* okay. More okay than before. Because JT was a good man—a man who knew when I needed to be held, and when I needed to be held down, when I needed tender truths and when I needed teasing.

In short, JT Wellbridge knew me better than I ever would have believed.

Which meant I was more screwed than I'd ever dreamed.

I ended the embrace quickly and stepped back to press a kiss to his cheek. "Thank you for that. For being... you."

"Baby," he began softly.

"Not now." I shook my head. "I can't anymore. Let's go to bed, okay? Nothing's gonna change tonight."

He nodded, and we moved together to the sink, where we brushed our teeth shoulder to shoulder in the tiny space. It wasn't until we'd made our way up to the loft and slid into bed with my head pillowed on JT's lightly furred chest that he spoke again.

"I had feelings for you back in high school, Firecracker. I had feelings for you three years ago. I have feelings for you now."

The admission was sweetly painful. It was good to know that I wasn't alone. Terrible to know that, just as I'd predicted back in Ogunquit, this disaster would end up hurting us both.

JT ran a finger over the crown tattoo on his wrist, tightening his arm around me with the movement. I'd noticed him doing that before when he was upset about something.

"Tell me about your tattoo," I said, trying to change the subject to something less devastating, less likely to tear my heart to pieces later.

He let out a huff of warm air against my forehead. "You asking for proof of my feelings for you?"

I propped myself up on my elbow to look at him. "What does your tattoo have to do with your feelings for me?"

He looked back down at the crown, bold and masculine. Permanent.

JT's long finger traced it on his skin. "This is you."

I grabbed his wrist and looked more closely at the tattoo, as if the design alone held an explanation. "I don't understand."

He tilted my chin up until our eyes met. The edge of his lip was curved with a kind of knowing that made my heart expand. "For years, you told me you were the king of the lake." He shrugged. "So I gave you a crown."

My world tilted on its axis until I felt like I would faint right there in my bed. No longer was it exhaustion pulling me down but the sheer heavy knowledge that I'd found my person. The man I wanted most in the world, the one who'd carried me with him for years on his very skin.

"But we can't... I mean you... I... it can't work... right?" My lips felt numb, and my fingers tingled.

JT blew out a breath. "I've been thinking on this for weeks, it feels like. There are parts of my job that are driving me crazy, like I told you before... but there are parts of it that I really like. It's part of my identity. I don't want to give all of that up."

I swallowed. "I would never ask you to. I feel the same about my business."

"I can't work remotely, and neither can you. And I've

thought about coming back here for the weekends, even though it's less than ideal..."

"But...?" I prompted.

"But I'm not going to lie. That commute would kill me. I can't imagine doing it every weekend. And the weekends are your busiest time anyway. So I don't know what the solution is yet. But I'm going to find one," he said firmly. "Trust me."

"Sure." I wanted to believe him. But evidence was not on our side.

"Let's just get through Brew Fest, then worry about it."

I made a sound of agreement, though I didn't agree at all. And if he thought I could simply not worry about it until after Brew Fest, he didn't know me very well.

In fact—I yawned hugely—I was probably going to stay up all night worrying about it.

But I turned out to be wrong because with JT's arms around me and the low, steady thump of his heart in my ear, I dropped to sleep in seconds... not knowing it was the last good night's sleep I'd get for a while.

Chapter Fifteen

JT

If you'd asked me Saturday morning whether I could possibly dislike any part of my weekend with Flynn, I'd have laughed out loud. How could I?

I'd woken at dawn, hard as a stone, with a sleepy, sweet Firecracker still cradled in my arms in the exact spot where he'd fallen asleep, as though neither of us had wanted to move even a millimeter apart in the night. When I'd pressed a soft kiss to his head, Flynn had woken immediately. He'd lifted his head to smile down at me, and then, without a word or a sound, we'd rolled over simultaneously so that Flynn was beneath me. We'd kissed and frotted lazily until we'd both climaxed, and Flynn's "Good morning" had been a breathy, satisfied groan as our heart rates returned to normal.

I'd spent years wishing the man would open up to me, and he finally had. I'd wanted nothing more than to feel like he and I were on the same page for once, and we finally were.

Nothing could kill my buzz.

By the midpoint of the Tavern's lunch rush that day, though, I was beyond exhausted and frustrated as fuck.

Flynn and I were on the same page, yeah, but neither of us could figure out how to turn it or what was supposed to happen next. And instead of cuddling Flynn or brainstorming solutions—ways to spend every other week in Honeybridge, maybe, or an apartment in Portland where Flynn and I could meet when our schedules aligned—I was pinch-hitting as a server at the Tavern because Amanda had come down with the same mystery bug Castor had caught the previous night, and I couldn't stand the idea of Flynn being even more overworked than he already was.

"JT? You good?" Dan demanded.

"Huh?" I blinked up from my thoughts. "Of course. Why?"

"Because I put the tray on the bar two minutes ago, and you're not delivering it." He nodded down at the bar top, where he'd placed a tray of chicken wings. "Brittany and Ciaran came for lunch, not dinner."

I scowled, though Dan was correct. And as I grabbed the tray and walked away, I heard him mutter, "Jesus. Alden wasn't kidding about the Wellbridge attitude."

Fucker.

It was obvious that Dan had a thing for Flynn, and he was jealous as hell. The guy barely knew me. He couldn't possibly know that I was worried and stressed that an invisible clock was ticking down while also feeling a little bit like an asshole with double standards because I was resentful that Flynn and I were going to be stuck working at *his* business all day instead of enjoying the weekend... when the whole reason we only had the weekend was because I needed to get back to New York on Monday for *my* business.

I did *not* have a Wellbridge attitude.

At all.

Still, I made a point of giving Brittany an overly bright smile as I set down their food. "Sorry for the delay. Enjoy!"

Wellbridge attitude? Fuck, no.

"Thanks, JT." Brittany popped a fry in her mouth, and her eyes rolled back. "God, the food here is so damn good."

"I'll pass that on to Kendall," I said in a chipper voice. "Will that be all?"

"Mmm. Actually, no." Brittany washed down her fry with mead and smiled brightly. "I had a question. What's it like working here?"

"Uh." I glanced around the room for someone else who could actually answer this, but when no one immediately came into view, I shrugged. "Nice, I guess. Flynn runs a tight ship."

She nodded. "He must if you left your New York job to work here full-time."

The bubble of startled laughter erupted from my mouth without conscious thought. "Me? Leave New York? No." I grinned. "Flynn and the guys are slammed preparing for a big event next weekend, and I figured I'd lend a hand while I'm home for the weekend, that's all. My actual job is working for a consumer products group specializing in beverage distribution, so it's not too far out of my wheelhouse, if you think about it. Helping out here has actually helped me understand my clients better."

"Oh." Brittany seemed bemused by my panic-babbling response. "No, that's cool. I was just wondering if Flynn was hiring." She shrugged. "I mean, *I* would *love* to work here."

"Right. Of course." I felt my cheeks go hot. "I'll ask him."

"Would you? Thanks! I gotta say, it's nice to have you back in town for a little while, at least. We missed you. And

I bet you missed us, too." She gave me a happy smile as she turned back to her food.

I clutched the tray against my chest like a shield and made my way through a throng of flirty tourists and back-slapping locals to the kitchen.

Brittany was right. I *had* missed Honeybridge. After just a couple of weeks, I'd come to realize that this town was much more than two camps at silent war. It was a diverse group of people with their own experiences and ideas. And those people—including Flynn—had been happy to make a place for me once I'd gotten my head out of my ass and stopped swanning from country club to garden party to marina like the entitled aristocrat my parents had raised me to be. I *could* be the new JT Wellbridge in my old town. I already was.

So why were you so defensive about Brittany thinking you worked at the Tavern?

The voice in my head sounded a lot like Flynn's, and the question was so unexpected that I froze in the doorway to the kitchen with the tray still in my hands.

There was nothing wrong with working at the Tavern. Obviously not. The place was gorgeous. The food was delicious. The mead was exceptional. And the boss was maybe the best man I'd ever known.

So why *had* Brittany's innocent comment made me defensive?

The answer hit me just as forcefully as the question had: because the lessons we learned from our parents were insidious. You could confront them, reject them, flee them, try to *kill them with fire*... and still, the roots remained buried deep.

And even at thirty-two, having long ago decided that I would make my own choices and be my own person... I'd gotten defensive because the son of Patricia Wellbridge and the Senator was supposed to be a high-powered executive at a major company, not a man who served at a *tavern* like one of *those Honeycutts*.

I *did* have a Wellbridge attitude. And it had been impairing my vision.

"JT?" Dan demanded irritably. "There a reason you're stuck in the middle of the swinging door? Pick a direction, buddy."

I nodded without really seeing him. The problem was that I didn't *want* to pick a direction. I wanted to be Frog, the Honeybridge native who enjoyed quiet mornings at the Retreat fishing with Pop Honeycutt, late nights at the Tavern kissing Flynn stupid behind the bar, and long, lazy backyard potlucks that became impromptu jam sessions with new and old friends. But I also wanted to be JT Wellbridge—the successful salesman who'd thumbed his nose at his parents' expectations, chosen his own life path, and gotten every bit as successful as his mother had wanted him to be... *without* her interference.

I didn't want to—*couldn't*—give up either of those things. And that was what my problem boiled down to, really.

"JT?" Dan said, irritation turning to anger when I still hadn't moved.

It was like the man didn't realize I was having important life revelations here.

"Yeah, sorry." I stepped aside, and Dan rolled his eyes before brushing past me.

After depositing the tray in the kitchen, I returned to the bar, hoping to steal Flynn away for a brief chat to help me process this... but Cas had taken over the bar while Flynn chatted with a table of tourists.

I was surprised to see Reagan sitting on one of the tall stools, nursing a lemonade.

"Hey," I said, moving close enough to talk over the bar without yelling. "I thought you were out at the lake with Brantleigh and that crew."

He shook his head glumly. "I left early. It's exhausting to be around people who are so shallow and immature."

I nodded. Until a couple of weeks ago, I'd have put Reagan in that category himself. Now I wondered why a guy who sometimes seemed so self-aware and insightful hung around with a revolving door of image-obsessed young socialites.

"Did something happen?" I wondered.

"Not really." He paused. "Or... kinda, yeah, I guess." He took a deep breath, and my stomach clenched, waiting to hear what kind of trouble Brantleigh and Dysen had gotten him into. "I got offered a job," he said in a rush. "Well, it's an internship, really, but it... well, it has potential."

"That... is not what I was expecting you to say. That's fucking amazing." I grinned hugely and leaned over the bar to give his shoulder a gentle shove. "Congratulations, bro."

"Yeah. It's... good." He sighed. "I'm excited. I think I might really like it."

"Yeah, you sound super excited." I snorted. "Like, shit, Rea, please try to keep the excessive celebrating down." I leaned my forearms on the bar. "What's the problem? Do you think Mother and Dad will give you shit over it? Because I know it's easier said than done, but you've gotta get over that. Stepping away from their expectations was the best thing I ever did."

Reagan shook his head glumly. "It's worse than that. I think they'll be *thrilled*." He wrinkled his nose. "Mother basically set this up. If I accept the internship, she's gonna gloat forever, and I'll never get her to stop interfering in my life."

"Ooooh." I winced. "I see. Yep. That's gonna suck. But

you can't turn your back on something amazing just because it might prove Mother right. That'd be just as bad as doing it because she wanted you to. You need to figure out how to not let them influence you at all, you know? Come up with your own definition of success and happiness, and— Oh."

I broke off midsentence and stared at Flynn as he approached the bar, shooting me a wink and a smile along the way.

"JT?" Reagan frowned. "Are you okay?"

"Yeah, no. I'm great." I ran a hand over my forehead. "Just... realizing I need to take my own stupid advice."

To define success and happiness *for myself*.

The simplest and most complicated idea ever.

"You gonna enlighten me?" Reagan prompted.

Before I could answer, the door to the Tavern burst open, and a new gaggle of people flowed in... led by the very assholes who'd gotten Reagan in his mood earlier.

"Omigosh! ReaBae and Jonny!" Dysen hurried over, holding out her phone triumphantly, with Brantleigh slinking behind her. "Check it! Rea, you left before the boat went over, but I caught it on video and put it on my TikTok. You *need* to see it. It's sick."

Reagan and I exchanged a horrified glance.

"The boat? As in, my father's 1938 Crosby catboat?" My palms began to sweat.

Brantleigh squinted his eyes. "I-D-K... the green one."

"*The Beetle Cat*," Reagan said quickly, shooting me a look meant to reassure me. He glanced at Dysen. "Tell me you righted it and baled the water out of it."

"Dude." Dysen threw up her hands. "I don't know what that means. But some asshole came buzzing over on a Jet Ski and made us swim to shore. I think he had people to fix the boat. It was lame, so we bounced."

I gritted my teeth, prepared to let loose on these disrespectful assholes, but before I could give them a piece of my mind and also kick Reagan's ass for leaving them unattended on our father's boat, Flynn came up beside me and laid a hand on my forearm.

"Take a breath," he said softly. "Not your circus, not your monkeys."

He was right. I didn't need to defend my parents' property. If they'd allowed Reagan's asshole friends on the boat, then the consequences were on them, not me.

"Thanks, baby," I said gratefully. "Hey, do you have time for a quick break? I wanted to talk to you about some crazy ideas I've been having."

Ideas that had me feeling truly hopeful we would find a way forward that worked for us both.

Ideas that blinded me to the reckoning that was approaching with all the speed and silent danger of a great white shark on the hunt.

Brantleigh came up behind Dysen and eyed Flynn's hand, then my face, which was probably stuck in some lovesick expression.

His cheeks flushed, and his expression immediately soured with jealous anger. "So, Flynn..." he said without preamble, in a fake-casual way that set my teeth on edge. "You must be really excited about Fortress's big investment in Honeybridge Mead, huh? Sounds like it could take you from—let's face it—practical *obscurity* to possibly being a recognizable name. Who'd you have to sleep with to get that sweet deal?"

What? No. No, no, no. This was *not* happening. Not now, when happiness felt like it was finally in reach.

My stomach dropped, and my ears began to ring. Everything slowed down around me. Brantleigh didn't—*couldn't*—know anything, I reminded myself, unless my mother had broken her promise...

Or he'd overheard us talking in the garden.

Fuck.

Flynn's face lost its smile, and his eyes lost their sparkle. "I declined their offer," he said with a forced grin. "Your information is out of date."

I opened my mouth to say something, to cut Brantleigh off before he could ruin everything, but he got there before I could.

"Hmm. That's not what JT said. He specifically said he wasn't gonna give up until he got you to sign, and Patricia agreed." Brantleigh gave a fake little gasp and covered his mouth with his fingertips. "Oh, noes! Did you not *realize*? Was JT keeping a *secret*? Tsk tsk tsk. JT claimed he *hated* secrets." He smirked. "Congrats on that promotion, by the way, JT. Patricia will be over the moon."

"I don't..." I looked from Flynn to Brantleigh to Reagan. "I haven't been promoted," I said hurriedly. I gave Brantleigh a look that should have singed the hair from his tiny Botoxed head. "What the *fuck?*"

Brantleigh shrugged. "Told you I don't handle rejection well," the asshole said with a wink.

I clenched my fingers into fists and glanced at Flynn in alarm. "Baby. It's not how he's making it sound. I can explain."

Flynn's eyes widened for one brief second before his expression turned to stone, telling me he hadn't necessarily believed Brantleigh's bullshit but that my own actions had given credence to them. *Fuck.*

"Flynn, let's talk in your office," I said. I could hear the thread of panic in my own voice.

Flynn's lips tightened. "Is it true? Are you still trying to get me to sign a contract with Fortress?"

My heart thundered in my throat. This wasn't what he thought. I was trying to help him. I was juggling a million balls in the air, trying to make this the deal of his dreams. But I needed a chance to explain that to him. "Can we—"

"Just answer the question, JT!" Flynn snapped, so loudly that all other conversations in the bar ceased. "You either *are* or *are not* still hoping I'll sign with Fortress. Yes or no?"

He could see the truth in my face, so there was no point in lying. "Okay, yes, but—"

Flynn held up a hand to stop me. "So you lied." The look of betrayal on his face was so horrible, I wanted to vomit.

"I didn't lie!" I argued. "I just... you assumed, and I..." I was digging the hole deeper, I knew it. I raked my fingers through my hair. "I wanted to tell you later. When the time was right."

He let out an ugly half laugh. "You mean after you made sure I lost Brew Fest?"

"What?" I demanded. "No! God. I would *never*. Flynn, come on! You know I... Flynn! Get back here and talk to me!"

But it was too late. Flynn had disappeared through the kitchen to his office. I raced after him.

"Let me explain," I said a split second before he slammed the office door closed behind him.

And locked it.

"Don't *do* this," I insisted, pounding my palm on the door. "Flynn, I know what you're doing right now. You're afraid, and you're hurt, and you don't want to hear my explanation because it's easier to be mad, but I—"

He flung the door open wide, sucking the air from the hallway behind me through the doorway and rustling some loose papers on his desk. "You think this is easier, Jonathan? Do you? And what's the fucking *proper* way to react when you find out that the guy you..." He swallowed hard, and tears filled those gorgeous green eyes. "...the guy you're *fucking* had an agenda he never shared with you and let you believe that business wasn't on the table anymore, when he was secretly... what? Planning to manipulate me into a contract after all?"

"No. *No.* No manipulation. I wanted to give you choices. I wanted to respect your boundaries." I winced as I heard the words come out of my mouth, and Flynn made a derisive noise. "I mean... your boundaries about the *terms* of the contract. See, I—"

Flynn held up a hand. "No. You know, Dan warned me you were just using me to get the business, and I told him he was wrong. That he didn't know you. That you would never do that to me. But I guess I'm the wrong one. I'm the one who didn't know you. I'm the sucker who thought..." His voice cracked, and he cleared his throat. I stepped forward and reached out to touch him, but he slapped my hand away. "Don't fucking touch me. If you care about me at all, you will go away and leave me the fuck alone. The most important event of my career is a week from today, and the last thing I need right now is this... this... *drama.* Fuck off, JT. Go back to New York and find another sucker."

He slammed the door closed again.

I leaned my forehead against the smooth, cool wood. The faint sounds of Patsy Cline's "Crazy" slithered through the sound system from the Tavern, mocking me.

"JT," Castor said softly from behind me.

I turned my head against the door to find Cas, Dan, and Reagan, all standing in the hallway, watching me. Cas looked hesitant, Reagan sympathetic, and Dan had his arms crossed over his chest.

"I need to talk to him," I told Castor. "This is a misunderstanding. Our whole relationship is littered with them. I need to explain."

Cas shook his head. "He needs to cool off first. He's not in a place to listen right now."

Castor meant well, but he was wrong. So wrong. "You don't get it. That's the mistake I've made in the past. I've left him without explaining. Last time—" I hesitated. I didn't know if Flynn had told anyone about what happened after Horace died. I wasn't sure he'd want me to tell them now.

Sweet Cas huffed out a breath and rolled his eyes. "I think there's a middle ground between giving Flynn space to collect his thoughts so that he's not speaking to you with embarrassed cry-eyes—which is only going to make him more likely to hold a grudge, FYI—and fucking off to New York for three years." He threw up his hands in exasperation. "And *yes*," he said, raising his voice so that Flynn could hear him through the closed door, "I knew that you two were together years ago. Who do you think made sure everyone left you alone that night? If *certain people* wanted to keep it a secret, destroying the second floor of the Tavern minutes after JT left town was probably not the most subtle way to go about it." He blew out a breath and made a sweeping motion toward the Tavern like a game show host. "Go on. Get out of here. Maybe use this time to figure out exactly what you're gonna say." He gave me a hard look. "And make it *good*."

Reagan lifted both eyebrows. I wasn't sure I'd ever seen Castor upset before. I wasn't sure I'd heard him swear before, even.

I took a deep breath and steeled myself against the pain that was lodged in my chest and throat. Then I turned around and trudged back down the hall.

Reagan squeezed my shoulder as I passed, then turned and walked out with me.

Flynn Honeycutt had asked me for space, so I'd give him space.

For now.

It took me about eight hours before I caved and tried again.

"Fuck Flynn Honeycutt, and fuck his space," I told Reagan before I stormed out of Wellbridge House.

"JT, when Castor suggested we come up with something eloquent for you to say, I'm pretty sure he was thinking of something a little more flowery than that," he called from the doorway. "Maybe more like—"

I shut the door to my Porsche and reversed down the driveway, cutting off the rest of his advice.

I'd spent the entire evening pacing a path down the center of my mother's expensive living room carpet. I was too frantic to think clearly. Too frantic to come up with any sort of plan. Too frantic to think about the best way to spin this or even present Flynn with a logical explanation, let alone some kind of flowery preplanned speech.

Turned out being a skilled negotiator—being a fucking *Rainmaker*—was impossible when you had your whole life and future on the line. All I knew was that my heart had removed itself from my chest against my will and was beating somewhere across town. I wasn't going to feel whole again until Flynn and I were together.

Besides, space was what had gotten us into trouble in the first place. He could take his space and shove it.

After verifying that Flynn wasn't in his house, I made my way to the locked front door of the Tavern and banged it with my fist until someone finally unlocked it.

It was Dan. The fucker.

"Where is he?" I asked without preamble. "Flynn's not home. I already checked. And don't even think about telling me to leave again because—"

"He's not here." Dan sounded tired. He stepped back and gestured for me to come in, which was... decent of him. "He took off after the last customer left and said he'd be back later to clean up. I figured I'd stay to do it for him since he's been so slammed."

Dan was doing a piss-poor job of being the villain I wanted to cast him as.

"Did he say where he was going?" I asked, grabbing a nearby chair to place on top of a table. I could tell Dan had been partway through the work when I'd shown up, and the least I could do to help Flynn—and Dan—was to help clean up while I interrogated him.

"You know... I didn't like you at first, JT," Dan began, eyeing me from over a set of chair legs before reaching for another. "I thought you were trying to sabotage Flynn's chances at Brew Fest."

"Yes. I know exactly what you thought." Since Flynn had screamed it at top volume earlier, the whole town might know at this point. "But it's not true."

"I got that." He ran a hand over his short hair. "I figured that out when I saw the look on your face earlier. You were helping us. It was nice of you."

I bristled at his generous use of the term "us" but appreciated his gratitude nonetheless. "I care about Flynn." Which was an understatement, but Dan wasn't the guy who needed to hear my truths or deserved my explanations.

"It seems like you do. Which is why I can't understand why you would keep this from him. This business is his heart. If you've known him as long as everyone says you have, how could you not know that?"

"I did!" I snapped, pushing away from the table. "I've been afraid of this all along, but I couldn't figure out what else to do. So don't fucking talk to me about knowing Flynn

Honeycutt, do you hear me? No one knows that man better than I do."

"Really?" Dan stepped forward and jutted his clenched jaw at me. "Did you know he has dreams to travel the world? To go to school and learn from the experts?"

"No he doesn't." I rolled my eyes. "No more than I want to be a baseball player."

"What?"

I shook my head, knowing that whatever else I'd fucked up, this one thing I'd gotten right. "That's not what he wants anymore, Dan. It might have been his dream once. And maybe I believed it still was, even a few weeks ago. But dreams change. People change. Flynn's real dream is to stay *here* in the place he loves most and help grow the town along with his business. He wants to support his family. He wants to build something that endures. He wants to make Honeybridge a place people want to come to and never want to leave."

Dan's face had morphed into an expression of surprise.

I let out a soft laugh, even though I felt like crying. "That's what I was trying to give him, man. His dream. That's all I was trying to do."

Flynn's voice came from behind me. "Then why weren't you honest?"

"*Flynn*," I whispered. I closed my eyes and breathed in and out. Just hearing his voice, filled with hurt and anger as it was, knowing he was in the same room with me, sent a wave of peace washing over me like Willow Honeycutt had just sprinkled me with relaxation mist while resetting my chakras.

I turned toward the man I loved, and in that moment, I realized my own truth just as surely as I knew Flynn's.

I had one chance to tell him. To make this right. But it was going to take a miracle to make it happen.

Chapter Sixteen

Flynn

I couldn't bring myself to look at JT's face. Dan met my eyes over JT's shoulder and tilted his head, silently checking whether I felt safe being alone with JT... while also telling me he thought I would be. Clearly, something JT had said changed Dan's mind about the guy. Maybe he'd turned on the Wellbridge charm.

I waved Dan off. "Go home, Dan. Gonna be a long day again tomorrow. Thanks for everything."

Thankfully, instead of arguing, Dan turned around and disappeared into the kitchen. A few moments later, I heard the back door close with a solid thunk.

Once we were alone, JT turned to face me. His face was drawn, and his blue eyes burned with some banked emotion, but he didn't speak. His hesitation was annoying as fuck. He'd done this to himself, so why the hell was he walking on eggshells now?

"I heard what you said," I admitted, crossing my arms in front of my chest to keep from reaching for him just to feel the solid, reassuring weight of him in my hands. "And you're right." He opened his mouth to speak, and I held up a hand to stop him. "So help me, if you say something smug right now, I'm going to punch you in the mouth."

"Not feeling smug right now, Flynn." JT's voice was hoarse.

He ran both hands through his once-perfect hair. I liked it better these days—a little long, messy and real, perfect for grabbing hold of. I hated myself for wanting to reach out and save it from his rough treatment.

He stared at me for a long moment, then shook his head like he was frustrated with himself. "Fuck. This is the most important conversation of my whole life, and I... I don't even know where to begin." He huffed out a breath that wasn't quite a laugh. "God, I'm an idiot."

"No arguments here." I propped my hip against the bar, keeping a solid ten feet of distance between us.

He did laugh then, a little, and scrubbed his hands over his face before meeting my eyes again. "Okay, let's start with this. I'm sorry. But I swear, Flynn—"

"Gonna stop you right there, Frog. An apology doesn't begin with 'I'm sorry *but*.'"

He nodded. "Okay, yeah. That's fair. I'm sorry, full stop. I'm sorry that I messed this up. That I couldn't figure out a way to be completely honest with you. I... I swear, I thought I was doing the right thing. I knew how good the Fortress deal would be for you. I wanted you to have that money, that exposure. You deserve that. Honeybridge Mead deserves that."

I inclined my head. He was right. We did deserve those things.

"And you said you wanted to keep the manufacturing here," JT went on. "So I decided I'd get you that, in addition to everything else in the initial contract, and then you'd have the freedom to do things. Hire people, expand, whatever you wanted. I found a property here in town. The Hornrath Chair Company is vacant and—"

"I'm aware," I interrupted. "First, because I'm not an idiot, and I had my eye on that place already for my own expansion plans." JT's face fell. "And second, because town gossip is going crazy about our fight earlier, and Alden's at the epicenter as usual. According to him, all of Honeybridge now knows you were working with Hayden to acquire the property." I rolled my eyes. Personally, I thought Alden was upset he hadn't been here to witness everything firsthand.

JT winced. "Yeah. I'm sorry for that, too. I didn't want people gossiping about you. *Us*. I knew you wouldn't like that." He cleared his throat. "Anyway. I submitted my idea to Fortress, and they've been taking forever to approve it, so I haven't been able to talk to you about it at all—"

"Why?"

He blinked, like the question confused him. "Well... so you wouldn't be disappointed if they said no. Obviously. I worried that you might feel—"

"Hurt? As opposed to how I'm feeling now? Smart thinking."

The pain on JT's face as my cheap shot landed didn't make me feel better. In fact, it made me feel worse.

"Did it not occur to you that *I* would say no, JT? Because I am. I don't want a distribution deal with Fortress."

He blinked at me some more. "But." He shook his head. "The manufacturing would stay here."

"Yes. I hear you. But I don't care. I don't want the deal under any circumstances. I didn't bring up the manufacturing location as a negotiation point. I only mentioned it to show you that you didn't know shit about my business, and I guess I was right. But you thought you knew better."

"No, I—"

"I'm fucking tired, JT." I shifted to lean my weight more fully against the bar. "All my life, I've busted my ass for other people, looked out for other people. I started working here to make money and stayed to help my grandfather when he couldn't do it on his own anymore. I raised my siblings when Huck and Willow fucked off to goddess-only-knew-where so they could live their dreams. I've sent Georgia money when her gigs didn't pan out in LA because she deserved to have her shot. I put Alden through his training courses so he could save his money to open his own business one day. And I've kept the staffing here as low as possible so I could afford to pay for PJ's rent at art school, because I couldn't stand to let his talent go to waste."

I could see my words were hurting JT, but I had to get them out anyway. They were drowning me. "This was my turn, Jon." I spread my arms to encompass my kingdom, such as it was. "Honeybridge Mead. The Tavern. This was supposed to finally be *my* fucking turn. Something all for me. I wanted this Ren Faire deal so I could afford to expand my own damned business *myself* without having to give up any part of what's mine. And last night, I was so excited to tell you about—"

I broke off with a headshake. I didn't want to tell him about my conversation with Thatcher Pennington anymore. I'd been so flattered and excited that the man hadn't wanted to acquire my business or any of the distribution rights; he'd been impressed enough with it to invest the money I needed to grow the business myself instead. Now, it was all I could do not to start crying.

"Instead of trusting me, JT, instead of supporting me and believing in my ability to do this without Fortress's help, you went behind my back and tried to yank my fucking dream right out from under me."

"No," he croaked. "Never. I support you, Firecracker. I believe you can do anything. I thought I was helping you."

"If you thought a big corporation from New York was any part of my dream, you were wrong," I said coldly. "And you sure as hell didn't know me at all."

"Flynn. Firecracker—"

"What was it you said last night about your mom thinking she knew what would make you happy better than you did?"

He shut his mouth with a clack, and his eyes squeezed shut. "Fucking Christ," he muttered, shaking his head. "I'm such an idiot. It's the thing with the frogs all over again." He huffed out a humorless laugh. "Pop was right."

I wrapped my arms more tightly around myself. I didn't know what he was talking about, and I told myself I didn't care.

"So... where does this leave us?" JT was hunched in on himself, defeat in every line of his body, his casual confidence erased.

I hated seeing him like that and knowing I had a hand in causing it. Part of me wanted to reach out and comfort him, which was probably a sign I'd reached my limit and then some.

If the whole concept of *us* had seemed impossible before, it felt doubly so now. I sure as hell couldn't handle another sad discussion like last night's, brainstorming ways to string together bits and pieces of our separate lives and call it a relationship. But I also couldn't handle ending things for good and knowing he'd fuck off to New York again permanently.

My stomach was full of swirling emotions, and I needed to end this conversation before I said or did something I'd regret. I didn't want any regrets with Jon.

Not this time. Not again.

"It's hard to think of an 'us' right now, Jon," I admitted. "I'm angry. I'm hurt. And I really need to focus on my own things. Brew Fest. My family. Building something that endures, like you told Dan."

JT's eyes narrowed and darkened. He took a step toward me. "Don't. Please, Flynn, I'm begging you, don't build those walls between us. Don't shut me out. Don't try to make yourself hate me again."

I held my hand up and took a step back to keep myself from leaning into his arms. "I don't hate you. I... I don't think I could if I tried." It was a simple statement of fact. "But you're leaving town tomorrow, right?" He blinked, like he'd forgotten that his real life existed, but I didn't need him to confirm it because I already knew. "You have your own Brew Fest prep to do."

"I can help you—"

"No." I exhaled sharply. "The Fortress team needs you. So go back to the city and do your thing, Rainmaker. It's for the best."

I couldn't bring myself to see the effect of my words on his face, so I spun around and headed for the front entrance, grateful for the auto-locking doors that let people out at night but not in. The cleaning would have to wait until tomorrow morning because I didn't have enough energy for one single minute more.

"Flynn?" JT called from behind me. There was a different quality to his voice—something resolved and determined—that made me pause without turning around. "Tell me this one thing. Do you really think I'd ever try to sabotage you at Brew Fest? That I was hoping you'd lose? That the deal was more important to me than your happiness?"

I closed my eyes. I didn't have to think—or overthink—about it. The truth was sitting right in the center of my aching chest, like a shiny coin peeking out of a vast pile of rubble. "No," I admitted. "No, I don't believe that."

"Okay." He sounded relieved. "Okay, then. I can work with that. I'm not giving up on us, Flynn."

I shook my head. I didn't know what he was talking about, and I told myself I didn't care.

Since I figured JT would come looking for me at my place, I only stopped home long enough to grab my keys before hopping in my truck and driving out to the Retreat.

Despite the late hour, McLean seemed to have a sixth sense that I was coming. I barely knocked on the door before he threw it wide, then opened his arms so I could walk straight into his big chest for a hug.

My brother held me tight and let me sob like a fucking baby until I was worn-out and numb.

And then he shoved me into his giant bed, where Lily curled up at my feet, and issued a one-word command.

"Sleep."

I slept. And when I finally woke up, the world looked a little brighter. At least, that's what I told myself when my mind wanted nothing more than to pull out every sweet JT memory and fluff them into a giant bed I could curl up in.

"Coffee's up," McLean called from the kitchen in his deep voice.

I threw the covers back and crawled out of bed. My body felt like it had been through the wringer, but I couldn't stop to nurse my broken heart. I still had loads of work to get done today before our supplies would be ready to pack into trucks to head to Brew Fest on Tuesday.

This was one of those times I was grateful McLean was the strong, silent type. We stood in companionable silence while we sipped coffee and stared off into space. Metric tons of unspoken words hung in the air, but I didn't feel pressure to deal with them. McLean, more than anyone, respected someone's need to stay inside themselves.

That was a good thing because I wasn't sure exactly how I felt.

I loved JT Wellbridge. That was a given.

He was a lying liar. That was true, too.

And I was hurt, angry, embarrassed, and not at all ready to have a mature discussion about boundaries and forgiveness, let alone about what our future might look like.

"What can I do to help?" Mac finally said. It was unclear whether he was offering to patch up my ailing heart or suggesting something more practical, like loading heavy boxes into the truck.

"Keep the Retreat running. That's help enough." Now that Huck and Willow were off to parts unknown, we needed someone here to keep things moving smoothly in their absence.

"Not a problem." He eyed me over his mug as he took another sip. "Hey, uh... have you heard from PJ lately?"

"No. The asshole keeps blowing me off." I frowned, feeling a pulse of unease. "Why?"

McLean bit the inside of his cheek, like he was deciding whether to speak. Probably deciding whether I could handle it, knowing how overloaded I was. "It's probably nothing, but... last night was the new moon."

"Okay?"

Mac fidgeted in his seat. "You remember Willow used to say that new moons were a time for wishes and dreams? I mean. I mean, I don't *actually* believe it," he said softly, his eyes shining in a way that said he really did. "But a long time ago—like, *years*—PJ and I started doing this thing where we'd, you know, make our wishes for the month.

Even after he moved away, he'd always, always call me on the new moon."

"And last night, he didn't."

McLean nodded somberly, and my heart sank. Our entire family was protective of McLean, despite him being older than the twins. PJ wouldn't have let him down unless something was really wrong.

I pulled out my phone and pulled up my messages. The text chain between PJ and me over the previous few weeks was full of garbage brush-offs.

Me: *How's the studio class going? Did you finish the piece?*

Daydreamer: *Yeah, great!*

Me: *Is the roommate situation working out okay?*

Daydreamer: *Absolutely!*

Me: *Hey! I've tried calling you several times this week. Where are you?*

Daydreamer: *Right here. Super busy. Everything's fine!*

Me: *Tried calling again. Willow and Huck couldn't get a hold of you either. They said to tell you bye and good luck with the semester.*

Daydreamer: *Cool. Thanks!*

Me: *Bro, wtf? Answer your phone.*

Me: *PJ, where are you? I feel like something's wrong and you're not telling us.*

Daydreamer: *Nothing's wrong. Everything's fine! Just busy.*

Me: *Too busy for a three-minute phone call? CALL ME DAMMIT.*

Me: *PJ?*

Me: *Bro.*

Me: *I'm working tonight, so if I don't hear my cell, call* *the Tavern landline and make someone find me. Promise me you'll call.*

I rubbed my forehead and sighed tiredly, shifting the mental burdens on my shoulders to accommodate one more. "The last I heard from him was six days ago."

McLean grimaced. "I dunno, Flynn. Maybe we should check on him. Just to be sure. We could ask Alden to go."

"Of course we need to check on him. I probably should have done it a long time ago," I admitted. *Would* have if I hadn't been so preoccupied with so many other damn things. "PJ won't talk to Alden, though. He'll give some bullshit excuse, and Alden will come back here saying PJ is fine... after stopping to squeeze in a Grindr hookup."

McLean shrugged, acknowledging this. Alden was loyal and he was fierce, but he wasn't warm or fuzzy. "Maybe we could send..." His voice trailed off, and I nodded in confirmation.

It had to be me.

McLean was too anxious to go, Castor too sweetly naive, Pop too busy with the store, and Georgia too damn far away.

McLean stated the obvious. "You can't. You leave for Brew Fest Tuesday. The day after tomorrow."

"I know." I took one last sip of coffee before placing my mug in his sink and brushing my hands together. "But if I leave here in an hour and the Sunday traffic isn't awful—and assuming my truck cooperates—I'll be in Boston by this afternoon. I can find PJ, make sure he's okay, and be home by tonight. Easy peasy." As long as I didn't sleep tonight, I would still have enough time to get my last-minute preparations finished by the end of the day tomorrow so I could load up the truck.

And maybe it would be a good thing to be out of town. Less temptation to drive to Wellbridge House, shake Frog silly, kiss him senseless, and try to work out all my frustrations in bed.

"Flynn," Mac said. "You're not alone. There are plenty of people you can ask for help. Alden and Cas—"

"Yeah." I'd already been counting on my brothers to help out, though Cas was still not feeling great, and Alden had his own work to do.

He firmed his jaw. "I can help too. If you need me to."

I nodded and reached for my keys and phone. "I'll let you know if I do, Mac. Thanks for being here last night," I said. His large, familiar strength was a comfort.

"Always," he said before stepping back. "Here." He took a fist-sized chunk of amethyst from his pocket, an apple from the bowl on the counter, and a small brown paper bag from the counter and handed them all to me, forcing me to juggle my phone and keys to hold it all. "If Willow were here, she'd try to offer you some advice. Since she's not, I figure I should make sure you have fiber—" He tapped the apple. "—protection from negativity—" He tapped the stone. "—and a snack for the road 'cause you know how you get when you're hangry." He smiled. "Find our bro, then kick ass in Portland. The other guys at Brew Fest won't know what hit 'em."

I leaned in to give McLean a hug, swallowing back the emotion in my throat. "That's the plan." I headed out the door before throwing a "Love you" over my shoulder.

If there was one thing I was grateful to Willow and Huck for, it was raising us to be demonstrative and unafraid of our feelings.

As I made my way out to my truck, I caught sight of one of the small signs in Willow's community garden that PJ had hand-painted with our mother's favorite quotes. The signs were so familiar to me I usually didn't notice them anymore, but today, I saw that one of them was nearly buried in a patch of Japanese knotweed. Eager as I was to get going, I still set my stuff on the dirt by the sign and knelt for a moment to clean it off. Then I smiled slightly as I took in the familiar words. Maybe Willow *was* sending me some advice.

"No joy can equal the joy of serving others," the sign read, which was a quote by an Indian spiritual master named Sai Baba, who lived over a hundred years ago. But what Willow Honeycutt always added to the guru's wise words was this: "And don't forget to give that joy to others by allowing them to serve you."

Every time she said it, she seemed to make significant eye contact with me in a way that implied I was stubbornly independent and prideful.

This was accurate.

But it wasn't as though I didn't allow *anyone* to help me. I had a select few people I could trust. Dan, Castor, Alden... though I supposed Dan and Cas were employees, and Alden didn't help often. And then there was...

I clenched my hands into fists as JT's face flashed through my brain. Despite my hurt and anger, I realized I missed him already.

I missed his embrace making the whole world warmer. His smile, energizing me when the task before me felt impossible.

I hated that I couldn't go in the next room and kiss his stupid mouth or pick up the phone and send him a ridiculous text, just to see his response.

In my mind, JT held me in my tiny living room and told a ridiculous story about mittens because he knew my limits. Because he knew *me*. And cared.

He tried to give you another option, a small voice in my head reminded me. *He tried to help. To support you in the best way he knew how since you wouldn't let him in and tell him what you wanted.*

I closed my eyes tightly. *Great.* My own brain was under JT's stupid spell and was revolting against me.

Isn't it time you stopped choosing the worst interpretation of his actions, Flynn?

"Ugh. Fine." I snatched my keys and my snack bag from the ground, leaving the rest of Mac's paraphernalia behind, and rolled my eyes heavenward.

JT and I would talk when I got back. Right now, I had way too many other things to do. A long drive to accomplish, a brother to find and lecture, a metric shit-ton of mead to pack up, a Tavern to prepare for my departure, and a Brew Fest ribbon to win.

All by yourself? the voice asked.

I ignored it.

As I took the final few steps to my old truck, I saw another one of my mother's ridiculous placards.

If you're looking for a sign, here it is.

Well, fuck.

I stood there, head bent, for twenty long seconds. Asking JT to spend a few hours packing things up at the Meadery today before he had to get back to the city would be smart. He knew the equipment, he knew my processes, and I knew he could do it right. I also knew without a doubt that he *would* help, at least until he had to leave town. Heck, he might even stay in Honeybridge until tomorrow, if Fortress could spare him.

But I still couldn't bring myself to do it.

The summer would be over soon. I didn't want a half-assed something with JT—I was pretty sure that would break both of us—and I couldn't think of another way forward. So even if I'd maybe—*maybe*—overreacted last night, was it really wise for me to trust and rely on someone who wouldn't be around long-term?

It wasn't about being proud or independent, no matter what Willow—or her signs—suggested. This was self-preservation.

So I headed to the salon to ask for Alden's help instead.

Chapter Seventeen

JT

"Jonathan! Jonathan, darling!" my mother called. The front door crashed closed behind her. "You will not *believe* what happened at the salon."

I glanced up from my laptop and exchanged a glance with Rosalia, who was preparing Mother's post-salon luncheon of fresh lettuce topped with tiny slivers of carrot. Her lips twitched, and I gave her a half-hearted smile in return.

It was good to know that, even when my own personal universe had just been tipped upside down and shaken, things in Wellbridge House remained unchanged.

"Jonathan!" My mother's voice carried down the hall, accompanied by the *tap-tap-tap* of her high heels on the parquet.

I sighed and closed out of my browser program. I hadn't been able to focus on work anyway. Catching up on Fortress emails—mostly annoyed demands to know why I was taking two days of unplanned time off right before Brew Fest—felt pointless when I couldn't think of anything but Flynn Honeycutt.

He trusted me, deep down—after his final admission

Saturday night, I knew he did. And I could see in his eyes how much he cared about me. He was scared and hurt *because* he cared so much, but he hadn't shut me out entirely. So I needed to show him that I was committed to making this right... even if I hadn't figured out exactly how to do that yet.

I'd decided that staying in town and heading directly to Portland for the festival Wednesday would be my best option. If Flynn wanted to talk, I wanted to listen. But since I'd also committed to not distracting him while he was doing his own Brew Fest prep, I'd limited myself to a couple of check-in texts a day, just to let him know I was around.

I was trying not to read too much into the fact that he hadn't responded.

"Jonathan! I've been searching high and low for you!" My mother and her cloud of Chanel paused in the doorway, but I didn't glance up until I heard Rosalia's shocked gasp...

And then I did a double take.

"Mother?" I demanded, jumping to my feet. "Dear god. Are you alright?"

My mother's hair was dripping wet and tangled, and she clutched a small white towel around her shoulders like a shawl. I'd never, in thirty-two years, seen her look so un-put-together, not even in her own home.

Mother threw her giant purse and keys on the countertop so forcefully that her Birkin bag skidded into the lettuce, and Rosalia had to rush to save it.

"Well, of course I'm alright." She moved a hank of dripping hair off her face with great dignity. "But I couldn't very well stay there for my blowout when I needed to get back here to strategize, now, could I? We don't have much time. I'm going to call Louise and Madeline to start mobilizing the Gentlepeople's Society. Vanessa Atanmo can help round up the diversity committee folks. Oh! And I'll contact Russell Cowgill and the others at the Log Cabin Museum—they're never busy on a Tuesday. Rosalia, dear, please fetch me my Rolodex. And one of my detox juices. I'm going to need it." She pulled out the kitchen chair across from mine and sat down heavily. She gave me a judgmental look. "Darling, don't just stand there. Contact your assistant. Alex? Alyssa? We'll need her help."

"Alice. But..." It was true that I'd felt brain-dead for the past thirty-six hours, give or take, but I couldn't follow this conversation at all. I sat back down. "What?"

Mother sighed impatiently. "I was at the salon," she began. "Alden is one of the most gifted stylists I've ever come across, you understand, even if he *is* one of *those Honeycutts*—"

"Mother," I warned.

She sniffed delicately. "I'm only explaining that I'd had to miss my yogaerobics class today so I could get a coveted Tuesday morning slot from him, so needless to say, when Castor Honeycutt came racing in, all in a panic, and Alden had to stop my shampoo massage and step away to calm him, I was *displeased*. So I..." She waved a hand. "I may have made a point of paying attention to their conversation when Alden dragged Castor behind the curtain at the back of the salon."

"You eavesdropped."

"Jonathan, honestly. My means of information-gathering are not the point of this conversation." She put her chin in the air and accepted the juice Rosalia handed her. "There's something happening with one of the other Honeycutts—the little one who does the fingerpainting—"

It took me a minute to figure out who she meant. "PJ? The one in art school in Boston? He's like twenty-three, Mother. Not so little anymore."

She waved her juice through the air after taking a sip.

"That's the one. He's missing. Which means Flynn had to..."

The rest of her words faded out. "He's missing? What do you mean?" I scrambled to find my phone. "Flynn must be frantic. I need to call—"

"No!" she barked. "Don't bother."

I blinked at her. She rarely took that tone with me. "Why the heck not?" I was trying to keep my cool.

She sighed. "Because Flynn left his phone here in town. Apparently, another Honeycutt boy—the quiet one, McLean—found it in their mother's garden Sunday afternoon, flashing with new text messages. Flynn dropped it before he left town."

"He's been in Boston since Sunday? What's he been doing for the past two days?" I sat up straighter. The man was stuck in Boston with no phone the day before he needed to be in Portland for Brew Fest? I couldn't imagine how he must be feeling—or, actually, I *could*. Out of control, worried, and therefore miserable... and alone, on top of it all. My heart ached for him. "You'd better tell me the story from the beginning."

"I'll tell you as much as I know, dear, though this is all secondhand, and you know I hate gossip." She leaned forward. "Apparently, PJ hasn't been responding to texts for some time—which, I do agree, is extremely worrisome behavior, and something you should keep in mind when you fail to respond to my—"

"Mother!"

She huffed but quickly went on. "Since PJ stopped answering, Flynn had to run down to Boston to check on him. He left Sunday, expecting it to be a short trip, but PJ wasn't at his apartment and hadn't been seen there for some time. Flynn was hoping to be back yesterday so he could finalize his preparations for some sort of quaint festival he's participating in—"

"Brew Fest."

"That's the one. However, he's not back yet, which has thrown a wrench into all of their plans. Castor was quite insistent that Alden *must* come help at the Tavern today so they can transport things to Portland. Alden said he'd already helped yesterday and Sunday because Flynn asked him to, and he had clients all day today. Also, he's supposed to be doing hair for a wedding at the country club tonight. Weeknight weddings," she scoffed. "Young people today are so—"

"Focus, Mother."

"Of course. *Well*, Castor was so upset Alden agreed to cancel his appointments this afternoon but said he *couldn't* miss the wedding tonight, which is quite fair, really. I don't know *what* Morrisey Huber would do since it's her daughter's wedding that Alden was supposed to—"

"Mother," I barked again. "I don't give a shit about Cate Huber's wedding hair. Focus, okay? Where is Flynn now?"

"Still somewhere in Boston, one assumes, trying to track down his rogue family member, only able to communicate with his nearest and dearest through the most primitive means." She lowered her voice and whispered softly. "Pay phones. Castor said this is Flynn's worst nightmare come to life—having to choose between his family and his business. But *Alden* said, for Flynn, there's no choice to be made. He'll always put the people he cares about first."

Yes he would. It was one of the things I loved about him.

"Which is why," Mother went on, "we need as many townsfolk as we can assemble to get over to the Tavern to help Daniel, Castor, and Alden finalize their preparations and pack up. Then you, Reagan, and I will get all of the Honeybridge Mead to Portland."

"We will?" I blinked. "*You* will? But—"

"It has to be us. Alden needs to stay in town for the wedding, and Daniel and Castor must run the Tavern."

Since when did my mother want to help Flynn Honeycutt? When was she willing to do *manual labor* to help *anyone*?

"Jonathan, we'll never get things sorted if you continue to be so easily distracted." She stood. "I'm going to make some phone calls." She eyed me up and down, crinkling her face when she realized I was in running shorts and a Brown University tee. "I guess you might as well stay in those grubby clothes if you're going to be lifting things, but please pack some decent clothes for the festival itself. I'll not have you representing Honeybridge Mead while looking like a baseborn tourist. Our town has a reputation to uphold."

"But—"

She huffed impatiently. "Jonathan. Are you or are you not madly in love with Flynn Honeycutt?"

"I..." I gaped at her in shock. I had never mentioned *love* to her. I was sure of it.

"And have you, or have you not, been moping about this house for the past two days, trying to figure out a way to show the man your affection and get back into his good graces after the *debacle* at the Tavern Saturday night?" She lifted a censorious eyebrow, and I winced. Honeybridge gossip was insidious... but in this case correct.

She nodded once, reading the answer to both of these questions from my face.

"Exactly as I thought. So, chop chop, darling." She put an arm around Rosalia's shoulder and ushered her from the room. "I'll need help packing my things, Rosalia, dear. What slacks do I have that will coordinate with the gold Honeybridge Mead logo? Thank goodness I look amazing in gold. That's our only saving grace."

I stared after her for a moment, then slowly smiled.

Patricia Wellbridge was annoyingly image-obsessed. Often petty. Terrifyingly vindictive. But when she cared about something or someone, she was an absolute juggernaut.

And I was proud as fuck that she was my mother.

I had many, many questions for her, but apparently, they'd have to wait. For now, I had a bag to pack.

Even knowing that Flynn had left his phone behind, I continued to call and text him updates all morning. Partly it was because I wanted him to have a status update on the Meadery, if he was able to get his phone back, and partly because... well, I'd gotten used to texting him often, just to make him smile.

I wanted him to know I'd been thinking of him when he read those messages in the future. I wanted him to know I'd meant what I said Saturday—I wasn't giving up. I was ready to fight for him—for *us*.

Now more than ever.

Me: *All the mead is bottled. Swag packed and organized. Just boxing everything up now and I'll see you in Portland.*

Me: *My mother is currently in the Tavern, talking to Dan, and trying to convince him to do Yogaerobics because his strong "Scorpio rising" energy needs an outlet. The look on his face, Flynn.*

Me: *Just talked to my boss. He went over my Brew Fest schedule. Apparently he thinks I don't need to eat or sleep. Remind me why I ever enjoyed that job?*

Me: *You know, I used to help out at Pop's shop a lot—*

probably more than you knew—and he'd make me sweep while I talked to him. Every damn time.

Me: *And I'd get so into whatever I was saying that I wouldn't pay attention to what my hands were doing, and he'd interrupt me. "I think you missed something, JT." or "You missed a big thing right there, Frog." Used to drive me crazy.*

Me: *But when I was talking to Conrad earlier, I swear I heard Pop's voice in my head. I've been missing the obvious.*

Me: *I've figured out a solution. A plan that will let both of us have what we want. And fuck, I can't wait to talk to you about this.*

Me: *I really, REALLY hope you'll give me that chance, Firecracker.*

"Are you sure he doesn't need one of us in Boston with him?" I asked Alden for the third time while we hauled the last of the Runway Brew into the back of the refrigeration truck.

I was pouring sweat despite the refrigerated air, but it was nothing compared to the nervous stomachache I had worrying about Flynn and PJ.

"I'm sure. PJ's probably just following his muse or whatever." He wiped his forehead with the back of his arm. "Flynn will track him down wherever he's hiding out, chew him out for going off the grid, then hotfoot it back up here in time for the first Brew Fest events. Hopefully." He chewed his lip. "Really wish he had a way to update us more often, though."

When I hopped out of the truck, my phone buzzed. I nearly dropped it in my haste to answer. "Flynn!"

"Noooo," Alice said suspiciously. "But if you're expecting a call from the mead maker, should I assume you have good news about the contract?"

I grabbed the bar rag from my pocket and swiped at the sweat on my face. "No. Definitely not." Flynn had made it clear that he wasn't interested in Fortress, period, so that was that.

"Bummer. But then maybe Mr. Shaeffer was right. After Brew Fest, you could make a lower offer and convince him that Fortress is where he needs to be—"

"It's off the table, Alice," I said firmly. "I don't do business that way. Conrad called me an hour ago to ream me out over taking yesterday and today off, and I told him the same. Not sure if he actually believed me or not," I added wryly.

"*Daaaamn*. I imagine he wasn't very happy."

Understatement. Apparently, all the business the "Rainmaker" had acquired for Fortress, the three years of sleepless nights and weeks without weekends, meant nothing to Conrad when I'd needed two days' personal time. He'd told me in a somewhat threatening voice that this wasn't "vice presidential" behavior.

I was finding it hard to care.

"I'm not very happy with him either," I told her. "His expectations are ridiculous."

"How unhappy?" she wondered. "Like, leaving-Fortress unhappy?"

I looked up from wiping my face to see the usual street scene on a summer weekday in Honeybridge. Families wandering out of Ollie's Fudge Shoppe with ice cream, delivery drivers unloading produce at Bixby's Market, kids biking down the sidewalk with tall flags waving off the back of their bikes to make them more visible, and teenagers loitering in front of the General Store in hopes of someone buying them beer or smokes, as if Pop Honeycutt didn't know the exact birthdate and age of every Honeybridger.

The sun was warm, but the breeze from the lake moved softly through town the way it always did, carrying the laughter of the volunteers who'd come to help us with the final, frantic packing effort and now stood chatting in the parking lot.

Those volunteers hadn't cared about Team Wellbridge or Team Honeycutt when they heard Flynn needed them. No matter how cutthroat they might be when it came to softball, or the Christmas Light Display, or… heck, even leaf peeping, Honeybridgers would always stand shoulder to shoulder against the world to protect one of their own.

That kind of loyalty was pretty damn rare in the rest of the world, but it was one of many things I loved about Honeybridge. And I'd missed it more than I'd realized.

For years, I'd told myself that I'd outgrown Honeybridge, when what I'd really outgrown was the person I used to be here. Maybe I'd had to leave town to figure that out—to figure *myself* out—and to really appreciate it. Now, I knew that I didn't want to be without it again.

Flynn had said the Fortress team needed me, but he was wrong.

I wanted to be Team Honeybridge now. I wanted to be Team Flynn.

As I'd packed and stacked boxes earlier, I'd realized that I needed to take the advice I'd handed Reagan the other day —to stop worrying about how other people measured success and decide what *I* wanted… then get it.

Flynn would probably tell me that was the most Wellbridge idea he'd ever heard… and he'd be right. But I was finally ready to embrace my inner Wellbridge.

"I'm not sure *exactly* what the future is going to look like," I told Alice finally. "But I've got an idea."

"I'd back your ideas any day of the week, Rainmaker," Alice said promptly.

I laughed. "It's really great to hear you say that because I'm going to need your help. How would you feel about hopping a flight to Brew Fest after all so we can discuss some things in person?"

"Hot damn! Will I get to meet your mysterious mead maker?"

"I fucking hope so," I said fervently. More than that, I really hoped Flynn was still mine.

"Are we planning to pillage the prospective clients at Brew Fest and sign Fortress so much new business that you'll be Conrad Schaeffer's new boss?" she demanded eagerly.

"No. Not at all. Here's what I'm thinking..."

Several hours later, I fell into a booth at the hotel bar. My shoulders and back ached from all the heavy lifting and carrying, but I was proud of the work we'd done getting Honeybridge Mead's booth set up. It looked amazing.

"I'll take a glass of Chablis, thanks," my mother murmured at the server who stopped to take our order. "Oh, and might you offer any kind of... amuse-bouche while we're perusing the menu? I passed peckish quite a while ago."

The guy blinked at her before flicking his eyes to me. "We've got potato skins. Is that what you mean?"

Mother's mouth opened, but I cut her off before she could offend anyone else today. "Yes, perfect. Thanks. I'll take a giant glass of ice water and an Allagash White if you have it. If not, surprise me with another local brew."

Once he was gone, my mother smoothed her hair down and sighed. "Must you be so... plebeian? Beer? How gauche."

I shot her a look. "I'm surprised that guy knew what

Chablis even was. No one has used that term since the last century. You might try ordering a chardonnay next time."

She sniffed and pointed her nose at the large, laminated menu. "And risk getting served a California wine? I don't think so."

I studied her unruly hair. After blowing it dry herself while I was busy loading the final truck at the Tavern, she'd looked like her usual self. But then the long drive in the convertible, followed by hours of ordering the rest of us around in a stuffy expo hall, had turned her perfect coif into a mess of curls.

"I like your hair like that," I said. "You should wear it curly more often."

Her sculpted eyebrows lifted, and her hand went to her hair again. "Really? You think so? Your father always preferred it straight."

It was strange to think of my father even noticing my mother's looks. I couldn't remember the last time he'd paid attention to anything other than his political ambitions. To be fair, those political ambitions were as much my mother's as his own. Still, it made me sad to think she'd been keeping herself a certain way all these years for someone who didn't seem to notice or care.

I thought of Flynn sitting across the breakfast table from me in thirty or forty years. Would I still notice him? Would I care what his hair looked like or what clothes he wore? Would I still want him?

I snorted softly at my menu.

Was it possible to be in the same room, the same state, the same universe and not notice Flynn?

Not crave his attention?

Not feel like he was the sun in the center of my personal solar system?

And not feel that jittery, heart-thundering sense of deep, deep *need*?

"Darling?" A little frown line appeared between my mother's eyebrows as she peered at me over my menu. "Are you alright? You're still breathing heavily even though the physical labor ended an hour ago. I think we need to get you in for a cardiac workup with Dr. Aldridge."

"I... no... I'm not alright. I want to marry Flynn Honeycutt." I grinned widely and felt the stress fall off my shoulders. "I'm in love with him, and I want to *marry him*."

She *tsk*'d and rolled her eyes before looking back at her menu. "Tell me something I don't know."

"You couldn't possibly know that," I retorted. "I've only just figured it out myself."

"I swear, you millennials act like we're the ones without a clue." She set her menu down and gave me a piercing look. "Jonathan, I have ridden many hours this day in your convertible, sans air-conditioning. My manicure has been ravaged so badly poor Corrine will disown me as a client, and I have knots in my shoulders that my massage therapist may never fully excise. Do not even get me started on the fate of my Aquarella Tieks." She stuck out one dusty, blue-soled shoe and sighed. "Do you think I did that because you had *affection* for your Honeycutt beau? Because you and he have shared..." She lowered her voice to a whisper. "*Carnal relations*, however satisfying?"

"Oh, god," I gagged. "Please, never say those words again."

"No," she continued, ignoring my interruption. "No, Jonathan, I did not. I did it because your happiness is my priority. And when you spoke to me about Flynn Honeycutt a week ago, I saw something on your face that I haven't seen there in a long time: true passion. The same passion that drove you to rescue frogs as a tiny child. The same passion that made you want to leave Honeybridge for college. I'd hoped you'd have that same passion for your work at Fortress, but..." She shook her head. "No."

"Mother." I shook my head, amused. "I appreciate the support, but you're wrong. I have been plenty passionate about my career."

"You were dedicated," she corrected. Her eyes perused the menu, though we both knew she'd order a salad. "The work was a means to an end, and that end was *success*. And there were certainly parts of it you enjoyed, I know. Perhaps, first and foremost, the opportunity to stay in New York." She shot me a wry look. "But the business itself? The lifestyle? No, dear. They never put that light in your eyes." Casually, she pointed to an item on the menu and pursed her lips. "Do you suppose they use imported mozzarella for these 'mozzarella sticks'?"

"Highly unlikely," I said, staring at her wonderingly.

"No, I suppose not. Well." She set her menu down again and folded her hands atop it. "I must say that I am very relieved that you've found your passion with your young man. It's possible to have a perfectly lovely life without it, of course. But one always wants the best for one's children, doesn't one?" Her voice sounded almost wistful, and it made me remember the story Marta had told me. I wondered if my mother had regrets.

Her prim and proper tone was back in place when she added, "Speaking of which, I would like grandchildren eventually. Ideally several. Honeycutts tend toward those monstrously large, boisterous clans, and I find I'm... not averse to that." She lifted her chin. "Though I imagine that with my influence, my grandchildren will be considerably more civilized. And, of course, your *inamorato* will want to name them after painters, but perhaps he'd be open to naming them after some good, solid English landscape artists—Gainsborough, let's say, or Constable—rather than those modernists."

She continued speaking, but my brain tuned out the rest as I focused on the heart of what she was saying.

Children. Grandchildren.

Building a life and a family with Flynn.

A family that was Wellbridge and Honeycutt together. Maybe the best parts of both.

The very idea lit me up from the inside out in a way that left not a single doubt about what I wanted or what I'd do to have it.

"Jonathan, do stop gawping, dear. You look rather like a bearded hippopotamus. Ah! The drinks. Finally. Thank you, dear."

She took her wineglass from the server and knocked back a healthy swig before making a sound of contentment and ordering her salad.

I followed her lead and took a deep gulp of my beer. I knew what I needed to do, but that didn't make it any less scary. Especially the part where I'd have to convince Flynn that he wanted it, too.

Before I could think too much about it, Alice came racing into the hotel bar, curls bobbing and bright red dress perfectly pressed, waving a stack of papers. "There you are. I've been looking everywhere for you."

"Sorry," I said, feeling guilty for forgetting she was arriving tonight. "My phone ran out of battery a few hours ago from overuse."

My mother sniffed. "Really, Jonathan. You should be more responsible."

"No worries," Alice assured me with a wink. "No mystery too great or small for your intrepid assistant. I have the draft of the business plan here, as well as your employment contract. I also 'backed up your files'—*ahem*—to a portable hard drive." She pulled a small black device from her handbag and placed it and the stack of papers on the table with a triumphant wink. "And I've scheduled seven more meetings here at the event with existing clients and prospects, plus made sure to move the ones already scheduled for tomorrow to the following day."

I moved over in the booth and gestured for her to join us. "You amaze me. Alice, this is my mother, Patricia Wellbridge. Mother, this is Alice, my—" I hesitated as my mouth was about to form the word *assistant* and smiled. "My right hand."

Alice smirked. "And don't you forget it."

Mother's eyes roamed from Alice's face all the way down to her red shoes. She nodded approvingly. "Nice to meet you, dear. I assume you're here to help Jonathan at the expo this week?"

"Yes, ma'am. I'll finally get to meet many of our clients in person instead of on a computer screen. I'm excited to be here."

I felt a familiar nervous swirling in my stomach. It had been happening on and off all afternoon. "They won't be our clients for much longer. Not after this week. Are you sure you want to make such a big move, sight unseen? Honeybridge is very small. Not much of a nightlife, especially during the winter."

Her eyes sparkled. "No, but they have a very active knitting group, a yarn shop, and a salon that does great hair. That's all I need."

"You've been googling," I said with a laugh.

"Research is part of my job description, boss."

The server stopped by to drop off the potato skins and take Alice's drink order. When he left, I turned to her. "I'm serious, though. If you want to take some more time to think about it—"

"No," she said, interrupting me before I could give her another out. "It's like that Jerry Maguire movie, where I'm Renée Zellweger and you're Tom Cruise, except we don't end up together because you're like my big brother, and that would be gross." She shot my mother an enthusiastic grin, and my mother blinked back uncomprehendingly.

I hid my laugh with another sip of beer.

"Seriously, though, JT, I'm excited. Half the reason I stayed at Fortress so long was because I learned so much from working with you. And we're gonna kick ass together, I just know it."

Mother finally put two and two together. "Wait. Wait just a minute." She held up her slender hand, the giant diamond and sapphire rings flashing in the low lights over the table. "Are you... Jonathan, are you considering opening your own business?"

"More than considering, actually." I grinned. "I already have a plan in place, and Alice has come on board to help me make it a reality."

"You're looking at the CEO of Rainmaker Holdings." Alice swept a hand toward me proudly. "The newest, most exclusive distributor of consumer products in the northeast."

I laughed. "The smallest distributor, more like. And none of the paperwork has been submitted yet, so it's not official."

"Not yet," Alice agreed. "But I'm gonna get the ball rolling this week. Harrison Yang already sent Fortress packing, and when I called to set up an appointment with him for this week, he was freaking thrilled." She wiggled her eyebrows. "Rainmaker is about to sign Archdale Vineyards as their first client."

"Our first client," I corrected.

My mother beamed. "And this will be happening..." Her voice caught. "...in *Honeybridge?*"

I nodded. "It's home," I said simply. "I don't need to go looking for success anywhere else. I can stay right here and build it for myself."

It had taken me a really long time to figure that out, but now that I had, I was committed.

"Even if things don't work out with your Mr. Honeycutt?" she ventured.

I swallowed hard. They *would* work out. I trusted Flynn, and I believed in us. But I also knew what she was asking.

"This isn't just about Flynn. It's about running a business I can be proud of. It's about believing in myself. It's about..." I broke off, searching for the proper word.

Mother studied my face for a long moment, and then she lifted her wineglass in a toast. "Passion," she said in a satisfied tone.

"Exactly," I agreed.

And when I fell asleep that night, I felt more confident than I had in a long time, not because I thought I had everything figured out, but because I'd been reminded just how many people I could rely on to support me through any storm that came my way.

I only hoped that, wherever Flynn was, he knew he could trust me to be that for him, too.

Chapter Eighteen

Flynn

By the time I found my brother in Boston in the wee hours of Wednesday morning, I was dirty and exhausted, not to mention out of my mind with fear. During the drive to the city, I'd convinced myself PJ had been snatched out of a dark alley one night and left for dead by criminals who had the false impression he might have money on him.

When I finally found him, after hours and days spent roaming the streets, showing PJ's picture to every random stranger I met and trying to get the police to take my missing person's report seriously, I wasn't that far off.

"PJ? What the hell?" I raced over to the too-skinny, too-dirty kid who vaguely looked like my baby brother. He was sitting in the flickering yellow light of a restaurant service entrance alcove that a homeless woman had pointed me to, with his bony arms wrapped around his knees. He looked over at me through the predawn gloom with a confused crinkle between his eyebrows.

"Flynn? Is it really you?"

"Shit," I said, closing the distance between us and skidding to a halt in front of him. I crouched down and pushed a dirty hank of hair out of his face. "Bro. Oh, thank god. I thought..." I broke off, not wanting to give voice to all the nightmares that had haunted me in the few hours of sleep I'd caught over the last three nights. "What the fuck is going on? Are you high?"

"No," he said firmly. "I don't do that stuff." But he shivered as he said it, like maybe he'd had a closer call with it than he'd have liked. "You always told me not to, and I listened, Flynn. I tried to make you proud." Tears filled his eyes.

I grabbed his chin and tilted his face toward the light. There were dark circles under his eyes and a faded bruise along his chin. "PJ. What happened, buddy? What the hell's going on? Your roommates said you moved out two months ago because you couldn't afford rent anymore, but that's not possible, unless—"

A tear slid slowly out of one of his eyes. "I lost it," he whispered. "The money."

My eyes widened. "What, all of it?"

He nodded miserably. "All the rent and more besides. I'm sorry. I'm *so* sorry. I was such an idiot. And I know how hard you worked. I... I wanted to figure out a way to get it back so you'd never have to know. I didn't want you to be mad."

"Mad? I'm not mad, Pollux. I'm fucking gutted. How could you be *homeless* and not tell me? And not ask me for fucking help?" My hands shook as I tried pulling him up from the sidewalk. He reeked of unwashed body, and his clothes were filthy. "Where's your stuff? We're going home."

He shook his head, but my usually cheerful, talkative younger brother shuffled out of the alley after me, meek as a puppy. "No stuff. Sold all the stuff. Sold my phone, too, last week."

PJ seemed numb. Tired in a way that implied he hadn't

slept well in weeks... maybe even longer. The only information I'd gotten from his drunken former roommates at his old apartment was that he'd moved out earlier in the summer and they hadn't seen him around campus since. One roommate had mentioned seeing PJ with an older guy —maybe a boyfriend, hard to tell—the previous semester, and I'd wondered if my brother was shacked up with some guy.

I hadn't imagined him alone. On the street.

"Daydreamer. Your art supplies? Your clothes?"

"Sold it all."

"Why?" I whispered.

He took a shuddering breath. "Don't make me tell you. It's too embarrassing, Flynn. I can't... I don't want..."

I led him back to the garage where I'd parked my truck. "I'm your brother. You can tell me anything."

But it was only a few moments of silence, once I'd finally buckled him into the passenger's seat and started the engine, that he finally spoke again. "I fell for a scam," he admitted. "One of my professors said I didn't have what it takes to be a career artist—"

"Bullshit," I snapped. "What the fuck? What professor tells someone that? And your talent is incredible, PJ. It's why the school gave you a scholarship!"

He waved a hand listlessly through the air. "Whatever. I don't care anymore."

"One person said bad things and it caused you to drop out?"

"I didn't drop out. I..." He swallowed. "I *failed* out because I stopped showing up. I found out about a gallery show—you know, a way I could prove I have what it takes— and I got conned into spending more and more time and money setting it up." PJ sighed. "It was a scam. To get money out of desperate art students. And it worked on me because I was stupid. Can we... not talk about this right now. I'm hungry and tired, and I just... I don't want to think about art ever again. I just want to go back to the Retreat and forget about everything."

"Yes, of course. Let's get you home," I said, biting back the million questions I had for him. Instead, I ducked into a deli to grab sandwiches and drinks before settling him into the truck and heading home.

PJ fell asleep an hour into the drive back to Honeybridge. Even with the windows down in the truck, the cab still stank of him. It made my chest hurt thinking of both what he'd had to go through in the past couple of months and why he hadn't felt like he could reach out for help.

PJ had always been like his twin, sunshiny and idealistic. Both PJ and Castor had somehow gotten all of Willow's artistic qualities and all of Huck's chill, which meant seeing PJ broken and sad was terrifying to me.

I'd always been able to count on PJ's happiness and simple devotion to his painting. Unlike Castor, whose shyness held him back from pursuing his singing, or Georgia, whose brashness had led her to move to LA for a music career with no preparation, I'd thought PJ had the perfect combination of confidence and natural talent to make it as a professional artist. It was why I'd worked so hard to support his move to Boston to get his art degree.

After hearing him say he was done with art forever, I knew something was seriously wrong. I wanted to sit and talk with him until I could set his head on straight about this again. But I didn't have time right then. I needed to hop in the truck and get to Brew Fest before the first press event started.

Alden had sworn up and down, the couple of times that I'd been able to find a phone and call home, that everything had been transported to the festival and was waiting for me. "Stop worrying," he'd said. "Trust and believe."

I hadn't had the time or brainpower to demand more details. Obviously, things wouldn't be as well prepared as they would if I'd done the setup, but I'd have to make the best of the situation.

By the time I pulled into Honeybridge, the sun was beginning to lighten the gray sky behind me, and I was desperate for coffee. Thankfully, McLean was already up and waiting at the Retreat, Lily by his side, ready to greet PJ with a worried hug and guide him to the shower to clean up.

"PJ," I called as he crossed the bathroom threshold. He stopped but didn't turn around. "You... you scared the shit out of me today," I admitted softly. "I wish you'd called me. Called any of us. I might have been mad—okay, I *would* have been mad—but I would have gotten over it fast because I love you. You don't ever need to be ashamed to ask for help from the people who love you. Okay?"

PJ's shoulders slumped, and he nodded. Then he shuffled the rest of the way into the bathroom.

Once he closed the door behind him, I sighed.

"Is Daydreamer okay?" Mac asked. He moved toward the kitchen, where the scent of glorious, glorious coffee called.

"He will be. Eventually," I said grimly, kneeling down to rub Lily's ears. "We'll make sure of it."

"Right." McLean poured coffee into a to-go cup and handed it to me. "Because it's okay to accept help from people who love you," he said pointedly.

I rolled my eyes. He wasn't subtle in the slightest. "Yeah, yeah. I know, I know."

"Do you? Hmm." He met my eyes over the rim of his own coffee cup. "You left your amethyst behind Sunday, along with this." He slapped my phone into my hand. The screen was dark, and the device was dead. I pursed my lips disapprovingly, and he shrugged. "I don't have a charger for this kind, Flynn. Maybe next time, make sure you don't leave home without protection and with no way to call your family."

I cleared my throat and clutched the phone in my hand. "I wasn't thinking clearly Sunday morning. About a lot of things."

If I had been, I would have called JT and asked him for help. I knew that now. I would have listened to his apology and made things right, even if he ended up back in New York for good. I was hoping I'd run into him at Brew Fest so I could tell him so.

Heck, who was I kidding? I'd hog-tie the Frog and stow him under the table in my booth until he listened to me.

"Hey, have you heard any details from Alden about Brew Fest setup?" I asked Mac. "The asshole kept telling me to trust and believe, but I kinda wanna know what I'm walking into."

Mac suddenly found a spot on the ceiling fascinating. "Uh. Well. Alden actually had to work a wedding last night, and he couldn't miss it."

I closed my eyes and winced. "So it's just Castor and Dan there today? Fuck. Did you have to close the Tavern?"

"Actually, um..." McLean scratched his head. "No. No, everyone kinda... pitched in and figured things out."

I stared at him. "Dude, you can't just give me that. I need specifics. Figured out how? How many people did Honeybridge Mead send to Brew Fest?"

"What? PJ? Is that you calling?" McLean demanded into the silent room. He hurried toward the bathroom. "You should probably go use Huck and Willow's shower, Firecracker. I'll hold down the fort here."

"McLean Honeycutt," I gasped. "What the hell is happening here? Are you seriously not gonna tell me?"

"Nah. I think Alden was right," he said with a gentle smile. "I think you need to learn to trust and believe. People love you, Flynn. And we have your back."

After I stomped across the yard to Huck and Willow's place to shower and change, I hopped back in my truck, plugged my phone in to charge, and immediately got on the highway. I debated stopping by the salon or the Tavern to demand to know what was going on, but I knew that would be a waste of time when I could soon see for myself.

Apparently, I wasn't the only one heading into the city today because the traffic was awful. When I finally found a place to park and hauled my sorry ass into the expo center, I felt shaky from lack of food and sleep mixed with too much caffeine.

I walked into the giant center and right into a wall of noise and people. The press event was hopping, with colorful signs everywhere and the scent of beer, wine, spirits, and food permeating the air.

This kind of event would normally energize me, but I was so bone-tired from the stress and effort of dealing with PJ that I suddenly wondered if I could do it... if I could even find my way to my own booth and speak coherently about my products. And the idea of having to do it again tomorrow, and the next day, and the next day made me want to get back in my truck and drive home.

When I imagined sweet Castor standing at the booth alone, though, trying to explain the intricate process of creating our craft mead varietals... that may have been the straw that broke the camel's back.

The sting of tears threatened, and my entire body began to shake. I looked everywhere for my booth location but couldn't spot it. *I couldn't find the booth.* I couldn't find my own damned booth in the event I'd worked so hard to prepare for. What kind of entrepreneur was I if I couldn't even find my fucking booth? The Ren Faire people would never want to do business with a man who was such a complete and utter disaster.

Where is it? Why can't I find it?

I spun around, looking for any sign of Honeybridge Mead, but all the colorful signs blurred together, and my head began to pound. Finally, I fumbled for my phone and dialed the one person I knew I could count on.

"Flynn?" JT's warm, familiar voice washed over me. I squeezed my eyes closed and felt the hot slide of a tear roll down my face.

"Hey," I croaked, suddenly nervous. "Uh. H-hey."

"Baby, what's wrong?"

Oh, shit. The relief of his words was a powerful drug—so powerful my knees trembled. Our relationship wasn't broken entirely. Not if he called me baby.

"I need you," I said simply. Two days ago, I couldn't have imagined letting myself be that vulnerable around JT. Now I knew that I couldn't do what I needed to do today without knowing he was on my side, even if he couldn't be with me physically. "*Fuck.* I have the worst timing anyone ever had. You're probably busy getting ready for Brew Fest, and you can't help me right now, but... I just needed to hear your voice, at least. I needed to tell you..."

"Flynn—"

"Wait. Let me say this." I grabbed a hank of hair at the front of my head and tugged on it as I walked aimlessly around the expo center. "Look, if you *must* know, I should have called you Sunday and asked you for help. I realize that, okay? I knew it even then, but I couldn't make myself do it. There's no shame in asking for help from people who care about you."

"No, there isn't. Flynn—"

"And I should have listened to what you were saying Saturday and not let my fear get in the way then either... though, I swear to Christ, Frog, if you say *I told you so*, I'm gonna make you eat fish sticks every day for the rest of our lives. The thing is..." I sucked in a breath. "I don't know if I can do this Brew Fest thing on my own. Not this time. I really wish you were here with me right now. I hate that I pushed you away." I huffed out a laugh and felt tears prick my eyes. "Hell, I'm so messed up, I can't even find my own booth."

"Ah, Flynn," he breathed. "Baby, I wondered why you'd wandered down this row three times already."

I stopped in the center of the aisle. "W-what?"

"Sweetheart," he said in a gentle, affectionate voice, the kind of voice that poured warm honey down through my chest and into my soul. "Turn around."

I closed my eyes and pivoted, almost scared to hope, but when I opened them, I saw the Honeybridge Mead display —literally fifteen feet away and looking incredible—and, even more amazingly, the handsome man standing out front in a Honeybridge Mead shirt.

"Jon?" I choked, lurching forward until I was safe in his arms. "You're here. Thank god."

He squeezed me tightly, one hand wrapped around my waist while the other sank into my hair. His scent—that expensive designer cologne that had become as comforting to me as any of Willow's candles or the yeasty oatmeal scent of the Meadery—made me want to shove my nose in his neck for the rest of our lives. I wanted to crawl inside him and sleep for weeks.

"I missed you. Missed you so much."

"Flynn, is PJ okay? Is he..."

"He's home. He's with McLean. I... I feel like I dropped

the ball and let him down, Jon. But he's safe." My voice broke on the last word.

"Shh." JT's voice rumbled through his chest, and my fingers tightened. "Ah, Christ, baby. You've had a shitty few days, haven't you? But I've got you now. I promise I do. And you don't have to do anything alone anymore if you don't want to."

I sniffed, annoyed at myself for dissolving so completely in his arms—though not annoyed enough to break away from his hold. It *had* been a shitty few days. And I was so damn tired of being strong. It was nice to let myself be held, especially by JT.

"Firecracker, I'm sorry," JT whispered. "I should have told you right away about the Fortress deal. As soon as I knew that you and I had understood things differently. But I swear, it wasn't because I don't believe in you or respect you—"

"I know. And I'm sorry I pushed you away. I'm going to work on that." I pressed my forehead to his collarbone and let my breath coast over his skin. "Every single thing you've done this summer was about empowering me and setting me free, Jon. I should have put my faith in that instead of knee-jerk reacting." I gave a watery laugh. "Thank you. For being here. For apologizing. It means a lot."

"So... you forgive me?" he demanded, his body sagging in relief. He pulled back just far enough to see my face. "Shit, baby. I thought I was going to have to make some kind of big speech. Write you poetry. Declare you *King of Brew Fest*. Promise you a million blowjobs—"

"Well, I mean." I dragged the heel of my hand under my traitorous, leaking eyes. "Let's not take those things off the table just yet."

JT's lips quirked, and then he full-on grinned, and— damn that smug, sexy, adorable, wonderful *asshole*—when he started laughing, I couldn't help laughing, too, right in the aisle of the expo center...

Because JT always knew how to make things better.

He was on my side. And whatever challenges life had in store for us, I would never doubt that again.

JT pushed my hair back from my forehead and grinned down at me. I swear I could see my future in those Wellbridge-blue eyes. "Only you, Flynn Honeycutt, could make me feel this chaotic and this fucking incredible. Loving you is going to be the wildest ride."

My heart skipped a beat. "L-loving?" I sucked in a breath. "Wait, you... what do you mean *love?*"

"Ah." He nodded with exaggerated seriousness. "Good call. Too many misunderstandings in the past. Let me make sure I communicate this clearly so there can be no doubt. I'm saying that *I*—as in, Jonathan Turner Wellbridge III—"

I choked out a startled laugh. "You," I repeated, annoyed and amused and ridiculously aroused, all at the same time. "The world's most aggravating, completely unsexy Frog—"

"Uh-huh. *Love*—as in, feel an overwhelming, life-altering, there-will-never-be-anyone-else-for-me passion—"

My throat made a clicking noise as I swallowed.

"For *you*, Flynn Honeycutt. My archnemesis. My soul mate. My unreasonable, prickly, gorgeous Firecracker. Is it clearer now?"

My stomach swooped and dove like a kite in the breeze, and I clung to him tighter. "Christ, you're an asshole. Seriously, *such* an asshole," I said with a sniff, lifting on my toes to press a hard, thorough kiss to his mouth.

And fuck, did I like him exactly as he was.

Jon's face went serious as he pulled back. "I love you," he whispered in a low voice. "You're the only man I've ever said that to, Flynn. The only one ever I want to say it to."

I bit my lip. When he looked at me this tenderly, it was impossible to stay prickly, even for me. "Well, that's good, then," I said, the words coming out hoarse and low. "Because I love you, too, Jon. So damn much."

He buried his face in my neck and held me so tightly it was nearly painful... and entirely perfect. "Just remember," he whispered in my ear, "who said it first."

I sputtered out a shocked laugh, and I might have argued—ah, who was I kidding? I totally would have argued—but when the man pushed me up against the edge of the booth and took my mouth in a savage, desperate kiss, I decided that maybe, just this once, I'd let Frog win.

Chapter Nineteen

JT

Holding Flynn and hearing him say he loved me was everything I could have hoped for. It wrecked me in the best way and made it impossible to focus on anything but him.

Which was probably why my mother felt the need to interrupt us.

"For the love of public decency, Jonathan, let go of the poor man's face. Mr. Honeycutt needs to *prepare*."

Flynn jumped away from me immediately, and his eyes went round.

"Jon," he warned, his gaze fixed over my shoulder. "Holy shit. *I think your mother is here.*"

"Yeah, obviously." I blinked at him. "Wait. Didn't you get my text messages?"

He shook his head once, not moving his eyes, like my mother was a predator who might attack without warning. "I left my phone in Honeybridge when I was in Boston, then it died, and then I was in such a hurry to get here—"

"So you didn't already know I'd be here for you, taking care of setting up the booth for the Meadery? But you called me anyway?"

"Well, yeah. Because I love you. And I missed you."

When my words finally processed in his brain, he shook his head and turned his gaze to me. "Wait, *you* set up the booth?"

He'd trusted me. I'd known it deep down, but the confirmation sent warmth spreading through my body from the inside out. I grabbed him against me again and turned him in a circle. "I love you, Flynn."

"I love you, too," he assured me. "But..." His eyes sought out my mother again, and he lowered his voice. "Am I losing my mind? Is your mother wearing a Honeybridge Mead T-shirt?"

"Well, of course I am." Patricia Wellbridge sniffed, rolling her eyes. "I'm not sure what sort of havey-cavey operation you were *planning* on running here, Mr. Honeycutt, but I'm here now, and I assure you that having your whole team in matching shirts elevates the look of the entire booth." She glanced at his button-down disapprovingly.

Flynn's eyes darted from the booth, where Reagan was chatting with a visitor, to my mother, to me, and then back again. I knew he was overcome with emotion when he didn't bother pointing out that he'd ordered the T-shirts himself for the very purpose my mother mentioned.

"You? Helped with setup?" he asked my mother in a shocked whisper.

"Indeed." My mother set her chin higher, a sure sign that she was fighting emotions, too. "Reagan, Jonathan, Jonathan's assistant Alice, and myself."

"But... why?" Flynn demanded, so honestly bewildered that I wanted to scoop him up, take him back to my hotel room, and not let him out until he understood just how amazing and valued he was.

"Because Alden had a bridal party to style last night," I explained instead, pulling Flynn against my side and draping an arm over his shoulder to keep him there. "And

Dan and Castor had to keep the Tavern open. My mother organized a whole troop of Honeybridgers to help pack things up yesterday, too. The Gentlepeople's Society, the volunteers at the Log Cabin Museum, and a few others besides."

"Wow. Thank you, Patricia," Flynn said softly. "Truly."

"Nonsense. No thanks needed. Honeybridge helps its own, and the town... loves you," she admitted. She straightened and tucked a strand of her blonde bob behind her ear. "Which is only fitting for my future son-in-law."

"Your future... *what?*" He sent a ferocious, adorable scowl in my direction.

Thank you, Mother. So helpful.

"Heh." I bit my lip, feeling my cheeks burn. "It's, ah... been a busy couple of days, baby. I've been doing a lot of thinking, and I've made some decisions that I really need to talk to you about—"

"But not now," Mother warned. She put an arm around Flynn's shoulders and steered him around the back of the booth, where there was relative privacy. "It's almost noon, and I've seen the Ren Faire people walking around already. Since Reagan and I only know the bullet points about the Meadery and Alice is off chasing down leads for Jonathan, you, Mr. Honeycutt, need a wardrobe change immediately so you can get out there. It's *showtime.*" She pressed a Honeybridge Mead shirt into Flynn's hand and gave him a small smile, then set her shoulders, shook her hair back, and strode out to greet the public like a modern-day Evita.

Flynn pressed the shirt to his stomach and frowned.

"Problem?" I asked, grabbing his free hand. "Is it my mother? She's a lot, but I promise she means well."

"No, I know. That's not it."

"Nerves again?"

He shook his head and looked at me wonderingly. "No,

actually. I'm waiting for the nerves to set in again, but they're not. I feel like I've got this." He squeezed our linked fingers. "*We've* got this."

I grinned. "Yeah, we do."

"*Boys!*" my mother called.

I loosened my grip, and Flynn pulled away from me reluctantly.

"We should get to work," I said, running my fingers through his hair to smooth it down from where I'd grabbed it during our kiss.

Flynn pulled off his button-down, giving me a quick glimpse of his broad shoulders and cut arms and chest. The sight made me harden instantly. "So the famous Alice is here?" He pulled his Honeybridge Mead shirt over his head. "Will I get to meet her?"

"*Ngh*," I said before trying to hide my reaction in a cough.

Flynn turned to look at me in concern, and whatever he saw on my face made him raise an eyebrow and dart a glance at my crotch. "Really, Frog? Now? Here?"

I nodded enthusiastically. "Always, baby. Anywhere."

He grabbed the front of my shirt and yanked me in for another fierce kiss, this one way too quick. "Next time we reconnect after an argument," he hissed, "could you please make sure it happens at a time when you and I aren't surrounded by hundreds of strangers *and your mother*, moments before I'm supposed to woo a bunch of Ren Faire judges?"

I pretended to think about it for a moment. "Or we could just... not argue at all."

Flynn pursed his lips. "We could try, I suppose. But... no arguing at all, Frog? Why on earth would we do that?"

I laughed out loud. Might as well tell a hedgehog not to be prickly. Our relationship had always involved rivalries and disagreements—passionate ones. But I wouldn't trade that passion for anything.

"How about I promise that from now on, our arguments won't involve either of us walking away without talking to the other?" Flynn suggested. "I won't push you away again—"

"And I won't be pushed?" I nodded. "Yeah. Yeah, that sounds pretty perfect."

His face cleared. "It does, doesn't it?" He unbuckled his belt so he could tuck in his shirt, and I forced myself not to get distracted. "So... I think we can figure the rest out, Frog. Don't you? Yeah, I know, I know," he hurried on before I could answer. "I've been the one saying that we couldn't work long distance for weeks now. But that was mostly me not trusting you. Not trusting *myself*." He shoved his shirt tails into his waistband and buttoned it again. "The truth is, it's gonna suck being apart. But giving you up entirely would be way, way worse. Keeping you in my life is nonnegotiable for me. So even if you're in New York on Team Fortress and I'm in Honeybridge, I want us to be together. I can travel sometimes, and you can— Wait, why are you shaking your head?"

"Because I'm not Team Fortress. I'm Team Flynn." I pointed down at my shirt. "Baby, I—" I took a deep breath and opened my mouth to tell Flynn everything.

"*Jonathan. Turner. Wellbridge.*" Mother appeared at my shoulder like an apparition. "Unhand Mr. Honeycutt at once. That *Boston Globe* reporter you contacted has arrived *and* three local reporters besides. While you're canoodling, we're being overrun!" She disappeared once again.

Fuck. "We'll talk about this later," I promised both of us. "As soon as possible."

Flynn's eyes met mine. "You contacted the *Globe*?"

"A college friend's husband. He was eager to come by—"

Flynn kissed me briefly, grabbed my hand, and towed me toward the front of the tent. "I love you. I don't know how I got lucky enough to have you come back into my life."

"It was mostly thanks to my mother," I reminded him.

Flynn closed his eyes and grimaced. "Dammit. I'm *really* gonna have to be nice to her now, aren't I?"

"Since I plan on you and me being together forever?" I squeezed his fingers before releasing him. "Yeah, maybe—"

"*Overrun!*" my mother whisper-hissed from way too close.

"But not too nice," I concluded, and Flynn laughed out loud.

From the moment we stepped into the booth, the afternoon flew by. Thanks to Frankie Hilo's magical Instagram posts, Honeybridge Mead already had a lot of buzz in the brewing world, and Flynn's booth was on the must-visit list for several media outlets covering the festival.

Alice came back soon, shooting me a wink that said her lead-chasing for Rainmaker Holdings had been successful, but I didn't bother asking for specifics. There'd be plenty of time for that later, ideally after I'd filled Flynn in.

The five of us worked side by side in sync for the next few hours, talking to people from the media and various other VIPs. Reagan lost no time charming Alice and joking with Flynn like they'd been best friends for ages.

Alice and Flynn got along even better than I'd expected. Apparently, Flynn had "sort of accidentally" learned how to knit one winter when business was slow and the local knitting club had relocated their meetings to the Tavern. He and Alice talked about yarn and patterns in the rare breaks between visitors.

My mother charmed the reporter from the *Boston Globe*

for a solid hour, telling him the backstory of our town and the Wellbridge-Honeycutt rivalry before smoothly segueing into discussion of the many varietals Flynn offered.

"So... you're a Wellbridge, but you're working for a Honeycutt? Are you saying this mead was good enough to end a centuries-long feud?" the reporter joked at length.

My mother fixed the man with a glare. "End the feud entirely? Why on earth would we do that?"

I darted a pointed glance at Flynn, who was deep in conversation with someone about the benefits of short meads versus those that aged longer. His blush and eye roll said he'd caught both my mother's comment and my look, but he didn't dignify either with a response.

I stifled a grin. He and my mother were more alike than either of them would admit, and I was going to tease Flynn about it mercilessly later. But first, I was planning a very leisurely, very thorough celebration of his success, followed by a long talk about our future.

I was done making assumptions about what Flynn Honeycutt wanted, but there was very little I wasn't open to considering, as long as it ended with the two of us together. In fact, I really hoped our future looked a lot like this—working alongside my family, friends, and the man I'd loved so long he'd become part of my DNA, teasing and laughing while creating something important.

I took a deep breath and felt the simple beauty of the moment sink into my bones.

The three Ren Faire representatives arrived and greeted Flynn with a barely concealed enthusiasm that told me they'd already heard plenty of good things about Honeybridge Mead, and their contract was Flynn's to lose. Flynn greeted them with his gorgeous smile and a smooth, professional confidence that made me want to get on my knees for him right then and there.

But before I'd even had a chance to pour them samples of Flynn's most popular varietals, a familiar loud voice distracted me so badly I nearly fumbled the bottles.

"Wellbridge?" Conrad Schaeffer demanded loudly, just as I was pouring the samples for Flynn. "Where the hell have you been? I must've called you a dozen times. Deb tells me you haven't even checked in at the Fortress booth yet."

Conrad's entire being bristled with anger, and Jeff Namath looming over his shoulder like a loyal, not-very-bright henchman only added to the drama.

The exact sort of drama Flynn didn't need at that moment.

Flynn shot me a worried look, but I shook my head. *This isn't a problem.* I tilted my head toward the Ren Faire people. *Get your contract, baby. Don't be distracted.*

"Conrad," I began politely, gesturing him to one side of the booth so we wouldn't interrupt Flynn's conversation. "I wasn't aware that you were coming to Brew Fest personally—"

Conrad would not be moved. "Well, I had to come, didn't I? Since my star employee threatened to abandon his post at the last minute."

I stifled a sigh. "I take it you read my email from earlier this morning, then?"

Conrad grunted. "Not sure what kind of hardball you thought you were playing, Jonathan, but it's highly unprofessional."

"Yeah. *Highly* unprofessional," Jeff echoed.

"If this was your way of expressing displeasure about our decision to delay your promotion, you've gone about it entirely wrong—"

"Yeah, *entirely*," Jeff said smugly.

"But if it'll get you to cease this tomfoolery about

leaving Fortress, then we're prepared to offer you the vice presidency," Conrad said grudgingly.

"Yeah, we're prepared to... wait, what?" Jeff gave Conrad a look of betrayal.

I darted a glance at Flynn, who wasn't even pretending to talk to the Ren Faire people anymore. All of them had turned their attention to my conversation instead.

Great.

"That email wasn't a threat," I said. I turned my head to meet Flynn's gaze. This was not the way I'd planned to explain things to him, but then... things rarely went according to plan for the two of us, and it had seemed to work out okay eventually, right? "It was my resignation. I'm leaving Fortress, effective immediately."

Flynn looked horror-struck.

Fuck.

Conrad waved a hand. "Nonsense. Here you are at the Honeycomb Mead booth, still working to sign the deal—"

"It's Honey*bridge* Mead," I said firmly. "And they're not interested in moving forward with Fortress at all. Neither am I."

Conrad's chin lowered, and his wide brow folded in confusion. His eyes flicked down to Flynn's logo on my chest before glancing back up at my face. "I don't understand. Why in the world would you be working here if you hadn't closed the deal?"

Out of the corner of my eye, I saw my mother move forward as if she was going to intercede. The fiery burn of anger singed my vision as I shot her a look that hopefully said, *"Do it and perish. Violently."*

"Because I believe in this product," I said calmly, willing Flynn to believe the truth of my words. "I believe in this company. I believe in Flynn Honeycutt."

He huffed out a laugh. "So you're leaving Fortress so

you can spend your time hawking the wares of someone from a little nothing of a town in nowhere, Connecticut?" he blustered.

Instead of correcting him—instead of reminding him that Flynn's mead was the vaunted "ware" that had become famous on social media because it had actually impressed someone enough to make a big deal out of it, and instead of reminding him of the name (and state) of my town—I simply shrugged. "Why not?"

"Jonathan." Conrad's tone turned conciliatory. "Let's not be hasty. If you need additional time off to spend in Honeybuns, I'm sure that can be arranged. And a small increase in salary—"

"Will change nothing," I interrupted.

Flynn stepped up next to me, his solid presence grounding me in a way only he had ever been able to do. "Jon," he said in a low voice. "Could I please have a quick word with you. Privately. *Now*?"

"It's all good, Flynn," I assured him. In a whisper only he could hear, I added, "I'm so sorry, baby. I promised I'd fill you in on everything later, and I will. Trust me?"

"Yes, but—"

"Finish your meeting, okay? Focus on what's important."

Flynn's face took on the stubborn, defiant look I'd seen so many, many times over the years. In one deliberate motion, he grabbed my hand, laced our fingers together, and pressed himself to my side. "I am," he said.

I sucked in a breath. I was going to love this man until the day I died.

Turning to my former boss, I continued. "What it boils down to, Conrad, is that I'm tired of working hard for someone else's gain. I've grown Fortress's bottom line for years, and instead of rewarding my hard work, you decided to give me extra challenges. I completely understand your desire to keep me hungry—it allows you to keep more of the profits for yourself, and that's your prerogative as the CEO. But it's made me realize that I'd like to be my own CEO. So I can run the business the way that works best for me. In a way that's in line with my values."

"Oh, *really*." Conrad's nostrils flared, and he darted an angry glare at the spots where Flynn and I touched. "I see what's happening here. Well, if you're planning to start a company in the beverage industry, you'd best think again. That would violate your noncompete agreement and cause you a heap load of legal troubles."

"*So* many legal troubles," Jeff agreed. "You'll be *toast*."

I felt Flynn stiffen in anger at my side, so I gave his hand a reassuring squeeze. "I expect you'll do what makes the most sense for Fortress. However, be aware that earlier this summer, when I was researching past contracts I'd negotiated for the company, I happened to take a look at my own employment contract. Turns out, I never signed a noncompete agreement. I requested red-line changes to it, and your attorney never got back to me with a new version to sign." I shrugged. "Seems like Fortress isn't so great with the follow-through."

Flynn clapped a hand to his mouth, and I felt his body jerk as he tried to hold back a snort of laughter. I relaxed against him, and he wrapped an arm around my back.

"*Hmph.*" Conrad seethed. "Don't bother coming back to the office after this, Wellbridge. You're *done* with Fortress."

"Done," Jeff stressed. "*So* done."

I shrugged again. In my email, which I'd also sent to HR, I'd stated that I planned to work out my two weeks' notice from home, but I was happy to let Conrad think it was his idea.

Conrad's jaw ticked. "You're making a huge mistake. Don't expect Fortress to clean up your messes when you disappoint whatever clients you manage to scrape together." He pointedly looked past me to the Honeybridge Mead signage, as well as the industry representatives and reporters currently filling the booth, and raised his voice. "We will make it very clear to our clients that if any of them leave us for you, we will not take them back when you inevitably fail to deliver."

"Thanks for the vote of confidence," I said with a cheery nod. "But I won't fail." And from the look Alice had given me earlier, as well as the conversations we'd already had with some soon-to-be-former Fortress clients, many people would rather take a chance on Rainmaker Holdings than deal with Fortress's business practices. "We'll be just fine."

"Can't say I'm disappointed to lose the Honeywax deal anyway," he bluffed. "Especially now that the chair-manufacturing facility's off the market, so there's nowhere to expand."

I tried to hide my surprise. I hadn't heard that the Hornrath Chair Company had been purchased, but I'd told Hayden days ago that the deal was dead, so he had no reason to keep me informed. I was sad that Flynn would lose the opportunity, but we'd find him something else. Something better.

Conrad couldn't resist one last bitter dig. "All in all, Honeydew doesn't live up to the hype, JT. You're welcome to it."

This time, I couldn't help giving him the reaction he'd been looking for. My hands clenched into fists, and my mouth opened in an angry retort. The fucker could say what he wanted about *me*, but Flynn—

Flynn's fingers pressed into my waist, anchoring and

calming me, and I managed to take a deep breath and bite out, "Honeybridge Mead doesn't need Fortress *or* me."

In my peripheral vision, I saw the Ren Faire people exchanging impressed looks.

Conrad smirked. "Don't underestimate the contacts I have in this business, son. Honeybunny might have a good reputation *now*, but once I explain—"

"Conrad, darling!" My mother swished forward and extended her bejeweled fingers for him to clasp. "So nice of you to stop by."

Anyone who didn't know my mother well would have believed her smile was friendly and a bit vapid, as if she and she alone had missed the spectacle Conrad had caused and the lingering tension in the air. I knew her well enough to see the wintery death gleam in her blue eyes, and it was almost—*almost*—enough to make me pity the man.

"Patricia," Conrad grunted, taking her proffered hand. "Wish I could say the same."

My mother laughed lightly. "Have you met Mr. Honeycutt yet?" She tilted her head toward Flynn. "He's the mastermind behind the hottest mead company in the country. Can you believe how many people are shouldering their way in here for a taste of his varietals? It's simply thrilling." She patted Flynn's cheek. "Such a smart boy... despite his questionable upbringing. He's like a son to me, you understand."

Flynn twisted his tongue in his mouth, but the edges of his lips still turned up. "You flatter me.... *Mama Wellbridge.*"

My mother's face went blank for one full second, which was an utter delight to behold. Flynn was right—too much getting along would be boring. It seemed my mother had met her match, and I was going to give Flynn the oral treat of his choice to thank him for demonstrating it.

She lifted one impeccably groomed eyebrow. "Not at all, Flynn. I'm excessively proud of your accomplishments," she said fondly. Then she turned back to my father's old friend, her eyes glittering in a way that reminded me why Patricia Wellbridge had always been a valuable asset on the campaign trail. "In fact, I plan to spread the word about Honeybridge Mead to *all* our friends and associates at our end-of-season victory party. The Dunkirks will be there, of course. Have you ever met Leticia Dunkirk, Conrad? She inherited controlling interest in one of the largest wineries in North America a few years ago. And the Sheas—you remember Gary Shea, don't you? I believe he's highly placed in the New York State Liquor Authority or some such thing now." She tapped her lip thoughtfully. "Pucky Dubour—pardon, *Governor* Dubour—will probably make an appearance. He loves my parties. And the Penningtons. The Patels. The Swenson-Taggarts—Stella Swenson is a columnist for the *Washington Post*, you recall, but her husband runs that giant shipping company that was rumored to have purposely held up shipments just to sabotage one of his son's political rivals. I never believed him capable of such *vindictiveness*, naturally, but then, is there really a limit to what one will do to protect one's son?"

With every powerful name my mother dropped, Conrad grew paler and seemed to shrink in on himself. "Well, I—" He swallowed. "I don't know."

Mother beamed. "I just *knew* you'd understand, Conrad. You and the Senator have enjoyed such a long-standing friendship, and we're so grateful for all that you've done for Jonathan—most especially sending him home this summer and indirectly helping these lovebirds along—"

"Lovebirds?" Flynn whispered.

"Go with it," I murmured.

"We'd be devastated if anything were to cause a rift in

that friendship." She tilted her head and gave Conrad a terrifyingly pleasant smile.

"N-no. No, of course not." Conrad nodded so firmly his jowls all jiggled at once. "Please assure Trent—er, the Senator—that our friendship will, ah... remain intact."

"Wonderful." Mother clasped her hands together. "Now, then. I'm sure we've taken up more than enough of your valuable time." She lifted her chin and made a shooing motion with her hands. "Please don't let us keep you any longer."

Conrad and Jeff flounced away, and I watched them go without a single qualm.

"Excuse me, ma'am." One of the Ren Faire people approached my mother with wide eyes and an awed voice. "Have you ever attended a Renaissance Faire? Because we have an opening for Queen Elizabeth..."

Before I could hear my mother's reply, Flynn grabbed me by the wrist and dragged me bodily around the side of the tent to push me up against one of the expo center's support poles.

"Your own *company*, Frog?" he demanded, green eyes snapping. "When you said we had things to discuss later, I assumed you meant something about *us*. A-a-a visitation schedule, maybe. Or asking me to make our relationship exclusive. Or maybe explaining why your mother is calling me her *son*."

I blinked. "Wait. Back up. Was there a chance we wouldn't be exclusive?" I growled, reversing our positions so that Flynn's back was to the pole. In the past, I'd never seen the appeal of commitment or monogamy, but when it came to Flynn... "It turns out I have very strong opinions about that."

"Well, no." Flynn blushed. "No, I want that. I just meant..."

I cupped his jaw and brushed my thumb over his bottom lip, unable to stop touching him. "You told me to let you know when I was ready to trade in my career for a position in Honeybridge. Well... I am."

Flynn's breathing accelerated, and I felt his pulse thrumming against the side of my hand like hummingbird wings. "You had a problem with the Meadery's benefits package," he reminded me softly. "No unlimited mead, no 401k."

"But what about unlimited access to the mead maker?" I demanded. "Are you willing to negotiate on that yet?"

Flynn's breath caught. "Don't," he warned, his voice raw and heavy with emotion. "Don't say shit like that, Frog, unless you mean it."

I stared down into those green eyes I loved. "Of course I mean it. I love you, Flynn. For maybe the first time in my life, I know *exactly* who I am and exactly where I want to be. Rainmaker Holdings will be based in Honeybridge. I'm moving there permanently."

"No." Flynn shook his head obstinately, trying to pull away. "No, JT. Absolutely not. You love your job. Y-your apartment in the city with the squash court. You love being that person. You told me so. And I won't let you give that up just because—"

I held him in place and gently covered his mouth with my hand. "Baby, listen to me. I'm not giving anything up. I'm giving myself the opportunity to do business the way I want to. To have the kind of community and relationships I want to. To wake up every morning and do something I'm passionate about—helping smaller companies make the connections they need to broaden their reach and grow their businesses—while also living conveniently close to the *man* I feel passionate about." I grinned. "I promise you, Firecracker, there is no sacrifice here. This—*us*—is success."

Emotions passed quickly over Flynn's face. Joy and fear. Elation and worry. Cautious, powerful hope.

"Shit, Jon. You'll love that." He pulled my hand away from his mouth and clenched it in both of his. "Are you sure? Please be sure."

"I'm absolutely positive." I gave him a half-smile. "And you know what I'll love more than building that business? Building a life with you." I caught him by the hips and pulled him closer. "I wanted to talk about all this tonight. As soon as possible. I was going to tell you everything I'd been planning and ask what *you* wanted our future to look like without making assumptions for once. I never planned to present you with the facts like it was all a done deal. You can check your texts if you don't believe me—"

Flynn draped his hands around my neck and pulled my face down to his. "That sounds *disgustingly* insightful and mature. I'll pencil you in for this evening."

I huffed wryly. "Yeah, well. It didn't happen quite the way I hoped. I'm sorry fucking Conrad came and spoiled things—"

"He didn't spoil anything." Flynn's lips brushed over mine in the barest, most tantalizing hint of a kiss.

"No, you're right." My hands shifted, resolutely pushing him away when I wanted to draw him into me. "The Ren Faire people looked really impressed, and if you get back out there right away, I'm confident you still have a strong shot at that contract—"

"Doesn't matter," he whispered.

"What?"

"I mean, it matters. Of course it matters. I want the contract, but..." Flynn scraped his bottom lip with his top tooth, and his fingers toyed with the hair at the nape of my neck. "I have a confession of my own to make. The Hornrath Chair Company? I bought it. Thatcher Pennington approached me about helping me grow the Meadery—he's an investor, you know?—and I agreed. Honeybridge Mead is poised to expand, regardless of what happens with the Ren Faire."

"Holy shit. Good god, Flynn. That's incredible!" I hauled him against my chest and spun him in a circle.

"Frog! Put me down!" he cried, though his face was creased with laughter. "A little respect, please. I'm a professional mead maker at a professional event."

"Fuck, yeah, you are." I set him on his feet but hugged him tightly, inhaling his familiar scent and letting it wash the rest of the stress away. "You're going to become a major producer of the world's best mead. And I'm going to get to be there to see it happen."

"Well, actually..." He gave me a nervous, excited smile and patted the Honeybridge Mead logo on my shirt. "I was hoping... I mean, now that you're staying... maybe you could help..." He scraped his lip with his tooth again. "Teach me how to find places to distribute it to? I don't need Fortress... but I definitely need *you*."

I let out a laugh so loud he jumped and glared at me.

"Baby, I'm going to sell the hell out of Honeybridge Mead. I'll put it in stores and taverns all across the country. If you'll let me represent your distribution side, I'll show you exactly what I can do to put Honeybridge Mead wherever you want."

"So the Rainmaker's winning streak is going to remain unbroken, then, hmm?" he teased.

"Unbroken?" I snorted. "No. As I recall, I was oh-for-three when it came to getting Honeybridge Mead to commit."

"But the mead *maker* is madly in love with you and ready to sign on the dotted line," he whispered.

"Is he?" My entire body felt buoyant, like Flynn was the

only thing tethering me to Earth. "You sure you've read the fine print, Honeycutt? Because you're signing up for a lifetime term. No limits, no take-backsies—"

"I accept," Flynn said firmly. Then he wrapped his strong, capable arms around me and kissed me to seal the deal.

Epilogue

Flynn

There was nothing quite like early fall in Maine to make a man feel grateful to be alive.

As I stood in the backyard of Wellbridge House, looking out over the sleepy town and the placid water of Quick Lake in the distance, I couldn't help falling a bit deeper in love with the ever-changing beauty of the town I called home. And I knew down to my bones that I could travel the whole world—stick a billion pins in Grandpa Horace's old map—but there'd never be anyplace that delighted my soul as much as Honeybridge.

Over the last few weeks, the vibrant summer green of the treetops had given way to bright flames of orange-yellow, scarlet-purple, and a dozen other colors only PJ would know the proper names of.

Out at the Retreat and in the Tavern, crowds of young tourists wielding sunblock and plastic floaties had been replaced by hordes of leaf-peepers and pumpkin-lovers.

The weather, while still clear and sunny, carried a crisp tang that warned us to enjoy the last of the mild temperatures because winter loomed on the horizon.

And the air, which had smelled of cut grass and growing

things just weeks before, was now thick with the scent of woodsmoke and...

"*Victoryyyyy!*" Patricia Wellbridge boomed into her microphone from atop the tiny stage she'd had erected on the far side of the lawn. In her hand, she hefted a wooden plaque bearing the words "Wellbridges: Softball Tournament Champions"—a miniature replica of the new rocker that had been installed below the Welcome to Honeybridge sign after Team Wellbridge's win in the final game of the season last week—like a conquering hero stabbing the sky with his sword.

"There are *so* many people I'd like to thank for this incredible honor," she gushed to the assembled crowd of bewildered New York socialites and long-suffering Honeybridgers. "In fact, I've prepared a brief but poignant speech..."

"Jesus Christ," I muttered under my breath in disgust. Okay, so not everything in Honeybridge delighted my soul. Some things were still barely tolerable.

"Awww, poor Firecracker." A pair of strong arms came around me from behind, and a voice whispered in my ear. "Losing is killing you, isn't it?"

I snorted, even as I leaned back against JT's broad chest and let my head rest on his shoulder. "Pffft. *No.* Not at all. Not even a little. I haven't given the silly tournament a second thought," I lied.

"Ah." JT nuzzled his face into my neck, and I tilted my head to allow him better access.

"Wasn't I the first one to congratulate Team Wellbridge after the game?" I demanded in a low voice. "And didn't I hand out free mead that night at the Tavern?"

"Mmhmm."

"Which, when you think about it, proves I'm not a competitive individual, Jon."

"Of course," he agreed solemnly. "Silly me."

"However," I was compelled to add in a whispered rush, "it bears repeating that the only reason Team Honeycutt lost that last game was because certain *Frogs* insisted on repeating inappropriate comments about my pitching skills being rusty and making offers to practice *catching* for me whenever I liked, which threw off my concentration. It was underhanded of you," I declared, as if we both didn't know I would have done the exact same thing if the situation had been reversed.

The vibration of his self-satisfied laughter rumbled through me.

"Also," I went on in the same low voice, unable to stop myself, "the way your mother is making an Oscars-level acceptance speech like she was the MVP of the team when she doesn't know a baseline hit from a foul ball is... irksome. On principle."

"Uh-huh."

"Furthermore, I can't help but feel that inviting the governor, three congresspeople, two Hollywood stars, and a Nobel Laureate to this celebration is a bit much. I mean, it was *one measly pitch*, Jon. Not like you rescued a bunch of orphaned kittens from a runaway locomotive while a horde of alien zombies threatened to destroy the Earth or whatever."

"Good to know what it would take to really impress you, baby," he murmured.

"And the fact that she invited Brantleigh Pennington, in particular, to this party, when she knows he deliberately tried to make trouble for us?" I whispered darkly. "Not cool."

The asshole had greeted me earlier with a smirky little smile and a request to "Introduce me to one of your brothers, Honeycutt. I need to see what Jonathan finds so impressive about you local boys." *As* fucking *if*.

"Yep, this is seriously, *seriously* killing you," JT sighed happily. "My prickly, competitive Firecracker."

"*Hmph.*" I managed to hold back my laughter, but it was a close call. It was uncomfortably wonderful to have someone know my flaws so well... and love me for them.

"Losing is never easy, Flynn," he said softly, his hands pressing flat against my stomach in a gesture that he'd probably meant to be soothing but instead made my dick perk up and take notice. "You played a great game, though—a great *season*—and next year, you'll get to try your luck again."

"I suppose you're right." I melted against him lovingly.

Then he went and ruined my vibe by adding in a sly voice, "And in the meantime, you can console yourself with the knowledge that you have a champion in your bed. Maybe I'll rub off on you."

I sputtered with laughter and lightly jabbed my elbow into his gut. I tried to turn my head to glare at him, but he held me firmly in place. "That champion won't be rubbing any part of me if he keeps running his mouth."

We both knew I was lying. I wasn't sure if JT's cocky attitude had always lit me up and I'd denied it or if this was a recent development, but either way, it was very, very real.

I could feel JT's smile against my skin... a second before he bit down gently on my nape. "You liked this mouth earlier today."

I shivered. He wasn't wrong. That mouth had trailed hot, sloppy kisses and breathed filthy, whispered commands over my lower back before he'd fucked me over an old wooden table in our new meadery building, and I'd liked it *very* much.

"If it makes you feel better, Mother didn't invite Brantleigh, and she was *not* thrilled that his father brought him," JT said. "She was the one who told Thatcher about his son's troublemaking last month, and from what she said, he's keeping a tight rein on him now. No more unlimited allowance and trips to the Riviera."

"Good. Brantleigh deserves it. And Thatcher's a straight shooter." Being in business with him, even just for a short time, had proven to be rewarding and educational. "Maybe he can help sort Brantleigh out."

"Doubtful. Oh, hey." JT straightened away from me just long enough to snag a couple of glasses from a silver tray carried by one of the phalanx of uniformed waiters circulating amongst the guests and pressed one of them into my hand. "Try this, baby. It's an apple bourbon cocktail. I had one earlier, and it made me think of that cyser mead you were dreaming up the other day. How great would it be if we tried aging that in bourbon barrels? I was reading an article..."

I grinned up at him, only paying attention to half of what he was saying. I loved knowing JT was my person at home and in my heart—the guy I got to eat dinner with every night, whether it was sandwiches in my office at the Tavern at the end of a long workday, or rutabaga-dogs at a cookout at the Retreat, or excruciating prime-rib feasts at the club while Patricia tried to give me remedial lessons in navigating high society—but it was a special kind of thrill that I got to share my business with JT, too.

As Honeybridge Meadery's new chief distribution and revenue officer, JT was already making things happen. He'd taken over the Ren Faire negotiation as soon as Brew Fest was over, and he'd scored us a way better deal than I ever would have been able to do on my own. He was also busy handling his own clients at Rainmaker Holdings, with Alice at his side.

Even though it had only been six weeks since coming

home from Brew Fest, JT already had contractors at the former Hornrath Chair Company building, giving us estimates on the work needed to get the new meadery production-ready. It left me able to do the supply sourcing, keep the Tavern itself running smoothly, and give JT insight into his clients' businesses based on my own experiences.

It turned out dismantling my defenses and letting JT in had made my life and my business stronger and more fulfilling. Who'd have thought?

He stopped talking midsentence. "What's that look for?"

"Look?" I asked innocently. "Which look?"

"The look that says you're madly in love with me and want to get me alone so you can take me apart piece by piece." He turned his back to the crowd of guests and not so subtly adjusted his pants.

"Oh, *that* look." I gave him a wicked, promising grin. "Was I giving you that look?"

"Drink up, Flynn," he growled. "We're leaving in an hour, tops."

"Your mother's never going to let you leave that soon," I reminded him. "Any good-son points you earned by moving home were wiped out when you presented her with that bouquet from Willow's cutting garden."

JT snickered, and the sound went down deep in my belly. His happiness turned me on no matter where we were.

"The look on her face when I handed it to her was worth the bee sting I got assembling it," he said before raising his voice into a semi-impressive Patricia Wellbridge accent. "Jonathan, darling, where in the *world* did you acquire this... *wilderness hodgepodge?*"

"She told *me* the arrangement was the 'prettiest thing she'd seen since the spectacle Willow concocted for Box

Day, Flynn.'" I shook my head fondly. Patricia was a connoisseur of the backhanded compliment. I was learning so much from her. It was much easier now that I understood snide comments were her love language. "I think Rosalia will like the flowers, though, and you and I both knew she'd be the one who ended up with them in the end."

JT dropped the teasing tone. "That woman deserves all the flowers. She's doing the lord's work by staying here with my mother despite socking away money all these years. I don't know how she puts up with... Oh! Senator Coglin." He turned toward the older man with a friendly smile. "Nice to see you, too, sir. Have you met my partner, Flynn Honeycutt?"

If I could go back in time and tell the Flynn Honeycutt of a year ago just how hard my belly would flip to hear Jonathan Turner Wellbridge call me his partner, in any sense of the word, the old me would die a thousand deaths. But the two of us together was a potent kind of magic... and I was pretty sure I'd always recognized that truth, no matter how long and fast I'd tried to run from it.

It wasn't that he *completed* me, or made me whole, or gave my life meaning, or any of that sentimental bullshit. I wasn't one of Pop's bargain-basement jigsaw puzzles with a missing piece, and neither was JT. But the way he supported and infuriated me, comforted and teased me, cared for me and *saw* me, made me more confident in myself than ever.

For the first time in my life, I truly *felt* like the Firecracker Pop had nicknamed me for, loud and colorful, shining bright, because there was no need to hide any part of myself. JT knew all the worst parts about me and loved me not in spite of them but because of them.

And if I ever tried to run from the scary, overwhelming

happiness we'd found together, I knew without a doubt that he'd drag me back.

As soon as we finished our polite chitchat and Senator Coglin wandered off to find someone else to bore with his stories, I turned to JT. "I remembered to ask the man about his equestrian daughter *and* his interest in breeding Norwegian Lundehunds, plus managed to discuss your mother's new yogaerobics studio with a straight face. That makes at least three blowjobs you owe me. Good ones. Not the quickie morning ones when I'm already hard for you."

His warm laughter made me smile. "You did that for my mother, not me. I never asked you to play politics for the Wellbridge family. In fact, if you recall, I specifically asked my mother to keep you out of it."

I shrugged. "It's not that bad. Especially since gladhanding some of her friends is what led me to my investor."

"Thatcher Pennington," JT grumbled. "Don't get me started."

I rolled my eyes knowingly. "You liked him just fine until he offered Reagan an internship in New York. I know you don't want to lose touch with your brother again. But I keep telling you, that won't happen."

"I don't *dis*like him... but there's something about the guy," he said darkly. "Mark my words, Thatcher's got secrets."

"Don't we all? Jeez, I was in love with an annoying Frog for years and kept it so secret even I didn't know." JT snorted, and I reminded him, "Thatcher's been an amazing friend and investor for Honeybridge Mead."

"Pfft. I guess. But he's only in it for the money."

"Which is why he's an *investor*, Frog. Would you rather him be in it for other reasons? Like maybe he wants to bend me over the worktable in the—*mpfh!*"

JT's lips on mine were never unwanted, even when they

took me by surprise, but he let me go again quickly and darted a frustrated look around the yard, like he wished we were anywhere but there. "*Thirty* minutes, Firecracker."

I brushed my fingertips over my tingling lips. "Really? You're getting all hot and bothered because I happened to mention Thatcher? I didn't even bring up that sexy salt-and-pepper thing going on at his temples, or his alluring ankles, or those seductive tattoos."

I had never noticed Thatcher's ankles in my life, and since his idea of a casual wardrobe was a button-down shirt and slacks, I'd seen more visible skin on monks. JT knew this.

He also knew I found it really fucking hot when he got all possessive and proprietary, and that since this rarely happened anymore, now that Dan and JT were BFFs and Dan had sworn off dating, I was deliberately playing with fire.

The banked flames in JT's eyes said I was going to get burned in the most delightful way.

"I'm *not* hot and bothered because of Thatcher *or* his magnificent ankles," JT informed me. "I'm hot and bothered because you were doing it again."

I frowned. "Doing what?"

"Giving me *the look* while I was trying to pretend I cared about Libby Coglin's dressage awards." He raised an eyebrow and glanced pointedly at my drink. "Twenty minutes now, Firecracker. Actually, make it ten."

"Oh, yeah? And exactly what happens in ten minutes?" I demanded breathlessly, as though my heart rate and breathing hadn't picked up the second those pretty Wellbridge blue eyes had fixed on me. As though I wouldn't let him do any damn thing he wanted to me, anytime at all.

"In ten minutes, we're gonna go park at the Retreat and

paddle out to the island for a little while before you head to the Tavern. You're closing tonight, right?"

I swallowed hard. JT and I had spent a very memorable afternoon out at Milk Bottle Island over Labor Day weekend, when the town had been so packed with tourists and family members that we hadn't been able to find privacy anywhere else. It had been the sort of afternoon that had caused me to leave a five-star review for JT's portable hammock and think very kind thoughts about Mrs. McLeroy, the den mother who'd taught our Scout troop's rope-tying class.

"I could ask Dan to cover tonight," I offered casually, taking a large gulp of my drink. JT was right—the beverage *was* delicious. I made a mental note to investigate bourbon-barrel aging. "He's been looking for extra shifts now that it's getting too cold to be out on the water. I think he needs a new hobby."

"What the man needs is to find a decent guy," JT countered,shaking his head. "And then to actually give them a chance for once."

JT was not wrong. Dan had only gotten grumpier as the summer turned into fall, and as his friend, I worried about him. But I was definitely not in the mood to talk about Dan's love life.

I was far too busy enjoying my own.

"Who knows? Maybe this will be the day a handsome man walks into the Tavern and changes his whole life." I gave JT an arch look and ran my fingers up his chest. "Happened to me."

He grinned. "Did it now?"

"Mmm. And now I might let that handsome man take me out to Milk Bottle Island... as long as he promises not to tip us into the water this time. It's getting damn cold for swimming."

JT rolled his eyes. "You make it sound like I tipped us on purpose the first time. That was sabotage."

He looked so disgruntled I snort-laughed. Just a couple of days after winning Brew Fest's Best of the Fest award, my family had thrown me *our* version of a victory party, which had involved Nat's Oreo cheesecake, a bonfire, and plenty of chilled mead. Pop had all but insisted that we take out his old wooden canoe for a victory paddle... and then had stood on the shoreline with my fool brothers, cheering and whooping as the little boat took on water. JT had upended us while trying to bail us out.

"Kiss him, Firecracker!" Pop had yelled once JT and I were both in the water. "Lay one on him and make the legend come true!"

"Poor Pop was so disappointed when nothing magical happened," I told JT now. "I think he hoped the water would turn purple or a buried treasure would bubble up from the surface. Maybe we *could* take a quick swim today. Call it... legend-fulfillment practice."

JT stuck one finger in the belt loop of my pants and hauled me behind a huge flowering hydrangea bush, giving us the illusion of privacy. I let out a stupid chuckle as I wrapped an arm around his neck. My chest felt giddy and light.

Shit, how much bourbon was in this apple bourbon drink?

"First off," he said, brushing his mouth against mine in the barest tease of a kiss, "I don't need practice to kiss you, baby. It's basically my favorite sport." He nipped at my lower lip. "In fact, next year, I'm thinking of asking the Town Council to get a Team Wellbridge: Best Kissers plaque added to the sign."

I shook my head. The love I felt for this man made my brain swim more powerfully than any bourbon concoction.

"I'd be down for that competition," I countered. I tilted my head to one side and regarded him thoughtfully. "How many folks do you suppose I'd need to kiss in order to win the victory for Team Honeycutt?"

JT's jaw dropped for a moment before he shut it with a clack. "Never mind."

I laughed out loud.

"And second..." JT's voice lowered in a way that made my dick hard—hard-*er*—and he pulled me tightly against him. "I think Pop got it wrong. I don't know exactly what he thought was gonna happen when a Honeycutt and a Wellbridge who love true kissed in Lake Wellbridge—"

"I believe you mean Kiss-Me-Quick Lake," I corrected.

One corner of his lips turned up, but when he met my gaze, his stare was different. No longer teasing but intense. Intentional. "I can tell you for sure, Flynn Honeycutt, that every time I get to kiss you—or hold you or fall asleep with you in my arms—it's really fucking magical."

My skin prickled with need, and my breathing tripped up. I wanted to make a snarky comment about him being so cheesy, to tease him in the way we both enjoyed... but I couldn't. Sometimes, like now, the love and trust and sincere affection shining in his eyes just swamped me, until there wasn't a single spark of sarcasm left.

Instead, I grabbed his wrist and pressed a kiss to his tattoo. The one he'd gotten so he could carry me with him always, long before he knew we'd be an *us*.

"Come away with me, Firecracker." He leaned in and pressed a soft kiss to my cheek a hairsbreadth away from my lips. He smelled so damned good, like expensive cologne and my own bedsheets. Like *home* and permanence and everything I'd ever wanted. "Let's have our own celebration. Team Flynn and JT: Best lovers ever."

"Yes," I said softly. I would say yes to him again and again. As long as he would be there to hear it.

Because the path that had gotten us here had not been easy, but being in his arms was the sweetest victory I could imagine.

Want to know what happens when a sunshiny stranger walks into the Tavern and changes Dan's life? Check out our FREE bonus story Sweetheart *now (https://subscribepage.com/sweetheart)!*

And don't forget to preorder Reagan's book, Mr. Important, *coming in 2023!*

A Letter from Lucy & May

Dear Reader,

Thank you for reading *Firecracker*! We are excited to bring you more adventures in Honeybridge. Up next is Reagan's story in *Mr. Important*.

If this is your first book by one of us and you'd like to read more, we suggest you start with *Fakers*, book one in the Licking Thicket series, or Lucy's *Borrowing Blue* and May's *The Date*.

We would love it if you would take a few minutes to review *Firecracker* on Amazon, GoodReads, or BookBub. Reader reviews really do make a difference and we appreciate every single one of them.

Be sure to follow Lucy and May on Amazon to be notified of new releases, and look for us on Facebook for sneak peeks of upcoming stories.

Feel free to sign up for our newsletters, stop by www.LucyLennox.com, www.MayArcher.com, or visit Lucy's Lair and Club May on Facebook to stay in touch.

To see fun inspiration photos for this book, check out the Pinterest board for Firecracker.

Happy reading!
Lucy & May

Also by May Archer

Love in O'Leary Series

Whispering Key Series

The Sunday Brothers Series

The Way Home Series

Licking Thicket Series
(cowritten with Lucy Lennox)

Licking Thicket: Horn of Glory Series
(cowritten with Lucy Lennox)

Honeybridge Series
(cowritten with Lucy Lennox)

About May Archer

May lives outside Boston. She spends her days raising three incredibly sarcastic children, finding inventive ways to drive her husband crazy, planning beach vacations, avoiding the gym, reading M/M romance, and occasionally writing it. She's also published several M/F romance titles as Maisy Archer.

For free content and the latest info on new releases, sign up for her newsletter at: https://www.subscribepage.com/MayArcher_News

Want to know what projects May has coming up? Check out her Facebook reader group Club May for give-aways, first-look cover reveals, and more.

You can also catch her on Bookbub, and check out her recommended reads!

Also by Lucy Lennox

Made Marian Series

Forever Wilde Series

Aster Valley Series

Virgin Flyer

Say You'll Be Nine

Hostile Takeover

Twist of Fate Series with Sloane Kennedy

After Oscar Series with Molly Maddox

Licking Thicket Series with May Archer

Licking Thicket: Horn of Glory Series with May Archer

Visit Lucy's website at www.LucyLennox.com for a comprehensive list of titles, audio samples, freebies, suggested reading order, and more!

About Lucy Lennox

Lucy Lennox is the creator of the bestselling Made Marian, Forever Wilde, and Aster Valley series, and co-creator of the Twist of Fate Series with Sloane Kennedy, the After Oscar series with Molly Maddox, and the Licking Thicket series with May Archer. Born and raised in the southeast USA, she is finally putting good use to that English Lit degree.

Lucy enjoys naps, pizza, and procrastinating. She is married to someone who is better at math than romance but who makes her laugh every single day and is the best dancer in the history of ever.

She stays up way too late each night reading M/M romance because that stuff is impossible to put down.

For more information and to stay updated about future releases, please sign up for Lucy's author newsletter on her website or join her exciting reader group here: https://www.facebook.com/groups/lucyslair.